IMAGE...

Aliens who want to get to know you—by trading memories.

A graveyard where riot cops must keep the interred from escaping.

You've been hired to have a baby, but you're a man.

A heroine kept in cold storage until the world needs her again.

That people in the future are so good, they must return to the past to learn what is evil.

You've chosen to become a prophet . . . to an alien race.

The cyborg at your bedside is both your enemy and *your enemy's worst nightmare.*

Seventeen talented science fiction and fantasy authors from around the world have already imagined these tales and turned them into breathtaking award-winning stories. Join them on distant worlds, in alternate realities, and in the farthest realms of the imagination. Here are stories that will thrill you, surprise you, make you laugh and even make you shed a tear.

Every story is illustrated by the finest new artists. All stories and illustrations are from this year's winners of the **L. Ron Hubbard Writers of The Future® Contest** and the **L. Ron Hubbard Illustrators of The Future® Contest.**

WHAT'S BEEN SAID ABOUT THE *L. RON HUBBARD Presents WRITERS OF THE FUTURE* ANTHOLOGIES

L. RON HUBBARD

PRESENTS

WRITERS

OF THE

FUTURE

VOLUME VIII

L. RON HUBBARD

PRESENTS

WRITERS

OF THE

FUTURE

VOLUME VIII

The Year's 17 Best Tales from the
Writers of The Future
International Writing Program
Illustrated by the Winners in the
Illustrators of The Future
International Illustration Program

With Essays on Writing and Illustration by

L. RON HUBBARD
EDD CARTIER
ALGIS BUDRYS
LOIS McMASTER BUJOLD
R. GARCÍA y ROBERTSON

Algis Budrys, Senior Editor
Dave Wolverton, Editor
Frank Kelly-Freas, Director of Illustration

Bridge Publications, Inc.

The Last Indian War: © 1992 Brian Burt
The Winterberry: © 1992 Nicholas A. DiChario
Boos and Taboos: © 1992 L. Ron Hubbard Library
Bringing Sissy Home: © 1992 Astrid Julian
Winter Night, with Kittens: © 1992 Sam Wilson
Invisible Man: © 1992 Larry Ferrill
Naming Characters and Why: © 1992 Algis Budrys
Surrogate: © 1992 M. C. Sumner
The Coat of Many Colors: © 1992 Christine Beckert
Timepieces: © 1992 Mike E. Swope
Notes to the New Artist: © 1992 Edd Cartier
Anne of a Thousand Years: © 1992 Michael Paul Meltzer
Subterranean Pests: © 1992 James S. Dorr
Getting Started: © 1992 Lois McMaster Bujold
A Cold Fragrant Air: © 1992 C. Maria Plieger
Blueblood: © 1992 Bronwynn Elko
Not Simply Blue: © 1992 Gene Bostwick
Write from the Heart: © 1992 R. García y Robertson
Scary Monsters: © 1992 Stephen Woodworth
Pale Marionettes: © 1992 Mark Budz
Running Rings Around the Moon: © 1992 Kevin Kirk
The Augmented Man: © 1992 Wendy Rathbone
More Than a Contest: © 1992 Dave Wolverton
A Note from Frank Kelly-Freas: © 1992 Frank Kelly-Freas

Illustration on page 11: © 1992 Evan T. Thomas
Illustration on page 32: © 1992 Matthew Stork
Illustration on page 68: © 1992 Jane Walker
Illustration on page 84: © 1992 Shaun Tan
Illustration on page 93: © 1992 Bob Hobbs
Illustration on page 118: © 1992 Darren Albertson
Illustration on page 139: © 1992 Evan T. Thomas
Illustration on page 147: © 1992 Omar Rayyan
Illustration on page 182: © 1992 Ira Crowe
Illustration on page 220: © 1992 Allen Koszowski
Illustration on page 243: © 1992 John Caponigro
Illustration on page 258: © 1992 Yevgeny Rzhanov
Illustration on page 274: © 1992 Allen Koszowski
Illustration on page 306: © 1992 Yevgeny Rzhanov
Illustration on page 337: © 1992 Matthew Stork
Illustration on page 357: © 1992 Omar Rayyan
Illustration on page 373: © 1992 Thomas Whittaker

Cover Artwork: "Palace City" © 1986 L. Ron Hubbard Library

ISBN 0-88404-772-5

Library of Congress Catalog Card Number: 84-73270
First Edition Paperback 10 9 8 7 6 5 4 3 2 1

Printed in the United States of America
Cover Artwork "Palace City" by Gary Meyer

CONTENTS

Introduction
by
Dave Wolverton

Welcome to the eighth volume in this series. As with previous volumes, we are wholly dedicated to discovering and
promoting talented new authors and illustrators from around
the world. Over the past eight years we have presented over
one hundred and twenty writers along with thirty-six illustrators. This volume contains stories from seventeen new
writers and twelve new illustrators. The Contests continue
to have an international flavor. Our writers and illustrators
come to you this year from the United States, Canada,
Australia, and the Ukraine, and one of our illustrators, Omar
Rayyan, was born and raised in the Middle East.

As Coordinating Judge of Writers of The Future, I had
the privilege of seeing thousands of stories while helping to
select those that you see in this volume. As I studied each
one I began by looking for a promising start—perhaps the
author promised adventure or a penetrating insight into the
human heart. Perhaps he or she promised a glimpse of a
strange new world or perhaps the author's facility with language itself promised a rich experience. It is the very first
test I make of a story. Each of the authors and illustrators
in these pages has made that promising start. That's why they
are here.

You will find in these pages artists who are polished, professional, and who often have a touch of genius. We believe you will find names that you will come to recognize and respect years down the line, and we hope you will find immediate pleasure as you peruse each story and illustration.

Over the past years, the L. Ron Hubbard's Writers and Illustrators of The Future Contests have become an invaluable institution in the field, discovering important new talent, and both Contests are still growing. No other program offers the unique combination of high-paying prize money, payment for publication, workshops with blue-ribbon professionals for the winners, along with continued promotion long after the Contest. We owe a debt of gratitude to L. Ron Hubbard who recognized the need for such an institution and who, in 1984, created and launched the program.

If you are interested in learning more about the Contests, you will find articles and instructions for entering at the back of the book. But for now, sit back, read the stories and look at the illustrations, enjoy. . . .

— Dave Wolverton

The Last Indian War

by
Brian Burt

ILLUSTRATED BY Evan T. Thomas

About the Author

Brian Burt of Portage, Michigan, was working on assignment as a computer programmer in Dublin, Ireland, when the urge to write finally overtook him. A combination of the scenery and the great appreciation the Irish have for the arts inspired him to pick up a copy of L. Ron Hubbard Presents Writers of The Future, Volume II, *and he began entering stories shortly thereafter.*

The Contest may have helped provide the impetus for him to write, but Brian supplied the talent it took to write this fascinating and thoroughly professional tale, which, as a first-place story qualifies him to win the additional $4,000 grand prize.

Brian says that winning first place in Writers of The Future has been the high point of his career by several light-years.

Yet Brian has a facile mind, combined with an innate ability to compose a satisfying story, so I suspect that we shall see him reach other high points in the near future.

About the Illustrator

Evan T. Thomas of Glencoe, Illinois, was born in Connecticut in 1965 and at an early age began to amaze friends with his ability to draw just about anything. Though he has never studied art formally, it has always been part of his identity.

One could describe Evan as a "Man of a Thousand Jobs." He has worked—among other things—as a bartender, waiter, night watchman, floor clerk on Wall Street, lifeguard, factory worker, English tutor, and in retail sales. For the past several years he has worked as a computer programmer—something that, like his drawing, started out only as a hobby. Yet he finds that in many ways it helps satisfy his creative urge.

Evan has many interests within the arts—sculpture, animation, drawing—and he also is a musician and songwriter. He says of his art, "Nothing satisfies like perfection. People often say that there is always tomorrow, but when I get into my work, I'm always conscious that there is no tomorrow. I have to do it perfectly, now."

It is an attitude that one commonly finds among the best artists, and—as he shows here and in his illustration for "The Coat of Many Colors" later in the book—Evan certainly promises to be among the very best.

The forest wrapped around **Joseph Soaring-Hawk like a thick, green blanket. The woodlands of Kelvyn were still alien to him,** still a little bizarre. Yet the soft rustle of leaves, the lush fragrance of vegetation, the springy bounce of living carpet beneath his feet offered familiar comfort. Corkscrew ferns twisted toward the sky in tightly bunched loops all around him, their giant fronds feathering out to catch the orange sunlight. The corkscrews amazed him, like nothing he had seen before. Each tree was a scale model of the forest, supporting a complete ecosystem within its massive coils. Unseen creatures whistled and chattered from a thousand leafy hiding places. He felt in tune with the rhythms of nature here, reconnected to the threads of growth and life woven into the very fabric of his soul. Endless months trapped in the sterile shell of the *Surveyor* had almost driven him mad. Every trip to a new colony site was cold and lonely, but the land never failed to embrace him.

Joseph sat on the base coil of a corkscrew to catch his breath. He was in better shape than anyone else in the *Surveyor*'s crew, but the strong gravity of Kelvyn sapped the strength from his muscles. He took three swallows from his water pack and watched in fascination as a nearby porcu-pine lured its prey. A brown flying-lizard not much bigger than a pigeon hovered between the branches, drawn by the aroma of honeysap that oozed from the porcu-pine's bark. As soon as the flyzard touched the sticky sap, the branches snapped together, impaling the tiny creature with a dozen needles.

Nerve venom in the needles quickly paralyzed it. Joseph reck-
oned it would take less than three hours for the tree to absorb
the flyzard's nutrients. Skin and bones would drop to the
forest floor, where scavengers feasted on the porcu-pine's
leavings. Nothing wasted. Nothing killed needlessly. Nothing
consumed to extinction. Life on Kelvyn was in balance. For
how long? Joseph shook his head and pushed on.

He came to the glade that marked the boundary of the
puffer-owl village. A cream-colored mousipede crouched in
the grass near the center of the clearing, nibbling on the fruit
of a bloodberry bush. The tiny rodent had no idea what a
dangerous place it had chosen to dine. Joseph studied the trees
across the glade expectantly. A few minutes passed before
the bloated outline of a puffer-owl glided from the upper
reaches of a towering corkscrew fern. It floated out across
the glade with silent stealth, riding the wind like a feathered
zeppelin. Suddenly it folded its wings and dove straight toward
the mousipede. By the time the little creature sensed the
danger, it was too late. It scurried halfway to the tree line
on its dozen stubby legs before the puffer's talons dug into
its back. It squeaked twice as its captor flipped it and sliced
through its tender belly with a scythe-like beak. There was
silence as the puffer fed.

The puffers were the strangest birds Joseph had ever seen.
Their round faces, large eyes, and thick bodies reminded him
of Terran owls. Their features had the same appearance of
dignity and wisdom, but there the similarity ended. They were
huge, some as massive as fifty kilograms. Because of their
size and the strong surface gravity of Kelvyn, they could not
get off the ground without the buoyancy of their flight bladders.
These inflated with hydrogen extracted from the air when the
owls rose, swelling them like balloons. Like most of Kelvyn's
creatures, they had limbs to spare. A broad pair of forewings
and a smaller pair of hindwings controlled their speed and
direction of flight. A third pair of vestigial wings resembled

tiny arms. Three pairs of jointed legs made their ground movements almost crab-like. Each leg had folds of skin that were used like fins to maneuver in the air. The puffers seemed to swim across the sky rather than fly. To the rest of the crew, they were ugly as sin. To Joseph, they were beautiful.

He watched the puffer carefully as it fed, studied the speckled plumage of brown and orange. A pair of blood-red mogre teeth dangled from its ear-tufts. He knew this one. This was the warrior-chief, the one he called Cochise. He waited for Cochise to finish, not wanting to interrupt the pleasure of the meal. When Cochise rose once more into the trees, Joseph slipped across the glade. As always, the village was silent. Only the whisper of leaves and the occasional murmur of wings broke the eerie stillness. He wriggled between the loops of a corkscrew so his presence would not disturb the puffers. The tree coiled above him like a giant wooden serpent. Far beyond his vision, a clan of puffer-owls had built their living chambers, piling section upon section as family and home grew together, intertwined. Nearly every corkscrew within four square kilometers housed its own clan, its own slice of tribal history. These woods carried the living heritage of Cochise's tribe. Of Shaman's tribe. He thought of the bedraggled puffer crouching in the corner of the lab aviary, mangled and dying. He felt a flash of anger, a pang of guilt.

Suddenly the tranquil world of Kelvyn exploded with the hungry roar of machinery. Joseph could not see the creatures hidden behind the leaves, but their terror and confusion buffeted him in waves. He cursed and squirmed out of his blind, breaking into a run. Within two hundred meters he was gasping for air, but he did not stop. He barely missed an outstretched porcu-pine branch as he labored back the way he had come, lean legs pumping against the grip of Kelvyn, black mane dancing in the wind. Only two kilometers to camp, but it felt like twenty, all uphill. When he staggered into the clearing, all ten pulverizers were already on-line, gobbling up the forest and turning it into mulch.

Joseph doubled over, sucking oxygen as fast as his lungs could manage. Through a fog of pain, he scanned the nearby units for Angus McIntyre. After a minute he spotted the crew chief near a field console, poring through schematics with a cluster of foremen. Joseph started toward them, winced as a charley horse bunched his quadriceps into tight, hard knots. He ignored it, dragged the screaming leg with him across the flattened, denuded soil. Several foremen stopped talking and turned in his direction. McIntyre followed their gaze, stroking the bushy red moustache that burned like fire in the orange light. Surprise and amusement played across his grizzled face.

"Hawk, you look like twice-baked shit. Those nature hikes are killing you, laddie. Maybe you should stick around here and suck dust with the rest of us."

The foremen chuckled as Joseph drew himself up, tried to catch his breath. "Mac . . . I told you not to clear any more . . . until I give you the OK. This area's not certified yet, and you know it. You . . . know the regs."

McIntyre shook his head. "Aye, I know the regs. I also know that Corporate is rattlin' their saber a little louder every day, and it's not your head'll be rolling if we fall behind. Now, Hawk, I know how you feel about the greenery. I love it, too, much as the next man. But the fact is, we've got to finish the shell structure here and then we're hyperspatial toward Avalon inside of two months, or it's my ass. It may not look like much to you, laddie, but it's the only one I've got, and I'm bent on keeping it."

The cluster of foremen broke into a gale of laughter as McIntyre bowed, a toothy grin spreading beneath his moustache. Frustration rose in Joseph like the color in McIntyre's ruddy face. The man was good-natured and popular, hard to dislike. But he was wrong this time. Dead wrong.

"It's not your ass I'm worried about, Mac. You can take care of yourself. The puffer-owls can't. You have read my reports. You know damn well we can't build here!"

The laughter stopped. "I read your reports, Hawk. Full of speculation and conjecture, nothing solid. Nothing worth killing a colony over."

"Nothing solid! What about all the video, Mac? The complex social patterns? The inside of the clan chambers? The use of tools? You're worried about killing a colony, but I'm worried about killing a race!"

McIntyre shrugged. "Ants have complex social patterns. Birds build nests. Otters and monkeys use tools. That doesn't make 'em sentient, now does it?"

Joseph's eyes glittered like chips of obsidian. "Those pulverizers don't make you sentient either. Every day you gobble up another chunk of their world. In another week, you'll swallow Shaman's entire tribal grounds. It's their ancestral land, Mac, and they won't leave it. Without my authorization, you'll be guilty of mass murder."

McIntyre smiled stiffly. "Mass murder, is it? The same tune you sang five years ago about those hairy little beasties on Rathgar? Well now, there's a thrivin' colony on that planet, and I don't believe a one of them that built it spent a slim second in lockup. Couldn't prove a word of your ravings then either, now could you?"

Joseph felt flames of rage licking at the edges of his face, tried not to let them show. His words came slow and heavy, weighed down by gravity. "No. I couldn't. It's hard to prove a race is sentient after it's extinct."

Tension swelled between the two men, as thick and menacing as the sudden silence. No one moved. Finally McIntyre let out a sigh. "I meant you no insult, Hawk. A blind man could see your sincerity. But I can't stop this operation on a whim. I'll make you a deal. You bring me proof of what you say, and I'll stop. You have my word, laddie."

Joseph studied McIntyre's face for several seconds. The foremen shuffled nervously behind them. "All right, Mac. I'll bring you proof. Then we'll see if your word means more than that bastard's on Rathgar."

He heard the angry muttering as he walked away, but he ignored it.

Joseph barely heard Cal Benton stumble into the lab, so drunk was he with euphoria. Benton stopped in his tracks, jaws hanging open like the village idiot. "Hawk, what the hell's gotten into you? I haven't seen you this happy since they ran Mac's shorts through the pulverizers. How come you're not out in the woods with your little owl buddies?"

Joseph spun from his terminal, flashed a smile at the geologist. Of all the people aboard the *Surveyor,* Benton was the only one with whom he felt any kinship. They were the oddball scientists, the geo-engineer, and the eco-engineer. Both were SEA independents who cared about more than a paycheck, and that set them apart. "Cal, my friend, the weather grounded me today, and am I glad it did. My little owl buddies don't fly when it's stormy out. They're scared to death of lightning. They call it 'fire needles.' "

Benton dropped his load of samples and grinned back. "Right, Hawk. How do you know what they call anything?"

"Shaman told me."

Benton glanced at the crippled puffer-owl behind the transparent wall of the aviary, luminous eyes studying its captors as if they were the ones in a cage. For the first time, Benton looked worried. "Hey, buddy, you been swimming in the booze again?"

Joseph's laughter rang against the walls, bold and unfettered for the first time since his arrival on Kelvyn. "I found something better. I found the proof Mac asked for, with some help from the computer. The key to Shaman's language."

Illustrated by Evan T. Thomas

Benton's eyes grew wide. "You mean . . . those critters really are intelligent? No shit?"

Joseph felt as if his smile would split his face. "No shit. I've got a whole dialogue on disk, just me and my feathered friend. They can't stop me now. I finally get to use the S.P.C. just like it's supposed to be used."

Benton beamed back. "Great, Hawk. What the hell's the S.P.C.?"

"Don't they teach you rock-sniffers anything? 'Sentients Protection Clause.' The one rule the SEA got right before they sent us out here. Any planet with indigenous sentient life is off limits to colonization. The puffers get to keep their planet . . . and we get out."

Benton whistled. "McIntyre's gonna pitch a fit when you tell him. And Corporate's gonna have his balls for breakfast when he tells them!"

"They can castrate whoever they want, but it won't change the regs. Corporate's lawyers know they lose their license to colonize if I prove the violation. They'll bitch a lot, but they'll get out."

Benton shook his head. "All that work down the chute. When are you gonna tell McIntyre?"

"I'm on my way now. Want to come?"

Benton unstrapped the rest of his gear in a hurry. "Are you kidding? I wouldn't miss this for all the platinum on Jarvis III!"

The pulverizers were roaring at full capacity when Joseph and Cal Benton reached the edge of the clearing zone. It didn't take long to locate McIntyre, but the noise made it impossible to talk in the open. The crew chief gestured toward a foreman's cube, and the three of them slipped inside. As McIntyre shut the door, sonic insulation enveloped them in blessed silence. Benton lowered his hands from his ears and grinned. "One thing about pulverizer crews—they're not gonna waste time gabbing."

McIntyre rubbed his moustache and grinned back. "You're dead right, laddie. Nor can I waste time gabbin' with scientists, so make it quick."

Joseph held up the disk in his hand. "You asked for proof that the puffers are intelligent. I've got it. I couldn't understand the lack of verbal communication in a species so advanced. I saw them stand around and stare at each other, but they never made a sound. Then it occurred to me. Maybe they were talking, but I just couldn't hear. I programmed the computer to scan the ultrasonic frequencies, and there it was. They have a musical vocabulary, pitched so high that the human ear can't detect it. They speak in song. Ants don't do that, birds don't, otters and monkeys don't. They're sentient, Mac."

Angus McIntyre scowled. "God in Heaven, I knew you'd cook up something like this. So they talk above the range of human hearing. How convenient for you, Hawk. Very creative, but not too believable."

Joseph dropped the recording disk on the table. "I've got a four-hour conversation with Shaman right there, electronically logged and verified. Not only are we in danger of destroying these creatures, we've already started. Shaman was the tribe's high priest, just as I thought from initial observation. When he saw us drop out of the clouds, he told his tribe that we were sacred sky spirits. After a few weeks with the pulverizers, we'd flattened half their hunting territory and driven most of the game away. The chief labeled us demons and declared Shaman a false priest. In keeping with tribal law, he was banished. He committed the puffer equivalent of hara-kiri—mutilated his flight bladders with a cured porcu-pine needle. They left him helpless on the forest floor, unable to fly, easy prey for the first razorbeak or mogre that lumbered by. He wandered into camp because he hoped he could undo the damage he had caused. *We* had caused. The computer can generate a complete transcript whenever you want. You can interview Shaman yourself, with the computer as translator."

"Log entries can be forged. Computers can be reprogrammed. This entire thing could be your elaborate hoax."

Joseph's temper rose like an eagle on the wind. "That's bullshit and you know it! I don't have the access or the knowledge to mess with *Surveyor*'s brain."

McIntyre rolled the hairs of his moustache between his thumb and forefinger. "I'm not convinced o' that. A bright, determined lad like yourself could do most anything if he felt he had no choice."

"Mac, you gave me your word. There were a dozen witnesses."

"I said if you brought me proof. You've brought me nothing."

"If you don't stop this now, I'll transmit all my evidence straight to the Space Exploration Administration."

McIntyre smiled. "You do that. By the time the SEA get off their collective ass, this operation will be long finished and the colony trebled in size."

Joseph stared at the stocky crew chief, knew with sick certainty that the man would not back down. He turned to Cal Benton, who could only shrug. The ghosts of a dead race shrieked in his temples. "Just like Rathgar. It's happening all over again."

McIntyre put a hand on Joseph's shoulder. "There's nothing you or I can do. Corporate needs the contract. I need the job. And you need to relax. If you're right about these beasties, then they're smart enough to go elsewhere. There's plenty of planet left for 'em."

Joseph slapped the crew chief's arm aside, black eyes glittering. "There'll be nothing left for them. When we rape a world, it's never the same again. It dies of shame and misery, then it rots around us until we leave. That's not going to happen here. I'll find a way to stop you, you bastard!" Joseph kicked open the door and left. The growl of the pulverizers swallowed McIntyre's curses.

It happened that night for the first time.

One section of the colony structure and three pulverizers were demolished while the crews slept. When McIntyre arrived at the lab with a pair of security goons, Joseph wasn't surprised. Cal Benton had examined the damage and tried to stick up for him.

"Come on, Mac, you know he didn't do it. Hell, we don't even know how it was done! The stuff is shattered into little pieces, but there's no burn marks, no trace of explosives. You think he smashed a titanium shell with his bare hands?"

McIntyre wouldn't listen. One look at the man's eyes told Joseph that evidence was irrelevant. He had threatened to stop the project, and now he was guilty by intent. McIntyre tugged so hard on his moustache that he nearly pulled it off. His words thundered against the walls of the lab. "I should have known better than to trust a man with a sentence for a name. 'Joseph Soaring-Hawk-Who-Sees-Far.' How far do you see, laddie? Far enough to wreck my equipment in the dark o' night without being noticed? Far enough to put the hex on my operation? Aye, that far at least."

McIntyre converted one of the storage cubes into a makeshift jail. Joseph went without argument after Cal promised to look after Shaman. The solitude gave him plenty of time to think. He knew McIntyre wasn't a wicked man, just frustrated and confused. To that Joseph could relate. He was fighting to save a culture, and he was losing. Soon Shaman's village would be a memory, and here he sat like a caged animal, cut off from the sweet breath of the land. Unable to stop the slaughter of a way of life.

Joseph knew little of his own Cherokee heritage, only scraps culled from thousands of history disks he had searched

over the years. He read of the Busk, the festival celebrating
first fruits and new fires, but the words had no flavor. He
read of Sequoya and others who tried to adapt to the white
man's customs, hoping to salvage some shred of their culture.
In the end their efforts brought nothing but blood and suffering along a Trail of Tears. Tales of broken promises, of
broken people, left him hollow inside. The essence of what
the Cherokee had been eluded him, like the dappled outline
of a lightning-buck darting through morning mist. He knew
that they had made peace with the land. They respected nature,
revered Her. Some spark of that belief still burned in him.
That was all. His ancestors called to him across the gulf of
time, but he could not hear. He was disconnected from the
past. He did not fit into the future. He was alone. He would
not let that happen to Shaman!

Cal shamed McIntyre into letting Joseph out the next
morning after it happened for the second time. Two more
pulverizers and two shell sections were destroyed during the
night. McIntyre had given Joseph an iron-clad alibi by lock-
ing him in a metal box. It was hard for a man like Mac to
apologize, but he did his best.

"I made a mistake, Hawk, I'll admit. You're not the one
wreakin' havoc on my operation, though we both know you
would if you could. And since it's not you that's wrecking
the place, I'll wager I know who it is. What it is. If you have
any influence with those fat balloon beasties, you better come
with me."

Joseph took a deep breath as Cal and McIntyre led him
outside. What a relief to see the sky! The tension in his body
unwound as the three of them ambled through the growing
maze of plasteel and titanium toward the far edge of the site.
The roar of the pulverizers swelled, much tamer now that half
their number had been reduced to scrap. As the trio came
within sight of the forest, McIntyre began to curse. Joseph
whistled in amazement. The trees and the row of structures

nearest to them were blanketed by puffer-owls. They wheeled overhead, diving and snapping at the crews, filling the air like a plague of feathered locusts.

McIntyre's face was redder than his moustache. "They're makin' a shambles of the entire area! Nipping at the clearing crews, dropping guano everywhere like shaggin' cluster bombs. We've only five pulverizers left as it is, and the lads can't make any progress with this commotion about. I want them out of here."

Joseph shook his head. "You can't blame them, Mac. They're just trying to protect their homes, their families. You're only a few hundred meters from their doorstep."

McIntyre shook his fist at a diving puffer. "Blessed Christ, Hawk, it's a big planet! Tell them to move. Tell them if they settle elsewhere, we'll leave 'em be. My word on it."

Joseph's eyes darkened into midnight. He couldn't feel the sun anymore, as if he were standing in his own shadow. While McIntyre smoldered, he turned to ice. "I won't tell them that, Mac. I won't lie to them. It's their land, and we're stealing it. If they go someplace else, we'll take that too, eventually."

Joseph had never seen a man any madder than Angus McIntyre. He looked far more like a cornered animal than the puffers that circled above him, singing their silent rage. "Damn it, Hawk, be realistic! I know how you feel, but we've no choice. Earth and Mars are choking, smothering under their own weight. If we don't spread out, we'll die!"

"So they die in our place? Are we really that pathetic? How many species do we eat to stay alive?"

"It doesn't have to be that way. But if these beasties want a fight, I'll surely give 'em one. They fired the first volley when they wrecked my machines."

Cal Benton broke in before Joseph could put his anger into words. "Mac, that's crazy talk. According to you, these things are just dumb animals. They don't have any weapons. They couldn't do that kind of damage in a hundred years! Maybe . . . maybe this planet has some weird localized tectonics, some kind of seismic hiccup that we haven't detected yet. I know you're frustrated, but give me time to figure this out.''

McIntyre's eyes were wild, paranoid. He took a step back, pulled a laser from his pouch. ''I expected you'd side with him, Benton. Spout some half-baked theories to protect his little pets. I don't want to hear it. I don't know how, but these devils are sabotagin' my operations. Damned if I'll stand around and watch 'em do it!''

McIntyre spun toward the nearest structure, a hexagonal dormitory shell. Puffer-owls covered every square meter of the roof, scowling down from the edges like living gargoyles. McIntyre raised his pistol toward them. A dreadful vision blazed its way through Joseph's mind. ''Fire needles . . . No! Don't shoot!''

It all happened in an instant. A rod of light leapt from McIntyre's hand into the mass of puffers. At least a score exploded violently, setting off a grisly chain reaction. One after another the owls burst into flame, like a line of bloody fireworks. Flaming gore and blackened feathers filled the air. Survivors climbed frantically above the inferno, but McIntyre kept firing, setting off a dozen smaller explosions. The smell of roasted flesh grew so thick it made Joseph gag. Blind with nausea and rage, he launched himself toward the wild-eyed crew chief. They fell to the ground in a jumble, Joseph clawing for the laser, McIntyre still trying to aim at the retreating puffers. Something white-hot and primitive stole into Joseph's body, chased all reason from his mind. Again and again he swung his fist at McIntyre's face. He heard yelling, but the words meant nothing. Hands clutched his shoulders. He shrugged them away, threw another punch. It took Benton and two burly roustabouts to pull him off.

The roustabouts held Joseph while two others helped McIntyre to his feet, the laser still clutched tightly in his hand. An ugly purple bruise bloomed on one cheek. A split lip bulged above a madman's crooked leer. Blood matted the bushy moustache. McIntyre's fury was gone, spent. Joseph's own icy rage had melted, turned to steam that boiled in his veins. He forced himself to look at the smoking carnage.

A mogre slipped like a shadow from the splintered tree line on six powerful legs, drawn into the open by the scent of fresh blood. Its feral eyes glowed with ravenous malice as it clawed through the blackened corpses. Massive crocodilian jaws snapped up the tenderest chunks, crushing them to pulp as they vanished into its maw. Shackled by the roustabouts, Joseph could only shout to drive the demonic creature back into the forest.

Cal mumbled something reassuring beside him in a shaky voice. Even the hard-bitten crewmen looked dazed. McIntyre's giddy brogue broke the stillness.

"That did 'em, lads. That showed 'em who's boss. Did you ever see the like? The Fourth of July right here on Kelvyn!"

Joseph tried to pull free, but the roustabouts held him tight. "You son of a bitch. Their bladders are filled with hydrogen. Hydrogen! You might as well hang bags of blasting gel around their necks! They never . . . never had a chance."

McIntyre glared back at him. "Oh, they had a chance, laddie. A chance to move out, go elsewhere. You wouldn't offer it. This is on your head."

Cal Benton took an angry step forward. "That's bullshit, Mac, heartless bullshit. What the hell's gotten into you?"

"A desire to keep my job, the jobs of all my mates." McIntyre touched his swollen lip gingerly. "You pack quite a wallop, Hawk, for a weak-kneed ecologist. Nice to see you've some fight in you after all."

Joseph struggled against the restraining arms. "If you

want more, there's plenty left. Or would you rather shoot me from a distance?''

McIntyre frowned. A fleeting ghost of pity slipped across his face. ''No, Hawk. Your brain's a wee bit softer than your heart, but I like you. I don't want to hurt you. I don't want to hurt any more of those beasties. If you really can talk to them, tell them to stay away from my equipment and my operation. If they show themselves again, I'll be cooking up a fresh flock o' fowl. You tell 'em.''

Joseph tried to douse the fire in his head. ''I'll tell you, Mac. It's a war now. You ought to think about leaving yourself.''

McIntyre grinned and ordered the crews back to work. Just before the pulverizers roared to life, Joseph heard him laughing.

The banging on his sleep-cube door didn't wake Joseph. He had been up most of the night, haunted by ghastly visions of Shaman erupting into flame. He crawled into his jumpsuit and released the lock. As the panels slid apart, Cal Benton's disheveled figure swam out of the orange twilight. Cal looked as if he hadn't slept much either. His straw-blond hair hung in tangled loops. His eyes were puffy with exhaustion. And something else. Shock.

''Hawk, you better get over to McIntyre's quarters right now. There's been an accident. A bad one.''

The two men jogged toward the section of temporary sleep-cubes where McIntyre and most of the foremen bedded down. Neither spoke. By the time they reached the scene, Cal was wheezing like an asthmatic. Joseph could see a large crowd gathered around the crew chief's quarters. He soon saw why. McIntyre's cube was gone, reduced to a pile of rubble. Joseph spotted Mac's deputy chief, Mike Marsalis, and headed for him.

''Mike, what's going on here?''

Marsalis stared suspiciously at the two scientists. Joseph could feel the eyes of the crowd impale him. "Maybe you should tell me. The chief's cube went to pieces last night with him inside. He's dead and already buried. Just a few hours after you told him he oughta haul ass out of here for his own safety. Seems kinda curious, don't it?"

There was an ominous buzzing from the crowd, but Cal Benton had managed to catch his breath, and he didn't hesitate. "Look, I know a terrible thing's happened here. We're all upset and a little scared. But you men are professionals, you know about demolition. All we've got is a neat pile of fragments and a couple guys who heard a loud crunch, like the cube just collapsed in a microsecond. What kind of machine could do that? What kind of explosive could do that without scorch marks, without scattering debris for fifty meters in every direction? You're an expert, Mike. You tell me."

Marsalis looked bewildered. The angry buzz of the crowd faded to an uncertain whisper. Finally Marsalis spoke. "I don't know. I guess you got a point. But something did this, and it might do it again."

Joseph saw his chance and took it. "You're right. Whatever's going on here, it's not safe for the crews until we figure it out. I think you ought to shuttle everybody back up to the *Surveyor* and stay orbital until we have an answer."

Marsalis glanced at the shattered ruins of the crew chief's cubicle, then nodded with obvious relief. The murmur of approval from the crewmen told Joseph he had won. These men did not fear anything in the galaxy they could see, but an invisible enemy was too much for them. They preferred to leave the unknown to the scientists. "Sounds real reasonable, Hawk. Who do you need to stay?"

"For now, just me and Cal. He's got some theories that the geology of this place might be responsible, and I'd like to stick around and give him a hand. The rest of you should get to safety and let Corporate know what's going on. We'll contact you at least once a day with a progress report, assuming we are around to give it.''

Marsalis nodded, his eyes wide. ''I'll start the evac right away. Shouldn't take more'n six hours to pull everybody off-planet. We'll send down supplies by drone when you need 'em.'' Marsalis stepped forward and grabbed Joseph's hand. ''You're a brave man, Hawk. Both of you. A lot braver than we gave you credit for.''

Joseph and Cal were in the lab four hours later when the last shuttle blasted off for the *Surveyor*. Both men went outside to watch it disappear into the clouds. Joseph clapped his partner lightly on the shoulder. ''Good riddance, my friend. Now we can get to work.''

Cal Benton looked thoroughly exasperated. ''Between you and me, Hawk, I'm stuck. I've reviewed every scrap of seismic data I have, and there's just nothing out of the ordinary about this chunk of rock. I don't know where else to look.''

Joseph smiled with a mixture of guile and sadness. ''Don't bother. You'd just be wasting your time.''

''What are you talking about?''

''I know what happened to the buildings, the machinery. To Mac. It's ironic, in a way. For all his paranoia, he was right. No seismic hiccups, Cal. Just the puffers. They may look soft and vulnerable, but they have one hell of a natural defense mechanism. Didn't you ever wonder why the mogres stay away from them? The mogres can climb. They could easily break into a clan nest and swallow a few tasty fledglings. But they don't. They know that the puffers can kill them with a song.''

Cal's eyes were soft with concern. ''Hey, buddy, take it easy. I know you've been under a lot of stress over this, but you're losing it.''

''I'm not crazy, Cal. Remember how the puffers communicate, in the ultrasonic range? Well, there's something else, something unbelievable. They have this instinctive ability to identify the natural period of vibration of a solid object. They can sing a note whose frequency just matches that period of vibration. Now one puffer alone can't do much damage, but fifty, a hundred? A thousand? They can create enough resonance to shake a thing to pieces. Even a thing like a pulverizer. Or a sleep-cube."

Cal raised a trembling hand to his forehead. "Are you telling me those things murdered Angus McIntyre?"

Joseph felt the ice forming around his heart. "What would you do if somebody tried to wipe out your entire race? They did what they had to do. And so will I, Cal. But I'm going to need your help."

Cal Benton swallowed twice. He studied Joseph with a new glimmer in his eyes: surprise, admiration, a trace of fear. Finally his features set in the familiar way that told Joseph he had decided. "What do you want me to do?"

Joseph sighed with relief. "You just did it. I need you to back me. Feed Marsalis and Corporate enough geological gibberish to keep them away. That'll give me time to get my evidence to the SEA, prove that the puffers are sentient. They'll have to grant an injunction against colonizing Kelvyn. Then Shaman and his tribe will be protected from the nastiest predator they've ever faced."

Cal nodded, tense but firm. "Okay. Hell, it's the right thing to do. I've always wanted to be a hero, even if it's just to a bunch of pudgy birds with thyroid problems."

Joseph laughed out loud, a sound as pure as forest air. "You'd make a great ecologist, my friend. Now I need your help for something else." Joseph crossed to the door of the aviary and opened it. Shaman scuttled out into the lab on his six spindly legs and raced past the two men. He paused just outside the science center, luminous eyes aglow with gratitude. Then he spread his two pairs of wings and inflated. While Cal Benton muttered in amazement, Shaman vanished into the sky.

Joseph felt as if he would burst with joy and pride. "I healed him, Cal. It took a while to figure out his physiology, but once I did, it was easy to repair the damage. Come on, let's follow him."

Cal Benton appeared to have had all the surprises he could stand for one day. "Where the hell is he going?"

"Home, Cal. He's going home."

It took just a few minutes to reach Shaman's village. Only a thin band of forest separated it from the outer edge of the colony site. Joseph's chest tightened when he realized how close the race had been. He saw the same wonder in Cal Benton's eyes that he himself had felt when he first walked among the corkscrews. He liked Cal better all the time. Maybe if Mac had seen this . . . No. It would have made no difference. The two men stopped just inside the stand of trees that marked the boundary of the village. Joseph pointed toward a massive corkscrew straight ahead of them. The upper coils were covered with puffer-owls of every size and color. "There. In the middle. That's their chief, Cochise. Beside him is Shaman."

"What's going to happen? I mean, didn't they banish him?"

"Yes. And now they'll welcome him back like a god. They have a legend about a warrior who was wrongly accused of cowardice in battle and banished from the tribe long, long ago. He crippled himself just as Shaman did, and the tribe considered him dead. A few days later he returned. Flying. Fully healed. They took it as a miracle and made him chief. The legend says he arranged a lasting peace between all the puffer tribes. Such a thing has never happened before or since. Until now."

Cal chuckled quietly. "Man, that's brilliant. So are we just here as spectators?"

"No. If I'm going to be able to save the puffers, they have to cooperate. They have to believe we're not demons, you and me. Right now Shaman is telling them that we helped him escape, and that we killed the rest of the metal monsters that were eating their forest. When he's done, I'm going to prove I'm worthy of their trust."

The two men watched the puffers rise in unison and glide forward to perch in the trees directly above them. Cal rubbed his arm nervously. "What the hell is this?" Joseph's voice was a jagged hiss. "Just . . . don't . . . interfere." He raised his arms to the assemblage, then bowed nearly to the ground. He walked toward a nearby porcu-pine tree. His hand disappeared into the pouch at his side and withdrew an ornamental knife. His arm struck out in a blur. A meter length of branch fell at his feet. Joseph knelt and grabbed one end, carefully avoiding the needles. He turned to the puffers and raised it above his head. Without warning he whipped it down across his legs, driving the needles deep into his thighs. Joseph collapsed with a shriek of agony. He managed to pull the branch loose and toss it away as Cal rushed to his side.

"What kind of a stupid stunt was that, you crazy bastard? I didn't come here to watch you kill yourself!"

Joseph struggled to speak, his mind adrift in a molten sea of pain. "Just . . . get me out of here. Please." Benton was a slender man, but he managed to sling Joseph over his shoulder and stagger back toward camp. Between rasping breaths, he cursed his stricken partner. "Of all the idiotic, brain-dead maneuvers I've ever seen, that one gets the blue ribbon. Decided to cripple yourself just like your little buddy Shaman, huh? If I'd known what you planned, I never would have let you go back there!"

Joseph's voice rose through a flaming veil of agony. "I know. That's . . . why I didn't . . . tell you. I needed to be there. And . . . I needed you. Put me down."

Cal Benton sank to the ground in exhaustion, laying Joseph on a bed of leaves. Joseph pulled a vial of medicine from his pouch and drank it down. The fire in his legs faded to glowing embers. His mind was clear enough to think. "Cal, listen to me. I helped the puffers defeat my own people. According to their laws, I'm a traitor to my kind. They could never trust me, and without their trust, I can't help them. I had to do my penance. There was no other way."

Cal shook his head in disbelief. "I don't believe you, Hawk. I don't believe how far you'll go to save these critters."

Joseph tried to smile, could only grimace. "Not just for them. For me, too. I wanted to do penance. The puffers collapsed Mac's cube, but how do you think they knew which one it was? This was Shaman's second trip back to his village. The first was last night. I told Shaman. Shaman told the rest. I murdered a man, a man more scared than wicked. I didn't see any other way, but that doesn't change it."

Cal stopped huffing. This time he hardly looked startled. "Jesus, Hawk. I'm lucky I'm on your side. Still, did you have to maim yourself?"

"Not forever. The porcu-pine venom doesn't work as well on us. I'll hurt like hell for a while, but I'll recover. Then I'll make an encore appearance in the village. Just like Shaman, risen from the dead. They might not trust an alien, but they'll trust an alien prophet."

Cal grinned and struggled to his feet. "You're some piece of work. You had it all planned out, didn't you? I better get you back so we can drug you up good. And so I can jabber some double-talk at Marsalis. We'll see this thing through together, buddy, then we'll get the hell off this rock!"

Joseph nodded as Cal hoisted him, but he did not answer. The pain in his legs paled beside the guilt that burned in him. Exploding puffers would haunt his dreams no longer. They had been chased away by a ghoul with hair the color of blood and a moustache of flame. Spectral eyes blazed at him, accusing, damning. His legs would heal, but this other wound? He did not know. Still, beneath the anguish lay a deep, cool well of peace. He glanced back at the green towers of Shaman's village. This time he had not failed.

Joseph closed his eyes, rocked back and forth with the rhythm of Cal Benton's strides. For a moment he was gliding through the ancient forests of America with his ancestors, strong and unbowed, sinews stretching down into the fragrant soil like roots. He would miss Cal. He could never explain why he was staying. Not to protect the puffers. Not for the sake of science. After so many empty years, he had found what he was seeking.

Joseph Soaring-Hawk had found his tribe at last.

The Winterberry
by
Nicholas A. DiChario

ILLUSTRATED BY Matthew Stork

About the Author

Over the past eight years, the Writers and Illustrators of The Future Contests have continually expanded. We've brought you prize-winning authors and illustrators from five of the seven continents—we are still waiting for winners from South America and Antarctica. Understandably then, the competition is so tight that sometimes a story comes in that we love and it somehow just doesn't take a prize and we feel that's a shame.

Nicholas DiChario's graceful "The Winterberry" is one of these stories.

Nicholas was born on Halloween in 1960 and works for a major health insurance company in upstate New York as a documentation analyst. He has a B.A. in English, and thanks to the State University of New York's Brockport Writer's Forum, he has been able to study with some of his favorite science fiction and fantasy authors—Nancy Kress, Karen Joy Fowler, James Patrick Kelly, and John Kessel.

Nicholas is rapidly establishing himself as one of today's best new writers. He has sold stories to Universe 2, Universe 3, *and* The Magazine of Fantasy and Science Fiction. *The powerful story you are about to read also appears in an anthology released in the summer of 1992 by TOR books.*

About the Illustrator

Matthew Stork of Grand Rapids, Michigan, tells us that he has been fascinated with art since age four or so, and that he reached a high reading level at an early age because he valued books with sex, aliens, and evil sorcerers more than the standard fare of "See Dick run." He first read Lord of the Rings *in the third or fourth grade. While others studied phonics, Matthew was exploring Middle Earth.*

Now as a beginning illustrator who recently graduated with his B.F.A. in illustration from Kendall College of Art and Design, Matthew will share what he has discovered in the realms of imagination with you.

May, 1971

It was Uncle Teddy who taught me how to read and write. I think it took a long time but I'm not sure. I heard him arguing with Mother about it one night a few years ago when I wasn't supposed to be out of my room, but I was very excited with the next day being my birthday and I couldn't sleep.

"He can do it," Uncle Teddy had said.

And Mother said, "He doesn't care whether he reads or writes. It's you who cares. Why do you torture yourself? Let him be."

"He's fifty-four years old," Uncle Teddy said.

"*Let him be!*" Mother sounded very angry.

I listened to Uncle Teddy walk across the room. "If you feel that way," he said, "why didn't you just let him die?"

There was a long silence before Mother said, "I don't know," and another long silence after that.

Something in their voices frightened me, so I returned to my room. I became very ill, and for several weeks Dr. Armbruster came to see me every day, but he wouldn't let anyone else come in because he said I was too weak to have visitors.

But some time after, when I was much better, Uncle Teddy came to visit and he brought a picture book with him which made me remember his talk with Mother. I'm glad Uncle Teddy got his way because now I read and write a lot even though I throw most of my writing away. I hide some of it though and keep it just for myself, and it's not because I'm being sneaky, it's more because some of the things I write are my own personal secrets and I don't want to tell anyone, just like people don't want to tell me things sometimes when I ask them questions.

December, 1977

I am very excited about Christmas almost being here. I am looking forward to Uncle Teddy's stay because he always has something fun in mind. Yesterday after he arrived he walked me through the house and showed me all of the decorations—wreaths and flowers and a huge Christmas tree near the front hall strung with tinsel and candles. He brought several boxes full of gifts, all shapes and sizes, wrapped in bright colors—red and green and blue and silver with bows and ribbons—and I knew they were all for me because he put them under my tree upstairs.

Our house is very large. Mother calls it a mansion. She doesn't allow me to go anywhere except the rooms on my floor. She says I have everything I need right here.

That's why sometimes at night I'll walk around when everything is dark and everyone is asleep or in their rooms for the night. I don't think I'm being sneaky, it's just that I am very curious and if I ask about things no one tells me what I want to know. I've come to know this house very well. There are many hidden passageways behind the walls and I know them all by heart. I will hear things every once in a while that Mother would not like me to hear.

There was a big happening in the house last night and the servants were very busy, although it did not look to be a planned thing because everyone ran around and Mother didn't come to lock me in my room.

I went through one of my passageways that led to the main entrance of the house and I peeked through a tiny opening in the wall and saw a very beautiful woman with dark hair

Illustrated by Matthew Stork

standing inside the door. She was so beautiful that I held my breath. It must have been very cold outside because she was wearing a long black winter coat and there were flakes of snow in her hair. When she spoke, it was the most soft and delicate voice I had ever heard. She said, "Merry Christmas."

I wanted to stay and watch the woman forever but I knew that Mother would be up to check on me so I ran back to my room and pretended to be asleep. Mother came in and kissed my head and said, "Sleep well, child," like she did every night. I listened very closely for a long time hoping to hear the voice of the woman again, but next thing I knew it was morning, and she was gone.

October, 1982

I heard Mother and Dr. Armbruster arguing yesterday. They were just talking pleasantly for a while and I was listening in my passageway to the low, pleasant sound of their voices. The doctor was saying things I did not understand about sickness and diets and so on, when all of a sudden he said, "But John is doing fine," and Mother just about exploded with anger.

"His name is not John, do you understand me? Don't you ever call him by that name again! John is dead! *My* John is dead!" I had never heard Mother get so angry except for that one time with Uncle Teddy. She made the doctor leave right away and told him he could be replaced, but I hoped that she wouldn't do that because I sort of like Dr. Armbruster.

I don't know who John is, but I felt very bad for Mother. I had never really thought about my own name before. Uncle Teddy and everyone call me Sonny because it's short for Sonny Boy, and that's good enough for me. But it made me wonder how someone could get a name like John. Uncle Teddy was probably named after a teddy bear. Mother was just Mother.

May, 1987

Today was a very special day. It was my seventieth birthday. Uncle Teddy came to visit and I was very excited because I hadn't seen him in such a long time. We had a big cake and a lot of food and we played checkers for an hour. Then Uncle Teddy took me outside for a walk!

I'll never forget it as long as I live. I think Mother was not happy about it because she did not want to let me go at first, but Uncle Teddy talked her into it and we went outside surrounded by men in black suits and ties and shoes. Uncle Teddy asked me if I minded if his friends went with us, and of course I didn't care. They came to my party and they had a right to have fun. In fact, I told them that if they smiled more they might have a nicer time all around, but Uncle Teddy said they were usually very serious people and were happy that way.

It was a sunny day. The wind blew in my face and stung my eyes at first, but it felt good. Uncle Teddy took me all around the yard and into the garden where I smelled the roses and touched the bushes and the vines. I listened to the birds calling and the insects buzzing. I never dreamed they would sound so loud and so near.

I touched the winterberry hollies which were very special to me because I could always see their bright red berries from my window, even during the cold cold winters.

After a short time I caught a chill and had to go inside, and I was weak for the rest of the day. But I didn't care—I had such fun! I'll always remember it.

August, 1996

One night I entered a storage room through my passage-way where there were a lot of tools and brooms and rags and buckets and things. I rummaged around in the dark and my hands found a flashlight. I thought this would be a wonderful thing to have so I took it with me hoping that no one would miss it. Now I can sit in bed at night and read and write as long as I like and not have to worry about someone seeing my light.

I have not seen Mother in a very long time. I wondered if she was angry with me even though I didn't think she knew about my passageways or my late-night writing. Mother would have yelled at me if she knew.

I've been seeing more and more of Uncle Teddy, so I asked him about Mother today and he said that she went away on a very long trip and I wouldn't be seeing her for a while.

I asked him how long that might be and he said not long. He said soon we'd all be seeing her and then maybe we'd find out whether we did the right thing, whether the choices we'd made over the years had been the proper ones. He looked very sad when he said this, and then he said, "I think there is such a place, Sonny Boy, a place where we learn why everything is the way it is."

I asked him if Dr. Armbruster had gone with Mother since I hadn't seen him in so long and I was seeing Dr. Morelande almost every day now, and Uncle Teddy told me yes.

I thought about how lucky Mother was to visit this place, a place where every time you asked a question you got an answer, and I could not blame her if she didn't want to come back for a while. I told Uncle Teddy so, and he seemed to cheer up. We played cards for the rest of the afternoon.

May, 1997

Today was my eightieth birthday. I have been very sick and I was afraid that I might not be able to have my party, but Dr. Morelande said it was okay so we had cake and games with Uncle Teddy and I had a very nice time even though I had to stay in bed.

It was after my party that I had a scare. I was very weak,

and I probably should have just gone to sleep, but being so excited all day and not being allowed to get up, I turned restless after dark, so I decided to take a short walk through my passageways.

I followed a path that led to the back of a closet in Uncle Teddy's room, and I saw some light coming through the darkness so I went up to it. That's all I was going to do—peek and go away—until I saw Uncle Teddy crying. I'd never seen Uncle Teddy cry before. He was in bed. He had a large, green book on his lap, and every so often he would turn a page and cry some more.

I watched him for a while, waiting for him to be all right, but he didn't stop crying and I couldn't stand to watch him any longer, so I did a foolish thing and I entered his room through the closet.

"Sonny Boy," he said, "what are you doing here?"

I thought he might be angry with me so I wanted to say that I saw him crying, and that I only wanted to help him and be a friend, but before I could say anything he said, "So you know about the passages," and he didn't seem to be upset at all.

"Come over here, Sonny," he said.

I went and sat on the edge of his bed. He was looking at a photo album. Mother had shown me some photo albums years ago, and I thought they were interesting and we had a lot of fun even though I didn't recognize any of the faces. I don't ever remember crying over them. But Uncle Teddy's album was different. There were newspaper pictures, and headlines, and articles.

Uncle Teddy was looking at a picture of a man and a woman. The man seemed very serious, and his right hand was raised like an Indian chief's, but he had on a suit and tie and no headdress. The man's eyes were closed.

The woman had short black hair with long bangs, and she was looking down.

And then all of a sudden I just about screamed. I knew that woman. I remembered her from . . . from somewhere.

Uncle Teddy said, "You know her, don't you? Think, Sonny Boy, think very hard. What do you remember?"

I did think very hard, and then I remembered where I had seen her. She was the beautiful black-haired woman I had seen at Christmastime in the main entrance of the house years ago.

But then there was more. As I looked at the woman in the picture something very strange came into my head. I had a passing thought of this same woman in a pretty white gown, with a white veil over her face. It was just a piece of a thought that I could not keep in my mind for very long, but I'll never forget it. I reached out and touched the picture.

"Always grand," Uncle Teddy said. "She was wearing a very dignified, raspberry-colored suit that day."

But that's not what I had seen. I had seen the white gown. I had seen something that happened before my room and my house and my passageways and Mother and Uncle Teddy. Was there anything before them? Yes, I think there was. It was more than a passing thought—it was a *memory*.

"Was I married, Uncle Teddy?" I asked him.

He smiled. "Yes, you were. You proposed to her by telegram, you know, from Paris."

I thought this was interesting, but nothing more than that. Uncle Teddy started to cry again.

"Please, don't cry," I said.

He held my hand then. "I'm sorry we couldn't tell her you were alive. We couldn't tell your children, not anyone, not even Father because we couldn't be sure of his reaction. Mother was adamant about that. No one could know. Just Bobby and Mother and myself—and the doctors, of course. Now there's just me.

"It was for the good of the country. Those were critical times. The eyes of the world were watching us. We could not afford hesitancy. We felt you would have wanted it that way. Do you understand?''

I didn't, but I nodded anyway to stop Uncle Teddy from crying. He was clutching my arm very hard.

He traced the newspaper picture with his finger. "She was a strong woman, Sonny Boy. You would have been proud of her. I remember her standing right next to Lyndon, solid as a rock, little more than an hour after you were pronounced dead."

I was very confused about Uncle Teddy calling me dead, and about what the woman in the picture had to do with any of it, so I closed the book and placed it on the floor. I remembered what Mother used to do to make me feel better, so I thought that maybe the same thing might help Uncle Teddy feel better too.

I pulled his bed covers up to his chin, brushed back his hair, kissed him on the forehead, and turned out his light. "Sleep well, child," I said, and then I went back to my room. I was sure Uncle Teddy would be just fine in the morning. It had always worked for me.

December, 2008

Dr. Morelande is the only one who comes to see me anymore. He says that Uncle Teddy is so busy he can't find time to stop by. But I don't think that's exactly true. I think Uncle Teddy went on vacation with Mother and Dr. Armbruster, and he is having so much fun that he is not coming back at all.

Dr. Morelande has tried very hard to make this a good Christmas, but I am sorry to say I am not very happy. I am tired all of the time, and I can't even move out of bed. Dr. Morelande asked me if I wanted anything for Christmas, but if I couldn't have Mother or Uncle Teddy, then there was nothing to ask for.

But then I thought about it and thought about it for a long time, and I remembered the pictures Uncle Teddy had shown me many years ago. I told Dr. Morelande about the green photo album in Uncle Teddy's room and asked him if he could find it for me. A little while later Dr. Morelande returned with the book.

Together we went through the pictures, and when we got to the one Uncle Teddy had shown me, the one with the man and the beautiful dark-haired woman, I made him stop.

"There *is* something I want for Christmas," I told him. "There is something I want very much."

I decided to tell Dr. Morelande about the passageways then. I didn't think that I would get in trouble. I made him put me in my wheelchair and take me for a walk behind the walls. He argued with me at first, but I refused to be put off.

I told him exactly which path to follow. He wheeled me all the way down to the wall at the main entrance. I looked through the small opening. I was sure that the beautiful dark-haired woman would be standing at the door in her winter coat. I was disappointed that she wasn't there. I thought that if I waited long enough she would certainly show up—she would come back like the winterberry, bright and strong even in the cold cold winter. There would be snowflakes in her hair, and she would say "Merry Christmas" in her lovely voice. So we waited.

Finally Dr. Morelande said that if I agreed to go to bed, he would wait for the woman, and bring her directly to me as soon as she arrived. I thought that this would be a good idea since I was so tired.

When she arrives, we will have many things to discuss. I have decided to make her my new friend. I think I will show her my book of writings. I think I will ask her about the white gown to show her that I have not forgotten, and then I'll ask her about the children Uncle Teddy mentioned. I won't tell her about the vacation place where everyone has gone without me, and not because I'm being sneaky, but only because I am very lonely and I would like her to stay with me for a while.

Boos and Taboos
by
L. Ron Hubbard

About the Author

One might say that L. Ron Hubbard wasn't just a writer. He was a phenomenon. He had an extraordinarily inquisitive and receptive mind, which led him as a youth to begin a lifelong exploration of the world and the nature of man.

He studied firsthand more than twenty-one different races and cultures; from the Indian tribes of North America, to the Kayans of Borneo and the Mongols living in the Western Hills of China. He was a licensed master mariner, a pilot of early aircraft and an organizer and leader of expeditions which carried the flag of the Explorers Club. Coupled with this insatiable curiosity and love of adventure was an ability to look at the world and, all in a glance, reach often brilliant and often startling insights based upon his observations.

L. Ron Hubbard began his professional writing career in 1930 scripting and directing action radio dramas. He was also a correspondent for a national aviation magazine before becoming a writer of popular fiction. Within a few years he had written a multitude of action, sea and air adventure stories and rose to the top ranks of published authors. His work carried a verisimilitude that most other authors could not match, for while they fantasized about faraway places, storms at sea and death-defying aerobatics, L. Ron Hubbard had lived those adventures. With remarkable versatility, he soon added mystery, *western and historical fiction to his growing markets. In the late 1930s, he began writing movie scripts for Hollywood and then turned to crafting tales of science fiction, fantasy and horror. He was considered a giant among authors of the Golden Age of science fiction and many of his works from that period are classics including* Fear, Ole Doc Methuselah, To the Stars, *and* Final Blackout.

In fact, Final Blackout, *a gripping adventure about a world locked in the throes of an endless war, has been called "The father of all Survivalist novels," and it will soon be the first book by an American author to have an initial printing of over a million copies in Russia.*

L. Ron Hubbard mastered writing. He mastered technique. He mastered storytelling. He knew and understood his audience and what they wanted and fulfilled their expectations time and time again with masterly skill. Each of the past Writers of The Future *volumes has contained one of his essays, and all of them are both practical and insightful. Though some of his articles were written in the thirties and forties for journals oriented to the aspiring and professional writer, the art of storytelling has not changed and his ideas are just as valid today as they were then—just as valid as they will be a hundred years from now.*

When Ye Editor recently popped up at an American Fiction Guild luncheon, she found me lime punch drunk against the bar.

Said Ye Editor, "Write me an article on something, will you?"

Said I, "Certainly, on what?"

Said Ye Editor, " 'Why You Sold Your Last Story.' "

I pondered it for a bit, couldn't remember what I had sold last, and then put the question to two very learned gentlemen of our exalted fraternity.

Said one, "Why did I sell my last story? Well, editors do go blind, you know."

Said t'other, "Why? Because I needed the money."

Said half a dozen more, "Because I needed the money."

Said Ye Editor, "Certainly, but you can't put that in an article. It doesn't make sense."

Well, here it is in an article, but neither does it make sense.

There was reason behind that last sale. Not facetious reason, but actual cold hard writing reason. Now that we get right down to the meat of it, the reason I made my last sale a few days ago was the farthest thing from your mind.

I broke all the taboos. Which brings us to the scene.

All writers agree on one thing. Strange but they do—on that one matter. Writing is the screwiest profession man ever invented—as witness our double existence. Writers were originally minstrels, of course, and the minstrels used to wander about sleeping in haystacks and begging their wine, getting paid only in gifts.

We have become elevated to respectability as far as the world is concerned but we still live that cup to lip existence of our long dead brethren, and our lives, whether we strummed a lyre or a typewriter, are pretty identical.

And every once in a while we like to upset our own traditions just to see what will happen.

So I broke some half dozen strict taboos and sold the story.

Now, of course, there's a hitch to all this which I must mention, later, even though it smacks of conceit.

But to the taboos. This particular house, in common with the other pulp dynasties, enumerates their taboos in no uncertain terms. But I don't think, after this experience, that they believe them any too strongly.

Their heroes must be strong, virile, upright.

Of heroines they will have none whatever. No love interest!

No first person whatever. All third.

And there were others which I can't name because they would identify the yarn too clearly.

This yarn, not yet published at writing, was told in first person by a gentleman whose deeds smacked of crime. He went to great lengths because of a girl, and was, in fact, entirely motivated by that girl.

Which makes a very unwholesome lesson. Pulp taboos have been handed down, down, down until they bind a story into a narrow, vise-like groove, and like water which runs too long in one place, the limited plots are wearing down like stone. In ninety percent of the present pulp stories, tell me the beginning and I'll tell you the end.

All too true. One day an editor told me that, grinding the editorial teeth, little suspecting the answer to it. And so I set out to write a yarn which wouldn't foretell its ending. To do that thing I found out I had to break a couple taboos. I shivered over it as a Polynesian shivers over his own particular *tabus*.

But the story sold. It was just enough out of line to be interesting, just enough inside to stay in keeping with its brethren. Like a golf shot which slices over out-of-bounds and then sails in for a landing on the fairway.

It is even possible to apply to detective stories—and that coming from an adventure writer, says a great deal.

These taboos! They're like fetters to a convict—and a writer chained to his mill is enough of a convict already. The story must not be over such and such a length. Well, you get to be an automaton after a while so that you can write without numbering your pages—as I do—and still arrive at the required length. A sort of automatic alarm clock which shouts "Ending!"

That's a taboo, to overlength something, but not very serious.

Another taboo consists of virile heroes. Anything but clean-limbed gentlemen with a gat in each hand wait outside. And some of the mightiest stories ever written have been about nervous, anemic, shivering shrimps afraid of their own cigarette smoke. But no, sayeth the pulps, the hero must be lithe, tall, dark, and handsome.

The heroine must always be pure as snowdrifts, unsullied, unsoiled, and the greatest worry is about the intentions of the big, bad, sneering, leering, rasping, grating, snarling villain. Dear girls. Most women are married in the mid-twenties. And with all due respect to everybody, the most interesting, witty, quick-thinking ladies are past that age. Dear me, can't we have some really interesting females in pulp?

One outfit puts a ban on anything where adventure fails to go after a reward of some kind. No mental rewards. The clinking clatter of gold and the brittle sparkle of jewels must be in the fore forever. I searched for gold once, twice, but any adventures I might have had, bad or good, dull or interesting, dealt with quantities far more intangible than gold. Esteem, self-respect, loyalty . . .

Ah, but I'm being too unkind. I could list taboos by the hour and boo at them, showing, of course, my great superiority over mind and matter, demonstrating that I dwell in a void high over all else. But I don't, honest, lady.

My cry is this. Writers are foolish enough, from what they've told me, to believe in a lot of those taboos to their own detriment.

As a consequence, what do we find? The rut, the pit, the caldron of lost hopes and the rain of sweat. That's a pitiful picture.

A man can clatter out just so much in one pattern before the pattern becomes as solid as a prisoner's bars. Don't argue. I've been through it. It gets so that you can't write anything but what you have written before. You lose all that delightful plasticity of ideas. You are hampered by vague demons who jump up and down and scream in your ears when you fail to place so many words of straight action in a story. You groan at the thought of writing something new, because you know the conflict which will take place in your own head. You'll drown in a sea of already written words, and the tide of youngsters will come up and sweep over you, and Davy Jones, in the form of the reject basket, will swallow your bones forever.

And mainly because of Old Man Taboo.

What courage it takes to break free! You stare at a vision of an empty cupboard. You seem to feel your toes peeping through your shoes, you already listen to the angry words of the landlord as he helps the sheriff toss your writing desk out into the street.

And you remember the taboos, and you know that if you fail to mind those taboos, if you fail to stay walled in and blinded by those ruts, you'll go broke.

And yet, if you don't jar yourself some way, then how will you climb, advance, put markets behind you and see others looming to the fore?

It's a bad spot. About a year into the game, every writer faces it, doesn't quite know what it is, groans and writhes about, and then, when the gentle news is broken—if he has friends friendly enough to break it, to tell him that his stuff is still in one place, that he must advance, for nothing can stand still—he is apt to lose months of work.

The taboos do it. You must mind the taboos, but if you do, you stand quite still for a space and then begin to slide—backwards. I wonder how many writers have wrecked themselves that way?

The solution wasn't rammed at me in the cold dazzle of day. It sneaked up on me through black nights of worry. "Damn the taboos!" And I thought about damning them. They were fetters. I couldn't actually face the fact that my stuff was juvenile. How could that be? Didn't I give it my all? And I tried to write for better markets. Markets I knew I couldn't touch. I had to make a break. I felt need of that plasticity of mind which would allow me to do something with a hero besides letting him bump off natives and kiss the girl, and I had to do something with the girl besides letting her kiss the hero and dread the villain.

But the taboos stuck and stuck until I deliberately set out one fine day and sorted out all the taboos of a certain market. Maliciously, I broke them, one by one, stringing out an off-length story.

But the thing retained its stamp. It was, after all, action for action's sake. It didn't live. It wasn't the best I'd done. And so I set out to break more taboos, bigger and better taboos.

For many, many words I wrote for the waste basket, and then suddenly I saw a change. Plasticity was coming back. Satisfied and smug, I sat myself down and wrote a yarn and sold it higher than I had ever sold anything before.

The formula to end all formulas had worked.

The whole summation is this. Any magazine, big or small,

will take something different, just off their beaten path, if that something is better to their own way of thinking than anything they have purchased before.

"What?" you say, "you mean you have to write twice as good for the same market? You mean you have to spend more time on a yarn? You mean you have to deliberately coax them out of their ideas with quality? Well, to the devil with that!"

Ah, but the glory of it! The feeling that you have done something real! And then those yarns can go higher and still sell lower the second time out. Not that I ever sell a reject, you understand. Oh, cross my heart, never. But you can sell a good piece of cloth to a native who dresses in gunny sacks and palm bark. You can sell a good fast cruiser to a fisherman used to a one-lung sloop. You can peddle can-openers to people who open their cans with an axe.

And you can sell a high class, fast action, counter-plotted, characterized, pulsating yarn to a mag which has heretofore purchased only the action.

It can be done, is being done, and to clinch the deal, unless you're one of those who likes to lie in a rut, keeps you from slopping about in the muddy plain of mediocrity. You'll get rejects, but when you sell, you'll be remembered. Never fear, you'll be remembered.

Give them all their own demands plus everything you want to put into a story. Do it so well that they don't even know their taboos are being broken, and through this escape from the pit. We'll all be saying, "Well, well, made the awards, did he? Yes, I knew him when."

Bringing Sissy Home

by
Astrid Julian

ILLUSTRATED BY Jane Walker

About the Author

A finalist can reenter the Contest until he/she wins a prize or until he or she has gone on to successfully publish more than three short stories and has happily disqualified himself as a novice.

Astrid Julian first appeared in our pages as a finalist in L. Ron Hubbard Presents Writers of The Future, Volume IV with the deliciously quirky story "Mother's Day." Astrid has lived in Germany and Canada, and currently resides in the Cleveland area where she works as a typesetter and attends a writing group with a number of past WOTF winners—Ken Schulze, Paula May, Mary Turzillo, Jay Sullivan, and Merritt Severson.

As if that were not enough to keep her busy, Astrid has a toddler and a teenage daughter.

None of which tells you what a charming, warm, and outgoing person Astrid is. Nor does it quite prepare you for this dark and stunning tale. We are delighted that she has returned to our pages now as a prizewinner.

About the Illustrator

Jane Walker of Beltsville, Maryland, was brought up on a dairy farm in Vermont, the seventh of nine children, and got her Bachelor of Fine Arts in illustration from the Rhode Island School of Design. She has worked quite successfully for several years illustrating fantasy and nature subjects.

She has one book cover to her credit, a reprint of The Broken Lands *by Fred Saberhagen and she has exhibited her art at the Prince George County Arts Council. She is an avid gardener and an amateur historian, specializing in medieval Europe and colonial America.*

02:30

Can't sleep.

It's usually like this the night before a hit, but tonight I seem to have a touch of fever. Can't be malaria. I haven't missed taking a Paludrine tablet since I got back to Africa. Has to be nerves. At twenty-eight, I've been in the business too long.

This afternoon I found a decapitated cat on my bed. A trail of fat red splotches led across the white bedspread to the nightstand and an opened sardine tin. Inside was the cat's head. Muzzle tied shut with tiny bandages. Both eyeballs punctured by rusty nails.

The landlord apologized, cleaned up, and gave me a crazy story about his new maid being fresh out of the holy forest. It gives me the willies thinking about an ignorant girl from the boonies making sacrifices to the voodoos in my room. But since this is my last night here, I decided not to press the issue and asked him not to fire her.

The mud walls of the house suck in cool ocean smells. My silk camisole and panties feel damp and clingy. Uneven clay tiles chill my feet as I walk to the veranda. There, a silver stripe of moonlight slashes the sleeping Atlantic and points an accusing finger at the city of Dakar and at me.

My assignment is Charlotte Abiola Kikelomo Jumake Adekunle, a Nigerian, Princess of the Yoruba, and heir to one of the world's greatest oil fortunes. I try not to think of her, but I can't stop myself. Tonight, she sleeps in the Club

Mediterranée's ultra-modern complex on the Pointe des Almadies. Tomorrow my librarian will stalk her through the market stalls of Dakar as she tries on silly hats with her aunts and her maids. It's not my fault her family has decided to marry her to Claude M'Bengue.

It's just . . . God, I hate this job. Ending a life is so personal. It should be done by family and friends, or by oneself, not by a stranger carrying a Heckler and Koch PSG1 with infrared image converter.

Heckler and Koch PSG1 is a simple tool. I call my rifle the librarian. Once my rifle closes a book, though, it can never be read again. Memories—the smell of a Sunday roast, the babbling of an infant son, the speech that rallies a nation to war, the screams of a soldier just before he agrees to cooperate—my H&K collects and ends them all.

Even the ending of my most notorious assignment, Abu Nidal, was sad and impersonal, although I was able to twist it to my advantage. It's nasty of me, but I'm rather proud of how I was able to make it look as if he'd been executed by the Iraqi military. Score one for my mother and for Sissy.

Charlotte Adekunle's book will be a short one. She's just eighteen, only three years older than Sissy.

Charlotte's skin is translucent brown. Like the tea the Senegalese shove at you in every little bistro and dibiterie of the Medina, Dakar's "African quarter" behind the Grand Mosque.

Watching the waiters pour tea from enormous heights into tiny glasses relaxes me. It's so hypnotic, the waiters imagine I'm flirting with them as they empty the tea back into the pot and then pour it into the glasses again. Back and forth until the sugar dissolves and white froth tops each amber-filled glass. Amber is the color Sissy's skin would be, if she weren't kept indoors all the time.

My own skin is black. Whether I stay inside or outside makes no difference. It stays as black as my father's. I like it, except when I'm back in Enterprise, Alabama, where Dad's family lives, or when I'm in West Africa.

Giggles mingle with the sound of the surf rolling onto the beach. A teenaged boy and girl, children of the fisherfolk that live in this part of Dakar, shyly hold hands and walk across the sand. That's the way it should be for Princess Charlotte, I think. She should be left alone to fall in love with some local boy back in Lagos, not forced into this marriage with a stranger. A marriage so upsetting to the powers that be, in general, and the pharmaceutical industry, in particular, that a contract has been placed on her life.

This job stinks.

Once more, I tell myself. Once more, and Uncle Sam can kiss my black ass good-bye. After this assignment I'll finally have enough cash to buy Sissy back. My bare feet pad back into the house. I close the louvered doors to the veranda.

06:00

Subh. First prayers of the morning. From the small mosque at the corner the muezzin calls the faithful. It's still dark when I walk outside to the bath house across the court-yard from my room. Very African, this having to leave your room to shower, but the fixtures are modern and the water hot, and I can blend into the background in this neighbor-hood. A black woman at Club Med still sticks out, unless she's a maid, or a princess.

On my way back to my room, I pass my landlord's *legba,* the concrete guardian of this compound. His face and head are smeared with blood that dribbles down onto his stubby feet. There, a ritual iron holds a freshly killed chicken head. The gods will transform themselves into birds and eat the offering throughout the day.

It's all so strange. To think I once entertained romantic

notions of emigrating to Africa. I'm suddenly hot again. The fever is returning.

A *gris-gris* hangs from my door knob. My landlord is concerned for my safety because I have been angering the gods, and even worse, the voodoos, with all my questions about his and his maid's religion. He's right, I think as I pull the charm from the knob. I should mind my own business and get on with my job, but I can't resist unwrapping the *gris-gris*. Inside the little red and white checked cloth, I find a raw egg, two feathers and a white powder that smells like pine needles. I wrap it in yesterday's newspaper and pitch it into the wastepaper basket.

I tie an ankle-length blue and white striped cloth over my western style khaki skirt and knot a yellow scarf with brown and green flowers around my head, trying to make the ends stick out at odd angles the way African women do. I achieve an acceptable result. Not too fetching. Not too different. Don't want to catch someone's eye. I have on a touristy-looking beige silk blouse that I cover with a gaudy *buba* made of the same material as my headtie. *Boubou,* I correct myself. I'm in Senegal now, not Nigeria. Use the Senegalese word.

I'm posing as Nigerian. Growing up in Europe has left my French good enough that I can be mistaken for a Nigerian cloth trader with a Senegalese parent. In Dakar that's good enough for me to fade into the background.

On the bureau is a Canon Sure Shot, a nice inexpensive little camera, along with a somewhat pricier Seiko sportswatch. Bribes, just in case there's trouble. For a day or two at least, the greedy landlord should hold off calling the police to investigate the missing cloth seller.

Lying on a hand mirror next to the camera is a brooch. A two-inch long, gray lump of man-shaped clay. Not quite representational, but about as good as my clumsy fingers are capable of. I call him Jan. Jan Sikorski, my death doll. He's been with me a long time. Since the Frankfurt debriefing after my very first action. Grossed Dad out when that old African custom was explained to him. Don't know that I myself really believe that Jan's soul is contained in the doll or that it's anywhere at all, but Dad's from the South. He was raised with a lot more religion than I was.

Actually I think Dad was relieved when Jan was killed. He never liked him. Said he wasn't about to let no commie marry his little girl. I never believed Dad's accusations. I mean, Jan's job at the Polish Embassy in London was to help Polish expatriates reclaim property that had been appropriated by the communists. Why would a communist involve himself in something that negated everything he believed in?

I pack my basket. Today the librarian's five-round magazine, action, and plastic stock rest on the wicker bottom covered by a length of blue-green paisley challis. I add a layer of garish, red-flowered cotton. On top of that, the barrel, freshly cleaned with a nylon parachute cord and oiled just last night, and the YAG laser scope coupled with the infrared image converter. Day or night, I can pick the time to close Charlotte's book.

In with my collection of thimbles, scissors and embroidery hoops, are two Winchester 308 cartridges which I have reloaded with less powder so the librarian will let them fly with only a subsonic pop and not a supersonic boom. The librarian rarely requires more than two cartridges for an assignment. Even Abu Nidal went down easy, with the first one.

In the beginning I used the suppressor my Uncle Sam supplied me, or else I made my own. But you don't drill your own holes in the barrel of an H&K PSG1. I went to Jordan in full chador and met with an Israeli gun trader just over the border. My mother, the women's libber, would have died to see me like that, walking around in a black tent, but how many black women have you seen walking the streets of Tel Aviv?

Stay invisible, stay alive.

I open the door to my room and walk outside. The canvas bag I sling over one shoulder contains a Canadian passport with my picture in it and a pair of hiking boots. It's also big enough to hide the librarian once my assignment is over. A rented Peugeot jeep waits for me in the parking lot at the railway station. By this evening I hope to be off to Mali, beginning my own Paris-Dakar rally, only in reverse.

The cab I called is an ugly Citroën with wooden bumpers. A crumpled left fender makes its slant-eyed headlights look crossed.

"Avenue Albert Sarraut," I tell the driver. Charlotte is meeting her future mother-in-law at the Novotel for breakfast. The hotel's view of the island of Gorée is said to be incredible. Gorée was the place where Dad's ancestors were loaded onto a slave ship and sent to America. I'd love to see it, but a four-star luxury hotel isn't the kind of place where Nigerian cloth sellers eat.

The cab winds through alleyways of white stucco-walled houses. I can almost forget I'm in Africa. Mismatched brown and red clay tile roofs with concrete patches remind me of western Poland where many of the buildings were also built by the French. Huguenots who found freedom from religious persecution in Pomerania. I spent my last weekend with Jan in Poland in a little clay-tile-roofed village north of Pila. Jan! I suddenly remember the death doll lying on the dresser back in the hotel.

It's stupid to waste time going back there now, I think. And Dad will be happy that I've finally stopped carrying it around. But then I think of the cat's head and of the voodoo girl using my room for sacrifices. I don't believe all that mumbo-jumbo about souls, but the voodoo girl will recognize the brooch as a death doll. I can see her gloat already, thinking she has some power over me, forcing me to be more respectful of her gods.

That little lump of clay and I have been through a lot. I warn myself that I can't afford sentiment and that no one can hurt Jan. Not anymore. But I can't stand the thought of the voodoo girl touching him.

I reach forward and tap the driver on the shoulder. *"Retournez chez moi. J'ai oublié quelque chose."* He wheels the Citroën around and heads back to my rest house.

When I get back to Europe, I'll drive out to Poland and bury Jan in the grass in a sunny birch forest. The Citroën lurches to a stop. I grab my basket and yell, *"Attendez!"* at the driver, then run into the courtyard. The basket is awkward but I can't take a chance leaving it with the driver.

The door to my hotel room is cracked open. The maid doesn't start work until eight. Instead of crossing the dusty courtyard directly, I walk along the veranda where I can remain hidden. I put my basket down on the concrete walk next to the door and pull my body flat against the wall listening for movement inside the room. I hear drawers being pulled open, but it's too dark to see inside. Then I get a break. Metal hangers squeak and scrape as they're being pulled back and forth across the steel bar in the closet. If the intruder is in the closet, I can get into the room without being seen.

I kick the door open with my foot so I won't be blinded by the sudden dark. He fills the closet alcove. I stare at his back and think, Christ he's big. If only I'd taken the time to pull some ribbons from my basket. With a garotte I'd have half a chance. Too late.

I jump up behind him and get lucky. He trips over a shoe on the floor losing his step long enough for me to get my arms around his head and twist. Three more seconds and I'll have his head at the angle I need to finish the job. A shorter man would be dead already. Then it gets weird.

He starts crying. A grown man. I lose my cool. This is either the dumbest thief in Dakar or the smartest spy in the world. Meantime he's bellowing like a cow needing to be milked. I hear the landlord yell to his wife as he runs across the courtyard. It'll blow my cover if they see me with a death grip on the guy's head, so I let him go and pick up the waste-paper basket, the lamp, the telephone and throw them one after the other at the thief.

He charges head first at the door, knocking the landlord flat on his ass. I scream and act shaken. I offer to pay for the broken lamp, but the landlord won't take any money. He's embarrassed that the thief, if that's what he was, got by him.

All I can think about is getting out of the hotel room and out of Senegal. Princess Charlotte must have been alert-ed somehow. I decide to find Charlotte immediately, if the mission has been compromised and she's hired a bodyguard, I'll take a cab straight to the train station.

I pin the death doll onto my *boubou*. Then I notice that the Seiko watch is missing. I can relax. The man was a thief after all. The landlord talks about calling the police. No, no, forget it, I tell him, the thief didn't get anything. The land-lord looks relieved. It would look very bad for his rest house if he had to file a complaint with the police.

A few blocks away from the Novotel hotel, I get out of the cab, hoist my basket onto my head and walk along the tree-lined avenue. Thick whitewashed tree trunks make the avenue seem quite bright even though the sun is just rising. In spite of the episode back at my hotel room there's no hurry. Mrs. M'Bengue is a devout Muslim and will be busy a while longer with morning prayers.

Charlotte will have a difficult time with the dawn prayers. She is a sleepy Anglican who keeps a few fetishes in her rooms at Club Med, but like all dutiful African wives, she will make her husband's religion her own. Compared to Sissy, she is lucky. The practice of female circumcision; the cutting away of the clitoris, has almost died out in West Africa. Both Muslims and Fetisheurs have abandoned it.

I shake my head and almost tip my basket. How easy it is to forget that after tonight there will be no Charlotte.

On the curb in front of the *Banc du Sénégal*, a group of vendors ready their trays and carts for the breakfast crowd of bank and embassy employees. I order a lamb brochette and lemon grass tea while I wait.

09:00

Charlotte drives up in a vintage Karman Ghia that any collector on the streets of Stuttgart would envy. The hotel valet opens the door for her maid. Charlotte gets out before the valet reaches her door. Good. She and the maid are alone. There is no bodyguard. The silver crucifix around Charlotte's neck glints in the sunlight as she turns and hands the valet her car key. She stops under the Novotel awning to brush the creases out of her pale yellow worsted silk dress. Her headtie matches her dress exactly. Something her mother picked out, no doubt. Hardly the sort of thing Charlotte goes in for.

The white Mercedes belonging to the M'Bengues pulls up a few minutes later. The driver waves off the valet and opens the door for Mrs. M'Bengue.

Fifteen minutes later, twenty-year-old Claude arrives on a bicycle wearing a grass-stained soccer jersey with the number eleven on it. He is followed by a small crowd of his fellow soccer-players who tease him about his breakfast date with his future wife. Claude blushes appealingly as he loads his bicycle into the trunk of the Mercedes and takes a dove gray suit from his mother's driver.

It does no good to wish that Claude could have been my assignment. He's just as sweet and appealing as Charlotte and he has five older brothers, any one of whom could be forced into a marriage with Charlotte. Charlotte is an only child. When she dies her fortune will be divided among the various branches of her family and will cease to threaten African stability. Claude's family, on the other hand, would use Charlotte's oil money to take their counterfeit drug company legit. AIDS and polio vaccines, malaria prophylactics, penicillin, birth control pills—American drug companies stand to lose a fortune, if the African pharmaceutical industry takes off.

But the M'Bengue's other business worries Uncle Sam more. Two of their factories, one in Dakar and another up north in St. Louis, are developing biological weapons. With Charlotte's money, Claude's father and uncle will be able to buy delivery systems for the biologicals. In two to three years the CIA expects M'Bengue missiles armed with biological warheads to be positioned in Zimbabwe, Libya and Mozambique.

I learned the hard way to trust the company analysts when they assign wet work. Back in Poland, too many people died because I tried second-guessing the analysts.

I rest my hand on the cloths covering the librarian as I sit on the curb sipping another lemon grass tea.

I'm saving the world.

This job still stinks.

11:00

The M'Bengues get into their Mercedes. Charlotte and her maid join them. They head west toward the Place de l'Independence. Good. I hail another crunchmobile and follow. There's nothing strange about a Nigerian cloth merchant heading in the direction of the Sandanga Market. I decide to take the driver into my confidence and order him to follow the Mercedes.

"Back in my country, mademoiselle has much money," I say.

This doesn't seem to interest my driver one way or the other. "Mademoiselle hasn't picked out the fabric for her family's wedding clothes. I will give you 300 French francs if you don't lose her." The driver grins at me in the rearview mirror and speeds up.

Somewhere along the Avenue Georges Pompidou, my taxi turns left and follows Charlotte into the colonial section of Dakar. Red bougainvillea drapes ivory walls. Paint on the old stucco mansions is peeling away from the walls exposing darker tan patches. The faded elegance of this quarter smacks of refinement. Like Mrs. M'Bengue and Claude. Claude's flashy father and uncle seem out of place here. The Mercedes turns into a black-iron-gated drive. My taxi pulls over to the curb and waits. The driver tries to talk to me. I ignore him.

The expatriate section of Kuwait City where my parents had their house was so modern it looked like an exhibit at a convention of Miami architects. Mom and Sissy were home when the Iraqis invaded.

Sissy had just entered the first grade in the local school. Dad had named her Yasmin, and for years he'd planned for her to be his Arab specialist, just as I had become his European specialist.

He sent me to school in Germany. Not an on-base American school with other Army brats, a full-fledged German school. He outfitted me just like the German kids. A knapsack packed with a hard roll and butter on my back, and in my arms a two-foot foil cone filled with candy. Later, he sent me to school in Holland, France and Greece.

When the Iraqis invaded, Dad, a retired U.S. army colonel, was on a consulting job in Alexandria, Virginia. His best friend had to sucker punch him and hide his car keys to keep him off a plane to Riyadh until I was able to get leave and fly down from West Point where I was a sophomore cadet.

Mom was a nurse at a Kuwaiti hospital, and she reacted to the invasion as if she were a smartass from Berlin and not the shy daughter of a penniless refugee from Breslau.

That's not fair. I'm sure if Mom had known Sissy would be taken from her, she would have gone into hiding right away.

Watching the execution of children in the streets of Kuwait made her snap. You'd think she would have thought of Sissy then, but in her mind things like that didn't happen to American kids, or German kids. At least they hadn't for a long time. I think she was already a crazy woman when the Iraqis moved into her hospital and shot the chief obstetrician and two pediatric interns.

She hauled out Dad's cellular phone, called Dad's friend in Saudi Arabia, and arranged for an uplink to CNN. If she wasn't sleeping or finding food for Sissy, she was talking on that damn phone trying to tell people what was going on in Kuwait. I heard her German-accented English on CNN myself. So did the Iraqis.

They kept her even after they released the other women and children. We allowed our hopes to rise when Saddam Hussein announced the release of the human shields, but Mom and Sissy were not among them despite numerous protests from the German and American chargés in Baghdad.

Dad never saw Sissy again, but three weeks into the war, Mom appeared on Baghdad TV. Her blond hair was hidden under a white scarf. Her face was swollen and her nose off-center. She called on the Coalition soldiers to lay down their weapons and stop their unlawful aggression against the peaceful people of Iraq.

Dad cried. Two days later he left for Saudi Arabia. I didn't argue.

Since the Red Cross brought her out of the theater of war, Mom hasn't been the same. She can't stand to be indoors where everything reminds her of Sissy.

Mom spends spring and summer with Dad in the little A-frame house Dad built just outside of Cody, Wyoming. She's taken a job at the local hospital helping out during tourist season, but she doesn't care about anything anymore. Even the furniture in the house, bought to replace what was lost in Kuwait, was all picked out by Dad.

Fall is spent in Enterprise, helping Dad's mother can her tomatoes and okra. Winter, she spends with her own mother in Nüremberg.

Christmas is the toughest on Mom. Late in the afternoon of each December twenty-fourth, she leaves her mother's apartment and walks the streets of Nüremberg until noon the next day.

12:00

Charlotte and her maid follow Mrs. M'Bengue back into the Mercedes. They head north to the Medina. My cab follows. Charlotte turns around and looks long and hard at my taxi. At least I think it's Charlotte. It seems a little ridiculous, though. She's only eighteen and full of smiles and giggles; too naive to suspect anyone would be following her.

The car stops at the Tilène Market. I thank my driver and let him go. A market is a good place for a hit, and there is nothing unusual about dropping off a cloth seller there. If I don't find an opportunity here, I know from her telephone conversations that Charlotte plans to tour the Grand Mosque at fourteen:thirty. I can catch a bus. It's on the main line.

The Tilène Market is very African. Only the *boubous* of the flower mongers can dim the masses of garish blooms. It wouldn't surprise me to learn that more than one of the women had a death doll or two wrapped in the handkerchiefs pinned to their blouses. Only in West Africa a death doll usually contains the soul of a child who didn't survive babyhood, not the soul of a former lover like Jan.

Haggling shoppers drown out the official French bartering

with the easy music of Wolof and Fula. Crude wooden stalls offer unglazed pottery, twig baskets, and exotic vegetables such as plantain and baobab leaves. The odor of sun-dried fish blends with the stench of sweat from the crowd. It sharpens the perfume of the floral bouquets stinging my nostrils.

Charlotte walks to a large stall at the end of the main aisle. Row upon row of mummified monkey paws stretch out at her feet. Wings of owls are arrayed with hundreds of little gray parrot carcasses. Goat skulls hang from the stall's roof like a bumper crop of grapes just before harvest.

In the center of the stall is a small table where wooden gods sit smoking cigarettes. Voodoos. Their skin bleached white during their sojourn across the Atlantic. At their feet are ritual offerings. Bottles of Charlie and Estée Lauder perfume. Red and white packs of Marlboros. They demand tribute in the currency of the lands where they became cruel and evil.

Stacked around all four sides of the altar are piles of burlap bags containing ampules of penicillin, birth control pills, steroids; all available without prescription, the source of the M'Bengue's modest fortune.

Two dogs tied to a corner post whimper as if they know they will soon be sacrificed to Ougoun, the Yoruba god of blacksmiths, hunters and motorcars.

The woman selling the magic charms and medicines smiles at Charlotte and kisses her hand. She pulls Charlotte further into the stall and places a necklace of cowrie shells around her neck. Charlotte leaves a little offering on the altar.

I'm curious to see what Charlotte has given the gods, so I wait for her to leave the market and walk to the stall. It's a relief when the slight, sweet aroma of decaying flesh from the little parrot corpses finally conquers the reek of the flowers.

A woman grabs my elbow and demands to see my samples. I smile at her and shake my head. "*C'est pas pour vous,*"

I tell her, but she won't leave me alone. People are staring.

I put my basket down and the woman bends to rummage through the folded material. Before she can find the librarian, I pull out a brightly embroidered cloth and name a ridiculously low price. The woman looks at me in disbelief, then smiles slyly and hands me some Senegalese francs. She bends again hoping to find another bargain to match the first. "*La prochaine fois.*" Next time, I tell her, and snatch the basket away, placing it back onto my head. She seems disappointed, but not enough to bother me again.

The woman in the medicine stall smiles at me and beckons with both hands. Her face is scarred by sinister geometric patterns, but her smile is all fresh air and sunshine. "Love potion?" she asks in Wolof. "Cure for a toothache?"

I shake my head and pretend to be interested in the vendor's statuettes, miniature Catholic saints ringed by eight-armed Indian gods. Many of the African gods and fetishes are familiar from my days at the University of London, when I still hoped to emigrate to Africa. Cheap ivory-colored, plastic crucifixes are jumbled together with garishly painted European mermaid dolls that are used by the Mami-Wata cult. Bata, the god of smallpox, has his brown skin dotted with white paint. Standing next to Bata are Edan, the snake god, who can send a snake to kill an enemy and Akiti, a particularly malicious fetish who causes mental illness.

The wooden crate next to the gods is filled with thunderstones, created when the metaphysical heavenly forces hurled lightning bolts down onto the physical world of man. The thunderstones symbolize the union of heaven and earth, the ordinary and the divine. Neither can exist without the other. Both form one-half of a whole, I was told by one of my Nigerian classmates at U. of London. But this union has no place for slaves, or the descendants of slaves.

I'd never understood why the Africans in my classes never talked with me, or why they turned me down each time I asked them out for coffee. It was the Nigerian in my Shona sculpture class who finally told me why. Her smile remained friendly as she patiently explained, as if she were talking to a very stupid child, that descendants of slaves have the souls of slaves. By definition they cannot be human. "Would you invite a screwdriver out for coffee?" she asked me. "Or a bicycle? Surely not."

My parents were relieved when I quit African studies and accepted an appointment to West Point. They had been against my emigrating to Africa, but I had been so determined. My mother would get angry and ask why I couldn't go to Silesia, after all I'm just as much German as African-American, but what can I say? When I look in the mirror, I don't exactly see Heidi.

"A ceremony?" the voodoo woman asks me. "A woman like you should be having three children already. Ten thousand francs and Mamissa will help."

I thank her, but no. Then she sees the death doll pinned to my *boubou* and clucks. "Next time you are pregnant, you come to Mamissa. She will keep the evil spirits far away from the little one."

I hardly listen as I shake my head. Charlotte has left something small and silver. An earring. *My earring!* A disc of beaten silver my friend Liz made for me in an art class years ago.

My heart feels like it wants to jump out of my chest. Like a voodoo animal about to be sacrificed. Calm down, I tell myself. Hadn't I lost one of my earrings? Yes. That day on the beach watching the fishermen dry their catch. But still. That's *my* earring!

It's suddenly very hot in the market. I feel ill again. The voodoo woman spills a smelly powder on me and my basket. Her grin grows wider, almost a leer. She acts as if it were an accident. "*Pardon, pardon. Comme je suis une folle,*" she apologizes, and begins brushing away the powder.

I remember enough of my African studies to know that the woman is a witch and that she has cast a spell over me.

It won't work. Descendants of slaves aren't human beings. Her magic has no hold over me. Not when it's compared with the magic of the librarian. I push her hands away and leave her stall. I rush down the market aisle towards the exit, shoving gawky shoppers out of my way.

At the end of the aisle I trip over a rolled up rushwork mat sticking out of a stall. I try to keep my basket from spilling the librarian over the market floor, and almost succeed, scraping both knees in the effort. My embroidery basket spills anyway. Agonizing seconds tick by before my black hand can dull the brassy gleam of the two Winchesters rolling across the concrete floor.

Lemon yellow pumps stop next to my basket. Hands reach under my left elbow to help me up. I know without looking, it's Princess Charlotte. At first, when I thank her, I think I see recognition in her eyes, but no. Her eyes glaze over and I'm just another cloth seller again.

But the earring!

You lost it on the beach. Remember, Stupid?

I have to get control of myself.

Oh God. She smells so clean. Like vanilla.

14:00

Suhr. Prayers again. I'm riding the bus to the Grand Mosque. The windows next to my seat have been broken out. When the bus moves, the heat, thick as honey, becomes bearable. I can't forget my earring lying there with the perfume and cigarettes for the gods. How did Charlotte get it? What does she know?

I should leave Dakar, but Sissy is so close now. This last hit, and I'll finally have enough cash. I tell myself I'm being

Illustrated by Jane Walker

silly. My imagination is running away with me. I saw a bit of silver, but it wasn't an earring. It could have been a coin. Yes, that's what it was, a coin.

I walk into the alley behind the empty house I checked out a couple of weeks ago. Cardboard boxes and rubbish barrels are piled in such a way that I can climb to the flat roof of the house. From here, I can see the forecourt of the mosque and look up at the minaret. An acacia tree grows over the roof, providing shade and camouflage.

The librarian snaps together with a reassuring series of clicks and hums as the computers and micro-motors realign the barrel and sights into the stock. The built-in collimator blinks green. I look through the sight and wait.

Sissy was adopted in Baghdad. We found out that much from the propaganda films. Saddam awarded a medal to a Muslim fundamentalist for adopting the child of the infidel and showing her the way to God.

After prayers, Charlotte and her entourage appear on the tower's little balcony and look down at Dakar. The crucifix is gone. In its place is a small brown pendant which Charlotte picks up with the fingers of both hands.

I load the modified Winchesters into the librarian's magazine. Charlotte is a dead woman, no matter what. If I don't do it, someone else will be sent, and they'll get the money that could have been used to help Sissy.

When I increase the magnification of my scope, I see that Charlotte's pendant is a miniature brown hand, a monkey paw. She presses it to her lips, then onto her forehead. Her maid gives Charlotte a small hand mirror which she uses to reflect light onto the various buildings surrounding the mosque.

I watch the light flit over store fronts, houses, workshops, trees and parked cars. When it gets to my house, the light freezes for a few seconds, then floats upward until it hovers in the leaves of the tree above me.

Through my scope, Charlotte kisses the monkey paw three times and says something which her maid answers. The laser locks onto Charlotte's forehead.

I feel the librarian get warm. And warmer. The plastic heats up like a metal car roof in the African sun. "Shit!" I scream, and let the rifle fall onto the baked mud roof.

I don't know what's wrong with me, letting mumbo-jumbo with a monkey paw get to me like that. This is for Sissy, I tell myself. Once more and Sissy will be free.

17:00

Asr. I hop a bus for Yoff that passes by Club Med. Charlotte will return to dress for dinner, as she has every night these past three weeks.

The bus drives by the tidy Muslim Cemetery. With its plain stone graves, all pointing to Mecca, it is very different from the City of the Dead in Alexandria. The mausoleums and catacombs of the City of the Dead have become a housing project for the increasing numbers of homeless poor in Egypt.

About three years after the war began, I was with Special Forces. Somebody needed a wife for an action in Ethiopia. On our return to Europe, Saad, one of our Egyptian operatives told us of a light-skinned black girl who spoke fluent Arabic with an Iraqi accent living in the City of the Dead in Alexandria. Sissy would have been nine. I couldn't pass up the opportunity. While the American contingent continued on to Frankfurt for debriefing, I headed for Alexandria. An unauthorized leave, but as it fell on a weekend, one that might go undetected.

For two days, I searched through catacombs and tramped into tombs, trading pieces of Wrigley's Juicy Fruit gum for information about a little girl in a wrinkled photo. I walked down the steps and entered the little mausoleum where three months before she had lived with eight other children. I saw the empty coffin shelf where she had slept at night. I placed my hand over turquoise hand prints running up the white stone walls and onto the ceiling. Hand prints, the other children told me, made by Sissy to ward off the evil eye.

A Palestinian had left her there, the children told me. Sissy spent months with them, begging. Because she was very beautiful and still spoke a few words of English, the tourists gave her much money, which she shared with the others. When the Palestinian returned for Sissy, the children told her not to go. The boy, Ismail, had heard stories. "He will put you on an airplane," he told Sissy. "And he will give you a pretty yellow radio and when you get up in the air, the radio will blow up and you will be killed." But it was what the girl, Nazli, had warned her about that came to pass.

Two months went by before I could get back to Alexandria. Saad insisted on helping with my search. My Arabic was poor at best, and the elaborate compliments Egyptians pay each other with even the most simple greetings meant that I would be perceived as rude or worse.

The house that Nazli led us to made me glad I hadn't confided in my parents. At first, I hadn't wanted to give them false hopes, but now I don't tell them where Sissy is, because it would kill my mother to know the truth.

A trail of small blue hand prints led across the white-and-beige-painted face of the house. The woman inside listened to my story with sympathy and offered the usual apologies for her profession. She made Saad angry, the way she made herself sound like a social service agency. If it hadn't been for her, she claimed, all twenty-three of the young boys and girls working the cubicles of her house would be sleeping in the City of the Dead and eating garbage.

Yes, she told us, Sissy had been there, but only for a few weeks. She was already too developed for the tastes of her clientele. And there was another problem. They tried to hide

it, but I could tell that Saad and his friend were horrified
by what she told them.

Saad, because he didn't know the English word for it,
told me how during Sissy's captivity in Iraq, those parts
giving a girl pleasure as she becomes a woman, had been
cut away. Then, he blushed as he explained to me how sensual
Egyptians are, and how unlike other Arabs, they mistrust
a *houri* without all of her sexual parts. Certain surgical
modifications had become necessary in order for Sissy to
practice her profession.

The woman just grinned placidly, as if Saad were explaining how to clip the tail and ears of a champion schnauzer.
I wanted to murder her. What had she done to my sister?

"What surgical modifications, Saad?"

He ignored me. His friend took my hand.

"Tell me!" I screamed at them. "What has the bitch
done to my baby sister?" I pulled my hand away and reached
out to grab the woman.

Saad held me back. "Hold on. Let's try and find out
where Sissy is, then you can beat her all you want."

Some man had taken Sissy to Cairo. Saad asked her very
nastily how much money she was paid for Sissy. The woman
just shrugged her shoulders. I stomped on Saad's foot and
lunged forward when he let me go. Things would have gotten
rough then, if five or six of her male friends hadn't shown up.

Out on the street, when I asked Saad again, he told me
the modifications were, "you know, to make her a woman
again."

We hit the bar at the Cecil Hotel and Saad's friend spun
stories of E. M. Forster and Cavafy. We drank to the wrinkled picture of the little six-year-old Sissy, and Saad's friend
flirted with me, telling me how Sissy and I were like Egypt.
I was a dark-skinned Nubian and Sissy with her light skin
was a Ptolemy. It wasn't just the *ouzo* that was intoxicating.

But I should have seen from the way Saad was hammering down the whiskies that he was lying. He hadn't told me everything that had been done to Sissy.

19:00

Maghrib. The sun is setting. I'm sitting on an empty metal barrel on the beach just outside the Club Mediterranée. Lighted arches from the restaurants and nightclub sparkle in dark ocean waters. The shimmering colors remind me of Berlin. Europeans and Americans in their white tuxedos and glitzy dresses laugh, drink, dance and smoke just like they do in Berlin. They play hard, totally absorbed in the game, never thinking of those who make it possible.

On the beach they walk by me as if I were an uninteresting piece of driftwood. Perhaps my African classmates were right. Perhaps I'm not really a human being.

Saad promised to keep trying to find Sissy, but he never meant to keep that promise. I think he decided that night in Alexandria that it would be better for me and my parents, and for Sissy, to just give up the search. He never returned my calls or answered my letters and postcards.

Three years after I left him in Alexandria, I walked into a café in Faya, in northern Chad, and found Saad sitting at a table in back with some uniforms. I didn't want to jeopardize a mission, but I wasn't going to leave without finding out what else he knew.

I sat and stared at him. He ignored me, so I bought him a drink. The waiter brought it over to his table and pointed back at me. When I lifted my glass to Saad, his laughing friends slapped him on the back. He pretended to his friends he was going to hit on me, with an Egyptian swagger so typical I couldn't help laughing myself. When I turned him down,

his friends roared with equal good humor. But before he re-
joined them, he dropped a slip of paper on my table. It read,
"Café Zanzibar, Berlin."

Berlin, the New York of Europe. I should have known.
Since the fall of the Iron Curtain it has become what it was
in the past—a marketplace of knowledge and beliefs, passion
and gluttony formed as the impecunious east and the rich west
collide. Not as xenophobic as London, not as conceited as
Paris, Berlin's syncretism rivals that of an African capital,
a Cairo, or a Dakar.

Only during the forty years of the occupation did it feel
like a place in Germany. Berlin is a piece of the world that
no single country can lay claim to. Now, as in the past, a
high percentage of Berliners are foreigners. Berlin was a "little
America" before there was an America.

I would have expected a whorehouse catering to an exotic
crowd to be located in Kreuzberg with its leather-clad
performance-artists, punks, and Turkish immigrants, but the
Café Zanzibar is on the Lietzenburger Strasse with the other
honky-tonks.

A five-hundred mark note got the bouncer to open the
door. I waited as he punched numbers into the security
system. Electronic locks clicked and dead bolts slid back with
loud snapping. The door swung inward.

Flashing lights from the amusement park Ferris wheel
across the street shone in through the windows of the night
club. The surly woman behind the bar refused to serve me,
but after I bought a couple of rounds of drinks the girls were
friendly enough, especially once they understood I was a
customer, not a competitor. That made the barkeep even
madder.

Two girls wearing matching black leather hot pants and
jackets with silver studs and buckles came on to me.

"I'm looking for something . . . special," I said and

shuffled a pack of crisp hundred-mark notes while I paid for another round.

"A friend of mine in Egypt gave me this address."

The girls giggled. The blond unzipped her jacket. An apple-sized, pink-tipped breast slipped out. A thick gold ring pierced the nipple. The other girl straightened the seam in her fish net stockings, waving her shiny leather-clad bottom at me.

I tipped them two hundred-marks each.

The blonde looked around nervously. "Madame Claudette keeps a girl up in the attic for special customers. We're not allowed to speak to her. Cook says she looks very young— maybe fourteen. Her name is Yasmin."

Yasmin! It had to be Sissy. Two drinks and another tip later, and they took me up to Madame Claudette's apartment. Three thousand marks bought me one hour with Madame's prize courtesan.

Two guards sat playing cards at a small table in the hallway. One picked up his Uzi from the table and stood guard while the other frisked me, then punched in the security codes at Yasmin's door.

The room was decorated like a Chinese palace. From behind a black lacquer screen painted with apple blossoms, a sleepy child's voice said, "*Guten abend.*"

Eight years, was all I could think of. I had spent eight years of my life searching for Sissy. What if it wasn't her?

I walked past the screen. A black-haired girl wearing a red brocade robe embroidered with purple and blue flowers and green leaves lay on the bed. It was impossible to tell the color of her skin. It had been painted white, like a voodoo initiate's. Her heavy eye make-up made her features look oriental. When she flicked on the lamp next to her bed, I saw that it wasn't just make-up. Plastic surgery had extended the epicanthic folds of her upper eyelids across the inner and outer angles of the eyes.

The red lipstick on her lips stopped far short of the corners, in a surprised "oh." She opened her mouth to moisten her lips with her tongue. A well-practiced gesture, designed to reveal to the client the tiny white pearl piercing its tip. As she extended her tongue out further, I saw that the pearl in the tip was followed by another, slightly larger than the first, and another and another. In all, a dozen pearls formed a line bisecting her tongue as she stretched its tip to touch her chin. A prostitute's promise of pleasures to come.

This bizarre creature couldn't be little Sissy, I thought. Then she smiled and dimples appeared in her cheeks, dimples just like Mom's. "Could you bring me a basin of water from the table?" she asked.

I turned to the table in the attic dormer and poured warm lemon-scented water from a blue onion porcelain pitcher into a large bowl. The bowl was heavy. I almost dropped it when I saw Sissy pull her robe up away from her legs. Her little feet were so small, they would barely have filled the palm of my hand. "Sissy!" I whispered.

She looked up at me strangely, but not with any sign of recognition. "Put the bowl down here, on the bed," she said.

I put the bowl next to her feet, as she asked.

"Now come here." She patted the pillow next to her, then took my hand. "I understand," she said. "You've had a hard day. Lotus feet are a mark of great beauty, but that's no reason for tears." She took a tissue from her nightstand and wiped my face. "Will you help me wash my golden lilies?"

I let her, a child, order me around. I had expected to tell her stories of Mom and Dad and to call in the police to bring her home, but what I found horrified me. Police would mean press. Mom would find out, and it would kill her, just kill her, to see her little baby play the temptress with such skill.

I watched Sissy take off her little black shoes. They were embroidered in many colors and so small they would not have

been too large for the doll Sissy had left behind in Kuwait
City. She made me unwrap the two-inch wide bandages. Ten
feet of bandage wrapped each foot. The toes were fat white
caterpillars bent around underneath the arch and suckling at
the heels. Her left foot was bleeding. The nail from her
middle toe had cut into her heel. I sponged her feet with
perfumed water, then dried them with thick, soft white towels.

She took my hand and slipped it into her robe, onto
her naked breast. I tried to pull away, but then I remembered
the City of the Dead in Alexandria, and how frightened and
hungry she must have been. When she showed me how to
rub and kiss her feet, I tried to leave. The tears in her eyes
reminded me of what the Alexandrian whore had said. People don't trust houris without all their sex parts. Sissy's lone-
liness was an icy desert wind that made me shiver.

Her tears worked. I watched her painted, rosebud lips
part with pleasure, as I licked and sucked her feet and tried
not to think.

It only mattered that she was safe, that I had found her.
She would never be used by strangers again.

20:00

Isha. The final prayers of the day. I watch Charlotte give
alms to the beggars at the entrance of the Club Med parking
lot. She will make a good Muslim, if she is allowed to keep
a few fetishes. Claude looks on indulgently and chats with
Charlotte's aunt.

What am I doing? Charlotte is so normal, so good. She
has every chance to lead a full life. Should she die to buy
freedom for an emotional and physical cripple? No matter
what happens, Mom must never know what happened to Sissy.
And Dad couldn't keep from telling Mom if he knew.

The small house I bought for Sissy is finally ready. It's

in a little village called Appeln about 20 minutes from
Bremerhaven. I like to imagine Sissy walking outside in the
sunny garden, showing off her koi pond to the neighborhood
farm kids.

After I retire, she will be safer in a small place. I have
nightmares of someone using Sissy to force me out of retire-
ment. The villagers will notice if someone hangs around
watching the black lady with the tiny feet.

My psychiatrist has warned me not to expect too much.
She may never learn to read well. Normal relationships are
beyond hope, but I can't stop hoping. Each time I have visited Sissy since, she tries to seduce me, but things have never
gotten out of hand like they did that first time, when the shock
of what had been done to her knocked me off-balance.

I've followed the psychiatrist's advice and paid outrageous
sums of money to take Sissy (along with Madame Claudette
and two armed body guards) for an hour or two to the zoo
or to the Ku'dam shopping. Things that normal teenagers do.

My greatest fear is that Madame Claudette will find out
that Yasmin is my sister. I don't know what I'd do if she
increased her price beyond my means. I've had to leave her
in that place too long already. Planning an action in Europe
is much more complicated than one in Africa. My friends
in Special Forces, German as well as American, would help.
I only have to ask. But during the past three years, I have
already killed too many people to win Sissy's freedom. And
there's always the chance, in an action, that Sissy would be
hurt.

An elderly Turkish couple fluent in Arabic, that I've hired
as housekeepers and tutors, already lives in the house in
Appeln. Sissy will learn to read Arabic first, then German,
maybe even English. Perhaps we can get her a wheelchair
so she can study at the university, the way Dad would have
wanted.

Quit stalling, I tell myself. I need to get on with this.

Princess Charlotte has had everything given to her. My
sister has had nothing. Not even a mother, a father, or a sister.
It isn't my fault Charlotte's family has decided to marry her
to Claude. They should know better. Claude's family's shady
business dealings are well known.

Claude's driver opens the door of the white Mercedes
for them. I flag a taxi and pretend I'm looking for a friend
whose address I can't quite remember. I will be back in Dakar
and in another cab before the first cab driver can realize I
am following the Mercedes.

After two taxi changes, the Mercedes parks by the Gorée
ferry, an enormous bit of good luck, since my Peugeot is at
the railway station just a few blocks away. Claude, Charlotte
and the aunt get out and walk with the tourists along the sea
wall, towards the station.

At the end of the west dock, next to the railway station,
is a kola nut warehouse. The second story is rarely, if ever,
guarded. I make my way through the crowd of drink vendors
and travelers to the warehouse.

The librarian's computers hum. As the micro-motors click
the action into the stock with cool precision, the metal barrel
catches the last glimmers of the setting sun. The YAG laser
picks Princess Charlotte out of the crowded square in front
of the station and locks onto her forehead.

I feel warm again. Heat washes through my body like
a wave, up from my feet and into my head where it lies
trapped. My hands are shaking. I must be coming down with
malaria. Paludrine just isn't doing the trick any more. I wipe
the sweat from my face with one of the cloth samples in my
basket.

Steady, old girl. The heat is deadly. I lock onto Charlotte again and squeeze the trigger.

The red neon Coca-Cola sign at the café across the street
from the station explodes in a shower of yellow sparks. A
white-aproned shopkeeper runs out and chases two boys whom

he thinks have smashed his light with stones. The laughing crowd turns to watch and cheers the shopkeeper on. All of them, except Charlotte.

She turns around to face me, then laughs, as I watch her through my scope. Laughs and waves her monkey paw at me. She is making me angry. Both my hands are shaking now and the sweat is pouring down my face. It's not malaria, I suddenly realize. It's her, Charlotte! How is she doing this to me?

The words of my Nigerian classmate ring in my ears. Descendants of slaves have no souls. They are not human. Is that how Sissy has been able to survive, because she is not human? My mouth is dry with heat. I need to get this over with. I turn my basket upside down and brace my arms on it to stop them from shaking. I find Charlotte's laughing face in the cross hairs and let the librarian close the book of Charlotte Abiola Kikelomo Jumake Adekunle.

Die, little princess, die. Sissy's coming home.

Winter Night, with Kittens

by
Sam Wilson

ILLUSTRATED BY Shaun Tan

About the Author

Sam Wilson of Chicago, Illinois, is a policy contract analyst for a major downtown insurance company, and has been a theater usher, short-order cook, dishwasher, day laborer, and worked for the Federal Reserve Bank of Chicago. He is also a part-time actor and has had lead roles in community theater plays by Shakespeare and Oscar Wilde.

He has been writing stories since childhood and made his first sale to Mike Shayne Mystery Magazine back in the late seventies. This publication qualified him for membership in a Chicago-based writers' workshop that included our own Contest judge and senior editor Algis Budrys, along with many other professional writers, where Sam benefited from the stern critiques. His second sale was to Rod Serling's The Twilight

Zone Magazine, *and the story was included in Arthur Saha's* The Year's Best Fantasy Stories #8.

After his second sale, Sam took eight years off writing to work on his insurance career. Perhaps he will now take some time to write more of his stories for us.

About the Illustrator

Shaun Tan is seventeen years old and hails from Perth, Western Australia. He learned about the Contest through Analog *magazine, and won two honorable mentions before becoming a finalist.*

He is also a budding young writer and has been a quarter-finalist in the Writers of The Future competition, and has won several state-wide writing competitions. He is earnestly striving to become the first person to win both the Writers of The Future and Illustrators of The Future Contests, and as you can see, he's over halfway there.

Shaun has published a number of illustrations in the Australian SF and F magazine Aurealis, *including one cover. Elsewhere in this anthology another illustrator, Darren Albertson, mentioned that as a child he had been inspired by the drawings of a high-school student. Now Shaun Tan is the kind of student who is inspiring countless others.*

He came from the far, far future, from a golden age, when all men were good.

When his time machine stopped the first thing to hit his senses was the foulness of the air. He had arrived on a winter night, in the middle of a snowfall. The full moon did not penetrate the clouds overhead, and in the sky above the city, there were no stars to be seen, not one. Not here ten seconds and already he was homesick.

He found himself on a street lined with trees and plots of grass, electric lighting and tall buildings. "High-rises," the buildings were called. The people of this time knew this area as a "good" neighborhood. His fingers brushed lightly over the time machine, a belt he wore around his waist. He stood there as the snow dropped around him. Alone in the street.

A car drove past him and pulled into an empty parking space not far away. He watched as a woman got out of the car and struggled to maneuver a cardboard box and two large, filled paper bags. She placed the box on the hood of the car and clutched both bags in one arm, then reached for the box with her free hand, but before she could touch it her purse slipped down her arm and one bag fell, bounced off an attempt by her leg to halt it, and continued its descent to the ground, spilling a few cans into the slush. She put the other bag next to the box, put her purse back on her shoulder, and stooped to return the cans to the bag. She picked it up. When she stood, he was there.

Illustrated by Shaun Tan

"May I help you carry that?"

She looked at him, startled at first; this was an age of fears, and he understood, and smiled at her. She saw goodness in his smile. The Dark Ages of Man had ended thousands of years before he had even been born, and he resonated with the cumulative effects of his history. She was no foolish innocent. A child of the city, she would never have responded to a man of her own time, a stranger, as they fell deeper into night. But this man: she smiled back at him.

"Yes," she said. "Thank you. Thank you very much."

The cardboard box was open at the top; he looked in and saw six tiny black kittens asleep on a pink cloth. He reached a hand in, not touching the babies, but feeling the radiant warmth of their little bodies. Then the woman handed him the bags, locked the door, and took the box from the hood of her car, and they proceeded down the snow-covered sidewalk together.

"I live just down the block," she told him. "I got these kittens from my church this afternoon; I volunteered to take them home—their mother belongs to the minister's family. He and his wife wanted them out of the house before the children got attached to them. Before they started giving the kittens names. It doesn't hurt to do a good deed once in a while, does it?"

"No, it doesn't."

"Well, I appreciate the good deed you're doing for *me*. You seem like a cat man. I don't suppose you'd like a pretty little kitty, by any chance?"

"Not at the moment," he said kindly.

"It doesn't hurt to ask. There's a notice up on the bulletin board at church, and I've got some nieces who are in the market for pets. Anyway, I'm not usually this disorganized, but while I was out running around I thought I'd get a little grocery shopping done, get some food for the kittens, too. Sort of kill two birds with one trip—"

She was a young woman, with curly shoulder-length blonde hair, extremely beautiful, in fact, by the standards of this time and place, the United States of America in 1991 A.D. Superficial attractiveness was important here, was considered *good* by these people. Where he came from, the human race had matured beyond that. Where he came from, goodness in its purest form was part of the fabric of everything. Goodness *was*.

"—And here we are!" she announced. "Listen, let's walk in fast so no one finds out what's in the box, okay?"

They walked up the steps and entered the lobby. The uniformed man sitting behind the bank of television monitors waved at her.

"Evening, Miss Chatterly," he said. He was a burly man with a pitted face. "Starting to come down out there."

"Hi, Joe," she said, not pausing in her stride. "This gentleman's a friend, he's helping me take my stuff up."

Joe waved them on.

Riding up in the elevator, one of the kittens started to cry. "Hush," she said to the box. "You guys are going to get me in trouble." To him she said, "The building doesn't allow animals, so this'll be our little secret, Mr. . . ."

"Avon," he said. "My name is Avon."

"Mr. Avon. Oh, forgive my manners. I'm Christina Chatterly."

There was an awkward moment at the door to her apartment as she handed him the box while she fumbled in her purse for the key, and then they were in.

"Let me get these now," she said, pushing the door shut with her foot and relieving him of the bags. He walked across the plush blue carpet to the sliding glass door that led out onto the balcony, carrying the box of kittens with him. He heard the rattle of paper and the clink of cans as she unpacked her groceries.

"Nothing's broken," she called from the kitchenette.

"Can I get you something to drink, Mr. Avon? Please have a seat."

He didn't speak. He stared through the glass. From forty stories up, this ancient city held a primal, twisted beauty. Snow swept across the land, a land crammed with the lighted shapes of buildings that seemed to want to tear themselves away from their earthly anchors and hurl themselves into the sky. The black sky. Heaven, with no stars.

If he could learn anything, it would be here.

He opened the sliding door and stepped onto the balcony. Icy air nudged him.

"—I said, can I get you anything, Mr. Avon?" Christina Chatterly said. She stood behind him. "I want you to know how much I really appreciate your help."

He nodded, and walked over to the balcony wall. He casually dumped the contents of the box over the side, watched the kittens tumble down only part of the forty stories. A few heartbeats later, he turned to her.

"Is this evil?" he asked, holding the empty box.

She froze. She forgot to breathe. Her intellectual functions were stunned, jammed, not working at all, but her instinct for survival took over. She screamed and turned to run, to escape. He was faster. He picked up a lamp and hit her on the head with it. The cord was yanked from the wall socket and whipped across the room and the lamp broke against her skull. The lampshade struck the carpet and rolled for an instant. He dragged her by the hair into her bedroom and threw her on the bed. He tore up the bedsheets and tied her arms and legs securely to the bedposts. He went to the kitchenette and found a bucket in the cabinet under the sink and he filled it with cold water. Then he brought the bucket and a kitchen knife back into the bedroom. He turned on the bedroom light and poured the water over her. When she came to, sputtering, straining against her bonds, eyes wide with terror, he ripped off her clothing and had her. She screamed

continuously. She only stopped screaming after he went to
work on her with the knife.

When he finished, he stood there by her bed, soaked
in her blood, knife in hand, and stared down at the lifeless
body of this random stranger. Cold air from the balcony
followed him into the bedroom.

"*Is this evil?*" he asked, for the second time that night.

He remained for a time, until he heard pounding on the
front door and shouts from the hallway. The pounding grew
louder and more insistent. Apparently people were gathering
just outside her apartment. He dropped the knife onto the bed
and shrugged, and the blood dried to a fine powder and fell
off his clothes. He touched the time machine at his waist and
the room plunged back into darkness. Leaving the bedroom,
he saw that the glass balcony door was closed and the lamp,
intact, was in its proper place. He left the apartment and
walked down the empty hall to the elevator. On the ground
floor he walked past Joe without a word. When he got outside,
he looked down the street, and waited. Very soon, he saw
a figure appear from out of nowhere. He walked down the
street and met himself.

"It's done," he said. "You can return to the departure
point. I'll come back soon, and our timelines will merge us
both back into one person, and you'll know the answer."

"Without actually having done it," his earlier self said.

"Because it never happened," he said. "Now go."

When his earlier self was gone, he walked to the empty
parking spot and met Christina Chatterly's car as it pulled in.

"If I were you," he told her, as she emerged from the
car, "I'd take the box up first, and come back for the bags."

She looked at him, startled at first. He smiled at her.
She thought about it, and nodded, and put the groceries back
into the car.

"You're right, of course," she said. "I'm trying to do
too many things at once."

"What's in the box?" he asked, and she told him, and soon he cupped a purring kitten gently in his hands.

"I'm sure you'll give it a good home," she said, smiling at him.

"Have no fear of that," he said, and walked away, and returned to the far, far future, to a golden age, when all men were good.

Invisible Man
by
Larry Ferrill

ILLUSTRATED BY Bob Hobbs

About the Author

Larry Ferrill of Columbus, Indiana, is twenty-nine years old, and like many writers has worked in various unrelated fields: as a documentation writer, baker, department store clerk, and he is currently an auditor and supervisor in a health insurance claims office.

Unlike most other successful writers nowadays, Larry says he has no formal training as a writer, but he has always considered it more than just a hobby, and he pursues it as much as possible during his spare time.

"Invisible Man," the second-place story from the first quarter, is Larry's first story to be published. He says it was "an honor and a thrill" to participate in the Contest, but we are the ones to be honored and thrilled.

About the Illustrator

At age ten, Bob Hobbs vowed to become an illustrator for Marvel Comics, *and promptly began creating his own comic books with his own heroes and villains.*

In high school, he began creating fantasy works that could stand on their own, and seriously considered a career in art. He studied art at five separate colleges in Rhode Island, Los Angeles, and Hawaii.

In the past two years, he has begun testing the waters in the fantasy market—and his list of credits is becoming so long that we can't begin to list them here. Who knows, perhaps he will make it to Marvel *yet.*

We walk through cold midnight
air, so silent that you can really hear your
footsteps. His patter along with firm, distinct
plops while mine occasionally shuffle. I hear the whisk of
rubber rubbing concrete and then make a conscious effort not
to drag, but that's hard to do after seven brews. It's like this
every time: I walk with my head to the ground, as if I'm
plowing my way through a snowstorm, afraid to look up
because I might see his eyes. You can always tell when he's
coming back; I'll be walking beside him, and his eyes become
the eyes of an older man, days or years more knowledge behind
them than was there a second before. And in that second you
wonder where he's been and how many people he's killed.

He's killed a lot of people, the invisible man, and he tells
me about most of them, exhales his confessions as if I were
a priest or something. He has no confessions tonight, however,
and that is strange. No confessions, no tales of adventures,
nothing for the longest time but that cold midnight silence.
We pass houses that are like comatose giants, some buckled
in prayer, some stretched out on the lawn, eyelids closed, walls
breathing sleep in and out. There are no sirens to wake them,
no screaming cars or kids with stereos cranked to the max,
nothing but nothing tonight.

After a while, I realize that I'm going to have to start
the conversation. "What was it like being King of the World?"
I don't bother to ask whether he actually *became* king or not.
The last time we talked, two weeks ago, that was his goal,
and I don't doubt that he achieved it.

Illustrated by Bob Hobbs

He laughs. "It was easy. At least, the Free World was easy. The Middle East was harder'n shit, like tryin' to pry open . . ." He searches for an analogy, then smiles when he finds one he likes. "Like tryin' to pry open Paula Matthews' legs. Remember Paula?"

I remember. From high school, the short sweet girl with the pony-brown hair. It seems odd that he should remember her, since they only went out once and nothing happened. His mind is stuffed full of memories of more adventures than I will ever see on TV, and yet he still finds space for some stupid girl from a long time ago. How long ago? For me, eight years. Not long. For him, though, it has been centuries.

"Whatever happened to her, anyway?" He seems genuinely curious. I begin to think he has memories of Paula Matthews that I don't know about. I wonder how many times the invisible man has raped her.

I shrug. We turn the corner and head down Wilson, just six blocks away from Central, where most of the motels are, where the highway cuts through town. The giants change now; they lie flattened, squashed by the slumber of the night. These are the houses that my father liked. We would drive through on Sunday afternoons, circling the streets until we found one that was for sale. And then we would stop and imagine what it would be like to live there.

"Like I said, the Free World was easy," he says, a bit impatiently, as if he's been waiting for me to keep the conversation going. "But them Arabs, they're stubborn bastards. You couldn't buy nothing; you couldn't even intimidate them, not by stockpilin' bombs, and not by cuttin' off their food."

"So what'd you do?"

He sighs. He seems bored with having to tell it, which is surprising because he usually recounts every detail. Perhaps he has told me all this before and gone back, erased it. "You can't intimidate them. We had to practically rip them apart, with bombs, I mean, and they salvaged some shitty old Russian hardware and did some pretty good rippin' of their own, but finally . . .'' He ends with that. I notice that he does not specify *nuclear* bombs, but I have no doubt that is what he used. So his death count rises to the billions. The invisible man has been busy.

"So I became king," he says, again implying that I have been quiet too long. Quickly I search for a question. I keep picturing him on a throne with a gold crown and ruling over a wasteland.

"How long did you keep it?"

"Not to the end. Five years maybe. Not that I was afraid. I just got bored, is all."

Only one time that he has told me about did he follow it through to the end. Once when he was at the twilight of his life as a film star, when he was on his deathbed with cancer, he waited until the very instant of death before he came back. He never said what it was like, if he caught a glimpse of God, or anything like that, but I got the impression that he didn't intend to come that close to death ever again.

"Oh, well." He kicks at a pebble, and it goes popping up the street. There is something he wants to say, but he doesn't know how. It's almost like we've both gone back, to the first night he told me about this ability he possessed, if you want to call it that. This thing that he could do.

He hadn't known how to say it then, either, and finally he had just blurted it out. "I can go back in time."

"Right." I didn't even bother to laugh. In high school he used to lie all the time, make up stories about himself and try to get people to believe him. Nobody ever did. He told some people he grew up in England and later moved to France, told others that he was raised by Eskimos. His father was either a spy who got killed smuggling documents out of Russia or a truckdriver who got killed when his rig jackknifed on ice.

"No, really, it's true," he said, and there was a level of sincerity in his voice that wasn't there when he told his other stories. But it wasn't enough to make me believe him. "I'll prove it to you."

"You wanna prove it to me, show me your time machine."

"I don't have a time machine. Alls I gotta do is close my eyes and imagine that—"

"Jesus, will you stop it? I mean, come on, just tell the truth once in your life, okay?"

"It *is* the truth. See that dude?"

A man was walking down the street, tall with bench-pressed shoulders and a haircut that said he was on leave from the service.

"I'm gonna waste that dude."

"Right," I said, but then he pulled a gun out of his jacket, a little pistol, and he grinned.

"Hey, this isn't funny. Put that away."

"It's cool."

"Put it *away,* before you hurt someone."

And something happened for a second that is hard to describe; his movements became out of sync, as if we were part of a movie that got edited with a chop. His head turned right when it had started to turn left and his feet strided forward when he had started to stop, making it seem as if he were skipping along the sidewalk. I noticed the gun was no longer in his hand, but I never saw him put it in his pocket. The dude passed us by without even noticing us, walking fast as if he were in a hurry to get laid somewhere.

"Thought you said you were gonna kill him, wuss."

"I did kill him. Shot him right through the head. Never knew what hit him. You threw up when you saw his brains leaking out."

"I think *your* brains have leaked out."

He thought that was funny. "The reason you don't remember it is because right after it happened, I went back in time, to just five seconds before I shot him, and this time I *didn't* shoot him. You don't have any memory of all that, because I erased it.''

''So that's your asshole proof that you can go back in time?''

''We're gonna go in Stone's Arcade and watch this dude play Zap Man. He's a little piss-ant runt with wire-rim glasses and stinky blond hair, but he'll score fifty-two thousand.''

''Fifty-two thousand on Zap?''

''You got it.''

And we went in Stone's Arcade and made our way through the dark room to the Zap machine on the back wall. We closed in on the crowd of high school farts who had gathered around it, watching over the shoulder of a skinny kid with long, greasy blond hair, bent over the screen, shifting his joystick, racking up points. He scored ten thousand on his first game, not bad at all, and added fifteen thousand on his next. The farts looked on in awe, their pimples glittering under the reflections of Zap Man's direct hits. Thirty-five, forty, forty-five . . . when the kid hit fifty thousand the crowd began to whisper about the awesomeness of this performance. The kid seemed to lose his touch after that. Zap Man flickered back and forth sluggishly, drunk, apparently, from his success, and died under a cascade of lights and blips. I looked up just in time to see the machine tally the final score. Fifty-two thousand. Nothing more, nothing less.

The kid turned from the machine and eyed the two of us coolly through his wire glasses, challenging the adults in the crowd. ''That's the highest rack in the state. Wanna take me on?''

I shook my head.

''Next song that plays on the radio will be 'Hotel California.' ''

I could barely hear the radio at all, what with all the games going at full effect. We moved closer to the corner where a speaker was nailed to the wall, just in time to hear the commercial fade, the station ID, and the first strumming chords of "Hotel California."

"Next it'll be Huey Lewis. 'Wanna New Drug.' "

He was right about that one, too. I didn't say a word, but got the hell out of that arcade right now.

"Fifth section of sidewalk up ahead will have three brown leaves on it. One yellow one."

I stared at him for a moment, refusing to move, hoping he would see how ridiculous this whole thing was, but he grabbed my arm and pulled me along, marching off the sections of sidewalk until we hit the fifth one. He stopped and crouched, the streetlight casting our shadows against the bank of someone's front yard. "One," he said, holding up a crisp maple leaf, as clean and compacted as if it had spent its death pressed at the center of a book. "Two." This one was bent and twisted, its stem perhaps afflicted with arthritis. The third one was not much more than stem, with crumbled patches of brown all around it. "And the yellow one," he said, producing a leaf from a different genus of tree, a yellow oval with red veins and a stem twice as long as the leaf itself. He dropped them all back to the sidewalk, stood and wiped his fingers on his jeans.

"The next car down the street will be a black Mustang. It'll stop right there and lay a patch—"

"Will you stop?" I said, turning back to the arcade. "If you're tryin' to prove you're psychic, okay, I believe. You're psychic. Now leave me alone."

"I'm not psychic. I haven't predicted any of this; all this has already happened to me."

We stopped out front of the arcade, in the gravel parking lot that seemed to contain more beer bottles than automobiles. "We've already done all this before," he said, his voice a hoarse whisper. "We passed that Army dude on the street, went into the arcade and watched this kid rack up points, walked on down the sidewalk a little ways. All this has already happened. Then I went back in time and did it all over. I can remember everything that happened, but you can't. That's how come it seems like I can predict all this stuff."

"You're crazy, man," I said. "You are seriously fucked up."

I didn't believe a word of it then, and I'm not sure really when I did start to believe him. But all I did that night was walk away, back to the house with the echo of some car squealing its tires behind me, and I never looked back to see if it was the black Mustang he predicted. That was eight years ago.

He stops walking, turns and faces me. I can't avoid his eyes this time.

"Sometimes . . . I don't know." He speaks as if there isn't much time. "Sometimes I wish I couldn't go back. You know?"

I wonder why he finds this so hard to say, since he is confessing out of boredom, not guilt. People can get bored with everything, I suppose.

"It's just . . ." He looks past me, seems to scan the stars for something. Maybe that's his next goal. He sighs and gives up, resumes walking down the street.

The priest should speak, I suddenly realize. "Don't go back anymore."

"What?" This stops him again.

"I said, if you wish you didn't have the power to go back, then just don't use it. Try to live a normal life." I say "normal" with a bit of acid, or at least it sounds that way to me. I didn't mean for it to come out that way. I didn't even mean to say it, really. It sounds so much like my father's advice to me that it scares me.

He laughs and claps his hands. "I couldn't live a normal life. No more than you could live my kind of life."

"Why not?"

"There's no excitement in it. No danger. I've been a movie star, a rock star, the President, a king, a mass murderer. I couldn't live your life any more than you could live one of those."

I shrug. "I don't have the talent to be an actor, or the education to get into politics. . . ."

"Shit, you don't need none of that. It's just a matter of bein' in the right place at the right time, that's all. An' bein' willin' to take risks."

I laugh at that. "Risk-taking's pretty easy when you can just go back and change your decision if you're wrong. I don't see much excitement in that."

"Maybe not. But you gotta have it in your blood, a desire to take a chance. People can't change that."

"People can change."

"Then I'll make you a deal," he says, and suddenly I feel trapped; he has traveled through this argument before and cornered me with my own words. "You do something risky, something that'll change your life and I'll try settlin' down and raisin' a family. Kill your wife, burn down your house, take a shot at the President, do *some*thing. If it backfires, doesn't work out, I'll go back and erase it. Deal?"

"No deal. I have no desire to kill my wife, or the President, or to burn down my house. You're one seriously fucked-up dude, you know that?"

He laughs as if he knows better than that. He slaps me on the back and trots on down the sidewalk. Then he stops again. Quiet settles on his shoulders. A moment later he turns, just like people do in those old horror movies after they've changed into a werewolf. He turns, and I see from his eyes that he has been somewhere, seen and done something that is now invisible to me.

He looks at his watch. That's a bad sign. "C'mon," he says, and he tears off down the street as if he hears someone calling him.

I don't have a chance to say anything, so I take off, too, and pretty soon I catch up with him.

"What's wrong?" I say between breaths, but he doesn't answer. We just keep on running.

We pass all the houses quickly now, then turn on Second and keep on chugging. We must be heading for Main, a narrow country road that widens as it passes through town. That's my only thought as we run, that we must be heading for Main, where the churches are. The giants change again. They are more run-down, with pale peeling skin and crumbling roofs, and not all of them are asleep. A few eyelids have opened to survey us with yellow pupils. We pass them all quickly.

At first it feels good, running like this. I used to run for the cross-country team back in high school, and after I graduated, I used to run for myself every morning, but I stopped a couple of years ago. I've forgotten that it feels so *good*. Then it doesn't feel so good. The pizza and beer we had before we left are not mixing well in my stomach.

He slows to a trot, turns the corner and then slows down even more. We are on Main now; just up ahead it meets Central. The street's only stoplight has become a blinker, and at the corner I see two figures moving. These streets are well lighted, and as I get closer I see that the figures are two girls. About high school age, or maybe just out of high school.

He marches toward them, passing the old storefronts, a barber shop, a men's store and a *Murphy's*. I fall behind. This is the side of town they are trying to revitalize by pouring new concrete and planting skinny trees. It looks kind of pretty in the street's yellow glow.

Closer, now: one girl is a short, curly-haired blonde who seems to be doing all the talking. The other one is fat, with straight dark hair. She laughs too loudly at what the other girl says, and her cheeks quiver and shine stupidly. She is the first to notice him; her eyes look up with surprise, but not fear. The blonde follows her glance. *This* one is scared.

He shouts at them. "Hey, don't I know you from some-where? Your name's Barbara, right?"

I fear the worst and stop. Not five minutes ago he was thinking about living a normal life, and now he is going to rape two girls.

The blonde is suspicious. Apparently her name *is* Barbara, but she lies anyway. "No."

"Sure it is. Your name's Barbara, all right. I read about you in the paper." He continues to shout, as if he wants some-one to hear.

"You did, huh?"

He steps closer to her. "Paper said you died tonight. Right here on this street corner."

She takes a step back. "Get away from me." I think I hear the fat one giggle.

"Get away from me." She starts to step into the street, but he grabs her and pulls her back. "Let go of me, you goddamn . . . bastard. I'll scream."

But she doesn't scream. He holds her there for only a moment, until a car comes shooting down the street, doing sixty or seventy, swerving from center line to sidewalk. As soon as it passes, he releases her.

"You're right, come to think of it. I guess I didn't read about you." He smiles and walks away, and I follow. As I pass the two girls, the blonde says, "Bastard. Goddamn bastard." The fat one definitely giggles.

He stops at the next corner and turns around, giving me a chance to catch up. "Fuckin' drunks," he whispers. His words are aimed at the darkness into which the speeding car has disappeared.

"I thought you were going to stop reading the papers," I ask when we start walking again. He'd once said he was going to stop reading newspapers, watching TV and listening to the radio because there was too much tragedy, too many things he couldn't change.

"I made an exception this time. I was reading the want ads of your little paper tomorrow morning, and couldn't help noticing the headline."

"Want ads? What were you looking for in the want ads?"

"Houses," he says, as if I should know. He is playing with invisibility again. "I decided to make good on my promise, settle down in your neighborhood. You know, live the 'normal' life." He says *normal* the same way I said it. With acid. "You kept your half of the deal; I'll keep mine."

"I kept my half of the deal?"

He laughs. "Like a pro, you did. Took you half a case of Miller to get up the nerve, but you did good."

"*What* did I do?" I could feel anger flooding my muscles, but thought I could control it.

He doesn't laugh this time.

"Spousicide. Took Karen in your hands and squeezed her skinny little neck till she dropped."

I believe him. Maybe it's gotten to the point where I'll believe anything he tells me, but there is something inside me that can't challenge the fact that I would kill my wife. "Karen's dead?"

"*Was* dead."

"You came back and erased it. How come? Just so you could save those two kids?"

"No, cause you called me up later on and begged me to erase it. The police were hot after your ass, I guess. They didn't believe that story you made up."

"Oh." I wonder what story I had made up. My hands are numb from the cold, so stiff I can't imagine bending them to fit Karen's throat.

"I'm a murderer."

"You aren't a murderer. It never happened; how can you be a murderer?"

"But it *did* happen."

"And I erased it. Don't worry about it." He seems

irritated by my mourning; he is not as comfortable with the role of priest as I have become. He changes the subject.

"You also said I wouldn't have to keep my part of the deal if I didn't want to. You feel that way now?"

"Do whatever you wanna do," I say.

He laughs. "This's a nice place to visit, but . . . I've got other plans."

"Oh, yeah?"

"Baseball." He laughs again. He was always shit city in phys-ed. "I'm gonna try out for the Cardinals. They'll be holdin' a camp in a couple of weeks."

I still think he's joking. "What brought this on?"

"The paper. I looked at the sports section and read an article about some slugger who said that hitting was all a matter of guessing and guessing right. He said if he knew what was coming to the plate every time up there, he'd have it made." He claps his hands. "I got it made."

Maybe so. Still, he's not exactly built like a home-run hitter, or even a utility infielder, for that matter. And isn't twenty-six a little old to get started? I'm not sure they will even let him in the camp. But perhaps none of that will stop him. I imagine watching him hit home run after home run, and reading about the greatest player who ever stepped on the field. It sounds exciting, even if I won't remember it after he gets bored.

As we walk, he twists his arms back and forth in the air, swinging an invisible bat at an invisible ball and hitting an invisible home run. Then he jogs on ahead, as if he can't wait to get started on his new life. He has been born again.

For me, though, depression comes. I always wish he did something that I could remember, since memories are all that keep his life invisible to me. After you do something, that's all you have left. The memory lives on. It's like this every time. He ends up born again, and I end up depressed.

Without so much as a good-bye, he vanishes into a

pocket of darkness. That's not hard to do if you know someone's steps before they make them.

I go into my house, expecting to find Karen's strangled body on the bedroom floor. But she is in the kitchen of all places, alive and moving in her little body, her skinny neck throbbing as she bends across the table to scrub away the remnants of our pizza and beer.

"Did he leave without saying 'bye to me?"

"He was in a hurry."

She gives me a look that must be resentment. She does not like my old friends. She smiles and makes them feel at home, but deep down she does not want to talk to someone who knew her man before she knew him. Before I smiled at her and spread her legs, and before she probed my mind. It makes her uncomfortable as hell.

I settle down in the family room, in front of the television where two o'clock talking heads are reading yesterday's news. Karen sneaks in and wraps her arms around me, rubbing my shoulders, trying to draw me back to her.

"You never told me what he does for a living." Her hands are warm and wet, and smell like dishwashing soap. "What does he do?"

"He does this and that."

"I think he's a drug dealer." She laughs. "Or a pimp. Is he a pimp?"

I sigh and she leaves me. Sometime after that, between the news and the old movies they show after it, I kill her again. Strangle her, like before, I suppose. The struggle she puts up is more like a shiver in my arms. She kicks once or twice, her butt ramming hard against my crotch, and then she dies. I don't like the feeling that she is dead, or knowing that I have killed her, but I know that it can always be erased. He will erase it when he finds out I have killed her again.

I must call the police, I say to myself, in order to make the story work, that I came home and found her like this,

on the kitchen floor. I doubt they will believe it. It's probably
the same lie I told before. But then I turn around and see
him watching me through the window, grinning between the
hanging plants and the candy-striped curtains. He gives me
a thumbs-up, then runs away.

By the time I get out the door he is already to the street,
out of sync again. He has started to stop, but then is moving,
going left from where he has been into an instant he's not
prepared for. The car comes out of a pocket of darkness, its
headlights just suddenly *there,* pressing down on him, and
you can hear the thump all the way back here. It sounds like
a basketball hitting the backboard, magnified a hundred times.

He is dead. I see his face in one clear second before
they cover him up, the long face of a kid eight years out of
high school, not the face of a president or a movie star or
a king.

"You know this man?" a policeman asks, waving his
flashlight at the body on the ground.

They have pulled someone out of the car and he is
staggering, trying to walk. He stops and throws up on the
policeman's black shoes. "He just come outta nowheres," he
seems to be saying, vomit spraying from his nose.

"Do you *know* this man?" the policeman says again,
pointing his flashlight at my dead friend.

"Yeah," I say. "The son of a bitch got what he deserved.
The son of a bitch just killed my wife."

I point back at my house and the house seems to point
back at me, yellow eyes staring at me as if it knows. It has
seen all the truths and all the invisible lies, and wonders if
this one might work. "She's in the kitchen," I say, and I try
my best to cry.

Naming Characters and Why

by
Algis Budrys

About the Author

From the Contests' inception until September 30, 1991, Algis Budrys was the sole Co-ordinating Judge and editor of the L. Ron Hubbard Presents Writers of The Future anthologies, overseeing the high quality of the program which has resulted in over 125 new talent discoveries. Today, Dave Wolverton has assumed these duties and Mr. Budrys has gone on to senior editor and advisor to the Contest.

As one of the most respected authors, editors and critics in the field, Mr. Budrys here contributes some key advice on an aspect of writing you may not have had fully pointed out to you before.

"Named characters are automatically interesting. Characters in motion
imply destinations."—Algis Budrys, in *Writing
Science Fiction and Fantasy,* © 1988, Algis Budrys.

Having said that, in an essay originally appearing in
New Dimensions, Jim Baen's book-shaped magazine—but
reprinted several times since then—I went on to enlarge on
it a little bit, and thought that was the end of it. But, no.
It requires some explanation.

For instance, named characters *are* automatically interesting. But what I could have gone on to say is that *if* you
name a character, for instance Sam Jones, you have got to
give him something interesting to do . . . more interesting
than if you had named him "the policeman," which in turn
is more interesting than if you had named him "*a* policeman," which in turn is more interesting than if you had
named him "a man," which in turn is more interesting than
if you had named him "a person," but which is more interesting than if he had not appeared in the story at all.

What I am saying is that characters are capable of fine
degrees of prominence, and that you have to assign the proper
degree.

How do you do that? A good rule of thumb is to see
how much motion the character is going to make in the story.

This is important. The motion a character makes—that
is, (A) the importance of the action, and (B) its duration—
determines his place in the story. If he or she only has one

thing to do, no matter how important that one thing is, it is unlikely that she or he is central to the story. In fact, he or she may not even have to be named, except as "a person," even if the *action* is central, if the action represents the only time she or he will appear in the story. But if the character is going to reappear at intervals, then logically you have to give him or her the importance that this implies; you have to confer a proper name. But you are once again dealing with a graduated scale; the most memorable proper name has to be preserved for the hero's use.

If he is the hero, you have to name him with a name that will stick in the reader's mind. "Sam Jones" is not going to do. A hero has to be named Grady Jones, at the very least. If he is the hero in a comedy, you might try naming him "One-ear Jones"—particularly if he is missing an ear, but possibly because he once fought a bull and acquired its ear as a reward. But you have got to name him *something* memorable. Otherwise, there will be a moment, quite likely repeated, in which the reader struggles to adjust *his* perception of the character with yours. That is, the reader will note that the character appears again and again, doing important things, and will have to adjust, each time, to the fact that you have named him Lou Smith, instead of, say, Bolivar Smith.

Now, as a practical matter, you will probably take care automatically to make sure the hero and the heroine have appropriate names. But you may not be so careful with secondary and tertiary characters. You may feel that it does not matter what you call them. But everything in a story matters. If a feature does not matter, it oughtn't to be written down at all. Conversely, if you have written it, the reader has every right to suppose it has a planned purpose. If the reader comes to realize the purpose was not well planned, he thinks less of your story.

• • •

Now, on the other hand, let us suppose you choose names essentially out of a hat. Clem Barnstable, say, is your postman, and he has been pestering you for years to "put him in a story of yours." Well, you don't, unless you are very foolish indeed, actually put him into a story, because you have no defense thereafter if Clem doesn't like the way you "put him in the story" and decides to sue you for every cent you have or are likely to ever have. But if you have known him for years, you are just liable to put *his name* on an unimportant character who—take out a little insurance— could not possibly be the real Clem Barnstable. It's still a poor idea, but you do it anyway; if people only acted on good ideas all the time, some of them might not ever act at all.

Or think of some other scenario; say you're the kind of writer who starts with a list of names—from a phone book, say—determined to write a story with, for instance, eight characters in it. All right. Here's this unimportant character with an important name. What happens? Well, any number of things, potentially. But the one we're concerned with is the effect of this character on you.

Because the naming of names does have an effect on you, the author. *You* are as aware as the reader of little jars between what a character does and what a character's name is, if they don't quite jibe. And what happens is that you begin assigning jobs to the character that you had not at first intended. The character "takes over"—that is, goes away from your original intention—and "insists" on playing up to the weight of his name. Pretty soon, *he* is "determining" which way the story will go.

Well, some writers have no other way of writing. They are not comfortable with a story until some character has taken it over, and they cannot finish a story until that happens. Chances are, they are not aware of the exact mechanism by which this happens, but that doesn't matter, to them. And it probably shouldn't, if what they produce is a professionally saleable story, and they continue to produce a steady stream of such stories.

The case is somewhat different if they are an amateur writer and for some reason the editors to whom they send their stories do not buy them. Editors *want* to buy stories, and if they have any smarts at all—and most editors do have smarts at all—they want to buy a hefty percentage of them from unknown writers. As I've said before, any idiot with a budget can buy stories from the established names; the measure of an editor is how quickly he can build his own stable of increasingly recognizable names from the pile of manuscripts that come in unsolicited every day. So any editor worth having is going to want to buy your story, *if he can*. If he doesn't, there's something wrong with your story. And the chances are overwhelming that it's not really because "it doesn't fit our needs at the present time." That *does* happen, but in the majority of cases, if the editor likes a story, he will invent a need for it.

So if you're an amateur who hasn't been selling despite determined efforts, you may want to look in the area of what you name your characters, and how, and what the characters do, and is it enough to suit their names?

Surrogate
by
M. C. Sumner

ILLUSTRATED BY Darren Albertson

About the Author

M. C. Sumner lives on the northern edge of the Ozark Plateau in Missouri, in ''the ugliest patch of woods to be found in several states.'' The household includes a cat, an iguana, a parakeet, salt water fish, various rodents, and occasional visiting critters.

Sumner has participated in the Writers of The Future Contest for some years, coming close to winning prizes four times before winning first place in the third quarter of 1991 with this smooth, lanky story.

Over the years, Sumner has written computer games, has been an environmental consultant, geologist, magazine editor, and a coal miner. By the time you read this, Sumner will have joined the ranks of past winners who are also published novelists, with a young adult novel.

About the Illustrator

Darren Albertson is the fifth Hubbard Contests winner from Provo, Utah. Other Provo winners include writers Virginia Baker, Shayne Bell, and Dave Wolverton, and illustrator Derek Hegsted—all of whom are first-place winners or grand prize winners.

Darren's love for fantastic art began in first grade; while on bus trips to and from school in Idaho he was impressed by a teenager who drew "exciting pictures."

While working as a medallion and graphic designer at Liberty Mint in Provo, Darren attended a science fiction and fantasy symposium and was awe-struck by an exhibit of Michael Whelan's work. This rekindled Darren's interest in fantastic art, and he soon began selling to markets such as the New York Review of Science Fiction and Fantasy *and* The Leading Edge Magazine. *He soon hopes to take the world by storm. We hope he does, too.*

"This mirror is very clever," she said, then she reached out a painted nail and clicked it against the glass. **"Part of the** conditioning? Make me see myself from outside?"

I smiled, knowing that in the swapping mirror, she would see her own face mimicking my actions. I told everyone that I used the mirror to protect my anonymity. I wanted to be known for my work, not for being the only man in a woman's business. The reality was that the mirror guarded only my pride; anyone wealthy enough to afford my services could easily brush aside the rickety screens that protected my personal data.

"That's part of it," I said. The reply would seem to be in her own voice, but many clients didn't recognize that.

She leaned back in the chair and pulled a cigarette from a wooden case. The sight of her lighting up made me long for a smoke myself, but the first thing I'd been taught about the business was to make the client think you'd take better care of their body than they did.

She was one of those few women who can smoke without seeming less attractive, the blue fumes hovering around her olive features. Of course, she was young and beautiful. I don't know that I've ever had a woman in my office who was not young and beautiful. Rich women these days always look good. But she didn't fit the standard. She wasn't a Smith or a Lane, or any of the other body families I could recognize. She had a look that was a century out of date—dark Mediterranean skin, brown eyes, a tremendous mass of dark curls. Not pretty, just simply beautiful. Just possibly, the beauty was her own.

"My name," she said, "is Evangeline Giscard."

"I'm Seldis," I replied. "I apologize for not shaking hands."

She smiled a bit at that. She had a quirky kind of off-center smile. "I understand, Ms. Seldis." Like almost everyone, she'd fallen into adding a "Ms." to my name. I don't mind. After all, that's what the swapping mirror was for.

"What can I do for you, Ms. Giscard?"

"Evangeline, please. I won't waste your time. I know what you do, and I'm in need of your services."

I nodded. "I appreciate your coming in early. I'll be happy to schedule . . ."

"No," she said. "I've got a clone prepared. I'll be needing your services very soon." A clone. Now we were talking real money. Buying a mass-produced body from the dealers was one thing, but a custom clone was a whole different league.

"How many months along is the clone?" I asked.

"None."

"I don't understand. The clone isn't pregnant, and you certainly don't seem to be pregnant. So why do you need my services right away?"

"I want you to surrogate for the full term," she said.

I leaned back in my chair. "I don't work that way. I go in a few hours before the birth is stimulated, and come out shortly after."

I knew some surrogates stayed longer. Myla Couldart had done a six-week job once a few years back. I stuck with the one-day schedule. Maybe because I was married to Myla Couldart.

"But you could surrogate for longer?"

"If you mean 'is it possible,' then yes, it can be done. Some clients do like to avoid the discomfort of those last few weeks."

"How much do you get for a standard job?" she interrupted.

"If there are no complications, I get a six thousand advance and another two when the tapes are completed."

"Eight thousand a day." She rolled her eyes back in calculation. "Say two hundred and seventy days, plus some recovery time, make it three hundred days." She looked back into the mirror. "All right, Ms. Seldis, I'll pay you two and a half million standard."

"You have that kind of money?" I managed to ask.

"I invest very well," she replied around a knowing smile. "We have a deal then?"

Sure, I get eight thousand a day, but I usually only work about six days a year. Two and a half million was more than I'd ever see. I could pay off the bills, get a decent house, a personal Sim unit, maybe even get Myla and me into a Perpetual Body Program. A PBP was practically immortality.

But a three-hundred-day job? "I have other clients," I said, "booked in advance."

"I'll pay for those, too, and pay your clients' way at another surrogate. A deal?"

Faintly, I heard my ears begin to ring, and I wondered if the expression she saw on the face in the swapping mirror was as confused as the one on my real face. "Where will I stay for nine months?" I asked.

She relaxed. She knew I was in.

"Great," said Myla, "nine months of you looking like some Cajun hooker." She tossed her cigarette into her dinner plate, where it landed on a piece of half-eaten toast. Smoke did not flatter Myla. "Going to play hell with our love life, Charlie."

"Two and a half million, Myla. We can retire. Hey, we can pay someone to have babies for you!"

She snorted and pushed her cooling eggs around with

the damp butt of her cigarette. "Don't want anyone having babies for me. I'm good at it." She looked up from her plate. "But not as good as you, Charlie. Why'd you have to be so damn good at it?"

"You got me started," I said. "You're the one that told me there was money in it."

"Yeah, but I never thought my husband would turn out to be a better mother than me."

"Come on. You know being a mother has nothing to do with it. It's just that I'm good at capturing the feelings. They like me because my recordings seem fresher. You've said before that it's probably because it's farther from my daily experience than it is for you." Myla gave me a cold look.

"Evangeline Giscard," she said slowly, then sat back, twisting her soiled napkin. "I've heard of her. She's in the Sim recording business."

"You did a long one once," I said, trying to change the subject. "You did Estaville."

"For six weeks," she said, "not nine months."

Later, when we were in bed, and I was almost asleep, she said, "Don't do it, Charlie."

"We'll talk in the morning," I said. But we didn't.

What do you pack for a nine-month trip when you know none of your clothes will fit?

Giscard had been in touch, and I knew something about the place where I'd be staying. She owned an island in the Mississippi Embayment, a chain in what had once been eastern Arkansas before the rising seas had turned it into an archipelago. She said I could bring along a friend, but Myla declared that she would not go. She didn't seem as dead set against the deal as at first, she just "needed more time to adjust." So I'd be making the trip alone.

When I left our apartment, Myla was still twisted up by the idea, but she made a big show of smiling and telling

Illustrated by Darren Albertson

me it was all right. At least we managed to part with a kiss instead of a fight.

Since, unlike my previous clients, Giscard wasn't approaching labor, we didn't use a med center. Instead, I got on the tram and made the trip over to Sammy's where she had the clone prepared. It's supposed to be the best body shop on the strip, but since I've never rented, all I can tell you is that it's a big place. Seems clean. They had a lot of rentals there, the standard long-legged beauties and square-chinned lunks, lined up in big acrylic tubes. I figured that was how they'd store my body while I was away.

It took the technicians a few minutes to attach the headset. Sweat kept screwing up the contacts. Funny how I was more nervous than I'd ever been on my previous surrogate jobs. On those other occasions, I had known I was headed for several painful, difficult hours. Now I was going on what, for the first few weeks at least, might be considered a vacation. If you had to pay for a thing like this, you'd spend fifty thousand on the rental body alone. Only thing was, on other jobs I went home at the end of the day.

I lay down in the reclining chair and closed my eyes. A few minutes later, I opened hers. You want to know what it feels like? Go get a rental. There's been more than enough press on the joys of transsex.

I don't get transfer headaches like most people do, and I adjust quickly. That's part of what makes me a good surrogate. Still, I found a couple of surprises.

The clone was several years younger than the woman who had been to my office. The face I saw in the mirror now was softer, less defined than hers. I never asked, but I guessed that the clone body was around seventeen. That amounts to about eight months in the speed-grow tubes. The other thing that surprised me was how good I felt, how healthy. I guess my job had given me the idea that women go through life in pain.

The body had been impregnated before I moved in, so at least I didn't have to suffer that indignity. I spent a few minutes in the back of Sammy's just getting used to things— yes, walking feels different, that much hair does get in your face if you don't keep your chin up, and brown eyes do see colors differently than blue. If you're a renter you're probably familiar with these things, but my work didn't usually leave much time for subtle observations.

A big Mauler liftcar picked me up at Sammy's elevated pad and we shot off to the northwest. I didn't see my body after the transfer, and I didn't see the real Giscard at all.

By three that afternoon I was comfortably marooned on Giscard's private island, which came complete with a house that was modest in size but decadent in furnishing, a pool, a mini-jungle of tropical foliage in the center and two kilometers of imported white sand beach around the edges. The only thing you could see from the island were miles of emerald water and the dark reefs forming around submerged buildings. Giscard's agents told me that the diving was good.

Inside the house I met the island's only other inhabitant, my maid, cook and companion, Rita. She was a matronly Hispanic woman who sported an Alto Mexicano accent too strong to be believed and seemed incapable of calling me anything but "Miss Evie." After a few minutes, I began to feel like the heroine in some antebellum drama.

Rita led me on the tour of the house and grounds and ended by showing me to my room. I found that my clothing worries were unfounded; Giscard had left me a closet full of casual wear. I unpacked the bag of books I'd brought and rested from a very full day.

And so, with my trusty companion and my private island, I settled down to lead the life of a kept woman.

Myla came about two weeks later and caught me at the mirror. Like any common rental junkie, I spent too damn much time at the mirror. I was ashamed of myself, but the glass seemed to exert some kind of magnetic pull. Every time I looked, it was startling. I'd tried on everything in the closet within the first three days.

When I got through blushing, I ran to hug her. It was funny to find her several centimeters taller than me. With no one familiar around for comparison, I hadn't realized how short I'd become. We managed a clumsy hug, but I felt the tension in her shoulders, so I backed off.

Neither of us spoke. Myla couldn't seem to decide whether to look away or bore holes in me with her eyes. Finally I said, "Well. What do you think?"

"Of you or the place?"

"Both."

"Lovely," she said. "Both of you, but I like the old Charlie better."

"Me, too," I said, and we both laughed a little nervously. Then I managed to work in some talk of food, and we went off to find Rita.

Rita never asked a thing about my relationship with Myla, and we never volunteered. She seemed happy to have more company and even happier to find Myla proficient in the "Spanglish" that they spoke around Rita's home. Soon the two of them were laughing together, and I got that isolated feeling you get when you don't "speak the language." I left them talking and went for a swim.

When I'd first pillaged Giscard's closet, the swimsuit had made me feel very uncomfortable. Even though it was an old-fashioned one-piece kind of thing, wedding white, wearing it made me feel queasy. Though only Rita and Myla were around to see, I wasn't brave enough to flaunt my temporary anatomy on the beach by going *sans suit*.

After I'd swum for an hour or so, Myla came strolling down the beach and sat cross-legged in the sand. She watched me for a while as I dove for chunks of rubble and bits of rusty metal from a big flooded store just off the beach. From what little I'd brought up, I hadn't been able to figure out what kind of store it had been. It took me a few more dives to work up my nerve, but finally I waded to the shore and sat beside her, wringing the water out of my hair.

"You holding up okay?" I asked.

"Lonely," she said after a moment. "I miss you, Charlie."

I tried to put an arm around her, but she leaned away. "Come on, Myla. You know it's still me."

She shrugged, and again we sat in silence for a few minutes, watching the waves wash Giscard's decorator sand into the bay.

"How do you feel?" she asked.

"Good," I said. "Physically, I never felt better. But I keep having this feeling that someone's going to pop up, point a finger at me and start laughing. I feel kind of ridiculous."

She gave me the kind of once over I'd seen her give other women at parties. "Believe me, Charlie. Anyone sees you now, they're not going to laugh."

"It all seems so strange to me. I'm just glad you're here."

"Yeah. Well, I had to come, didn't I?"

I didn't know what to say to that. Myla got up and walked back toward the house. I brushed some wet sand from my tan legs and followed.

Rita had already prepared a room for Myla. Late that night, when Rita had gone to bed, I knocked on Myla's door. She didn't answer.

Myla stayed for two months. She helped Rita get me through a three-week bout of morning sickness, and she came to my bed on several nights when she heard me crying out from nightmares, but she would not sleep with me. Whenever I tried to press her beyond a sisterly hug, she shied away. Gradually, I stopped trying. I'm not sure I had ever really wanted it. Maybe I just wanted to prove to Myla, and myself, that it *was* still me.

Other than that, we seemed to be getting along famously. We spent a lot of time on the beach. Swimming seemed so effortless, easier than ever before. Women are built better for it than men.

It was Myla who brought up the old golf clubs and fishing lures that led us to conclude that our little Atlantis had been a sporting goods store. She also convinced me to take a "safari" into the treacherous hectares of the island's interior, where we were threatened by nothing more dangerous than some plump mosquitoes. We began talking more and laughing more. At night, we sat up and watched the vid. Rita smiled at us and called us her "girls." I thought things were going well.

Then I got up one morning early and found Myla struggling down the hall with her suitcases.

"I can't take it, Charlie," she said before I could get out a word. "I can't take having a husband that looks like my little sister." She glanced back my way. "Only prettier. You know who Evangeline Giscard is?"

I shook my head. "She's in recording, you said."

"She's the head of TrusCom, the gray market Sim company. They probably plan to put the whole pregnancy on tape, selling motherhood in a box."

I knew that Giscard had this body implanted for full time recording, but I'd been forcing myself not to think about that. It was bad enough to know that one person would experience every moment of these months on the island; millions of voyeurs was something I didn't want to consider. "It's only a few more months," I said.

"I'll see you then," she said. When she opened the door, the taxi had already settled soundlessly on the pad. I moved out the door behind her, trying to find the words that would call her back, but they wouldn't come. She didn't wave.

Maybe she had caught me in front of the mirror once too often, because two days later I got a separation notice. On the back Myra had scrawled, "Keep the money, Charlie." In my bedroom I had a picture of me, the old me, and Myla. That night I looked at that picture for a long time. Over and over, my throat tightened and I felt on the verge of sobbing, but the tears never came. Finally, I opened a drawer and put the picture away.

With Myla gone, the days became monotonous. I read a stack of books. Watched hours of old flat films on a viewer in Giscard's study. Ate a lot of Rita's food. And I thought about the baby.

The scale said I was gaining weight. I examined myself critically in the mirror, contemplating the gentle bulge pushing against the taut skin of my belly. I felt only a vague sense of movement from within, a profound feeling of life, a warmth I had never experienced in my painful bouts as a labor surrogate.

After a few more days of laziness, I decided to get out and do some more swimming. The white suit had become awfully snug around the middle. I was starting to feel a little clumsy on land, but in the water my expanding waistline didn't seem to be a problem.

I stroked out to the old store, enjoying the way the water parted smoothly around me. Wearing goggles, I dived under the waves and through the collapsed roof. Blue light filtered in and played across mounds that had once been aisles of goods. I spotted something glinting and got my hand around a solid metal bar, apparently untouched by corrosion, and began to pull.

That's when the first cramp hit. I tugged at the bar again, but the pain in my abdomen grew stronger—disorienting. I released my grip and clawed my way upwards. I reached the surface and took a deep breath. That helped the pain for a moment, but then I felt something warm against my leg. I looked down; a dark stain swirled away in the water.

Blood.

When I reached the shore, the pain doubled me over. I managed to knock the water-filled goggles from my eyes and stagger toward the house.

"Rita!" I fell to my knees as the next wave of pain hit. "Rita!" I cried again, just a gasp. I rolled on my side and cried as knives dug at my insides. As the peak of the pain passed, I managed to get back on hands and knees. The wet sand beneath my knees squeaked as I tried to crawl to the house.

Evangeline Giscard came to see me at the med center.

The doctors had gone, and I had finished crying. At least, I'd finished my first round of crying. There was a rap at the door, and I looked up to see a young woman standing there. It took me a moment to realize that the face was one I had seen in the mirror so many times. Evangeline sat beside the bed.

"I am sorry," she said.

I nodded.

"Of course, I will honor the contract. You will be paid in full."

"I'd like to try again," I said.

"That is not necessary. I know what you have suffered. While you were sleeping, I had the recording chip extracted."

I ran a hand through my long hair, feeling the tiny port at the base of my skull. I was astonished that she could get the doctors to agree to such an intrusion without my permission.

"There is no need for you to go through that again," she continued.

"I *want* to try again."

She gave me an unsettling smile. "No. I have changed my mind about having a child. I must get to an important meeting. Whenever you are ready, you can retrieve your body at Sammy's. Again, I am sorry it ended this way." She stood up and started to leave.

"Wait a minute!" I called. "Wait a minute."

She glanced at her watch. "Yes?"

"You planned it this way, didn't you?"

"I don't know what you . . ."

"This miscarriage. This is what you wanted."

She hesitated. "I have what I want."

"Myla tried to warn me, but I didn't want to listen. You're sick!"

"Not me. The public is sick. A tape of a pregnancy, yes, I could sell that, maybe a few million tapes if it's done well, but this—the pain, sorrow, even grief." She leaned in very close and put her perfectly manicured hand on my arm. "All of which you have captured so well, my dear. From my brief sampling I can say that I'll sell many millions more of these tapes. A novel pain is always worth more than a pleasure. It's the nature of the business."

I jerked away from her. If I had felt even a little bit better, I'd have climbed out of that bed and done my best to strangle her.

"Anything else?" she asked and she flipped her hair back with a gesture of such studied elegance that I understood for the first time that this was not her natural body.

"Yes," I said. "There is something I want."

"What is that?"

"This body," I said. "I want to keep it."

She laughed. "Yes, it is good, isn't it. Top quality, limited run. And very expensive, I'm afraid, worth well over a million. Even in, shall we say, a used condition?"

"Take it out of my pay."

"If that is what you want." She gave me a last mocking smile and left.

I rolled over in bed and hugged my legs tight against me.

The Coat of Many Colors

by
Christine Beckert

ILLUSTRATED BY Evan T. Thomas

About the Author

Christine was born in 1946, a leading-edge baby boomer who drowned herself in books. She grew up in the Midwest but eventually moved to New England, which she now considers to be her home.

Throughout her youth she continually wrote fiction. She says, "I was writing science fiction in high school, of the 'The planet's inhabitants called it Earth' variety; gloomy mainstream stuff in college, the kind where everyone dies; and slightly better science fiction in my early days as a technical writer." At that point, she began receiving kindly rejections from editors, but withdrew from fiction for almost twenty years as she taught English, encouraged other writers, and turned out textbooks, newspaper articles, essays, and reams of notebooks with ideas for future stories.

Recently, though, her desire to write fiction has been demanding release, and she is garnering more than kindly rejections. She has been published in After Hours *and* Midnight Zoo, *and will soon be published in* Pulphouse. *Christine is wise enough to know that many of our finest writers start late. "To find myself in the pages of* Writers of The Future . . . *turns me again into a ten-year-old dreaming of someday. Being forty-five doesn't matter; I am a writer of the present and the future."*

•   •   •

Christine Beckert's illustrator is Evan T. Thomas.

Martha Malone was on her lunch **break when she saw the sign: The Coat of Many Colors. It was odd that she noticed it—she still** roamed the streets at noon and after work, but she did so with her arms tight around her, her eyes too purposeful or too dazed for detail.

It had not always been like that. When she had arrived here in Boston, emerging from a small town in the western part of the state, from an almost forgotten branch of the state college, from a marriage that hadn't worked, her eyes could not see enough. When she roamed then, she eagerly watched the people and the movement of the city. She studied the clothes and the gadgets; she visited the pubs and the parks; she watched faces and hands and feet on the move, always on the move. Though she loved food, she forgot to eat, living on the smells in the city, the odors of dreams and sausage and fine, dry wine.

But no matter how quickly her eyes darted, no matter how briskly she walked, she seemed always a pulse out of step with the beat of the city.

Now, she lived in an apartment, old and dim, and if truth be told, rather seedy. People had posted notices at work, looking for roommates to share larger, nicer apartments, but Martha was afraid to pursue them. What if she didn't like the people—how could she say no after she'd talked to them and walked through their private places?

So she stayed in the building owned by a friend of Aunt Rosa. Only one tenant, Lois Galloway, had shown any friendliness when Martha moved in, had bustled over and introduced

herself and steered Martha away from a particular neighborhood shop. "The prices are too high there, dear. I'll fill you
in on which are the good ones. I'll even introduce you to my
hairdresser. Aren't I a good recommendation?" She preened
for a moment, patting her hair, thick and gray and bristly as
a winter bush. Martha grinned and nodded, but she never got
that introduction, because the next day Lois Galloway had a
stroke and was carted off to a hospice. Most of the other tenants
were retired people, watching for their social security checks
and terrified of being robbed. They kept to themselves. They
muttered and withdrew their eyes from Martha and harbored,
she thought, a dark suspicion that she was a scout for a gang
of thieves. She could feel her pale face heat at the thought,
feel the spray of freckles across her nose glow angrily.

Martha worked for an insurance company, processing
incoming claims, checking the account status, referring rou-
tine claims one direction, large claims another, suspicious claims
upstairs. She was good at her job—very few of her decisions
returned to her desk with sharp notes of criticism—but she had
to watch as others were promoted over her, others who weren't
as fast or as good but who went out of their way to flatter the
director or make friends with the supervisors.

Martha didn't have time for that. Always the stack of
incoming claims rose higher than the hours left in the day and
so she smiled politely when someone stopped by her desk but
ducked her head when the inevitable gossip began. She sat with
her acquaintances during her break, but she rarely knew anything about the people or movies or restaurants they talked
about, and so she listened for bells that didn't ring.

She had not thought, when she came here, to storm the
city, to conquer. But she had thought to grow, to glitter a little.
She had not starred in Windsor, but she had not been lonely
either. Everyone knew everyone; everyone cared and took care.
They took care of her. After the divorce her family and friends
had clucked and held her in their arms, though they could not

make her forget how Greg had laughed when she told him she dreamed of harbor lights and how beautiful those words were— "harbor lights"—how they beckoned away.

But here in Boston the harbor lights seemed more distant than ever. Martha woke, worked, wandered, slept—and no longer, with sleepy morning smiles, recalled her dreams.

Until she saw the sign.

It was hanging in the window of a small, dark shop on a narrow, dark alley linking two main thoroughfares. Martha had often cut through the alley but had never noticed the sign or, for that matter, the shop. Today, perhaps because she was walking slowly in the baking heat, she did: a small sign, hand-lettered, with only the five words: The Coat of Many Colors. Martha stared at the words, her mouth open. The words repeated themselves over and over in her mind, like the clacking of a rolling train: the coat of many colors the coat of many colors the coat of many colors.

Finally she focused on the display in the window: a couple of dingy dresses, a misshapen coat. Above the shop was a faded sign: Pre-Owned Clothes of Distinction. Perhaps at one time the shop had recycled designer gowns their owners disdained to wear twice, but Martha doubted its stock today had any distinction whatsoever.

And yet—The Coat of Many Colors, said the small card.

Martha glanced up and down the alley, but there was no one. It was still and quiet here. As if the alley were a tunnel, light and noise and crowds passed on the two ends, distant, unreal, the image wavering in the heat, like moving pictures on cut-off screens. Reality centered here, in the hushed, dim alley, and most specifically on a little sign: The Coat of Many Colors.

Martha entered the shop.

It was dimmer inside, and cool. July shimmered outside, but here it was October or November—Martha knew which it was made a difference but she could not decide for sure. The shop was dusty—not dirty, exactly, or creepy, but—dusty, like the attic of an old couple, comfortable in their knowledge of what lay up here but disinclined to come disturb the dust. Racks of old, drab-looking clothes hung along one wall, and crudely labeled boxes—Sweaters, Shirts, Ties—crowded shelves on the opposite wall. Across the back a battered display case offered old, tired jewelry. Behind it sat an old man reading, a goose-neck lamp on the counter angled to light his book.

He looked up and rose as Martha stood uncertainly inside the door. "Hello," he said. "Can I help you?"

He couldn't be real, Martha decided. No one could so perfectly fit this shop—short and slightly bent, a fringe of thick, yellowish white hair circling his head and rimless bifocals perching on his nose, suspenders holding up baggy pants but allowing his shirt to escape at several points around his middle.

Martha shook herself a little and gestured at the sign in the window, feeling a little foolish.

"Ah, the coat," he said, nodding as if he knew it all along.

"Uh . . . what exactly *is* the coat of many colors?" asked Martha, furious at the flush she felt suffusing her face, at the freckles that lemon juice did not lighten.

"You're not here by referral then?" asked the man.

Martha shook her head. "No, I just saw the sign and . . . came in."

"Mmmm. Yes. Well, then, I'll have to show you."

He moved to a curtain that hung across a doorway at the rear of the shop, lifted one side, and revealed a tightly shut glass door. Martha caught only a confusing glimpse of sparkling light. She walked to the counter and leaned on it.

And was transported to Windsor, on a crisp October day with the sunlight dazzling in the air of the hills, transmuting the maples and oaks and ash and birch, shattering into the jewels of a queen's ransom, ruby and topaz and gold. But no— not October in Windsor, no—the Impressionist room at the museum, the one Aunt Rosa had urged her to visit and where she had almost drowned in points of light and color more real than the sun and the prism. No—no. July in Boston, in the back room of a dusty alley shop—a greenhouse, backing into some other alley and filled with green growing things as a backdrop to hundreds, thousands of butterflies.

Martha realized her knuckles were white on the counter she was gripping. She loosened them and made as if to walk to the end of the counter and back, into the dream beyond, but sudden alarm crossed the old man's face and he hastily dropped the curtain and stayed her with a hand on her arm.

"No—" he said. "It's private."

"But I don't understand," said Martha, her mind reeling with flecks of drifting, roving, flying color. "Are they really butterflies?"

"Yes," he said, pulling out a box from behind the case. "Sit down there and I'll show you."

Martha sat in the rickety chair he indicated and waited as he brought a large, flat case covered in glass. She gasped. Lying on a background of black velvet were some of the most beautiful butterflies she had ever seen. They were not arranged formally, with little tags announcing their species, but almost haphazardly, their outstretched wings touching and even overlapping slightly, angled, turned, to create a dizzying flow of light and color.

"They're—oh, 'beautiful' isn't enough," breathed Martha, pushing her pale brown curls back to glance up at the shopkeeper. "They're like—splintered rainbows."

"No," he said. "They may look perfect, but they're not. Even though they're preserved, their color isn't what it once was. Your eyes wouldn't see the difference, but I know what they can be. Even the glass over them, even that, subtracts something."

"So that's why—" Martha gestured to the back room.

The man nodded. "Till recently only a handful of collectors around the world have had—lepidopteries, I suppose you could call them. But public ones have opened in a few cities."

"But where do you get them? Do you travel, catch them?"

He barked shortly, gesturing around the room. "Does this look like I could afford to travel?" he asked. "No, I do some collecting around New England on weekends—I even get some from U-Mass, from discarded student collections. Then I trade—there's a network, you know. Still, it's an expensive hobby, and that's why. . . ."

Martha pointed to the box. "You mean—the coat? Like this?"

"The coat."

"But . . . but . . . how?"

The man's eyes glittered a moment—Martha shivered a little. "Surely you don't think I'll tell you that, do you? Never mind—it can be done."

Martha stared at the box, her eyes greedy, tilting it back and forth so she could focus the light on first one bright wing, then another. Something like fear woke in her. She didn't know if she could bear the coat, but she knew she had to have it. "The price," she said. "How much do you—"

"One thousand dollars."

Air left her. A thousand dollars—it might as well be a million. She had exactly three hundred sixty-two dollars in her account and her car needed a brake job. A thousand dollars.

He seemed to see her thoughts. "I'm sorry, but I don't make many of them, you know. And I can't trade for everything. Oh, and one other thing—" Martha looked at him inquiringly— "something of yourself."

Martha recoiled a little and laughed uneasily. "You mean, like a pact with the devil? Do you want my soul or something?"

"Or something," he said. "I don't know you, but you'll find something. At least, it usually works out that way."

He was looking at Martha strangely, with that glitter that surely must be just the reflection from the lamp in his glasses, and she felt an impulse to flee, but—the coat.

Now the old man shook himself a little, as if shaking off a mood, a moment, and said briskly, "There's something else you should know—the coat lasts only about twelve hours."

Martha had no idea what he meant.

"You understand—even under glass the colors die, a little. In a coat, worn by a woman, sat upon, danced in . . . you understand."

Martha nodded. A thousand dollars for a coat that would last a night, no, live a night. Reluctantly, she handed the box back to the man and rose.

"Give me a month's notice if you want it," he said. "The coat goes together quickly—you understand—but I need to gather the materials."

"Yes," whispered Martha. She moved dazedly toward the door, but then stopped. "Yes," she said, too loudly, blushed, and turned. "Yes, for New Year's Eve. I'll take it. I—I'll write you a check, for a deposit."

"Wonderful," said the man, pulling out an order blank and beginning to write as Martha walked back to the counter. "The coat of many colors, one thousand dollars, for pickup New Year's Eve at—" He looked up inquiringly.

"At eight o'clock," Martha said firmly.

"Eight o'clock. Deposit—" He glanced at the check Martha pushed over to him and his voice lost some of its approval—"three hundred dollars."

"I'll bring the rest as soon as possible," said Martha humbly.

"Yes, well—I won't begin until it's paid in full, you know."

Martha mumbled a reply, grabbed her receipt, and almost ran for the door. At the last moment she turned. "Goodbye," she said, "and thank you."

"You're welcome," said the old man.

As Martha stepped out, the heat seemed to knock her awake, as if she had been dreaming, or as if she had been floating in some still, dark channel beneath the sea. It couldn't be real—but there in the window was the sign, the coat of many colors, and in her hand an ordinary receipt, the coat of many colors.

The coat of many colors the coat of many colors the coat of many colors.

The litany whirled her through August and September, blinded her to October, warmed her in November. One of the elderly women in her building asked her to help her take out an old table for the rubbish, and Martha did so but only nodded vaguely and walked away when Mrs. Borelli thanked her and invited her in for cake and tea. Howard Keller, from the office, asked her if she'd like to go to the symphony with him, but when her mind swiftly computed the cost of the dress she would have to buy, she shook her head. "No," she said finally, moving away from him. "No, I can't afford it." She didn't even notice the puzzled look on his face. She thought of calling home, of asking her mother for the money, but her mother was all prose and biscuits; she wouldn't understand the coat of many colors and Martha wouldn't lie to her. But when some of the women in the office asked her out for Chinese and a movie, she hesitated and then hurried away. "No," she said. "No."

One evening she stopped into Finnerty's, the neighborhood pub, for a now infrequent glass of wine, but she barely noticed when Sam LeCourt, one of the regulars, greeted her as if he'd missed her.

"Hey, where you been keeping yourself?" he asked, lightly boxing her shoulder.

"Oh, around."

"You been sick?"

"No."

"Well, you look kind of run down. Not enough beer, kid! Gotta get you fattened up. Forget this stuff—" He pushed aside her wine spritzer and gestured to the bartender. "Two drafts, Gene."

Martha focused her attention on what Sam was saying. "Run down . . . really? Do I look bad?"

Sam seemed uncomfortable. "Well, yeah," he said. "You look . . . well, pale, skinny, you know? You been eating right?"

She shook her head, and for a moment was tempted to tell Sam about the coat of many colors. He would be goggle-eyed and laugh and call it terrific. Instead she waved aside the beer, mumbled an apology, and fled.

The coat of many colors the coat of many colors the coat of many colors.

On New Year's Eve Boston becomes a zoo, say some; magic, say others. The city celebrates ends and beginnings, old and new, dying and being born. Streets are closed to traffic and events sprout in halls and churches and parks. Raucous rock blares on one corner, while a quartet in evening clothes plays Mozart on another. Minstrels and troubadours, fiddlers and spoon clackers wander the streets, and vendors hawk festive ephemera and spicy foods. Crowds sway and dance and snake line; lights glitter in the cold air. Confetti flies, and noise-makers whistle or squawk. Clowns vie with police officers for the right to direct movement.

Martha stepped out of the shop into the alley, a tunnel of abandoned quiet linking the glitter and gaiety at both ends. She was dressed warmly in a black turtleneck and slacks, but over them hung the coat of many colors, a flowing robe with long, wide arms, galaxies of color within its folds—thousands of butterflies caressing her body. She twirled there in the alley and watched the butterflies dance in the dim light. Her own color was high, hectic, and she laughed as she danced down the alley and into the street . . .

. . . where crowds parted before her and little eddies of silence surrounded her and whirled into murmurs of delight, where children ran up to her and reached out their hands but stopped short, afraid to touch, where musicians missed a beat and then picked up with something new in their music, something wild and sweet and crystal clear, where clowns bowed and minstrels became her attendants, walking a little, running a little, dancing a little, twirling often to let the coat of many colors swirl around her, where performers on platforms opened a way for her to step up and curtsy and raise her arms and direct their play before she whirled down and off, ever toward the waterfront, where the harbor lights glittered and laughed in the water as the symphony played, and where people strolled or danced or sat and drank in the cold night air like a tonic and hugged a stranger and craned their necks when Martha came into view, gliding like a swan, hovering like a hummingbird but always dancing, dancing, dancing with a thousand butterflies fluttering about her every move . . .

. . . and she thought her heart would burst unless she let it free to ride on her shoulder, and it lurched as she realized how much the old man in the shop had understood and what a goose she was.

She thought of Mrs. Borellị and knew she would call the older woman and invite her out for pastry and tea, and talk to her about—

Oh, but that wasn't enough, and then, across the boardwalk—impossible in this crowd to spot someone you knew, but there he was, Howard Keller, standing alone, his hands in his pockets and his mouth agape, staring at her, and she whirled over and took his hand and pirouetted. "Next week," she called over her shoulder. "Come over and we'll put Schubert on the stereo and eat sausage and learn German."

Someone had seized her hand and guided her into another pirouette, and another pair of hands, and another, dizzyingly, until she shook them off and darted away and looked back and saw Howard, grinning as he watched, suddenly fall into a bow, his arm parting the air in gallant homage.

Illustrated by Evan T. Thomas

And that wasn't enough either, but suddenly there began the loud tolling of a bell, and silence moved like a wave over the crowd and eyes flew to the conductor as the drums picked up the count and the people stood and flung their arms around each other and their voices merged—ten, nine, eight, seven, six, five, four, three, two, one—

"Happy New Year!" And the rocket exploded above the harbor and burst into a million slivers of delight and Martha was forgotten—she forgot herself—as the old year shattered and reformed in a jubilant burst of sound from the orchestra and from the throats of thousands of people glad to be alive and greeting the passage of time.

Martha stood still, the coat of many colors light on her shoulders. No one grabbed her in an embrace, but that made no difference. The butterflies hovered patiently and the harbor lights nodded. All the bells were pealing now, mad with celebration, and Martha knew.

She thought of a place she had passed a hundred times in her roamings, the hospice a few blocks over where Lois Galloway had gone to die. She turned and moved away from the harbor, her feet reluctant but carrying her through the crowds and beyond, into a quieter area where the party had not spread, some houses lit up but most dark and dreaming. Around the corner was the hospice, soft lights in the lobby, dim ones marking the corridors on each floor. Martha faltered and shuddered a little, looking up at it, and then entered.

"Could I speak to the director, please?" she asked the startled nurse on duty at the desk.

"He's not here," the nurse said, reaching for the phone. "I'll call Ms. Hawkins, the night supervisor."

Ms. Hawkins gasped, too, as she emerged from an office and caught sight of Martha standing in the coat of many colors.

"Please listen to me," Martha blurted out, afraid her will would change and whirl her back into the endless party. "I know it's late, but please tell me—well, is a woman named

Lois Galloway still here? A patient? She used to be my neighbor and I—''

She broke off when she realized how crazy she sounded, when she saw both Ms. Hawkins and the nurse stiffen in outrage. "No, no," she said. "Listen to me. This coat—well, it really is butterflies, but it won't last much longer, it'll fade, but I thought—well, it's the new year and I've worn it all evening and now—well, I thought I'd like to give it. . . .''

Her voice trailed off, but when she saw comprehension dawn on Ms. Hawkins's face, her shoulders rose a little higher. "Come with me," said the supervisor, turning down the corridor, leaving the nurse still open-mouthed at the desk.

The woman did not speak as she led Martha to the elevator and the second floor, but she paused outside Room 204. "Lois was a good woman," she said, "but in all her time here, no one's come to visit. She gloated in giving advice, until she had the second stroke. We don't think—"

Martha nodded, and Ms. Hawkins opened the door.

A startled attendant stood from the chair where he was reading by the light of a hooded lamp. Martha approached the bed and looked down at Lois Galloway, sleeping, her thick gray hair spread out on the pillow, her face slack, one side drooping a little, moisture escaping from her closed eyes.

Martha slowly lifted her hand and undid the ribbon at the neck of the coat of many colors, slowly lifted it off her shoulders, slowly raised it to let it fall softly and lightly over the sleeping woman. Even in the still air the butterflies seemed poised for a moment in flight, as if they would flutter away forever, but then a small sigh escaped from Lois Galloway and they settled, soft and light. A flicker of something—a lost memory, an old jest, a soft kiss—crossed her face and then was gone.

Martha watched a moment longer, but turned when Ms. Hawkins touched her elbow. Quietly they left the room and retraced their steps. Ms. Hawkins walked with Martha to the street. "Well, goodbye," said Martha, stretching out her hand, "and thank you for letting me in."

The older woman gripped Martha's hand in both of her own. "Thank you," she said. She looked at Martha quizzically. "You're awfully thin, you know," she said. "You should eat better."

Martha laughed. "I intend to," she said. "I'm starved."

She could stop by Finnerty's on her way home. Perhaps Sam would be there, but even if he wasn't, she could find sandwiches and popcorn and beer. And tomorrow—tomorrow was all perhaps and harbor lights she could kindle herself. Tomorrow shimmered more brightly than the coat of many colors.

Timepieces
by
Mike E. Swope

ILLUSTRATED BY Omar Rayyan

About the Author

Mike Swope is a graduate student in the Master of Fine Arts/Fiction program at Wichita State University, and says that he doesn't know whether his story even qualifies as science fiction—certainly it is not like some of the stories that he particularly admired in Volume VII. In that, I think he's right. He's unique. I'd call the following story an extended allegory with SF overtones—a modern man's myth—but it certainly does fit within the realm of SF and Fantasy, where uniqueness is a valuable commodity.

Mike says he has only been writing seriously for two years, though he has won prizes for his writing in college, and he has published a number of poems.

There are as many successful ways to write as there are successful writers. Mike mentions that "I must have at least four hours time to begin writing so that I don't have interruptions that impede my movement from one sentence to the next. Writing, for me presently, is mystical." Certainly, his *technique works, and I think you will feel the mysticism as you flow through "Timepieces."*

About the Illustrator

Omar Rayyan was born in Amman, Jordan, and spent most of his youth moving about the Middle East—Saudi Arabia, Qatar—along with a short stint in Texas. He says that when he was four, his mother once drew him a picture of a horse and sent him galloping into the magical world of art.

At age sixteen he graduated from high school with honors, and went on to study architecture at the Rhode Island School of Design. After several months of saturating himself in the study of turn-of-the-century art, he changed his major to illustration and soon began selling his work at science fiction conventions, where he had earned many awards.

He now lives at Martha's Vineyard, Massachusetts, where he works for a paper, paints murals for local businesses, and he has recently earned his first assignment illustrating for a major children's magazine.

"What's this?" I remember asking Mother when I was four, interrupting my play and pointing to the thing in my chest.

"That's your Timepiece, dear," I remember her reply.

"Does everyone have one?" My finger pressed against the round, clear glass that's like the hollow of a test tube.

"Yes, dear. Everybody's got one just like it."

"How come yours is different?"

"It's not, dear. It's just like yours. See?" She unbuttoned and opened her blouse about six inches to expose her Timepiece like a third breast. I'd seen hers before when she took me into the bath with her, but it wasn't like mine.

"No, it's not, Mom. These lines are different on yours. They're in a different place." I pointed to the hands on my Timepiece. I didn't know to call them hands, then, like on a clock.

"Oh." She got real quiet after that and buttoned her blouse back up. "That's an answer for another time," she said. "No more questions, okay? Mommy's tired of questions. Let's just play. What do you want to play? Want to play Tow Truck? No? How about Horsie? Let's play Horsie."

So I climbed on her back and we played Horsie. I didn't ask any more questions then, and she was a little sad about something. If I'd understood, I'd have kissed her before climbing onto her back.

The next time I said anything about the Timepieces I was five.

"Mom, my numbers are the same as yours," I said as I came in from school.

"What, dear?"

"My numbers are the same as yours. See?" I'd pulled up my shirt and was pointing at the five. "That's a five, just like yours."

She stared at me for a minute with this look on her face, but she wasn't mad. When she didn't say anything, I let my shirt fall back down.

"What's wrong, Mom? Didn't I learn good?"

She kneeled down until she was my height and said, "Oh, yes, dear, you've learned good. And Mommy's proud of you." Then she hugged me. "I'm so proud of you. You learn so well. Mommy loves you very much."

I hugged her back. "I love you, too, Mom."

She relaxed and pulled away from me. "Now go on upstairs and put on your play clothes. As soon as I get through with supper, we'll go work in the garden before the sun goes down, okay?"

"Okay, Mom. I'll be back in a minute." And I went upstairs and changed, and later we worked in the garden.

I can see now, looking back, how that last year had worn on Mother. Her hair hadn't yet begun to turn gray, but it was as if she knew so much more than she wanted either of us to know.

I learned more about the Timepieces during the next six years. I learned on my own what all the numbers were and that the hands moved in the same direction as the hands on a clock, but that they counted from 31 to 0. I couldn't ask Mother about the Timepieces because she always got that look on her face that grew sadder each time I asked, so I waited for the sixth grade sex education course to learn anything more. I'd noticed, too, that my Timepiece now read 19, and hers 4.

Illustrated by Omar Rayyan

"We'll start with something all of us already know something about," said Mr. View after the girls had been taken to another room, "our own bodies. We're all boys, or males. Who can tell me what that means?"

No one raised his hand, although all of us knew the answer Mr. View wanted.

"It means, boys," Mr. View explained, "that all of us have a penis."

We giggled at this, but he went on, telling us about the male body parts, how they worked, and their purpose. None of this was new to us, though, because Bobby Jones' dad subscribed to *Playboy, Penthouse,* and *Hustler.*

"If there are no questions," Mr. View ended his first lecture, "we'll discuss the female body tomorrow."

I almost raised my hand at the last moment to ask about the Timepieces, but I didn't want to embarrass myself in front of the other boys. I thought they already knew and that Mr. View would explain the Timepieces sometime during the next two days.

On the second day of the course, Mr. View gave a lecture similar to the previous, this one on the female body, but he didn't discuss the Timepieces in this lecture, either.

"You're awful anxious today," Mother said when I came home from school after the second day of the course. "And you were anxious yesterday, too. Anything you want to talk about?"

She thought I wanted to ask about sex because a notice had been sent home about the course, but I couldn't tell her the truth about what was making me nervous. I remembered the sad looks that crossed her face whenever I'd asked about the Timepieces before. "No, Mom, there's nothing I want to talk about."

"You sure?"

"Yeah. Can I go out and play now?"

"Change into your old clothes first," she said, "and don't forget to put your good clothes in the basket."

So I slipped out of my school clothes, into some old ones, and out the door to play.

The next day, on the third day of the course, Mr. View discussed the mechanics of sex, but again never mentioned the Timepieces. After class, after everyone else had gone home, I quietly approached him at his desk.

"Mr. View?" I said.

"Jack," he acknowledged.

"I have a question I didn't want to ask in front of everybody."

"I'll do my best to answer it. What is it?"

"I expected you to answer my question in class, but you didn't."

"Yes."

"It's about," I was embarrassed to ask about the subject, "the Timepieces."

A concerned look crossed Mr. View's face before he laid down his pen.

"I'm sorry, Jack, I want to help, but I can't tell you anything about them."

"Why? All I want to know is what they're for."

"I just can't, Jack."

"But, look. Mine says 19 now, and last year it said 20, and the year before that 21. And Mom's says 4. And every time I ask her about them, she gets this sad look on her face, but doesn't say anything. What is it? Why won't anyone tell me about them?"

"Because they can't, Jack. Not yet. You have to be six-teen or a father before anyone can tell you."

"Why? I'm near the top of my class. I'll understand."

"I know, but it's the law. You're not mature enough yet."

"Why not? I'm mature enough to know about sex."

"It's not the same thing."

"It's not?"

"No. It's different. A lot different."

"Then what are they for?"

"I can't tell you. Look, Jack, when you turn fifteen you'll contract, get married and have a child. It's only after you're married and have a child that anyone can tell you, and not before. There's a good reason for it, but I can't tell you that, either. You'll probably come to understand on your own. You have to wait to find out anything more, okay?" He leaned forward in his chair until his elbows rested on the desk. "I'm sorry. You have to trust me. There'll be plenty of time to worry about it later."

I knew the conversation was at an end when he picked up his pen again.

"I'll see you on Monday, Jack," he said, and I left the building more frustrated than before.

So Mr. View knew more than he was telling, too.

I contracted on my fifteenth birthday with Mother's help. It was April Third, and we had the customary cake and ice cream at home, then made the trip to the post office. We sat at a table in a small room and filled out the required forms. The points of the contract were simple: I must marry within seven days; my wife and I must attempt to conceive within the first six months of marriage; and we must have no more than one child, unless otherwise blessed. The terms appeared reasonable enough at the time. Everyone had to follow them.

After signing and dating the contract and handing it to the postal clerk behind the counter, we were given a large spiral-bound volume.

"What's that for?" I asked Mother.

"It's the Listing. It's how you're to choose your wife. It lists every girl who's eligible this week."

She resignedly handed the thick black notebook to me, which I opened. I'd heard rumors about the black book; there were many legends about it.

On the inside cover was a white index card stamped with the week's date. On the facing page were the color photographs of three young women, all of them fifteen like me, and next to the photos were short biographies.

"What happens to the girls if there's any left when the week's over?" I asked as I read the first biography.

"Their names and photos are held and reprinted at the front of the next Listing."

"So, I'm looking at the girls left from last week?"

"That's right," said Mother.

"Is there anything wrong with these girls, Mom, that they're not chosen the first week?"

"No, Jack, of course not. They just weren't chosen for one reason or another. A lot of them weren't what that week's boys were looking for."

The first girl, a cute brunette with round, high cheeks, was Rachel Aachen. Her father was Chief Mechanics' Engineer for Coastal Pacific, her mother a homemaker like mine, and her two brothers headed for careers in the Marine Corps. She was a triplet. She had an IQ of 132 and ranked at the top of her class. Her lifetime goal, the entry said, was to teach college mathematics and engineering.

I tilted and turned the Listing toward Mother.

"What's wrong with this one? Why wasn't she chosen?"

"I don't know."

She took the book from me and read the entry.

"It might be she wants a career and wouldn't have been content to sit at home. She may not have been chosen because she'd have been too independent for the likes of most husbands."

"What's wrong with independence?"

"Nothing, nothing at all."

I took the book back and thought for a moment.

"Mom, I want this one. I want Rachel."

"Are you sure? You haven't looked at any of the others."

"I'm sure, Mom. She's cute, smart, and ambitious. There's nothing else I want."

"You're sure."

"Yeah, I'm sure."

"All right, Jack."

I took the book to the postal clerk and handed it to him, opened to Rachel's photograph.

"I would like her," I said, pointing.

He entered her Identification Code into a terminal and waited for the results. "She's clean," he said after the code had been processed. "Nobody else has taken her. She's all yours." He slid a laminated card across the counter to me. "Here's her phone number and address. You need to contact her to make all the arrangements." He winked at Mother, who looked away. "Good luck," he said as she led me down the hall.

Within the week Rachel and I married because, by law, no girl could decline an offer. As required, the wedding took place downtown in Matrimony Hall, an old church that had been restored sometime in the past by the state. Scheduled by the city clerk with a phone call, four officers performed ceremonies in rotating six-hour shifts, twenty-four hours a day, seven days a week.

It was an old officer who married us, his hair the color of steel, his Timepiece reading 4 as it protruded between the folds of his black robe.

Mother, her Timepiece near 0, sat faithfully alone in the first pew reserved for the marriage couple's families because Rachel's parents had died only the day before.

"Have you, Jack Benedict," the officer read from a book as the wedding march ended, "through the exercise of your own free will, chosen Rachel Aachen to be your loyal and lawful wife?''

"I have.''

"And you, Rachel Aachen, have you been chosen to be this man's loyal and lawful wife, as set forth by government?''

"I have.''

"And the two of you have been counseled concerning the expectations of this union you are about to enter, that all attempts must be made to produce a child within the first six months, and that at the time of the birth both of you must undergo sterilization?''

"We have.''

"And the two of you understand that if a pregnancy does not result within the allotted six months the two of you will voluntarily submit to sterilization at that time?''

"We do.''

"And do the both of you understand that a divorce or annulment will not be granted at any time for any reason, that the marriage union is until death?''

"We do.''

"Then, with the powers invested in me by law, I pronounce you husband and wife.'' The officer closed his book as Rachel and I kissed for the first time. Our Timepieces read 16.

Mother cried quietly in the pew behind us, I guessed from happiness.

Two days later, on Mother's birthday, I found Mother lying on the kitchen floor. I'd stopped by to get the rest of my things after Rachel and I had been lucky enough to find a small apartment in the want ads. There was only an armload or two of things I'd left after the first day of moving, and I wanted to wish Mother happy birthday.

"Mom,'' I called as I closed the front door behind me.

"Mom,'' I called again when she didn't give the familiar

order to remove my shoes. "It's me, Jack," I said, but she didn't answer.

I left my shoes beside the door and walked toward the kitchen, where I'd always found her before.

"Mom?" I called once more before stepping on a sharp object near the kitchen doorway and yelping in pain. Favoring my foot, I sat on the arm of the couch and pulled a small piece of curved glass from the ball. I took off my sock and limped toward the kitchen to find Mother, the toes of my foot pulled back.

"What'd you break, Mom? I cut my foot on a piece of glass in the living room."

It took a second to find her in the kitchen because she was partially hidden by the table, lying face down on the linoleum floor on the other side of the room, a pool of blood beneath her. Her glasses lay beyond her outstretched hands. Shards of glass like the one I'd pulled from my foot littered the floor, which kept me from rushing across the kitchen to her. I looked for signs of life from the doorway, but she lay absolutely still, her chest never expanding.

I picked up the phone from the wall beside me and dialed 911 as I'd been drilled over the years to do, but it took three tries to get the number right.

"9-1-1," a recorded message answered, "if the victim is immobile and there are weak or no signs of life, please call 9-1-2, the crisis line. If the victim is responsive, please hold on the line and an operator will be with you as soon as one becomes available."

I hung up and dialed 912.

"9-1-2," a dispatcher announced.

"It's my Mom," I told the woman on the other end. "She fell and and she's bleeding, and I don't think she's breathing."

"Calm down, sir," the dispatcher said. "Everything's going to be fine. What's the name of the injured?"

"Angela Benedict."

"Her age?"

"Thirty. No, thirty-one. Today's her birthday."

"Her general health?"

"Well, it's not so good right now. She's bleeding and she's not moving."

"I mean before the injury, sir."

"Oh! Great. She's always had good health before."

"And the address of the emergency?"

"1812 Pembroke Lane."

"Nature of the injury?"

"I don't know. She's bleeding from her chest. I think she fell and broke her Timepiece."

"All right, sir," she said, "stay calm. Don't worry. Emergency Life Support will be there in a few minutes. We recommend that you clear the immediate vicinity and let the personnel do their task."

"All right. Okay. Thank you," I said and hung up, stepping outside to wait.

Emergency Support pulled up three minutes later as I sat to one side of the front porch nursing my foot. The moment the van came to a stop three men rushed from the cab, each grabbing an orange first-aid kit from the back and sprinting toward the porch where I sat.

The medic who drove the van stopped to attend me while the other two entered the house. "She's in the kitchen," I told him as he bent over me.

"In the kitchen," he called to the others inside.

"It's only a small cut," I told the driver, referring to my injury.

"Well, let me see, and we'll fix it."

I leaned back, resting on my elbows, and gave him my foot. As he turned to get supplies from his kit, one of his companions came out the door, rushed through the small crowd that had begun to gather, got a stretcher from the van, and ran with it back inside.

"There you go," the driver said as he stuck one last strip of tape to my foot.

He'd just closed his box when the front storm door swung open and banged against the house. The two medics who'd been inside emerged, each carrying an end of the stretcher that held Mother. They'd covered her with a blanket. The medic who'd attended me held the door open for them and, when they'd cleared the doorway, went inside. He reappeared a moment later with his buddies' first-aid kits, one under his arm and the other in his hand. He bent down to take his kit into his free hand and told me someone would be calling about Mother's condition, then he was in the van with the others and they were gone.

Rachel and I began to have problems after Mother's death, although the authorities had called and reported that her death was natural, that it wasn't the glass from her Timepiece that killed her. The nightmares about the Timepieces began the night she died. In them, the Timepieces were living things, growing until their bubbles became prisons. The people, now prisoners, pounded at the glass, their lips moving, but not a sound would break through. I'd wake in the early hours of the morning and have to sit up until dawn because of the nightmares. I wanted to tell Rachel about them but couldn't because I didn't want her to know I was afraid. They haunted me and that was enough. As the days wore on, I kept more and more to myself. To her, my troubled state seemed rejection, and one evening, two months after Mother's death, her wits finally broke as she did the day's dishes.

I sat at the table, arms folded, silent as I'd become, when before we'd always talked about how our days had gone.

"Damn it, Jack," she hissed, shattering a plate against the back of the stainless steel sink and spinning around, "I've had it! No more! I'm your wife, remember? We may not have to love each other, but we have certain obligations to fulfill.

We're in this together. Just because your mother died doesn't mean you have to, too.'' When she finished, she dried her hands on a towel, threw it into the dishwater, and left the apartment. It was the first time she'd ever left the house angry. She returned a few hours later to find me sitting up in the dark, like she had so often before.

"Are you okay?" I asked as she removed her shoes, one of my habits she'd taken up.

"Yes," she said.

"Are you sure?"

"No."

"What's wrong?"

"You tell me," she said.

"I don't know."

"You've been distant these past two months," she explained. "There's been something eating at you that you haven't shared with me. If you don't want me around, just say so. They may not grant divorces, but we can arrange something. I can't go on feeling as if I'm living this life alone. Especially not now."

"What's that mean, 'especially not now'?" I asked. "What else is wrong?"

"I went to see Dr. Andrease yesterday about the sickness I've been having, like you wanted me to."

"What did he say?"

"Jack, I'm two months' pregnant."

"You're what?"

"That's what he told me."

"You're pregnant?"

"I didn't think you'd be happy about it," Rachel said.

"No. No. I mean, yes. Yes. Yes, I'm happy about it." I stood and hugged her. "It just took me by surprise for a moment. I hadn't expected this."

"Why? Why does it surprise you? We've never tried to prevent it."

I took my arms from around her and stepped back.

"I know, but I just never dreamed, never imagined."

"The vomiting alone should have struck a chord."

"I did notice. I wasn't totally oblivious."

"How could you miss it? You were up and sitting in the chair every time I rushed to the toilet. You must have heard me."

"I've had a lot on my mind," I said.

"You really didn't notice that I was sick, did you, until I said something?" she accused.

"No," I admitted. "I'm sorry."

"What bothers you so much it wakes you in the middle of the night?"

"Nothing."

"No, Jack. Tell me. I need to know."

"The Timepieces," I relented. "I've been having nightmares about them ever since Mom died."

"What are they like?" she asked, settling into the chair I'd previously occupied and leaving the floor to me. She knew I'd need the space once I got worked up.

"Remember how I found Mom," I said, "lying face down on the floor with her Timepiece shattered beneath her? That sticks with me. I can't get rid of it." I began to pace. "There's a dream I have where there's only one Timepiece. When the dream begins, it's small, about the size of a wristwatch, but then it begins to grow and every day it gets bigger.

"I try to stop it by pressing against it with my hands, but it's like squeezing a balloon and the air inside rolls to another place. Then suddenly, as I'm pressing, the giant Timepiece starts to fall. It seems like forever until it strikes the ground, and, when it does, it explodes, destroying everything—buildings, cars, people—everything.

"In the dream, I'm always the last to go and must watch as everyone dies."

Rachel seized my hand as I finished. "It's only a dream,

Jack," she said, her head thrust determinedly forward and upward toward me. "Everything's going to be all right."

I gave a short, nervous laugh. "It's gonna have to be now, hunh, now that a baby's on the way."

She made a weak attempt to smile as she got to her feet. "Forget about the Timepieces," she said. "You have other things to dream about now that you're going to be a father."

So I was, but the knowledge helped little since I still dreamed about the Timepieces, waking in the middle of the night. The only difference was that I forced myself to lie in bed instead of sitting up until daybreak.

At some point during the next seven months, in spite of the nightmares, I began to sleep further into the night, although I always woke before dawn. When I felt especially energetic, I made Rachel breakfast in bed. We chose names for our daughter and son during one breakfast after Dr. Andrease informed us Rachel carried twins, deciding at last on Alexis Renée and Zachary Ryan. Surprisingly, neither Rachel nor I felt guilty that she carried two children instead of one. At the time I didn't notice the calm that had settled within me. Later, while reading one evening, I came across these words by the poet David Thomas, which summed up how I'd come to feel: "But sitting here with my words and wonder/I'm amazed I knew all the time there was peace."

Finally the time came. Dawn had not yet appeared and I'd been lying awake when Rachel shook me and told me to get up. I found a suitcase, helped her into her robe, and quickly gathered our things while she went down to the car. As we hurried to the hospital, I rested my hand on her stomach, something I'd grown fond of doing when we were alone. This time, though, I knew that in a few hours our daughter and son would soon be born.

At the hospital, two orderlies hurried forward from

emergency to help Rachel onto a cart. When they had her safely aboard, they wheeled her around and rushed her inside, me trailing, my hands filled with an empty suitcase and the bundle of clothes I hadn't yet thrown into it.

By the time I got inside, Rachel had already disappeared. At the admissions desk, I filled out the necessary forms and was assigned a room with two beds, another requirement, the clerk said, because birth exhausts both parents.

As directed, I scrubbed and slipped into a sterile gown after depositing the empty suitcase and clothing in our room, a precautionary measure to insure a sanitary environment for Rachel, Alexis and Zachary, although I would observe from a separate booth above them.

The nurse led me into the observation booth and motioned for me to sit down in the only chair there, but I protested when he began to strap me in.

"Another regulation," he told me. "We have to secure you. But," he lowered his voice, "you appear harmless enough. If you'd like, I can leave your legs free."

"I'd appreciate that," I answered and let him strap my arms to the chair.

Through the Plexiglas window I watched Dr. Andrease enter the room. He glanced at Rachel aching to give birth as he slipped his hands into a pair of sterile gloves. I was both fascinated and appalled. Broad canvas bands held Rachel upright against the inclined table, crossing her chest and Timepiece, crushing her breasts. Her hands gripped the edge of the table so tightly her knuckles turned white. Sweat trickled down her neck and beneath her gown. Dr. Andrease gestured as if talking, trying to soothe her.

"Why can't I hear anything?" I asked the nurse, who'd taken position behind my chair.

"I haven't turned the audio on."

"Why not?"

"Most of the fathers can't bear to he͟ heir wives in

pain and ask me to leave it off.'' As an afterthought he added, ''I can turn it on if you'd like.''

''Please,'' I asked.

I heard the rustle of his uniform and a shuffling foot-step, and suddenly the room was filled with noise. I heard the intake of air into Rachel's lungs as her chest expanded, and the rush of air out as her lungs collapsed. I heard her hiss, bear down, and finally howl as she pushed to get Alexis and Zachary out of her body and into the world.

I hadn't expected the birth to be so intense, and I watched in awe as Alexis' fragile head appeared first, then her neck and shoulders, her arms, her waist, her legs, and finally her feet, followed almost immediately by Zachary. Dr. Andrease gently clamped and cut the umbilical cords that attached them to their mother. That accomplished, Alexis and Zachary finally shook to life and wailed, shaking the walls of the observation booth, and as Dr. Andrease reached down to take them into his hands, I saw they had no Timepieces. He carried them to a small table in the far corner while two nurses followed to assist. Alexis and Zachary's cries softened then ceased beneath Dr. Andrease's administered anesthetic.

The remaining nurses bathed Rachel with soft, saturated sponges, her strength entirely spent from the labor. The nurses assured her that the babies were healthy and beautiful before she fell into an exhausted sleep and was guided out the door and to our room to rest.

The delivery, though, was not yet over. I nervously watched Dr. Andrease's shoulders work as he carefully labored above Alexis and Zachary for another four hours before taking a damp, sterile towel and wiping them down. He removed his latex gloves when he'd finished cleaning Zachary and donned a fresh pair while the nurses dried and powdered the infants.

With clean gloves Dr. Andrease and a nurse picked up Alexis and Zachary's unconscious forms. They held them close, one hand beneath them, the other across their backs. Dr. Andrease turned around and looked up at me strapped into the chair, the nurse following his example. With a proud smile and the slightest movement of his thumb he motioned to me that everything had come out all right. As if to prove his point, he carefully slipped his hands beneath Alexis' arms and lifted her up, her face toward me, for me to see. The nurse did the same with Zachary. In the center of their chests now protruded Timepieces like mine and their mother's.

I remember that Mother only got angry with me once when I was a boy. At six I broke a vase Dad had given her. I tried to glue it back together so she'd never know. The sound of the vase, though, as it collapsed on the dinner table was like skeletons knocking together. When Mother scolded me, the only things in focus were the table, the pieces of vase, and my own hands, so that the effect was like lying in a long glass tube. I felt the same when Dr. Andrease and his nurse held Alexis and Zachary up to me.

In the observation booth I felt nauseous and heavy, like a stone, and must have asked, What's this? because the nurse behind me answered, "Your children. They're beautiful, aren't they? Birth's the only time I know their Timepieces to shine like that. I think it's the lighting they have down there," he said.

In a moment my nausea turned to anger. At that instant all I wanted was to shatter the Plexiglas window and to hear the satisfying crunch as it struck the floor in the room below, the fragments bouncing across the tile like pebbles. I raised my legs and began beating at the window with my feet. The window shook with each blow, but didn't break. The nurse behind me rushed forward and tried to restrain my pumping legs with his weight, but caught a heel to the nose instead and fell to the floor, where he bled across the white of his uniform.

Below, Dr. Andrease and the nurses frowned, lowered Alexis and Zachary to them, and left the room.

Still I kept at the window.

Less than a minute later the door opened and the room filled with officers, all trying to stop me from breaking the window that wouldn't break anyway. Four of them went for my legs, which they finally restrained with their combined number, but not before I heavily bruised their bodies. I remember hoping they'd hurt for a week. The others, who by this time had released the straps which held me into the chair, seized my arms, and together they carried me still struggling from the room. In the hallway, Dr. Andrease injected me with a sedative, and the police laid me on a cart against the wall to rest while two nurses held Alexis and Zachary to their Timepieces, as if the children would suckle.

During Rachel's last visit, she begged me to plead temporary insanity. Her eyes were wide, not with fear for my safety, but with the knowledge of my insignificance.

"Please, Jack," she implored through the Plexiglas partition, "do it for Alexis and Zachary. You're not a traitor. Be the father you never had."

"I can't, Rachel. Maybe if I'd had a father."

"Is it so much to ask that you become a father yourself, then?"

"It's asking too much. Do you realize what they've done?"

"Of course I realize, but everyone's in the same boat. You're no different," she said as she pointed through the partition to my Timepiece.

"But I am. I value life. No one has the right to rob another of it."

"That's just it, don't you see. Other people value life, too, but they try to make the most of it while they can. They don't make examples of themselves." She leaned forward until her nose almost touched the partition. "You'll die at thirty-one like everyone else, only you'll have forfeited your freedom, like your father, and I'll get a registered letter in the mail when it happens."

When I said nothing, she pulled back and stood up, sliding her chair back with her knees. "I guess you already know I can't attend the trial."

"Yes, I know."

"But I'll wait outside the room. Please, do what's right," she said.

"I will."

And then she turned and was gone.

The courtroom was not crowded the day of my trial. The judge sat behind the bench, gavel at hand, his Timepiece ticking merrily away from between the folds of his black robe, the material a little thicker and a little stiffer than that of the clerk who'd married us. The twelve-person jury sat on his left in its small but elegant oak corral, each Timepiece ticking as carelessly away as another, a slap in the face to which they were oblivious. The only other people in the room were the bailiff, myself, and my lawyer, a plump public defender appointed by the court. The media was not allowed in the room, as in all cases involving treason. Rachel waited on a bench outside the room as I went in, and would be there as I left.

"Does the defendant wish to change his plea?" asked the judge, his voice deep and hollow, echoing in the courtroom.

"No, your Honor," returned my attorney, "the defendant does not."

"The defendant's final plea of guilty, then, is entered into the record," noted the judge. "Has the jury agreed upon a verdict?" he asked.

A tall man stepped forward in the jurors' box. "We have, your Honor," he said. "In light of the violence with which the defendant attacked the window of the observation booth, and in light of the animosity with which he resisted arrest, and in light of his final plea of guilty, we, the jury, have no choice but to find the defendant, Jack Benedict, guilty of the charge filed against him.'' When he'd finished speaking, the juror quietly took his seat.

"This court, then," the judge addressed me and my attorney, "has no choice but to find the defendant guilty, and to sentence him, accordingly, to life imprisonment without parole. It's important, Mr. Benedict," he said to me, "that you realize the danger into which you've placed yourself and the lives of others, and reflect upon it." He struck the bench with his gavel. "Bailiff, please remove the defendant from the courtroom."

And so I was taken from the room and hugged Rachel for the last time before being led away. "Please," I tell Rachel now each time she visits, "let Alexis and Zachary know their father is fine and that he loves them, and explain to them about the Timepieces." I hope she's able to explain so that they understand and some sort of acceptance is achieved. But, if Alexis and Zachary are anything like their father, they'll never understand the Timepieces ticking away within them. And, I ask, who could blame them?

Certainly not me.

Notes to the New Artist

by
Edd Cartier

About the Author

Edd Cartier comes to us as a judge for the Illustrators of The Future Contest with over fifty years experience in the field of illustration and commercial art. His illustrations are classic, and in "Notes to the New Artist" he offers some timeless advice.

Edd was instructed in art at the Pratt Institute in Brooklyn back in the 1930s by artists who also illustrated for pulp magazines. One of his teachers was the art editor for a famous pulp publishing house, Street & Smith. Even before he graduated, Edd began working on illustrations for magazines, and upon graduation he was immediately assigned to one of the foremost pulps, The Shadow.

Among his thousands of pieces, Edd has illustrated in such magazines as Unknown, Doc Savage, and Astounding, along with Red Dragon Comics, and he illustrated covers for Gnome Press and Fantasy Press Books. He illustrated covers for virtually every major author of his time including L. Ron Hubbard, Isaac Asimov, Theodore Sturgeon, Jack Williamson, Gordon R. Dickson and many others.

A limited-edition collection of some of his works, Ed
Cartier, the Known and the Unknown, was published in 1987.
In 1990, Edd Cartier won First Fandom's Hall of Fame
Award.

When asked to pen a few words of advice for new science fiction and fantasy illustrators, I wondered what I could possibly add to the mass of "how-to" information that seems to be inundating the country today.

The problem, so it seemed, was that my art was first published in 1936 and it was a far different world back then. The pulp magazines were flourishing as the greatest form of mass entertainment the world had ever known. Newsstands literally overflowed with such magazines as *The Shadow, Unknown, Planet Stories, Doc Savage, Other Worlds, Black Mask, Wild West Weekly, Fantastic Adventures, Weird Tales* and all the others. And there was a steady need for new artists to illustrate them.

Of course, the great pulp magazines of the past are long gone. Photography has taken over the job of illustrating most stories in most magazines. Yet, there is still a large market for science fiction and fantasy illustrations in comic books, paperbacks and magazines like *Analog* and *Isaac Asimov's Science Fiction*. But for the novice illustrator, these are not enough. That makes it much harder to break into illustration of any kind, especially the speculative fiction market.

And that is why I agreed to Frank Kelly-Freas' request for my participation as a judge for L. Ron Hubbard's Illustrators of The Future Contest. From the very beginning, the Contest seemed a marvelous way to break down the barriers and to open the doors to new science fiction and fantasy illustrators. Now, years later and in conjunction with L. Ron Hubbard's Writers of The Future Contest, the idea has proved its worth and now Volume VIII of *Writers of The Future* is published. Both Contests have been marvelously successful and are doing exactly what they were designed to do.

So, what advice can I give to the new artist of today? As it turns out, there are some things that still apply and have changed little during the years.

The main thing that hasn't changed over all these years is you, the new artist. What I would like to do is to point out a few mistakes that I made as a beginner and to offer a few suggestions about the "business" of illustration—and about the novice artist's "relationship" with those who judge and publish science fiction and fantasy illustrations. I will leave discussions of materials, techniques and creativity for another time or another Contest judge.

Keep Good Records

My sons insist that I first mention something that has come back to haunt me and that has thwarted fifteen years of their research: It is the fact that I never kept thorough records. I never kept copies of the magazines my art illustrated. And I rarely kept copies of the books I illustrated.

Simple as that. And frustrating as that! If you do the same and try to find copies years later, you will know what I mean by the word "frustration"! (And by "expensive." Just try buying original copies of *The Shadow* from the 1930s!)

Why didn't I keep copies and why didn't I, at least, keep good records of where my illustrations were published? It just didn't seem important at the time.

Now I know that it was very important. That's why you, the new illustrator, should start your "archives" today. Keep careful records of your art and carefully preserve the magazines and books it appears in.

For that matter, carefully preserve your original art—no one prefers to look at, or buy, art that is torn, creased, smudged or mildewed.

Keeping your personal archives also pays off, years down the road, when a publisher calls to ask about reprinting your work. This is simple advice, with the guarantee that in 20 or 30 years (or much sooner) you will be grateful you followed it. Even if you are not, your children or your children's children may be very grateful. My sons certainly wish that someone had said the same to me. I suspect that there are other illustrators who will agree wholeheartedly.

On Business

Don't ignore the business side of the art of illustration. A starving, cheated artist is not a pleasant thing to see or to be—even if it has a somewhat mythic aura about it.

The art of illustration also includes the art of business. Take my word that records, accounting, taxes, contracts, bills, copyrights and all the rest are more important than ever.

As is the preparation of a professional portfolio. You do not want to show disorganized and out-of-date samples of your work to an art editor. Nor out-of-focus transparencies of your art.

Learn to be businesslike right from the start; your career will never be hurt by professionalism. Though I hate to see an illustrator kept from the task of creating, I must emphasize that taking care of business is a necessary evil.

There are excellent books and articles written for artists about the business and legalese of the visual arts. (Start by contacting the Copyright Office in Washington, D.C., for information. Today's copyright laws are finally on the side of the artist—if you follow them.) There are artist guilds, associations, societies and other organizations that offer information and assistance; they help prevent the feeling of standing alone against the business world. There are college and university courses that will help, too. And, of course, there is professional legal and financial assistance, as well.

Know Your Market

As a judge for the Illustrators of The Future Contest, I have seen entries that seemed to have very little connection to science fiction or fantasy. Some of these have been excellent illustrations showing talent and style, but they suffered when I judged them because they were not apparently relevant to the judging criteria of "appropriateness to science fiction and fantasy illustration."

It seems unimaginable to me why a contestant would harm his or her own chances by submitting something inappropriate. There is an old phrase which still applies after all these years: "Know your market!" It means that you don't submit an illustration of cans of soup to a science fiction and fantasy contest. (Unless those cans are in the hands of an alien creature on the third moon of the planet Bok!)

"Know your market!" That advice has been repeated and repeated; yet some beginning artists choose to ignore it. Of course, the phrase was originally meant about the business world, but it applies just as well to contests and to new artists trying to get their first illustrations published. Remember it and you will have a better chance at winning the Illustrators of The Future Contest and in getting your art accepted by magazines, book publishers, ad agencies or wherever you intelligently submit it.

Dealing with Editors and Authors

In the science fiction and fantasy pulps, I had the great fortune to work with a brilliant editor, John W. Campbell, Jr., and to illustrate stories for many top-notch writers including Theodore Sturgeon, L. Sprague de Camp, Jack

Williamson, Poul Anderson, Isaac Asimov and, of course, L. Ron Hubbard.

Admittedly, there were times when Campbell and others offered criticism and suggested revisions of my illustrations. They were not artists, but on occasion they were absolutely right. On the other hand, my explanations often put them back in agreement with what I had illustrated.

This "give and take" of criticism and explanation was a learning experience for all of us. Remember this and you will not look at your editor (or the story's author) as the "enemy." It can lead to those joyous, memorable occasions when someone like an Asimov or a Hubbard will write or phone to say, "You drew that thing just how I imagined it . . . you captured every last nuance . . . I'm thrilled that you illustrated my story." When that happens, it is total satisfaction for you, the artist. For the readers, it means that you have superbly communicated the author's ideas and, perhaps, expanded upon them. That is what illustration is all about!

When I first began illustrating *The Shadow,* the magazine's art editor insisted that I copy the style of my predecessor, Tom Lovell. I grudgingly agreed when the editor explained that he didn't want to jolt readers with any new look for the character of the Shadow. At first, I felt that the editor was suppressing my abilities. Truthfully, I'm still not pleased with my very earliest Shadow illustrations. As good as Lovell was, my work only mimicked his. It did not show my skills or my style. Looking back, I can see that at the time I was just a beginner in illustration. It had to be that way until the Street & Smith art editor was sure of my abilities.

But soon I started adding my own touches to things in the background. He didn't complain. Then I changed minor characters to how I pictured them. Finally, after a year or so, the look of the Shadow himself was as I envisioned him. There were no complaints from the editor because by then I had proven my talent to him and, thus, to the readers.

I suspect that other illustrators have also found that pleasing the editor is a terrific way to please the readers. This works because if an editor is any good, then he or she knows what the readers want. If not, the editor loses his job or the magazine loses its readers.

Retaining Artistic Integrity

You must never forget that the most important thing about an illustration is communicating the story; demonstrating your talent is always secondary.

Some of you may not want to compromise the integrity of your art. Some of you may even have been told not to compromise it. That's fine if you can afford it. Who knows, you may even triumph in the end. But I would rather see your work being published now—not "in the end." Again, my advice here is about winning the Illustrators of The Future Contest and getting your first illustrations published. Remember, right now you are a beginner.

I was influenced by the work of illustrators such as Frederic Remington, Charles Russell, Arthur Rackham, Dean Cornwell and Howard Pyle. In turn, other artists have said that my illustrations influenced them. Sometimes I see this in their work—and sometimes I don't!

Of course, there is nothing wrong with being influenced by another artist's work. Appreciating and, perhaps, imitating something from another artist's style can help you recognize and define your own. There is no shame in that. In the end, a truly talented artist will develop his or her own uniquely individual illustrations.

If each new artist was not progressively influenced by what came before, the caves of Lascaux might have remained the pinnacle of artistic endeavor. Besides, as someone who has been imitated, I can reaffirm that old cliché: "Imitation is the sincerest form of flattery."

Get Your Training

There are artistic geniuses who illustrate quite satisfactorily (sometimes spectacularly, as did Russell) even though they are self-taught. These artists have the innate ability to observe and remember what they see around them—that which nature and man have created. They see the world so clearly that when they are called upon to illustrate, they can take their observances and use them as a superb guide to the interpretation of an author's writings. However, the talent of a Charles Russell is a rare thing. Most new illustrators will benefit tremendously from artistic schooling and training.

Over the years I have often been congratulated on my ability to depict extra-terrestrial and horrific anatomy: "Believable, living and breathing creatures" according to the critics. For those types of science fiction and fantasy illustrations, my imagination helped and my observations of the world around me helped, too. But, taking anatomy and life drawing classes helped just as much. If you are good to begin with, just imagine what you could do with more training. If you are self-taught, my advice is to take some art courses— an understanding of human and animal anatomy is invaluable.

The Goal of the Illustrator

As an illustrator, I tried to not only capture a character or scene from a story, but also to capture the reader's attention, inducing him or her into reading the story—and then pulling that reader even deeper into it. Doing this for works of speculative fiction is much more challenging than for any other subject of illustration. That is because there are no "set rules" in science fiction and fantasy. However, when you succeed it is a very special satisfaction.

To the new artist, my best wishes for your success with L. Ron Hubbard's Illustrators of The Future Contest—and in seeing your science fiction and fantasy illustrations published soon.

Anne of a
Thousand Years

by
Michael Paul Meltzer

ILLUSTRATED BY Ira Crowe

About the Author

Every once in a while, we find in these anthologies that there are themes running through the lives of our writers and artists—seeming coincidences. For example, Michael Paul Meltzer works at Livermore National Laboratory in California developing ways to prevent environmental pollution, and has his Ph.D. in Environmental Engineering from UCLA. He is one of several writers this year whose concern for the environment has led him to a career where he does more than talk, gripe, or even demonstrate for the environment. In a sense, he's trying to help save the world.

Perhaps what I find most intriguing about Michael, along with our other winners who are also environmentalists, Gene Bostwick and M. C. Sumner, is an inherent optimism about the future. Together, they present visions of a future that most of us, I think, would enjoy.

Michael does a fair amount of folk dancing, hiking, traveling, and he studies Tai Chi. Several of his recent stories, like the one you are about to read, are heavily influenced by Tai Chi attitudes.

In the third grade, Michael was influenced by Heinlein, and has been in love with science fiction ever since. He has seriously been working to develop his skill as a writer for three years. His story won first place in the first quarter, and this is his first sale.

About the Illustrator

Ira Crowe earned his Bachelor of Arts in Fine Arts and minored in theology and literature. After college, he spent thirteen years as a minister and pastoral counselor, then returned to the secular life and committed himself to reviving an artistic career.

In 1991, Ira put on a one-man art show at the Celebrity Center of Washington, D.C. Since then, he has entered other shows and contests with favorable results. His interests include Celtic music, ancient history, philosophy, and his friends. He currently lives with his wife and four children in Arlington, Virginia.

After six days of thawing out, Annie woke from the dead. For over three years, she'd had no pulse. She hadn't breathed. Even her neuroelectric activity had been undetectable.

Annie felt a gush of warmth course through her body as Vincent replaced her fluorocarbon blood substitute with the real thing. Annie looked up through the milky aerogel top of the cryotank, and saw Vincent's craggy face smiling down at her. He looks like a seedy version of God, she thought. She watched his hands fly over the control panel making adjustments. He pushed a button. She felt the tingle of ultrasonic fingers tickling her head, then passing ever so gently over her face and down her body, stimulating long unused muscles.

I hate the waiting, Annie thought as she lay in the tank hour after hour, her muscle control gradually returning.

When she could move her arms enough to sign to Vincent, he cracked open the seals and swung the top of the cryotank back on its hinges. Annie climbed out with Vincent's arm around her for support. Her legs could barely hold her.

"Thank you, Vin. What's up? Why did you wake me?"

"Aziz is coming," said Vincent. He wrapped a robe around Annie's body and guided her into a pair of slippers. He walked her out of the cryonics vault, and into a corridor of the monastery, where an electric car waited. As they glided soundlessly down the eight-hundred-year-old corridors, they passed Nepalese monks on their way to prayers, and the scientists on their way to seminars. Both appeared equally oblivious to the passing car, though it came within inches of them.

"Aziz again," Annie commented. "I haven't seen him for thirty wakings."

"You did, temporarily. But now he's made peace with his former enemies and put together the biggest horde in Asia. He's knocking on our door at this minute."

"What do you mean?" asked Annie.

"He's right on the other side of the Khyber Pass, getting ready to march on India with an army of two million."

"That's incredible. The hordes have never unified against us before. They've never been more than bands of roving raiders."

"Things have changed since you went into coldsleep."

"Still, what can they do to us? If necessary, we can blast anything that comes across the pass, though I hope there's a better way to handle Aziz than that."

The open door to a meeting room revealed half a dozen men arguing over a set of equations on a chalkboard. In the next room, black-robed initiates knelt before Buddha's image, their foreheads resting on the floor. In a third room, more men and women in black glided through the postures of a tai chi form, striking the air in controlled slow-motion punches and kicks.

"Aziz won't be quite that easy to stop. He's got three GR-7's aimed right down our throats," Vincent said.

"Those are kilomegatons," Annie said. "What's he got to deliver them?"

"Near-sentient rockets. They're too tricky to track. He can wipe out a fifty-mile corridor from the Himalayas to Delhi. They give a neutron wallop, so they pretty much kill everything in their paths, but leave the factories, weapons, and even the farms intact."

"Mother of God! How did he get a hold of them?"

"He had an army of agents spread out through Baghdad

before it fell. They snatched the bombs from the royal armory, and whisked them out into the desert. We don't know quite where they are at the moment, but we suspect they are in three rather well-guarded silos primed and ready to fly."

"So why did you wake me? I don't do commando shit. You know that. I have trouble killing."

"We don't want a ninja for this job. We need a Cadre Member's skills. Subtlety will be required. Also, you've met Aziz."

Annie's thoughts drifted back to a night spent under desert stars in the arms of a wild-eyed young chieftain whose band of renegades picked fights with anything that moved. She had wanted to stay with him longer, but she was due back in the tank the next evening. One more relationship ruined by her profession. They didn't wake her again for another year, and by that time, Aziz had been declared outlaw and gone underground.

"Let's get you into a warm bath and scrub that dead skin off. You look like hell."

"Thanks, Vin. You look older." She glanced at her arm, and rubbed a patch of dry, peeling skin.

"I am. By three and a half years."

"My God, I've been in coldsleep for that long? What have I missed, other than the rise of Farouk Aziz?"

"Plenty. The reentry tapes must have filled you in when you were warming up."

"I don't mean news events. What's happened to my family? When I went into the tank, my sister Kim had just gotten engaged, and my old friend Lawrence was ice climbing in Antarctica. . . ."

Vincent looked at his friend with compassion. "Annie, Kim has a baby. A year and a half old. And Lawrence and his wife lead those expeditions jointly now. Climbers fly in from all over the world."

"Oh." Her eyes filled with tears. "I used to climb with Lawrence." I could have been leading those expeditions with him. At his side. Instead . . .

"You haven't done so badly for yourself, Anne Carlisle," Vincent said.

Annie sighed and followed him into the bathhouse.

"This is my fortieth awakening from coldsleep," Annie complained. "Why do you put me through basic training like I was still a novice?"

"Chi Gung exercises are for novice and intermediate and advanced Cadre Members. No exceptions. Besides, you may need this stuff in the desert." Vincent got up, went to the door of the workout room and peered out around the jamb. Then he closed the door and returned to Annie, who knelt on a meditation cushion. "There are three men coming down the hall. Describe them."

"Shit. I'm going to get a migraine from your exercises." She closed her eyes and centered herself. She put her hands on her thighs, her fingers pointing towards the door. Vincent felt a slight tingle across his skin as she extended chi energy out of her body, focusing it with her fingers. He could almost see her energy field move forward, through the wall and into the corridor beyond. He heard a shuffle outside as the men walked by.

"The first man: small, wiry, and old. His chi is unsteady, as is his walk. The one behind him is much bigger. Fat, and tall, too. He lumbers down the corridor like a bear. He is strong, but lacks grace. One of our laborers, perhaps?"

"Exactly. He works in the hydroponics vats."

"The third man is also big, but he moves like a leopard on the prowl. His chi field is powerful, though untrained. I don't think he's even aware of my probe."

"That's because he has been here only ten weeks. By your next awakening, he will be more sophisticated."

Illustrated by Ira Crowe

"He's ninja material, isn't he? You will teach him to kill or maim with any part of his body."

"We cannot instruct him in your skills, Annie. He does not have the potential to learn them." Vincent turned his back to her and held up two fingers on his right hand and one on his left. "Now, how many fingers am I holding up? And on which hands?"

Nicolas Kessler, the Director of the Solutions Institute, sat behind his gray steel desk studying Annie, who fidgeted from foot to foot. He did not invite her to sit. The sleeves of his rumpled white shirt were rolled up to his elbows, exposing a pair of muscular forearms, furred with hair the same shade of gray as on his head.

"What we want, Cadre Member Carlisle, is for you to find Aziz."

"We already know where his camp is," said Annie. "It's hard to miss; it must hold over a million people."

"Closer to two million, actually. And Aziz hides among them. He sleeps in a different tent each night."

"So you want me to get to him. And do what? I'm no ninja."

"I know that. We don't think it is necessary or advisable to cancel him. It would just create a martyr." Kessler reached forward and fingered something on his desk. The office lights dimmed. The wall on his left lit up, revealing the head of an Indian-looking man with finely formed, almost effeminate features, an impeccably styled longish haircut, and a slight graying around the temples.

"That's Ramaj Singh, the Deputy Minister of War, India Section," said Kessler. "He's highly respected by New Pentagon circles. The Confederacy Council in Honolulu considers him a real comer. He's the man you'll be reporting to. He recorded this message an hour ago." Kessler twisted something. The head on the wall started talking.

"Cadre Member Carlisle, the mission on which we have asked your esteemed Solutions Institute to send you is a highly dangerous one, but essential for the well-being of the Confederacy." Singh spoke in a clipped, cultured voice with only the slightest trace of North Indian nasalness in it. "This man Farouk Aziz has gathered hungry, desperate followers from all over Central Asia. Their credo is common hatred of the Confederacy, which they blame for all of their troubles. They think they can stream over the Khyber Pass, take prime farmland away from us, move into our factories, and send those presently settled there down the road.

"What we want to know is, what does he hope to gain by leading a nation of people, including many mothers and children, on a suicide march guaranteed to get them all butchered by the Indian Army? We have tried to ask him this, of course, but Aziz refuses all contact with us. Tell us what he's really after, Carlisle, and maybe we can avert a war."

As the message ended, Kessler turned on the lights, stood up and walked around the desk. He put his hand on Annie's shoulder. "Get your kit together tonight, Annie. We'll have a hummer waiting for you tomorrow morning in front of the Institute. It will take you over the mountains to within a few miles of Aziz's camp. I don't think he can detect the approaching craft, so we trust he won't know about you. You're to make your way into camp and find his headquarters, which may take a few days because he keeps moving it. You are to somehow get past any guards he has, and probe him. Then you are to get out of his camp alive and report to Singh."

"How long do I have to perform this miracle?"

"Six days. By that time he'll reach the Khyber Pass and we will have to fight him."

"I'm going to need a disguise," Annie said, fingering her blonde hair.

"I'll say. You look like a California beach girl, not an

Afghani bedouin. The boys in Makeup are going to have fun with this one. They're expecting you right now, by the way. Good luck, Annie. Come back to us in one piece, you hear?''

Annie lay back in a recliner, inspecting the rich caramel color of her hand with approval. She decided that she also liked the long jet-black hair that spilled down past her shoulders.

Someone tapped on the door of her room. She opened it. Vincent walked in, and stopped, an embarrassed look on his face. "Oh, I'm sorry," he said. "I was looking for Annie Carlisle. . . ."

"Annie sent me to entertain you tonight." She giggled.

"You witch! You're unrecognizable."

"So, do you like what you see?" She twirled.

Vincent extended one hand toward her face. "That nose, it feels just like skin and cartilage."

Annie slid into his arms and leaned her head against his chest. "I leave tomorrow," she told him.

"We were supposed to have two days together!"

"I'm sorry," Annie said. "The situation has become critical. Aziz is ready to attack."

"Then let's not waste any more of the night," Vincent said, and kissed her on the lips.

In response, Annie pulled his shirt from its waistband, and slid her hand underneath across his belly. She pinched him. "You're getting soft, Vin." Her eyes grew moist. "I thank God that every time I come out of the tank, you're there. At least something stays constant in my life."

"Not really. I'm getting older."

"How long has it been since I joined the Cadre?" Annie asked.

"Twenty years, my time. About one and half years as far as your body is concerned." Vincent ran his hands over her shoulders, down her sides, and cradled her buttocks in his palms. He sighed. "It's been three and a half years since I've touched you."

She pulled his hands away, stepped back and peeled off her shirt.

"I see that they rubbed that pigment all over you," he said. "Now that would have been a fun job."

Annie laughed and threw her T-shirt at him. "Get naked, Vincent Petersen, and enjoy the new me."

He did so, and she moved into his arms once again. She buried her face in his fuzzy chest, and exhaled against it. He kissed her open mouth, and thus locked together, they made their way across the room, collapsing onto her bed.

Annie awoke in the middle of the night. Vincent's sleeping face was illuminated by the Himalayan moonlight streaming in the window, reflected off of the snowfield below. Vincent looked pale and old.

I just touch the surfaces of those I love, and then they go. Or rather, I go. Back into the cryotank. Soon, my friends will start dying, and I will be all alone.

They woke with the first predawn light. Annie peered out the window, and saw the hummer getting fueled on the airstrip. Dressing quickly in a heavy black caftan, she headed down the corridor to the elevator. Some monks were already at their prayer wheels in the rooms she passed.

The elevator deposited her on the main floor of the monastery, where she met her Tibetan pilot, Genzing Yurda. Three-foot-thick steel doors opened as they approached. They entered the monastery's lobby and walked across its polished marble floors, Annie carrying her small gearbag over one shoulder. The bag was made of a piece of coarse muslin, and looked like what a poor fedayeen woman might carry.

Annie glanced up at the arrays of surveillance equipment and antiterrorist weaponry mounted on the ancient stone walls around her. She knew that no arms could be brought past them undetected into the heart of the monastery, and in fact no person could walk by the instruments without first being weighed, blood-typed and gene-scanned, all without ever being physically touched. Only then would the heavy steel inner doors of the monastery unlock.

She'd heard that about fifty years ago, a saboteur had attempted to smuggle a grenade into the Institute. The surveillance array had him made before he'd taken two steps into the lobby. Before he'd taken four more steps, fast-acting nerve gases had paralyzed him like a statue, allowing the cleanup crew to carefully pluck the explosives off of his belt.

By seven in the morning, Annie had stowed her gear under her seat in the hummer and they were accelerating down the two-mile strip of plasticrete that had been blown free of snow just half an hour before. Taking off and making a sharp bank to the right, Genzing guided the hummer skillfully down a narrow corridor formed by towering peaks. This long, tortuous canyon provided the only land access to the monastery. If necessary, explosives that had been mounted on the cliffs above the canyon could knock enough snow and ice off to blockade the monastery against any ground attack.

After twenty minutes in the air, they reached mach 2, emerged from the canyon and climbed to thirty-five thousand feet. The only sound they heard was the rush of wind over the fuselage and the hum of the magnetic drives. They circled to the north, towards the plains of Afghanistan, and Farouk Aziz's hordes.

Annie pressed herself back into the thick cushions of her seat, watched the snow-carpeted ridges sweep by beneath her, and wondered why she'd ever been stupid enough to join the Cadre.

She had been only 25 when Nicolas Kessler offered her Cadre membership. That was beyond even her dreams. She'd get to see the future, move through time while staying young, and live to be one thousand. But most of all, she'd get to do things that mattered. Cadre Members change history. Of course she signed up.

What they didn't tell me, she thought, was how much it hurts watching my friends grow apart from me. I wish to hell I had more leave time after a mission. Two or three days is barely time to see what I've missed the past couple years, and then it's back into the tank.

As the crags of the roof of the world gave way to gentler mountains, foothills, and finally rolling plains, the hummer descended sharply, following the contours of the slopes, and flying no more than one hundred feet above the ground. This maneuver plus the nonmetallic, sleek hull design protected them from any radar detection. They touched down ten miles from Aziz's camp. Annie leaped out and began walking. The hummer quietly took off and headed back to the Institute.

By late afternoon, as the shadows crept across the high desert plains, Annie had hiked to within a mile of the camp's edge, and stood on a ridgetop several hundred feet high. The term "camp" did not fit the scene before her. It was more like a movable city. An ocean of drab brown and black bedouin tents stretched out to the horizon. She could see tiny figures and beasts of burden making their way down the aisles between the tents.

A day later, Annie thought that she'd worked her way to within a few hundred yards of Aziz's tent. She stood at the intersection of two alleys, thick with traders hawking food, clothing, tools, jewelry, and weapons. Annie drifted from one goods-laden blanket to another, drawing the merchants into casual conversation while admiring their wares.

"I see important-looking men walking down this lane," she said to one, jerking her head in the direction they had gone. "Are they going to talk with the Wise One?"

The man she addressed averted his eyes, picked up a pot and began discussing its merits. "It is light and strong and will not warp even in a very hot fire. A good addition to your traveling kit, wouldn't you agree, my sister?"

Annie extended her chi fields, their feather-light fingers taking the measure of the man's fields. She asked him rather loudly, "Why is it that you won't tell me where the Wise One resides, good sir?"

His fear field, a dark green, pulsated wildly. He looked around to see if anyone had heard what she asked, terrified of the attention she gave him.

"Don't want to talk about it, I see. Well, I wasn't heading after those men anyway. My family lives in the opposite direction," Annie said, sensing relief in the man's field. Fearful green replaced by cool gray. She did walk in the opposite direction until she was out of sight of the merchant, and then turned down another walkway and doubled back.

Hour after hour, Annie used chi probes to readjust her course. A martial arts instructor, a dried fruit merchant, a mother doing her family's wash by hand, all gave her bits of useful information without knowing they had.

Then she was nearly run down by an electric car filled with four grim-looking men in caftans noticeably cleaner and finer than those of the masses. Annie probed their fields and was startled by the ferocity she found there. The chis of these men mapped blue-black in her mind, and felt like those of angry bulls pawing the ground, ready to fight. She followed the car, trying not to be too obvious, until it rounded a corner. She reached the corner, and in the distance, the car turned left into another alley.

By the time Annie reached that turn, there was no car in view. "Oh, shit," she said, then looked to see if anyone had noticed the unfamiliar colloquialism. She headed down the alley. At the next cross-alley, a man stepped from the shadows and blocked her way. He was one of the men who had just passed her in the car. He stood almost six and a half feet tall, and must have weighed close to three hundred. He crossed his arms and stared at her.

Annie dropped her eyes, stooped her shoulders and hoped she looked like a submissive bedouin woman. She tried to walk around the man. An arm like an oak branch blocked her way. She looked up into eyes like black holes, a pock-marked face and a thick-lipped mouth exuding garlic fumes. ''Turn around, woman, and go back to your tent. You have been asking too many questions.''

''I seek justice from the Wise One,'' Annie said. ''I must see him.'' She tried to dart past again, and this time extended her chi as she did so. Once more the arm stopped her. As she pressed against it, the red of anger appeared, and green fear. Was he afraid she would slip past and threaten Aziz? He must be very close then.

Leaning against the guard's arm, she swiveled slightly to the right. The fear level dropped a little. Then she swiveled left, and up went the intensity of the green. To her left sat a large tent, with more open space between it and its neighbors than any tent she'd yet seen. Two nervous-looking men equally as big as Garlic Breath stood outside, watching her.

Bingo.

''Tell Farouk Aziz that I bear a message from an old friend,'' Annie said.

''What old friend?''

''Anne Carlisle.''

''Liar! You have been telling people that you are a poor bedouin with a murdered husband. Instead you spy for the Confederacy.''

''I am no spy.''

"Achmed," Garlic Breath called. One of the tent guards came running. They grabbed Annie's arms just above the elbow. She did not resist as they hustled her away from Aziz's tent.

She waited in a storage tent for what seemed like hours, among piles of dried figs, sacks of flour, and heaps of saddle blankets and leather harnesses reeking of camel sweat.

Finally, Garlic Breath returned. "Give me your message," he said gruffly. "The Wise One does not allow Confederate lackeys near him. He does not trust them."

"He will see me."

"Oh? And why are you so different?"

"Ask the Wise One if he still has the agate that Anne Carlisle gave him. The sea-green agate."

This time, Garlic Breath was back in less than ten minutes. "He will see you," he said, looking puzzled. "I think you have made him curious. I will be right next to you the whole time, with this pointed at your head," he said, exposing a thick-barreled thermal gun. At low power, Annie knew, the weapon only set your hair on fire. Turned up to high, it boiled your brains within your skull.

"Now take your clothes off," the big man told her.

"What?"

"I must search you for weapons."

Her face red, Annie unbuttoned her dress and let it fall to the floor. Garlic Breath did his job, probing very thoroughly in all possible hiding places for weapons. His fingers felt like rough sticks of wood inside her. She wanted to scream.

Before she had finished dressing, one of the other guards walked into the tent. He looked at her bare shoulders hungrily. Annie quickly pulled the dress up to her neck and secured its fastenings.

How old he looks, Annie thought as she was roughly ushered into the presence of their leader. Aziz sat on a worn divan, his hands in his lap, studying her. She remembered a man with a stallion's mane of shiny black hair, a smooth, handsome face, and enormous eyes of a soft, liquid brown. His hair now was mostly gray, and his forehead deeply lined. His cheeks looked like cracked leather. But his eyes were unchanged.

Annie expanded her chi to fill the room, testing the emanations from Aziz and Garlic Breath like a boatman gingerly feeling out the currents of an unknown river. She felt the close scrutiny of Aziz, his energy field relaxed but alert. She sensed no fear from him. Rather, he exuded a wariness and cunning, like that of a fox.

Probing deeper, she felt an empty, hurting space at the center of his field. He had been a boy forced to be a man too young, Annie remembered. By the time he was twenty, he rode at his father's side, second in command of a band of twenty thousand seasoned desert fighters. A year later his father died in a skirmish with another band, and the mantle of leadership fell on young Aziz.

Annie sensed the mistrust, and, yes, the fear emanating from Garlic Breath. What did he fear? Annie couldn't read the hidden compartments in his fields. He reminded her of a viper, his beady eyes watching for an opening, his body tensed to strike.

"He must leave," Annie told Aziz. "The message is for you alone." Aziz looked surprised. Garlic Breath hissed a curse at Annie.

"You have searched her, Hamid?" Aziz asked Garlic Breath.

"Of course. But Cadre Members can kill without weapons. Do not let this slut . . ."

"That will be all, Hamid." Aziz reached into his caftan and withdrew a laser pistol set with a jade handle and mother-of-pearl on its barrel. "I am able to protect myself. Leave us."

Garlic Breath glared angrily at Annie as he left.

Aziz studied the woman. "You have a message for me?"

"Yes. It is a message of concern, motivated by memories of a special night sixteen years ago. Anne Carlisle does not want you and your people slaughtered like lambs, Farouk Aziz. Give up this plan of attacking India."

"Your voice . . ."

Annie felt the empty space at the center of his being throb painfully.

He sighed. "I will attack India because I cannot watch my people starve and do nothing to help them. We have only enough food for a month."

"What happened to your herds?"

His expression changed. Annie felt the cold hatred spill out of him and envelope her. She shuddered at its intensity.

"You should know the answer. Your people did it. You are from the Confederacy, aren't you?"

"I'm from the Solutions Institute. We owe allegiance to no nation, but to all people on earth. We resolve conflicts, not start them."

"She was from the Institute. She came from the special branch that lives forever."

"The Cadre."

"Yes, that was it. She was a Cadre Member."

"Aziz, what killed your cattle? I only know what Ramaj Singh told me in my briefing. That it was some plague."

"They were poisoned."

"You can prove that?"

"We almost did. I caught two men from Agra, sneaking among our herds, sprinkling something on their fodder. We fed some of the tainted grass to healthy cattle, and they took sick within hours."

"Do you still have the poisoners?"

"They died before we could find out anything useful."

"I will report this to Singh."

"What will that do? The report will be filed away on

some shelf, and my people will still starve. Unless, of course, we force our way into India. We need a homeland,'' Aziz continued. ''We must strike while we are still strong.''

''But you'll die. The Indian Army will butcher you.''

''Then we will die with honor. And maybe, just maybe some of us won't die.''

Annie knew that he wasn't telling her something important. He'd planned this attack for months, and he was not a stupid man.

She probed him with her fields. She sensed strength and determination, and clear intent. To do what?

''Show me your cattle,'' she said. ''Show me some who are still alive, but sick.''

Annie stroked the head of the stricken lamb. Too weak to move, it looked up at her with soft eyes, as if pleading for release from its suffering. Annie closed her eyes and probed its field. It was flickering like a candle about to burn out. Throbbing pain, and fear. Normal for a dying animal. Then Annie sensed something that made her skin turn cold. Immovable gray clenched the lamb's life force like an iron fist, slowly squeezing it dry. This was no viral infection. It had, rather, the character of something manufactured to do a job. A non-organic constriction imposed upon the lamb's body. Annie tried to get inside the gray swirl, sense its nature, and find a way to neutralize its energy. But she couldn't make a dent in it.

Annie examined another animal, and others after that from different herds. In each case it was the same. ''I've never felt anything like it,'' she said. ''I can't do a goddam thing to help them.'' She leaned her head on the dying lamb's neck. She cried until she felt a hand on her shoulder, and looked up into warm brown eyes, big as saucers.

• • •

Annie filled the bath with hot water from the solar-heated storage tanks, pouring in the solvent when her bath was full. The hotter the water, the better the solvent worked. Then she climbed into the bath and rubbed the treated water into her skin and hair. She watched the artificial pigments dissolve. Finally, she dipped her head under, and felt the plastiform nose enlargement and cheekbone enhancers begin to come loose. She stayed in the bath the required fifteen minutes, then emerged, toweled dry and slipped on the silk pantaloons that Aziz's cousin had loaned her. Not bothering to put on the shirt that went with it, she walked out from behind the screen, her golden hair radiant in the lamplight.

Aziz, sitting on a pile of skins on the floor, slowly sucked in his breath, his eyes devouring her until she felt that she would melt. Then he arose, and Annie saw that though his hair was now gray, and his face deeply lined, his body was still the wiry, taut body of a cat. Annie walked over to him, and as they wrapped their arms around each other, Annie pressed herself against his hard chest and felt his long sigh come from deep, deep within.

The camel struggled to its feet, Annie balancing on top. Aziz and his lieutenants mounted other beasts. Aziz led them through the camp, the dark brown tents rippling in the frigid wind from the Himalayan high country to their south.

From her vantage point on the camel, Annie noticed the numerous patches and mends in the tents. Riding into a wider section of the alley, Aziz motioned for her to pull abreast.

"You will bring us food, Annie?"

As the camel train strode down the rutted alley that comprised the main thoroughfare of Aziz's encampment, Annie watched the tapestry of his new city on the move flow by in front of her. She saw men and women haggling over chickens and goats, and little children chasing each other up and down the narrow walkways between tents, leaping over the guy ropes and stakes that anchored the dwellings. And she saw class after class of instruction in the arts of war. They were not just for the young and strong. The elderly, mothers with little ones hanging onto them, and children as young as seven or eight attended them.

She wanted to see these people live. "I will bring more than food," she said to Aziz. "I will find an alternative to your war. But you must tell me what you really plan to do when you march on India. Farouk Aziz would never lead his people to the slaughter. I think you've figured out a way to win."

Aziz smiled slightly. "You spend one night with me, and you can read my mind."

"Not exactly, but close."

"The price my people will pay for survival will be very high."

"What will it be?"

"Death, but not immediately. We have modified the GR-7 warheads. We added plutonium."

"That's insane. You'll destroy the land you want to settle on. It will stay contaminated for decades."

"Which is what we want," Aziz answered. "No armies will dare attack us."

"They won't need to. The radiation will kill your soldiers."

"We've calculated the plutonium dose very precisely. Most of us will live for about two decades. This is enough time to raise families, cultivate farms, and build factories."

"That's a cruel plan. Think of the children."

"I am thinking of the children! They will be sent far from the dangerous areas until we are too sick to work. Then they will return, and inherit what we have built for them. By that time, the rains will have cleansed our lands. It will be hard on our children, but they will survive. It is better than what they have now."

The hummer met Annie in a plain just beyond the camp's edge, and as she climbed in, she looked back once, and wondered if she'd ever again see the man with the flowing gray hair and the huge brown eyes.

Annie flew south, toward Delhi and the offices of the Deputy Minister of War, India Section.

Ramaj Singh's personal office was filled with rich antique wooden furniture. It looked more like a sitting room in a Victorian mansion than the nerve center of a sizable armed forces group. One wall was all window, little squares of glass set in rosewood frames. It must have cost a laborer's yearly salary just for that window, Annie thought.

Singh gazed out the window toward his gardens, tended by what seemed to be an army of gardeners. Annie noticed that the grounds were designed in the formal English style, the contoured edges of the flower beds ending precisely at the emerald-green lawns, and the topiary of the hedges perfect and geometrically precise. She sat drinking a cup of tea in an elegantly carved oaken chair. Though exquisite to look at, it was rather hard and uncomfortable.

"Cadre Member Carlisle, I don't think you understand this warlord," Singh said, his back to Annie as he surveyed his domain. "He is most sly. He has killed many people to get where he is."

"I think that the rest of the Cadre will back me up on this, Mr. Singh."

Singh still looked out his window, studying something in his garden. Perhaps he saw a clod of dirt in one of his flower beds. The man held a riding crop, and wore jodhpurs and boots. But the boots were spotless, and too perfect. Annie was willing to bet they'd never come close to a horse. "The idea of extending ally status to some outlaw band is ridiculous, Ms. Carlisle. Ally status in the Confederacy of Nations is a very precious gift. It entitles the country to the protection of our armed forces, and access to our universities and technology.''

"Which is just what Aziz needs to build a nation. He could be a valued ally on the Confederacy's North Asian border, Mr. Singh. The border we always get raided from.''

"I am quite able to defend our borders without the help of a roughneck land pirate.''

"Aziz commands a nation of two million people, over half of which are fighters. His followers revere him and would die to protect him. He could be of use to us. The hordes from the north would have to fight him before they ever get to India.''

Singh turned and pointed his riding crop toward Annie. "Your thinking is dangerous, Carlisle. It encourages the Asian hordes to threaten us at every opportunity, and then try to negotiate a favorable peace.''

He makes me uneasy, Annie thought. She probed, and found a shifting pattern of chi, continuously changing shape and color, masking its true nature. "I can't argue with that, Mr. Singh. Except, there's the matter of justice. You see, his food supply has been destroyed,'' Annie said.

"By some sort of virus.''

"Not at all. His cattle were poisoned. I examined them.''

Just for a moment, Singh's composure dropped. His foppish stance stiffened, and Annie caught a burst of real fear from his field. Just as quickly, he covered it over with an indulgent smile. "If they were poisoned, although I doubt this very much, I am sorry for his people's misfortune. But treachery is a way of life on the Central Asian plains. Why should we extend our protection to this man, and not some other tribe?''

"He caught the poisoners.''

Singh's smile stiffened. His left eye ticked a couple times. Even without her chi extended, Annie felt his terror. He's been caught out, she realized. Then his fear transformed into something quite different. He became like a cornered weasel, dangerous and sly. The man's expression barely changed, but it was as if his eyes narrowed, and he took a step back into the shadows, snarling at the woman he'd just recognized as an enemy. Waves of menace emanated from him. "Does Aziz still have the poisoners?" he asked, his voice carefully controlled.

"No. They died during interrogation."

Singh's fear field instantly receded, to be replaced by his usual shifting energy fields so difficult to read, and a concerned expression. "This matter must be investigated at once. If citizens of the Confederacy are involved, I will see that they are prosecuted to the fullest extent of the law," he said with righteous indignation.

Annie commended him on his zeal, and forced herself to drink another cup of tea with him, when what she really wanted to do was run from the room, or even better, shove that riding crop down his lying throat. They roughed out the plans for an investigation. Oh, there would be an inquiry all right, but the subject would be the man standing in front of her. Just wait until she made her report to Kessler. If there was any connection between the poisoned cattle and Singh, Kessler would root it out.

They finished their planning and embraced. Annie promised to initiate the inquiry as soon as she got back to the Institute. She left and caught a pedicab to the airport.

She tried to locate Genzing, her pilot, but he was out looking for parts for one of the jet turbines, which was dangerously worn. They'd leave in the morning, then. She went to a phone to call the Institute and make her report, but it was dead. Delhi, she thought. Nothing ever works here.

Annie returned to her hotel and called the Institute number from her room. All she got was static, and then a recording explaining that a storm in the mountains had temporarily cut off communications to that region.

Annie took a shower, toweled dry and put fresh clothes on. She thought about trying one of the Tandoori restaurants she'd heard about in Delhi, then she realized how exhausted she was. She turned off the light and decided to lie down for a minute. In seconds, she was asleep.

The attack came an hour later. Annie sensed them coming fast down the hall outside her room. She woke instantly and rolled from bed to floor just as the door burst open. She flattened herself behind the bed, and heard the sizzle of a laser burning into the mattress above. Murderous chi emanated from two men in the doorway.

Annie wriggled around the bed on her stomach and got as close to them as she could while staying out of sight. Then she gathered her legs under her and launched herself at them. They did not expect it, and probably couldn't see her well in the dark room. She came in low and rolled. The beam from the laser pistol flashed above her. As she came out of the roll, Annie struck with her foot. Her chi, preceding her bare toes like a headlight, told her just where to aim. The darkness did not matter. She caught one man square in the crotch.

He screamed and struck downwards, trying to protect himself. The blow lifted him off the ground and threw him into his partner, who cursed and squeezed off a shot that hit the ceiling.

Then Annie went for the second man; her right-hand fingers jabbed him in the eye. She grabbed his gun arm with her other hand, bent it behind his back. She jerked, and the arm broke with a snap. She pinched a nerve in the side of the man's neck and he collapsed.

The first man had recovered enough from Annie's kick to pick up his gun. Annie leaped on him, smashing her fist into his skull until he lost consciousness.

She picked up the men's guns, then sensed more hostile energy approaching. Lots of it. At least six assassins, very close. Annie ran as fast as she could, and barely made the corner of the corridor before they entered the hall.

Once in the street, Annie considered her options. She could run for only so long. She could make it to the airport, maybe, but Singh's men (at least she assumed they were from Singh) would guess she'd do that, and would be guarding the plane. If only she'd had a few more seconds, she could have grabbed her distress beacon from her kit, and summoned a Cadre team to pick her up. Damn!

She found a public phone and dialed the Institute emergency number. "I'm sorry," the recording said. "This number is temporarily out of service." The Institute emergency number was never out of service.

Again, she felt the sense of menace approaching. The call must have signaled them. She ran, using every ounce of chi to propel her faster toward the shadows across the street.

A cruiser screamed around the corner and screeched to a halt next to the phone. Four very large uniformed men jumped out.

So Singh controlled the police too.

She kept close to the wall of the building, scampering from shadow to shadow. Her pursuers aimed their infrared sensors into nooks and crannies, trying to pick up her scent.

Somehow, she had to get to the Institute. Or signal them. The Institute was thousands of miles away. Jet or suborbital were the obvious choices to get there in a hurry. But they were obvious to Singh as well. Air and rocket ports would be well guarded. And he'd blocked the phones.

Sooner or later, he'd catch her.

The KLJK radio station grounds were lit by four floodlights, and surrounded by a razorwire fence. But the gaps between the wires were large enough for a small body to wriggle through, and the station grounds were patrolled by only one guard. . . .

• • •

Vincent Petersen had just settled himself into a very hot bath that he'd liberally sprinkled with his favorite herbs. Bar of sandalwood soap in hand, he was all set for a good half-hour soak when the intercom in his bathroom crackled to life.

"Oh shit," he said.

"What was that, Petersen?" came Nicolas Kessler's bass voice over the line. "I haven't disturbed you, I trust," said the Director of the Solutions Institute.

"Of course not, sir. Nice of you to call at . . . " He looked at the clock set into the tiles on the wall of his shower. "Twelve-thirty A.M."

"Annie's emergency code just came in. From a radio station."

"From a what?" The sandalwood soap fell from Vincent's hand and skittered across the bathroom floor. Vincent felt a cold chill move down his body, despite the warmth of the bath.

"You heard me. From a one-hundred-kilowatt Delhi rock station, blasting all over the Himalayas so that anyone with a handheld transistor could have heard it, although they would never guess what they were hearing."

"Well what are we wasting time talking for? Let's go get her, dammit," said Vincent, struggling from the bath and reaching for a towel.

"The hummer's being wheeled out now. Be down at the field in five if you want to join in the fun."

"I'm working on it," Vincent called back, struggling into a pair of thermal underwear. "From Delhi, you say. Why the hell isn't Singh looking after her?" Let her be all right. Please, God, don't let her be hurt.

"She didn't say. The station broadcast a thirty-second multifrequency focused bleep that all but blew down our antennas, and probably exploded their transformer bank. All the signal contained was her emergency code. Aren't you dressed yet?''

"I'm coming, I'm coming." He snapped shut the last flaps on his down parka on his way out the door.

The brown-uniformed men scurried around the radio station grounds, setting up projectile tubes and searching among the shadows. The station personnel sat handcuffed in the back of a khaki van. "Are you sure she's still in there?" a man with sergeant's stripes asked another, who'd just come out of the van after interrogating the handcuffed men.

"They say she was there when our copter landed. She must still be inside."

"Then blast it, Corporal."

"Sir?"

"The station. Blast the station. Now."

"Yes sir." The corporal removed a two-way radio from his belt, and spoke into it, then counted down from five. When he reached zero, the four projectile tubes surrounding the station fired simultaneously. The building exploded into flame.

By the time the Institute's hummer skidded to a stop at the gate to the station enclosure, four fire trucks were squirting water and fire retardant on the blaze. But it was a losing battle.

"Are there any survivors?" Director Kessler asked the officer in charge.

"Just those," he said, pointing to the handcuffed men in the van.

A rumble issued from the skies loud enough to drown out the sound of the fire. Four large copters appeared, hovered and landed. Men in black uniforms spilled out, laser rifles cradled in their arms. They quickly located the officers in the khaki corps and arrested them, rifles aimed at their hearts. Then they began herding the other khakis, who were outnumbered five to one, toward one corner of the parking lot.

When the radio station, or what remained of it, was firmly in the control of the black troopers, Ramaj Singh emerged from one of the copters.

He walked over to the khaki captain, held at bay by the black-suited gunmen, and approached to within a foot of him. Then he slapped him across the face. "I arrest you in the name of the Confederacy of Nations for the pursuit and murder of Cadre Member Anne Carlisle. This act of terrorism will not go unpunished!" he screamed into the captain's face. "Take him away," he said disgustedly. The captain, a shocked, uncomprehending expression on his face, was wrestled off into one of the copters. His platoon was handcuffed one by one and led off into the night. Singh, his face a caricature of righteous wrath, approached Director Kessler. "I want to express my deepest regrets over the loss of your Cadre Member. I grieve that I wasn't able to sniff out this heinous plot an hour sooner. It might have saved the poor girl's life."

"What the hell happened here?" asked Kessler. Petersen's face was ashen. He looked as if he were going to be sick.

"Some of my officers were engaged in extracurricular activities," Singh began. "Your agent Carlisle apparently unearthed some dirty secrets involving an attempt to precipitate a war with one of the Asian hordes. They attacked her in her hotel room earlier tonight. She escaped, but they ran her to earth . . . in there," he said, pointing to the charred ruins of the radio station.

A small soldier in a black uniform came up beside Singh. The soldier held something wrapped in cloth. "We found out about this mutiny not an hour ago," Singh continued. "If only my timing had been a little better." He shook his head sadly.

"I think that your timing was exquisite," said the little soldier in a high voice. The soldier let the cloth fall away from the object within. A laser pistol pointed directly at Singh's abdomen. The soldier's back was to the rest of the black soldiers; none of them could see the gun. "Why don't you come over to our hummer, Ramaj Singh, and have a nice cup of tea with us."

"Annie," said Vincent Petersen, tears in his eyes. "I thought . . ."

She met him on the same plain, by the edge of his tent city. Her golden hair streaming out behind her, Annie ran into Aziz's arms. Clutching each other tightly, they walked to the waiting camels.

At a joyous dinner that night in Aziz's tent, attended by his family and served by his bodyguards, Annie told him what had happened at Delhi, and how they'd captured Singh. "An official apology is on its way from Hawaii, Farouk. From the Chief of Staff of the New Pentagon. This is terribly embarrassing for them. I think that ally status for your nation is a sure thing, if only to buy your silence."

"Can I trust the Confederacy?" Aziz asked.

"It's willing to let you keep your missiles in place for a year. After that, you be the judge if they are trustworthy. Meanwhile, your people will eat. And with the Confederacy's technology, you can build a new life on even these plains. You know, it was this region that Singh wanted all the time."

"What do you mean?"

"He meant to provoke you into an attack, so he'd have a good excuse to annihilate you and then set himself up as military governor of this region. To 'protect our northern border against further barbarian attacks.' It was all in the notes that we found when we raided his office."

"If I'd launched those bombs, I would have given him exactly what he wanted," Aziz said. "He didn't know about the plutonium in them, though."

"We also found the poison he'd used to wipe out your herds. It was developed in his laboratories, which were supposed to be working on nerve-gas antidotes," Annie said.

Aziz's strong-breathed guard leaned over the table and poured sweet coffee into silver cups for Aziz and Annie. His pungent exhalations made Annie wince.

"What he did," Annie continued, "was use a normally harmless bacteria with an affinity for stomach tissue. He mutated it and 'taught' it to synthesize corrosives as byproducts of its metabolism."

Garlic Breath put a silver platter of date bars rolled in coconut in front of them. Annie turned to him. "But then you know all about that, don't you, Hamid? In fact, you used the poison on the two prisoners from Agra before they could say anything embarrassing."

Her chi sensitized and extended, Annie felt the rush of terror and shame burst out of the guard. She *felt* rather than saw his hand go for his weapon. She stood up quickly and danced away as Hamid pulled the blade from his *jalaba* and lunged for her.

"Hamid!" Aziz shouted. He drew his own laser, but with a scream of hatred Hamid turned and threw the knife as hard as he could at Aziz.

Annie saw the flash of silver bury itself to the hilt in Aziz's forearm, the point emerging with a spurt of blood out the other side. Aziz cried out and dropped his pistol. His sisters screamed and scurried to his aid, one pressing a wadded-up napkin over the wound and the other shielding him with her ample body against further attacks. His mother stood up and shouted instructions and curses in Afghani.

The other two guards in the tent, momentarily stunned at what their leader had done, drew their own lasers. Before they could aim, Hamid charged them, desperate. Ducking under the hastily shot bolts from their guns, he crashed into them. The larger of the two landed flat on his back and lay there gasping.

As Aziz retrieved his gun with his left hand, Hamid

sprinted out the door, surprisingly fast for his size. The one guard who was still able to get up ran after him, sounding the alarm.

Aziz looked down at the blade skewering his arm like a piece of ka-bob. His face was white.

"Get his physician," shouted Annie at the alarmed servants who clustered around. Then she turned to Aziz and gently eased him back into his seat. His chi pulsed purple with pain and rage.

She stroked his arm and shoulder, soothing him as best she could. But it was like trying to gentle a wounded leopard.

He snarled and hissed for an hour as his physician fussed over him. Aziz directed his fury mostly at himself, for being "clumsy as a ruptured yak" and allowing Hamid to best him.

And when the guards slunk into the tent to report that Hamid had made it to the edge of the camp and escaped into the desert, Aziz's ranting began all over again.

Finally he grew tired, drugged by the doctor's narcotic. Steadied by Annie, Aziz staggered to his bed and collapsed onto it. He clutched Annie's shirt tightly with his good hand as he drifted into sleep.

She stayed with him through the night, cradling his head in her lap, thinking of the future that they might have had together if things were different. When he woke up moaning, his wound throbbing, she gave him another injection of the narcotic and rubbed his temples and the back of his neck until he fell back asleep.

In the morning as golden sunlight drifted in through the tent flaps, she kissed him long and hard on the mouth, and then left. She met the hummer at the edge of the camp. By noon, she was back at the Institute.

"Annie, don't cry," Vincent Petersen told her as she stripped down and climbed into the cryotank.

"I'm sorry. I'm just sick of watching everyone I love age in front of my eyes, while I get to live another millennium without them. I'm lonely, that's all."

"Think of the things you'll see. Centuries of historical events, and you'll get to take part in some of them. They'll write about you, Annie. By the time your contract is up, you'll be a legend ten times over."

"Yeah, I guess. I also get to say goodbye to a lot of people who are special to me. Like you, and Aziz."

"Someday, centuries after I'm gone, you'll finish with the Cadre, pick a nice time to live in, and get married and live a totally normal, boring life. Except you get to pick the time and place to do it. Most of us just get to pick the place, if we're lucky."

"Goodbye, Vincent. Wake me soon, if you have any say in the matter. I happen to like this century, and want to live in it all that I can." Annie lay back and made herself comfortable in the blood-temperature saline solution. Vincent turned to his control panel, and prepared to send Annie into the future one more time.

Subterranean Pests

by
James S. Dorr

ILLUSTRATED BY Allen Koszowski

About the Author

James S. Dorr of Bloomington, Indiana, is a semi-professional musician who plays the tenor recorder at Renaissance Fairs. He worked as a technical writer and editor for several years, but in 1983 his interests turned to fiction. To support his fiction habit, James works at an optometry clinic while he writes fantasy, science fiction, horror, dark mystery and poetry.

James has sold to Fantasy Book, Aboriginal SF, Pulphouse, Alfred Hitchcock's Mystery Magazine, and Avon Books' Borderlands II anthology.

This list of publications gives ample evidence that you will be seeing much more of his work soon—within, oh, six months.

About the Illustrator

Allen Koszowski of Upper Darby, Pennsylvania, is a self-taught artist and a life-long fan of the science fiction, fantasy and horror genres.

He is married, with two children, and is an ex-marine and a Vietnam veteran with Purple Heart and other decorations. Allen has published art extensively in fan and small-press magazines, and has won the Small Press Writers and Artists Organization *best artist award nearly a dozen times. He has also been a finalist for the* Balrog *and* British Fantasy Society *best artist awards, and because of recent changes in the economy, is considering a career as a full-time illustrator. In that, we wish him the very best.*

She brought the smell of winter
with her. That was the first thing Ambrott
noticed when she slipped, almost furtively, into
the dimly lit interior of his store. He had nearly lost sight
of her, in fact, in the play of brightness and shadows outside,
when he heard the screen door shriek and—there was the
smell. Stronger, even, than the dusty metallic odor that seeped
from the bins and shelves around him.

It was, he thought, a smell like soil that had lain without
turning for too many months—of fallen leaves resting under
the snow. He had been watching through his front window
when he first saw her striding across the churchyard that cut
off the end of Main Street, which separated the old part of
town from the subdivision that lay beyond. It was, he thought,
a *good* smell in its way.

"You miss the farms, don't you?" the woman said. Her
voice had a hint of an accent about it, a lilting tone that he
couldn't quite place.

"I beg your pardon?"

"The farms that used to surround this town, before the
city people came and bought up the land. Back when you
were younger. You miss the odor of dirt and sweat, of good
honest work on a day like this when farmers would be out
in their fields, getting their crops ready for the harvest. Now,
you are Mr. Jacob Ambrott?"

He nodded slowly. Outside the store, she had walked with
a purpose, tall and thin, all bone and angles, dragging a large
square suitcase behind her. But now she stood quietly, soft

and attractive in her own way, her long black skirt almost covering the case where it lay on the floor. "Yeah," he said— he glanced up at the window, its sign, "Ambrott's Hardware," showing through in reverse gold letters. "And you're Ms., uh . . ."

"*Miss* Celaeno." She smiled at him, then heaved her case up and, letting its weight help drag her around in a half-pirouette, laid it on the counter behind her. "I'm old-fashioned in some ways," she said. "Nevertheless, one must still move along with the times. That right, Mr. Ambrott?"

"I . . ." Ambrott stopped while she opened the case, revealing rows and rows of bottles in an assortment of shapes and sizes. He suddenly realized that she had come to his store in order to sell him something, yet, unlike most salespeople he saw, she hadn't driven up in a car. Instead, she had walked in, like in the days when his father had first opened the store and people still used the Greyhound bus, getting off at the side of the highway west of town.

"Now, Mr. Ambrott," the woman said, "how's business these days?" She smiled again, her white teeth contrasting with the dark, tight curls of her hair, and he smiled back this time in spite of himself.

"Could be better," he started to answer.

"But not much worse, yes? Like I say, a person's got to move with the times. Back when your father ran this store, you sold farm implements, fertilizers, tack and harness for the horses—store was so crowded I bet you couldn't find room to stand. What you did then was you sold things tailored to people's problems. Now, though, look at the cabinets around you, covered with dust. . . ."

Ambrott laughed. "Now look, Miss Celaeno—yeah, business is lousy. But don't tell me you're going to turn it around. Just with a sample case full of bottles . . ."

"Garden products, Mr. Ambrott. And I am. City people don't have farms—you know that. What they do is destroy farms, but, when they're finally settled into their houses, then they plant gardens. Bet you even sell some of them seed.''

She paused, waiting for him to answer.

He finally nodded. ''Well . . . yes,'' he said. ''But most of them go to the shopping center. . . .''

''Because they carry the same goods, yes? And they sell them cheaper. What you need to have, Mr. Ambrott, is a gimmick. Something to draw people into your store.'' She paused as she rummaged through her samples, then brought out one of the larger containers. ''Something like this, Mr. Ambrott, to solve their *new* problems.''

Ambrott took the bottle from her and squinted at its faded red and yellow label. ''MOLE–B–GONE,'' it said in letters a half inch high, then, underneath, in smaller printing, ''also effective for prairie dogs, gophers, and other subterranean pests.''

''This some kind of poison?'' he asked.

This time Miss Celaeno started laughing.

''Oh no,'' she finally said. ''Like all my products, this is environmentally approved—tailored for today's modern market. What that means is it doesn't *hurt* moles. After all, you poison a mole, you still have a body you have to dispose of. Rather, it does what the label suggests. It makes them be gone.''

''You mean''—Ambrott tried to remember—''you mean like moth balls when I was a kid? I had an uncle who, sometimes, when he had trouble with gophers, used to put moth balls down their holes. Said they didn't like the smell, so sometimes they'd leave. But, Miss Celaeno, nobody farms any more these days. So why would they need it?''

''And sometimes they'd stay,'' Miss Celaeno said. ''The gophers, I mean. But yes, Mr. Ambrott, this product works along those lines, except that they *always* go away. And as for the need, you've had a dry summer. Insects and things that moles like to eat have been dormant this year. Meanwhile, though, people have still been working on their lawns and gardens and, now that the weather's getting cooler . . .''

"You figure maybe they'll start to have moles?"

Miss Celaeno had been persuasive, Ambrott thought when he left the store. He walked west on Main Street, toward the church where he worked as a sexton on evenings and Sundays, feeling the dryness of the autumn air. She had been right about the weather at least, he thought—it had been dry ever since the trees had been cut and the farms cleared for building. But she had also been right about him, about how he missed the rural feeling the town had once had. About how he disliked the city people.

He shrugged and continued into the churchyard, checking the grave plots for signs of weeds, then pulled out his key and went into the church. One good thing about the dryness, he thought as he climbed the steeple ladder, was that it kept the weeds in check. The weeds and the moles—at least that was what Miss Celaeno claimed.

She had ended up giving him six sample bottles of Mole-B-Gone, along with a card with a box number on it for ordering more. "Send this note with your order," she said, "and you'll only be charged a dollar a bottle. You, in the meantime, can charge $6.98 or more—$6.98's the suggested price, but I guarantee that you'll be the only store that has it. I won't make any money this time, but, what the heck, if your customers like it, it's building my trade."

"Yeah, if there *are* moles," Ambrott had said, but he'd ended up taking the card and the samples. When he had asked where he could contact her if he needed to see her again, she said that she always checked up on her prospects.

"I'll be around if you need me," she'd said.

Then she'd disappeared in the sunlight and shadows of the street outside, just as she'd been hidden the instant before she had first come in. He shook his head as he remembered, then continued his climb up the ladder into the tower.

Once at the top, he checked the mountings of the bell, adding a drop of oil here and there, then stretched and gazed through the louvered windows out over the town. He loved the view, especially east where the older business section lay, most of the buildings dating back to before he was born. In fact, it was the view of the town and the memories it brought, seeing it laid out beneath his feet, that had made him take up the sexton's position. It sure wasn't the pay anyhow, he thought with a chuckle.

Still, the pay helped. Everything helped, even the little trace of dampness he thought he had felt in the air in the churchyard. Maybe Miss Celaeno was right. Maybe moles *would* attack the newcomers' lawns and gardens.

Before he went down, he crossed the tower and looked through the louvers to the west, out toward the bypass. He tried to imagine the farms before the subdivision had been put in. In one way it wasn't that different—the checkered lawns resembled fields if he looked at them right. To Miss Celaeno, in any event, they were farm-like gardens.

He tried to name the houses' owners: Bronston the nearest, then McMichaels, then Smith and Lewiston and Palmer. Out toward the highway, Zekuski and Davis. These were the real, non-subterranean pests that had come to infest his town.

He shrugged and started to climb back down, wondering, idly, if Miss Celaeno had anything that worked for unwanted people.

The next day the air was decidedly cooler and, that night, it rained. On a hunch, he wrote out a check the following morning and ordered a full case of Mole-B-Gone. It came on Friday the following week and then, that Sunday, while he was sweeping up the church vestibule after service, he overheard Mr. Davis complain to his wife about moles.

"You know," he said, putting his broom down, "I've got a product that's good for moles."

"I beg your pardon," said Davis, a plumpish, prosperous-looking man.

"I didn't mean to interrupt," Ambrott said, "but I thought I heard you talking about moles. My name's Ambrott, of Ambrott's Hardware just down the street, and I got a product in only last Friday that's guaranteed to get rid of moles."

"Maybe you ought to try it, honey," Mrs. Davis, a pale, blonde woman, said to her husband. "It wouldn't be any trouble for me to pick up tomorrow, and I know how proud you are of your garden."

"You say this stuff you got's guaranteed?" Mr. Davis asked. "Like I get my money back if it doesn't work?"

Ambrott thought for a moment, then nodded. "If you want, I'll open the store up for you today. Just do me a favor and let your friends know where you got it. Then, when you use it, if you have any trouble, just give me a call."

Wednesday morning he got a call, not from the Davises, but from their neighbor, Mrs. Zekuski. She wanted to know if he could deliver two bottles of Mole-B-Gone to her home.

He argued a little, but finally agreed to stop over during the time he would normally close up the store for lunch.

Three hours later, he pulled his truck into the Zekuskis' driveway. He stopped once on his way to the door to inspect what looked like a couple of mole tunnels on the front lawn, then rang the doorbell. The woman who answered, he couldn't help noticing, looked a little like Miss Celaeno, except that her hair was a bright orange-red.

"M-Mr. Ambrott?" she said as she ushered him into the house. Also, he noticed, unlike Miss Celaeno, the clothing she wore—shorts and a halter—was perfectly modern.

"M-Mr. Ambrott, I'm *so* grateful you could come. This morning, before he went to work, my husband was so mad. . . ."

"Now just slow down a little," he said. "You have some mole damage in your front yard, but it doesn't seem all that bad. Not enough to require two bottles."

"I-it—you mean they're in the front yard too? It's Mr. Zekuski's garden in back I was worried about. B-but—you know the way this stuff works? Mr. Davis finally told us, after my husband *really* got mad. You don't just put the stuff in the tunnels, but sprinkle it over your entire yard. That way you make sure you've got 'em all. At least that's what it says on the label."

Ambrott nodded. He actually hadn't read the directions on the label. In fact, he'd begun to have second thoughts after he'd ordered the case. But, if it took so much for just one application—he started to smile. Maybe he'd sell the whole case after all.

He realized then that Mrs. Zekuski had started to cry, and tried his best to look serious again. "Uh, maybe if you show me the garden. I mean, I could help you spread it around. . . ."

The woman nodded, then led him back to the kitchen door. *Tight* shorts and halter, he couldn't help noticing as he followed, but when she led him out into the back yard he suddenly realized why she seemed so frightened.

This was not just one or two mole tunnels. The yard was crisscrossed, from side to side—and some of the tunnels were larger than normal. Moreover, the lawn—and the garden behind it—were littered with planks. Planks and tools, some from a shed that had been knocked over, some from the wreck of a picket fence that had once stood between the Zekuskis' yard and the one next door.

"Over there," Mrs. Zekuski said as she poured the contents of one of the bottles into a mister. "That's the Davis' back yard. All *he* had were one or two tunnels, like you say are in the front now. But then, Sunday afternoon, he used that stuff and . . ."

"Uh huh," Ambrott prompted as he accepted the mister from her. She shook her head and he waited while she filled a second, then led him to the ruins of the fence and showed him how to spray the liquid, back and forth in careful arcs, so that when they had crossed the yard every inch would be covered. "And then what happened?" he prompted again, as soon as she'd finished her explanation.

"What happened was nothing—at least at first." She walked alongside him, directing her mister's spray to the left while he sprayed to the right. "I understand from Mrs. Davis that Mr. Davis was fit to be tied until she read the directions again and told him what the really small print said. What it comes down to is that it takes a couple of days for the Mole-B-Gone to 'permeate'—I think that's the word Mrs. Davis used—to kind of seep all the way into the soil. It's like spraying the whole yard the way we're doing, in order to make sure *all* the—what's the phrase they use on the label?—that 'all subterranean pests are affected.' "

Ambrott nodded. The work went fast—especially with Mrs. Zekuski working next to him—and they'd already completed most of the yard in back. "And after a couple of days—then what happened?"

"Oh—oh, Mr. Ambrott!" Mrs. Zekuski was in his arms. "I-it was horrible, Mr. Ambrott"—she pushed away, but not until after he had been able to give her a hug. "I-I'm sorry, Mr. Ambrott. Here—we'd better start doing the side yard. Anyhow, Tuesday afternoon, about the time Mr. Davis came home, the moles in the Davis' yard just went crazy."

"What do you mean?" They finished the side, then turned the corner into the front yard—at the rate they were using the spray, Ambrott realized the two bottles of Mole-B-Gone he'd brought would be barely enough.

"They—they just sort of came out of the ground. Mrs. Davis called me as soon as it started, so I saw it too. They came out of the ground, just sort of popping out of their tunnels—more moles than you could possibly dream could have been in one yard—and they started running around in circles, jumping up and down and bumping into things as if they were blind. Mr. Davis explained it's because they live underground—they really *are* blind."

"Well, almost blind, yes," Ambrott agreed. "And the bright light must confuse them terribly." They completed the lawn in front and started to spray the final side yard, working back toward the kitchen door. "But did the moles just keep running around, or . . . ?"

"One of them actually *bit* Mr. Davis. He went out in back, thinking maybe that, now that they were out of the ground, he'd be able to catch them or something. All my husband was doing, meanwhile, was watching and laughing from the back yard on our side of the fence, while *I* was the one who had to go over to help Mrs. Davis take care of her husband."

"That why you wanted me to bring the stuff during the day? You were afraid, if they came out later, maybe they'd hurt your husband too?"

Mrs. Zekuski began to laugh, just a little. "Actually, that part was kind of funny—with Mr. Davis. But, honest, the reason I called was because I was afraid for myself to use it tonight when my husband's back home. Because of what happened after it started to get dark last night. All of a sudden it got real quiet, and then the moles—it was like now they could not only see, but they had been communicating somehow before. That they'd gotten a plan. All of a sudden they all disappeared—back into the ground—and then it was like the *ground* started moving. All of the moles started moving at once, making new tunnels, all of them in the same direction. They went through the fence—knocked it down—

Illustrated by Allen Koszowski

my husband barely got in the house himself in time—then all of a sudden all of them were destroying *our* yard. . . .''

Ambrott took the woman into his arms again. "Take it easy now, Mrs. Zekuski. We're all finished here. Maybe you'd like a drink of water. . . ."

He led Mrs. Zekuski back into the back yard, then whistled when he saw, again, the damage the Davis' moles had done. And now that this yard had been treated—whose was the yard that was next to this one? He started to think, as he and Mrs. Zekuski continued up the back steps and into the kitchen. Maybe the next neighbor would need three bottles, and maybe the next one down the block would want to have four. And he had a whole case of Mole-B-Gone that he didn't have to sell for *just* $6.98 a bottle. . . .

He almost didn't notice it when Mrs. Zekuski, still holding onto him, thrust a cold can of beer into his hand. He more than noticed what she did after she'd kissed him, though.

Sure enough, a few days later, Ambrott received a telephone call from Mrs. Palmer. Then, shortly after that, Mrs. Lewiston stopped in his store and, a day or two later, Mrs. Smith called. Ambrott, meanwhile, hired a boy to help wait on customers while he did house calls—as Miss Celaeno had predicted, his other sales started to increase as well once people rediscovered his store. All in all, he should have been happy.

After all, the Mole-B-Gone worked exactly as it was supposed to. It solved people's problems and if, in doing so, it just passed them on to new people, well, it was able to help *them* too. Nevertheless, that last aspect did bother him a little. That, in one sense, the product he sold was in itself a cause of the very ill it had been intended to cure. That and the rather large profit he made on every bottle, not to mention the occasional . . . um . . . "gratuities" he'd been receiving from other housewives besides Mrs. Zekuski.

Perhaps in part because he was bothered, he found himself putting more and more effort into the work he did at the church. He began to take a special interest in making sure the graveyard remained in tiptop condition, even polishing some of the older stones by hand. And then, one afternoon, he noticed what looked like it might be a burgeoning tunnel just on the other side of the churchyard's low, iron-barred fence.

He wondered—whose property would that be? Who had he sold a bottle to last? He rushed into the church and climbed the ladder to the tower. He looked through the louvers to the west, to the setting sun. He saw, to his horror, the mole-wracked yards of half the newer section of town arranged like an arrow—a wedge of destruction—pointing directly toward the churchyard.

Slowly, he climbed back down the ladder and, for the first time in many weeks, he sank to his knees in the nearest pew. He looked to the pulpit, above it the play of light and color through the west-facing stained glass window. He tried to think.

He had just sold a product. Just hoped, at first, to help his business. To help people too.

Was he now to have sacrilege on his conscience?

No, he thought. He had *just* sold a product. He left the church and ran to his store. A product that could be used in the service of good as easily as that of evil.

Once in his store, he reached to the shelf where the last few unsold bottles of Mole-B-Gone stood on display, and gathered them all up into his arms. He placed them in a cardboard carton and, grabbing a large-capacity mister as he went back out the door, he returned to the church.

He started to work in the darkening churchyard, applying the Mole-B-Gone in a slow, methodical manner. What was effective in chasing away moles after they were already established *ought* to be even better in keeping them out in the first place. He hummed a tune, an old church hymn, as he covered every inch of the grounds. And, as he neared the end of his work, he smelled a wintry, humus-like odor that made him think of Miss Celaeno.

The following Saturday was cold—cold enough for Ambrott to have to put a jacket on when he went to the church-yard that afternoon. Autumn is really on us, he thought, as he started to work, sprucing up the grounds. There was to be a wedding Sunday, just after the morning service, and, even though the yard was neat and clean as always, he wanted it to look extra special.

He hummed as he worked, another church tune, and thought about moles. The tunnels had stopped, just as he had hoped, on the other side of the low, iron fence. Over the two or three days that had followed his soaking the graveyard with Mole-B-Gone, the approaching tunnels had widened out and seemed to flatten, as if whatever creatures were under the ground had dug in, like soldiers preparing to mount a siege. But the tunnels *had* stopped.

Ambrott weeded around the fence, then, putting his trowel down, he started to rake between the graves. Some of the trees had turned already, their leaves quickly gone through red and gold, and some of the leaves had already fallen. He looked at the sky—an October sky, still crispy clear but with the first traces of oncoming winter—and it occurred to him that Hallowe'en was only a few weeks away. A time when the newcomers' kids would be going out in costume to beg for candy.

A time for tricks, it occurred to him. And a time for treats, too. The Mole-B-Gone was a treat, in a sense, if the dug up lawns in the subdivision ended up driving some of the town's newcomers away. In fact, a few "For Sale" signs had appeared already.

But only a few—the non-subterranean pests in the town were like soldiers as well, dug in for their own siege. A siege of increasing traffic through town, of subdivisions and shopping centers, of decreasing business and rising taxes. . . .

He shook his head and continued raking when, out of the corner of his eye, he thought he saw one of the gravestones move. He turned to inspect it—were some of the kids playing tricks already?

The grave erupted.

He found himself covered with leaves and mud, staggering backward, tripping over a second stone that rose to meet him.

He rolled to his knees, saw a hand reach to him. Looked to the fence, saw a wave of moles explode out of the tunnels, press over the fence and flow into the graveyard.

And all around him the graves opened wide as long-dead corpses clawed to the surface.

He swung at the nearest corpse with his rake. The corpse ignored him, gaping instead at the autumn sky. Screaming horribly and clutching at its eyes.

He dodged past the corpse—others were joining it, looking up toward the sky and shrieking. While at his feet the moles jumped and ran in crazy circles, just as Mrs. Zekuski had described them when he had helped treat her yard.

He dodged right into a second corpse, pushed it from him. Smelled the stench of rot and corruption. He pushed past a third, ducking, running. Seeing his way to the churchyard gate blocked, he scrambled, screaming himself, to the church.

When the sun rose the following morning, Ambrott's first thought was that there would be no wedding. Not at that church, and not on that Sunday. He shivered, and not from the morning cold, as he remembered barring the church door, then hearing the stained glass windows shatter as he locked himself in the minister's tiny office.

Once inside, he had called the sheriff. What else could he do? He had argued at first that he hadn't been drinking, but then other people had passed the churchyard and gone to the sheriff.

Eventually, the sheriff arrived, and shortly afterward the town's fire department had come. Fire hoses pushed the corpses back long enough for Ambrott to get to safety.

And then the *real* siege began.

Trucks with searchlights were brought to the streets surrounding the churchyard, keeping the gravestones brightly lit so the moles and other . . . the other subterranean pests could be held at bay. Sheriff's vehicles raced through the night, bringing generators and floodlamps. Inside the churchyard the corpses milled, but outside, on the side of the living, the hastily rigged ring of light held firm.

When dawn finally came, the sheriff refused to talk to Ambrott. He ordered his men to remain on call, but otherwise to try to get what rest they could. And, as the first of the sheriff's cars left, Ambrott, all but unnoticed now, decided he'd better get back to his store.

He walked, alone, down the town's main street, not quite knowing why. All he knew was that he was bone tired—tired and frightened. Frightened of what would happen the next night—or the next night after that—when, finally, like the moles on the other side of the iron-barred fence, the denizens of the town's ancient churchyard would grow tired themselves of waiting.

He almost didn't notice the humus-like, wintry smell that greeted him when he entered the store.

He saw the square black sample case first, lying open on the counter. Then, behind it, the familiar, darkly dressed figure of Miss Celaeno. She seemed to be rummaging through the bottles that were arranged in neat rows inside. Searching for something. Oblivious to him until he moved closer.

"Ah, Mr. Ambrott," she said, looking up. "I understand you've started to have a problem with zombies."

"More than just a problem," he answered. "Yesterday afternoon, the corpses in the churchyard . . ."

"I'll bet you tried to use Mole-B-Gone on them, yes, Mr. Ambrott? Mole-B-Gone isn't good for zombies. It just makes them angry." She pulled a bottle of Mole-B-Gone out and handed it to him, pointing to a tiny legend, etched in the glass above the label.

"You see, Mr. Ambrott?"

He squinted at the almost microscopic letters, reading the words out one by one. "Not to be used on churchyards, graveyards, cemeteries, or hallowed ground."

"You see, Mr. Ambrott?" she said again. "Zombies get mad when you treat them like pests. Things like Mole-B-Gone hurt their feelings, so they climb up, out of their graves"—she paused a moment and smiled at Ambrott, then lowered her voice—"and, just between you and me, Mr. Ambrott, sometimes they act even worse than the moles do."

"But these *aren't* zombies," Ambrott protested. "These are just ordinary corpses—at least they were. And you didn't tell me about not using the stuff in graveyards. . . ."

"Corpses, zombies, once they're moving around, what's the difference? And the warning *is* on the bottle. Just think of it as doing business, Mr. Ambrott. We're both salespeople, you and I. We solve people's problems—modern problems, for modern times. But we can solve old-fashioned problems as well."

"You mean like zombies," Ambrott said.

Miss Celaeno nodded. She reached inside her case again and pulled out a smaller bottle this time. "I think this ought to help a little, Mr. Ambrott," she said as she placed it into his hand.

He looked at the label. "ZOMBIE–NOT," it said in inch-high silver letters and, underneath, smaller letters added, "for use on ambulatory corpses, wraiths, were-beings, and other two-legged animations.''

"Stuff really works, does it, Miss Celaeno?'' Ambrott asked.

The woman nodded.

"As well as Mole-B-Gone worked, Miss Celaeno?''

"Of course, it *is* a bit more expensive, but you understand. People's problems often tend to breed more problems, and those, in turn . . .''

"Of course, Miss Celaeno. Perhaps, then, two cases— two to start with?'' He reached for his checkbook and, finding a pen in his jacket pocket, he turned to the light of the store's front window.

Outside, the sky was a steel-heavy gray and, even though it was still just October, Ambrott could tell there was going to be a long, hard winter.

Getting Started
by
Lois McMaster Bujold

About the Author

Lois McMaster Bujold was born in Columbus, Ohio, in 1949. She has been married to her husband John for twenty years and has two children.

She began writing seriously in about 1982 and won a place as semi-finalist in Writers of The Future in 1985. Lois tells us that the encouragement she received from the Contest "gave me a big boost" at a time when she wasn't getting much encouragement from other sources. Shortly afterward, Lois made her first three novel sales to Baen Books and hasn't looked back since.

In just a few short years Lois's skills have garnered her a number of honors. Her novel Falling Free *won the Nebula Award for best novel of 1988, and "Borders of Infinity" won both the Hugo and Nebula for best Novella in 1990. Her novel* Barrayar *is currently a finalist for the Nebula Award, and for 1992 she will be publishing her first fantasy novel with Baen Books,* The Spirit Ring, *a novel of magic set in the Italian renaissance.*

Lois has an eye for intrigue and adventure, but the thing that gives impetus to her books is her tremendously likable and human characters and a remarkable ability to draw life as it really happens. Lately, if you listen to writers talk or if you read articles on writing, you will find that time and time again you hear the same advice, "Do it like Lois McMaster Bujold." Obviously, she is someone you can learn from.

My writing career was inspired by my friend from seventh grade on, Lillian Stewart Carl. She, like myself, had been in a creative fallow period while starting her family. She began writing again, a few fan stories, a novel, then her first professional sale. I was at that time beached in a small town in Ohio with two children ages 4 and 1, no job, and no prospect for getting one. So not just writing, but making a living writing, was my goal from the very beginning. Happily, writing required no more initial investment than pencil, paper, and the useless miscellaneous education lingering in my head.

I did not quite dare begin with a novel, though the basis of one was already forming in my mind, from an old scenario I'd worked out years ago to entertain myself while driving to work, pre-children. Instead I wrote a novelette and mailed a copy to Lillian, who sent it on for another reading to Patricia C. Wrede, a fantasy writer whom Lillian had met on the con circuit. Pat too was recently published, with unclouded memories of how hard it was to get started. She wrote me back a 14-page single-spaced letter of critique and encouragement, which was more attention than I'd gotten from one human being in years. I did some rewriting, packed up my story and sent it to a magazine, calculated my pay (7 cents per word times 13,000 words), and waited anxiously. It never did sell.

In December '82 I began *Mirrors,* My Novel, not yet perceived by myself as my *first* novel. As sections were finished I would send off carbon copies to Pat and Lillian, who would reward me with letters back in my mailbox—a nice change from "You may already be a winner" and "If you have already paid, please disregard this notice"—and chapters of their own for me to comment on in return. They were nearly the only contact I had with the outside world at that time.

I wrote intensely, 450+ pages in nine months. I overshot the ending, and had to back up and search it out, having been told that editors were resistant to 600-page manuscripts from unknowns. I rewrote the opening and other scenes four or five times. I started without chapter organization, and had trouble finding proper dividing points. I was learning everything the hard way, by trial and error. Pat and Lillian advised extensively on submission etiquette, cajoling me to be brief and professional in business correspondence.

That summer I sat down in my kitchen with my back to my family and began the "final" draft, plus carbons, on my old college report typewriter. The temperature hit 103 several days that August. I struggled with my conscience for postage, and sent the finished manuscript to an agent. A month later I began my second novel, *The Warrior's Apprentice*.

The agent kept the manuscript six months and then returned it with a kind letter, but declined to represent me. I sent it to its first publisher on my own. A month later, having never got back my postcard of receipt, I wrote inquiring if it had ever arrived. I received a curt note on a return postcard that my book had been "received and returned," which meant that NOT ONLY was it rejected BUT ALSO it was lost in the mail. Only unsubmittable carbon copies remained to me. Six more weeks of retyping at least. This was also the day that my confused two-year-old, then undergoing toilet training, crawled out of his crib during his nap, took off his diaper, dumped on the floor, and stuffed the evidence down the hot-air register.

Reasoning that it could only be uphill from here, I

continued with my second book, now well underway, resolving to retype the first one later. Much to my surprise, the top copy of *Mirrors* turned up three months later in my mailbox, complete with a personal rejection letter from the editor. It had never been lost in the mail after all, just in the publisher's office.

I finished the second novel and packed it off, then turned my attention back to *Mirrors*. The rejection letter included all of two lines for suggested revisions (do "serious tightening" and "add a couple of twists on the plot"), plus a hint that the editor might be willing to look at it again. Directions how to boil water would contain more information, but I resolved to try. I could make no sense of the second instruction, but I did go back and tighten till it squeaked, cutting 80 pages. It took two months. I also retyped it on my new word-processor I had begged from my father. (No more lost top copies!)

In fact, the cutting was an excellent learning experience; I've written more tightly ever since. And I don't think I could have done the editing job I did without the experience of writing the second novel, during which I finally gained command of chapter and scene structure.

Eventually, both the slimmer *Mirrors* and *The Warrior's Apprentice* came back rejected from that same first publisher, and were sent out again to others. I made my first short story sale and started my third novel. *Mirrors* cycled through again.

In August '85 I sent *The Warrior's Apprentice* over the transom at Baen Books. In October, I made my second sale ever—all three completed novels. All previous rejections were immediately reclassified as well-disguised blessings. *Mirrors,* now retitled *Shards of Honor,* was published in June of 1986, just six weeks before my father died.

My advice to new writers working on their own first novels thus stems from my own experience. First, finish the thing. There is no defect greater, more guaranteed to render it unsalable, than not to be finished. Revise as best you can, but then stop diddling and go on to the next project. As well as dividing your ego into two water-tight compartments, the second may teach you just what you need to know to fix the first. Don't stop with one book and wait for it to sell. It was my second novel, not my first, that caught me my publisher, though luckily it took the first in its train. Other writers have broken in with their third, or fourth, or more.

The only proper place to store a manuscript you are not actively revising is in the mail or on an editor's desk. Besides the fact that most New York publishers' turn-around times are geological, luck can only fall on those who are in position to receive it. Persistence is a necessity. Everything I've written since my first novel has sold eventually, but only lately on first submission. My personal record is 14 rejections for a short story. Editors are idiosyncratic. One editor's indifference may be the next one's delight, all without your changing a word. Unless you agree that they have identified a fixable fault in your story, it is a waste of time to revise to the last editor's taste unless the book is going back to that same editor. (Spelling and grammar are not matters of taste.)

Publishers are not just looking for a good book, they are looking for a writer who can produce several books. The pace of today's paperback market, which is the arena of action if you hope to make a living writing, is frankly frenetic. If you can't write at least a book a year, they think you've died. Writers who can write faster have an edge, which you can discern by examining the shelves of any well-stocked SF section in your local bookstore. (A twenty-year headstart also helps.) But the heavy competition also means that you can't afford to write a bad book, especially if, like me, you just can't write fast enough to beat the daunting market rhythm. My own delay in getting published, distressing as it was at the time, gave me an artificial appearance of rapid production. My first novel alone would have been buried, which is exactly what happens to all too many first novels; three, all published in the same year, were an assault-in-force that supported each other and thus survived.

Imitate the best. I looked around at writers I admired—Zelazny, C. J. Cherryh, Poul Anderson—and thought, "Waiter! Bring me a career like *those* people are having!" Thus I avoided a current pitfall of the journeyman novelist, when book packagers, spotting a hot new talent, sidle up with blandishing offers to you to be a junior collaborator on some shared-world project. I did not wish to be a junior anything. Looking at the names in the big print on those collaborations, I realized that they did not get there by doing the task I was being offered. They did it by writing original work that went out and won Hugos and Nebulas, interspersed with solid, steady, workmanlike yearly novels. Every package deal I ever turned down would have displaced something of my own which did precisely that, advancing my career and no one else's.

So head in the direction you wish to arrive. Don't divert or divide yourself for a degree in English (unless you want to be a teacher) or articles for the local paper (unless you want to be a journalist). You became a fiction writer by writing fiction. Your own fiction.

The other, most subtle and difficult thing for a new writer to learn, is what advice to *ignore*. I don't "write for myself"—I write for a reader—but I do write *from* myself. Originality, or an original twist, comes not only from surface detail, but from your personal world-view. I myself pass early drafts around to test-readers, and many new writers get involved with workshops at some stage. You can sometimes discover your daemon, that inner voice, in your response to well-meant revision advice. If you slap yourself on the forehead and cry, "Why didn't *I* think of that!", the advice is probably sound. If it's clearly fugg-headed, you can just ignore it (politely, of course). But there is a middle ground, more ambiguous, that can include both excellent and fatal suggestions. They *sound* logical, and it can be a good writing exercise to try to incorporate them. But if, at the end, you look at your well-written revision, applauded by your writer's group, and experience a strange, deep unhappiness—the first draft was better.

A Cold Fragrant Air

by
C. Maria Plieger

ILLUSTRATED BY John Caponigro

About the Author

As a child Connie Maria Plieger read many books of fairy tales and folk tales, and perhaps rightly concluded that she is a changeling—not of this world. Few good writers are of this world.

She lives in the country near Prince George, British Columbia, where some years back she made and sold soft-sculpture dinosaurs and dragons, but gave this up to pursue writing.

Her only formal instruction in writing has been through the Writer's Digest School correspondence course, where her instructor was James Kisner. She says that, "Placing third in the Contest has been both exhilarating and scary. I've finally written a successful story; no more excuses, now I have to do it again." That's the fun of it.

About the Illustrator

John Caponigro, who resides in Cushing, Maine, has many artistic interests—writing, drawing, painting and photography— and he has studied the arts at both Yale and at the University of California at Santa Cruz, where he received his B.A. in Art and Literature in 1988.

In his work, John explores the relationship between images and text, and his art reflects his intense interest in the natural world and a fascination with mythology and sacred writings. John's drawings and photographs have been carried by various galleries around the U.S.

John often shares his expertise with others by writing art reviews for Preview! *magazine. He will share his expertise with you in his illustration for "A Cold Fragrant Air," which follows.*

They were all waiting for David. Around seven-thirty, Frankie had tucked foil around the pieces of five-spice chicken in the oven. This did nothing to keep the aromas from seeping out to the living room, where the hot canapés had run out, and one of the three guests was becoming noticeably tipsy.

Frankie peered out between the drapes at the long white driveway curving away into blackness, between inky spruces and pines. Where *was* he? It had begun to snow again, tiny flakes that twinkled briefly in the slat of light from the window before plunging into darkness. Behind her in the living room, with its earth tones and pottery lamps, the tipsy guest, Brenda, laughed shrilly. Frankie let the drapes fall, turned, and asked her husband, "Was the road sanded?"

Keith had taken the kids over to his mother's earlier. "No," he said from the hearth-slab. Firelight etched the bones and muscles of one side of his face. "It was damn slippery going until we hit the highway." He turned to the guests, who had driven out from the city. "They don't bother much with these side roads on weekends, when the school buses aren't running."

"But we'd risk our lives for your cooking anytime, Frankie," said John, his bread-dough features clumping together in a grin.

Frankie smiled faintly. "Well, I guess we'd better eat, then."

John's wife Brenda said, "Michelle refused to drive with us." She teetered to her feet. "She followed us in her car."

The quiet, dark young woman beside Brenda smiled. "I like to have my own wheels." She stubbed out her cigarette and rose lithely.

John, lumbering like a Saint Bernard, ice cubes tinkling in his glass, led the way into the kitchen. "Wonder what happened to ol' Dave," he said, sitting down at the table set for six. "I know he wouldn't miss out on your cooking for anything, Frankie."

Frankie peeled back the sheet of foil from the chicken. John asked, "Think he smelled a fix-up?"

"Shush," said Brenda. The slender young stranger, Michelle, looked up. The light from the overhead swag lamp glanced off her cheekbones. Michelle had her dark hair boyishly cropped, and she dressed like a teenager in a floppy black sweater over tight black leggings.

"It's no big deal," said Brenda. "We just thought we'd get you two together and see what happens."

Frankie pictured the mushroom rice upended, oozing, over Brenda's frizzy blond head.

A noise; Frankie looked up. Only the wind, slapping snow against the window over the sink. A million tiny ballerinas twirling through her ghostly reflection in the black pane.

"What's this 'we' business?" John said. "It was all Brenda's idea; we couldn't talk her out of it."

Michelle looked bemused, not the least bit flustered. She is a cool one, Frankie thought, spearing crisp brown chicken pieces onto a platter. David will probably like her.

The five pounds Frankie had put on at Christmas suddenly felt more like twenty. She wished she hadn't worn the long peasant skirt that usually made her feel gypsyish, but tonight made her feel matronly.

She brought the platter to the table and said, "Dig in." Keith had already brought the rice and the almond vegetables; he was good that way. So good in every way. She sat across from Michelle, who looked up at her with intensely dark blue eyes. Blue contact lenses, Frankie decided, over brown irises. Michelle's eyebrows swept upward across her forehead like two perfect wings. The place beside her was empty.

Frankie unfolded her napkin. "Brenda says you're a dancer."

Michelle's shoulders twitched. "I dance a little. Mostly, I wait—" She tensed, her eyes widening at something behind Frankie. Frankie's heart lurched, and she glanced around at the window. Nothing. Only the snow, dancing as it fell.

The wind was rising. Evergreen boughs scraped at the house, scratchy violins.

Michelle relaxed, with a soft, low laugh. "Thought I saw something. Just a trick of the snow."

"Michelle waits tables," Brenda said between mouthfuls, "at the place where I grab lunch. She just started there last week. We got to talking, and I thought. . . . Well, don't you think she and David would just hit it off?"

Frankie's ears rang faintly. The kitchen was too hot.

A certainty gripped her suddenly that David was nearby. Outside, in the cold, smelling her cooking. Why didn't he come in?

"This is wonderful," Michelle said, nibbling on a chicken wing. "I don't get to eat like this very often. I'm a terrible cook."

"Frankie's such an earth mother." Brenda giggled. "Did you grow the rice yourself, Frankie?"

John growled, "Can it, Brenda."

"Excuse me," Frankie said, rising. She fled into the bathroom and splashed cold water on her face. Her cheeks in the mirror looked flushed, and too round. I used to have bones, she thought wildly. Where are my bones? I should never have quit smoking.

Brenda was getting to her. John and Keith had been friends since college, and Brenda knew she was just along for the ride; so she took it out on Frankie, for some reason. Envy,

Frankie supposed, for her outwardly idyllic life.

The doorbell. Was that the doorbell?

Frankie scurried down the hall, the long skirt swirling around her legs. In the kitchen, everyone was still eating and talking; only Michelle looked up; she gave Frankie an oddly intent look. Frankie padded past, down the hall, into the stairwell. She wiped the fog from the pane in the front door with her hand and peered out. Nothing. No one.

The pane was improperly sealed, and a snowy perfume seeped around its edges—*a cold fragrant air.* She knew that phrase from somewhere; Joyce's "The Dead," she thought; she had written an essay on it in college. She used to write poetry, too, back then; a night like this would shake it from her in spates, like the wind snatching snow from tree branches. It was terrible, effusive stuff—she'd come across a batch of it recently; all the same, it had a strength and depth of feeling, a fierceness, she'd lost.

David hadn't given it back to her. He had only made her realize it was missing.

They weren't lovers, exactly, yet; Frankie feared that would spoil it somehow. Besides, she still loved Keith, and told David so. Also, David and Keith and John were all friends. That didn't stop David from wanting her, though. Or her from wanting him.

Outside, the wind gusted, parting sheets of snow. And then she saw him.

He stood at a little distance, under one of the big spruces, gazing up at the house. Only for a moment; then the curtains fell back, obliterating him.

She yanked on her coat and boots and flew out, past the three cars pulled up to the house, past Michelle's boxy black Landcruiser parked farther down the driveway. The wind tore at her clothes. As she struggled up to David, the boughs above and on either side of him lifted with a mighty rushing sound, like huge black wings. His dark-blond hair, whipping over

Illustrated by John Caponigro

the sheepskin collar of his jacket, was bedraggled and wild, and his face was oddly dim, the features obscured, despite the scatters of light from the house.

When he spoke, his voice was the voice of the wind. "I had to come. I had to see you."

Around them the great wings flailed and trembled. A mysterious shyness held her back. She tried to answer, but the wind filled her mouth.

"I don't have long," he soughed, raising his blurred eyes.

"There you are," said Michelle.

She stepped out of a frenzied waltz of snowflakes. She wore only her black sweater and leggings, and a pair of thigh-high black boots. She wasn't looking at Frankie, but at David.

"Here I am," he answered slowly, as with dawning recognition. "There *you* are."

"I'll be gentle." Michelle's voice tinkled like wind chimes. She brushed past Frankie and grasped David's arm.

"No," said Frankie. "Don't." She inserted herself between Michelle and David. "You can't have him." But a terrible cold at her back forced her aside.

"Sorry, Frankie," said Michelle, leading him away. "He's mine now. Don't worry, you'll forget this ever happened. Do you know the *lambada*, David?"

David doesn't like dancing, Frankie thought. He likes my cooking.

"Wait!" She plunged after them.

"Don't," Michelle said, as Frankie flung herself at David. "Don't, Frankie."

Frankie felt herself falling; there was a moment when she thought she might fall forever. But something caught her: a cold resistance, like thickened air, or a blast of wind. Icy, tingling lips met hers.

And something breathed through David, into her. Snow and wind and darkness, filling her.

When she pulled away, her insides felt like a snow globe,

dancing and sparkling. "You shouldn't have done that," said Michelle. "That was dangerous."

"I don't care," Frankie whispered, as Michelle and David trudged toward the black Landcruiser. She watched them drive away. She watched the wind fill the Landcruiser's tracks.

After a while she couldn't remember why she was standing there, and went in.

" . . . not authentic Chinese cooking, of course," Brenda was saying. She saw Frankie and added, "Not that it matters a bit." She and Keith and John were filing into the living room, carrying steaming toddies.

Keith asked, "Where the hell have you been, Frankie?" His voice softened. "I made you a hot rum."

She gazed at him, his adorable, anxious face, and thought, Where the hell *have* I been, lately? She took off her coat. "I'm back now."

"We thought we heard a car drive away," said Brenda. "But all three of them were there." Something sly and hard came into her eyes. "For a moment I thought you went looking for David."

Frankie smiled at her. Color crept up Brenda's cheeks. Frankie said, "There's hot orange tarts for dessert. With sour cream."

She headed for the kitchen, wondering what had gotten into her. That walk in the fresh air had done her good.

Too bad David hadn't shown up. He'd missed a great meal, if she thought so herself. Pure culinary poetry.

She was distracted by the leaping and capering of the snow outside the kitchen window. Spellbound, for a moment she felt herself soaring upward, through the white flakes. Then she fell back softly.

Someone had cleared the table. Five rinsed plates were in the sink; another, clean plate sat on the counter—David's plate. After puzzling for a moment, she shrugged and put the unused plate away.

Blueblood
by
Bronwynn Elko

ILLUSTRATED BY Yevgeny Rzhanov

About the Author

Bronwynn Elko was born in Racine, Wisconsin, but in 1974 she escaped to the Yukon Territory where she spent the following thirteen years exploring the wilderness by dog team. One of her true adventure stories sold to Alaska Magazine in 1985.

From as early as age eleven, when Bronwynn began filling pages of notebooks with prose, she knew that she would be a writer. She has sold several nonfiction articles, has written a number of short stories, and is doing research for her first novel.

She currently lives in Vancouver, British Columbia, with her partner John and a part-wolf dog named Sadie. Between writing and developing her own practice as an astrological counselor, Bronwynn plays electric funk guitar. The dark and compelling story ''Blueblood'' was inspired by her studies in myth.

About the Illustrator

Yevgeny I. Rzhanov was born in Kiev, Ukraine, in 1958, and graduated from T. G. Shevchenko Art School at age nineteen.

For the following eight years he worked as an advertisement designer until he went back to school at the Ivan Fyodorov Poligraphic Institute, where he graduated in 1991.

While at the Institute, he met and befriended last year's Grand Prize Winner, Sergey Poyarkov, who introduced Yevgeny to the Contest. We are honored to have him as a winner and to present his work to you.

Two things I remember most about Carl are his voice and his blood. Ah, the blood.

Bright as poster ink flooding a board, it splashed onto the pillowslip in large, thick globs of magnificent color. How surprised we were, he and me; he could not believe the soft gurgle rising from the wound, the half-formed words bubbling through the blood; I was amazed at how easily his throat parted under my inexpert stroke.

But it's his voice I vividly recall—a wildly euphonious thing only he could tame. As I watched him struggle soundlessly I knew that nothing devastated him more than the loss of speech at the last moment of his life.

First and foremost Carl was a talker. And he had been right after all; killing was astonishingly simple.

On that first sweltering day in August, his rich contralto penetrated the sticky air effortlessly. Muscular as a snake. "Todd Barrett? Is this the poets' group?" he asked the doorman, who pointed toward the men at the front of the room.

Little Mona nearly swooned when she saw his dark figure enter the constricting, oak-paneled room where we held our weekly poetry meetings. Shoulders rippling under the black silk shirt, he crossed the floor to join a clot of male members circumscribed around the podium. They seemed to shrink under his approach, their shoulders sagging beside his broad, straight back.

"Carl! So glad you could make it," said Todd. His voice sounded anything but glad.

"Took your advice about not being a stranger. Thought I'd read some new stuff I've been working on." He sounded maddeningly confident, as if he knew Todd could not refuse. His teeth glinted. "If that's all right."

His smooth, creamy voice slid into my ear and much further, much further, almost becoming a caress on the inside of my thigh. My blood quickened, just a little.

Todd replied after an awkward silence of perhaps three seconds, his perfect face a perfect blank, "Fantastic. We'd love to hear it. That's what our little group is all about, sharing."

I almost laughed. Todd conducted all his relationships under a cloud of suspicion; terrified of his own emotional weaknesses, he resented any situation that might trigger them. Feelings were not shared, they were exchanged like objects for barter. Whatever I revealed to Todd was turned against me, despised as an intolerable defect of feminine character.

I had loved him until I realized he considered my spontaneous expressions of affection an embarrassment. My wild howling during sex disturbed him; he equated heightened excitement with a bestial sensuality that evoked in him a sense of powerlessness and repression.

Todd took the same approach to both lovemaking and poetry: He made all the right motions without any *emotion*. His poems, like his cock, meted out emotional impact with a steady, predictable beat, like timed strokes from a grandfather's clock.

Todd was president of the poet's society and it showed: all of our poems were inert lumps of prose, soulless, riddled with quasi-feelings about pain and love. We knew precious little about love—nothing at all of pain. We could afford *not* to. Or so we thought. Lately, I wasn't so sure.

The room swelled with anticipation when Todd announced Carl would read some of his poetry. Even the men flushed slightly—or was it the heat of jealousy?

Todd reminded us of the society's picnic next weekend and then introduced Carl with a few tepid words.

Carl's fabulous body panthered up to the scrolled teak podium with just enough cultivated nonchalance to make me squirm. He was too damn aware of his riveting power. Arrogant. Bastard.

"Great ass," moaned Mona under a cupped hand.

Distracted by Mona's whispering I didn't hear his first words. It wasn't just his brutish style that bothered me, nor the lithe intelligence I could sense pacing under the cool, aristocratic exterior. There was something opaquely dangerous under the glinting smile and pewter-blue eyes.

His sonorous voice gently abraded my thoughts.

> " . . . webbed my feet and
>   birdwings scraped softly my soul.

> "Immortality is now
>   and evermore desirable.
>   Brushed with ravenspeak
>   and dew sperm and the sperm
>   of dragons."

Immortality, a smear of dragon sperm? My thighs stirred. He went on.

> "I am the dragon,
>   climbing the purple peaks
>   of the blueblooded mountains
>   of my tribe.

> I am the genius of my blood's
>   desire, brooding into the future."

Yes. My blood felt reptilian, lying in wait, preying . . .

> "I am the fornicator of taboo,
> lighting the cerulean fires anew.
>
> I am the lost bird tribes
> Cretaceous, ascending the scaly
> evolution of Logos.
> I am wanton and
> wanting, transmuting primal
>
> red into blue, into a
> banquet of desire."

At the mention of ancient wantonness Mona's sweat quickened. Even William's glazed boredom was corrupted in a trice. His little mouth plumped up, and he shot me an artless simper. My skin felt hot.

> "I am the wings and
> the blood of the ravenhearted.
> Taking flight into
> the fires eternal,
> drinking the eternal wine of life.
> I burn and drink alone.
> Perched and waiting,
> I suckle the breast of the Divine Beast
> in atonement for life everlasting."

A soft moan effused Mona's exhalation. I felt feathers stroking my thighs, gooseflesh sprouting on my shoulders.

> "Ravenhearted and hungry
> I am waiting.
> I am waiting.
>
> Will you come?"

It was so quiet you could hear pores perspiring. The air was like an eggshell waiting to split on the edge of a frying pan. Finally it broke and everyone applauded. Carl nodded, flicked a wayward coil of dark hair off his smooth brow and glided off the dais.

His last words, "Will you come?" still clung to the backs of my eardrums. I could smell every woman's body oil answering an emphatic yes. Which sulky priss among us would dare go?

Will you come?

Someone would go. Of that I was certain.

Would it be Sara? Or perhaps Clarice?

I gave each a sidelong scrutiny. So did their men. No way they'd get a chance tonight. Mona's latest lover, Cary, sidled to her possessively.

Perhaps William then. His cherubic cheeks sheened a luscious pink as he spoke to Carl.

" . . . *so* enjoyed your use of the dragon as a metaphor for desire. And blood's passion as genius is so *exciting*. I . . ."

Carl watched the vein go up and down in William's throat. Then he glanced my way, lips drawn over his teeth in an almost imperceptible smile. I wanted to kick him. And kiss him at the same time. What had those dark lips touched? They seemed unnaturally dark—brimming with blood. I think I actually blushed and shivered with loathing and excitement.

"Aren't you going to meet him?" breathed Mona into my ear. Like everyone else flocking around him, I wanted to take him deeply inside me. Yet the very thought of it made my juices curdle. I left, angry and confused.

His damn lips were so virulently conceived they haunted my dreams for a week.

The annual picnic finally arrived under moody shanks of cloud and the smell of autumn rain.

Little striped pavilions grazed amid the exotic greenery of Todd's imported lawn like a herd of zebra. Freshly cut lotus flowers bobbed in the brackish pond, looking pretentious among skunk cabbages which the landscape artist had left behind, vainly hoping to blend neo-exotica with the local flora. Caged on three sides by a thick bamboo grove, Darcy, Guy and a few others languished in chairs, making feeble attempts to play computer games on tiny monitors perched on lap tables. Their drinks sloshed gently when they jiggled the mouse to make a move.

Mona hunched nearby, angry at Cary, who was well past coherent inebriation. There was no sign of Carl anywhere.

I felt slightly annoyed by his absence—and was that disappointment sleuthing about under my relief? And fear? My antennae were poised, expectant. I imagined him as I last saw him—eyes locked on William's throat.

I crossed the lawn to join Todd, who wore a ridiculous party hat that bobbed up and down as he spoke. His clear baritone sounded slightly ruffled. "William was supposed to bring his mother's famous pâté de foie gras, but I haven't heard from him since last week. Lilly will be so disappointed if he doesn't show."

"A week? Don't you find that odd?" A tiny chill scampered up my neck.

"Oh, he's probably avoiding Lilly by lying low at one of his seaside hideaways."

He turned and scanned the crowd. "By the way, where is Lilly? Did she leave already?" An unfamiliar dent crouched between his brows. He would have been horrified to see his reflection in a mirror; a quirky jaw muscle jerked his mouth down into the line of a hooked fish. "And where's Carl? One minute he's admiring her long, white neck and then they're gone. It's vulgar of them to leave so early."

His words stunned me.

What did Carl say about "drinking the eternal wine of life?" I pictured him staring at Lilly's long, curving throat, pale under the beige powder she used.

Then I knew. Without doubt, William was dead.

And Lilly, silly bird, was probably being plucked right

now. She had always wanted to provide erotic essence for another's poetic license. Now it seemed she would finally attain that status, albeit posthumously.

While Todd rambled on about the delicacies of goose pie and Carl's appetite for women, I mouthed some platitude about the temperamental angst of my Siamese cats. "Given their mood, I think I should go home before they rip each other's eyes out."

"But Melanie darling, that's the whole point of the new therapies. You're not supposed to worry about such things. Let nature take its course and if they lose an eye or an ear you get them another one," said Todd, with a tinge of ennui.

I backed off through the usual circuitous route of polite excuses and walked to my car. What was the line in his poem . . . "I am the fornicator of taboo . . . I am the wings and the blood of the ravenhearted, taking flight into the fires eternal."

Was he Dionysos or Pan? Or was he the damned?

Perhaps he was all three . . . I had a feeling he was something far more complex. But what? I steeled myself—I would find out, one way or another.

Controlling my terror with an ample supply of scotch, I prayed he would phone. He did—but not until after he had taken Clarice.

Her disappearance sparked a tirade at the club, bringing the total number missing from our group to three. William, Lilly and now Clarice. Where were they? Just what the hell was happening?

Todd suspected Carl, yet he wouldn't give specific reasons. The others scoffed. When pressed to reveal details, Todd raged, exposing his jealousy. He stormed out of the club, jaw twitching. I could barely suppress a smile.

Baffled authorities conducted interviews, filed reports and remained ominously silent, waiting to see what happened next.

Throughout the next week, I waited by the phone, filing my nails into sharp points. There were no bodies, I mused. But somehow I knew—Carl's dark lips were too dark. They had touched something profane. I wanted to—what? I didn't know exactly, only that I would. Just this once.

When the phone finally rang I was so nervous my hands shook.

"Melanie. I believe it's time we meet."

Of course I knew his voice as soon as I heard it. Just hearing him say my name sent ripples up my spine. I breathed slowly, deeply, then spoke.

"Your penchant for words is only surpassed by your flair for dramatics," I said, shearing a torn nail. Could he hear my heart skip? "Todd suspects you, you know. Thinks you're responsible for the others. He's so upset he actually made a fool of himself at the club. I could never imagine Todd being *that* shaken. It's quite a feat, really."

"Ah Melanie, your amusement is charming. But let's not dwell on trivialities— It is such a waste of your passion, your feral wine . . ."

Feral wine? Does he mean my blood? I plunged on.

"The 'eternal wine' of your poem, I suppose? Thirst is like passion . . . it's unpredictable."

He laughed a great belly laugh. "You *are* sweet."

He *does* mean blood. My thighs felt watery, pressed together in prayer, a delicious feeling marbled with terror.

He sounded warmly delighted, as if he were aware of everything I felt, sensing my lust and fear and finding it to his taste.

"If you only knew how truly insightful your understanding is. I really appreciate the animal intelligence of your nature. Life *demands* a feral embrace of fear."

He paused. "Modern man dilutes everything. There is nothing left and he thinks life is safer." He laughed harshly.

"The others in your little group," I could hear him

shrugging those magnificent shoulders, "were so passive, so *benign*. Killing them was merely redundant. It's tragic really, killing humans. Too easy. It doesn't satisfy . . . anything.

"You are . . . full of the dragon, Melanie. I'll give you what you want. And more."

My mind was reeling. "How do you know I want anything? Especially from you."

"How could you not want it? The freedom of eternal fire, ever transmuting, evolving . . . The fire you feel now is nothing. Come *burn with me*."

He must be joking—this wasn't real. But no, my head pounded with blood. I gripped the phone to steady myself. "How do I know you won't, ah, manhandle me? Why should I trust you?"

He laughed. "It's not trust you want." His voice was hollow, dry. "Trust only your instincts. You want the midnight soul but are afraid. To write poems of passion, Melanie, you must enter the lair of the beast."

I paused. He knew he'd touched my trigger bang on. I would do anything to become a real poet.

"Let's just say an hour? The Hotel Empress, room 703."

I drove with the windows rolled down through a torrent of rain, the cold pellets of water distracting me from an insistent simian alertness of the night's perils.

The hotel's huge lobby was deserted. My finger tingled as I pressed the elevator button for the seventh floor.

I entered quietly, without knocking, hoping to catch him unawares. Flames scorched the antique gloom, telescoping the immense room around the Victorian fireplace. Shadows leapt like African dancers, weaving sinewy rhythms onto the vaulted ceiling and brocade-covered furniture.

He stood erect by the open grate, head slightly inclined, and I felt him absorb my presence without turning around. His voracious inspection penetrated my senses with a palpable smack. For a wild moment I thought he would swoop upon me. I nearly burst a vessel when he finally spoke, his voice brilliant and explosive.

"So glad you came. Come drink the fire with me."

For a moment I couldn't respond; his whole manner enthralled me past the point of all sense. His gleaming lips were shadowy purple wings fluttering against his dusky skin, shivering in and out of the firelight in penumbral flight—a flight I felt compelled to join. I could taste his fecund scent, lush as tropic leaves after rain. He breathed unnaturally deep, as if to inhale me. Suddenly his lower lip erupted into a tremble of whispering, evoking instant thirst and fright in me. Understanding nothing he spoke, I heard his sounds deep within my body and became spellbound. Flames splintered his unwavering pupils into chasms of chaos. Watching his soul rise to the rim of his eyes, I knew instantly that his pain and desire were alien to all I had ever known. He was a beautiful dark angel burning in an indigo fire.

He smiled suddenly, without warning, and handed me a drink of warmed brandy. Why can't I remember him pouring it? The smell drained my head of blood.

"'I burn and drink alone.' Is that it?" I spoke from some dank place inside I hadn't known existed, some part of me possessing night vision. I felt something wet and scaly stirring within my gut. Terrified, I drained my glass.

"We are always alone," he said, looking at me for the first time. "There are alternatives to death, but not isolation. It is my greatest source of pain." I vaguely wanted to know what he meant by alternatives. I was too captivated to ask. "It's peculiar . . . how such a thing brings us together, like moths. I have dared to touch the flame . . . yet this isolation cannot be extinguished."

My throat was parched. I watched him swig his brandy, entranced by the muscles of his arched throat.

"Funny," he said, sadly, "I always thought the years would lessen the pain." His eyes shone darkly. "Melanie,"

Illustrated by Yevgeny Rzhanov

he said, murmuring my name over and over. His lean hands entered my hair with long, gentle strokes. ''Come taste the night.''

His burning lips seared into mine, our tongues thrusting between beds of hot, wet flesh. My nails tore sweetly into his soft inner thigh. But all else blurs beside the memory of his blood bleeding into my open mouth.

''Drink me,'' he said, and I remember taking him at his word, biting his neck in a moment of frenzy. The strange flavor spurred my hips to whip his groin ferociously. I must take him. I longed to drink all his desire, all his strange blood and dark despair.

The evening slid away into phantom shapes indistinctly remembered, unfocused, dream-like. Yet I sensed some part of me was adapting to and transforming the light and darkness inside my being.

I burned into wakefulness the next morning, my intestines so hot it felt as if a red hot poker were being thrust up my rectum. Lice seemed to crawl under my skin and I shivered violently, despite the heat in my loins.

I writhed on the antique bed, calling him, conscious only of pain and the empty echo of his name falling back off the high ceilings, unanswered.

The bastard was gone. What was happening to me? It wasn't the physical pain I feared; for the first time in years I wanted to cry. My ancient rage exploded; all that was locked away, forsaken, felt alive and screaming.

Hours passed and the pain eased, only to be taken over by an insidious itching that escalated by the minute.

What started as a mild burning sensation in my lower back, quickly spread up my spine. Fierce prickles gnawed upwards from under my shoulder blades, scuttling along nerves and tendons. I scratched vigorously, tearing at my back with my nails, rubbing against the rug and furniture until I was raw. My skin bubbled and burned.

Abruptly, it stopped.

I whimpered, suddenly overwhelmed by fear laced with a strange anticipation of what the next moment would reveal. Blood heaved up against my left temple in waves.

Naked, I went into the bathroom to find a mirror.

I screamed. Again and again.

Huge long hives snaked along my upper back in vertical rows running from my neck to the S-curve of my spine. The crest of each hive weeped a sticky, bluish fluid from the lips of an open sore. The dark edges around the lips pulsed and shimmered under the ooze. What horrible mange was this?

Shaking, I put on my clothes. My blouse grazed uncomfortably against my back as I ran down the empty corridor of the hotel and caught the elevator to the main floor. I dashed past the astonished desk clerk and bolted into the parking lot, fumbling for my keys.

The hives rubbed and hummed beneath my shirt. I put the car into gear, and stepped on the gas, hard.

When I entered the apartment my answering machine was beeping, followed by the yowling of my cats. I ignored both, tearing my clothes off on my way to the shower.

I emerged feeling much better and forced myself to look in the mirror. Soothing water had cleansed the welts thoroughly; they had shrunk a bit and the pores had tightened. The air cooled my skin and I decided not to dress.

Wrapped in a towel, I went to the liquor cabinet where I kept a hearty stock of scotch, poured myself a triple and went into the kitchen to feed Grendel and Dot. They were almost hysterical with hunger, whipping my legs with their thin tails and nibbling my ankles with sharp little bites while I got their food. I placed their bowls far apart and reached over to turn on the message machine.

I had just pressed the play button when Grendel swiped Dot a vicious blow to the ear for pushing her way into his food dish.

As Carl's smooth recorded tones filtered through the apartment, blood spurted out from Dot's wound, sprinkling the green tiles with splotches of red.

At the sight of blood, I was thrown to the floor by a sudden frenzy of itching that ripped open my pores.

I could feel the hives raising their heads above the skin, puckering the edges of their lips.

"Melanie dear, I know how distraught you must be."

His voice mocked the loud humming of the hives reverberating over my skin like maddened bees. I thrashed wildly. Dot spit, raking her claws across Grendel's cheek.

"You are probably wondering what is happening to you, blaming me no doubt. It's a pity you must suffer like this."

I convulsed on the floor, grinding my back on the tiles. Cat blood rained around me. Grendel went for Dot's eye. Carl sighed deeply.

"But then, most of life is suffering . . . the slow crush of death and decay. It's absurd." He sounded angry. "Rotting in the flesh while being alive is just one of life's cruel jokes I'm afraid." He hesitated and then his voice lifted. "Make no mistake, Melanie, life is passion and *hunger*. We are thirsty yet refuse to drink. . . ."

The hissing of cats strobed between the lines. The hives extended their heads another inch. I writhed and *heard the lips suck, gasping and empty.*

"Listen to the dragon, Melanie. It speaks your true desire. You must drink if you would live as the ravenhearted."

Before I realized what I was doing, I grabbed Dot by the throat and milked her streaming eye socket onto the tiles. Her eye bulged and popped onto the floor where it lay quivering on globs of red and white mucus. She flew from my grasp, screaming.

But I was already rolling in her greasy blood, exalting in the slippery feel of it sliding past the lips and into the throats of the hives, and down further, past the ribbed muscles suctioning her gore into the new little bellies perched above my soul. My internal darkness sighed.

Darkness spread over my inner landscape, a vision of sable wings, black on black. A beak darted out from between the wings and plucked out my mind's eye. I screamed.

". . . the indigo heart is the midnight soul, the nadir of existential pain. Can you feel it pounding your ribs, like a clapper tolling in a bell? Go into the sound, Melanie, into the pain . . ." I heard a sound like a muffled sob. "I am sorry, truly sorry." He laughed nervously. "But you are strong and getting stronger. Can you feel it?"

Drinking every drop, the hives bloated outward into a series of humped, scaly ridges. Bones were shifting around my heart, squeezing my left ventricle. Spears of ice punctured my veins. Sobbing, I ripped a tile loose with my bare hands. My tears flowed freely with blood smears on the floor. Slowly I struggled upright, driven forward by an irresistible force exploding inside my skull, my blood stampeding through my head, hot and dry.

". . . temperance has laid waste the soul, our hooded companion of spirit. What is light without shadow?" He sighed heavily. "At one time I thought, but then . . ." His voice rose excitedly. "Can you see the ravenless sky above your heart? Your longing could fill it with wings. Have you risen from the abyss? I am waiting."

I flexed my back tentatively and stumbled toward the bedroom, quickly showered and pulled some panties on over my damp groin. I reached up to grab a bra off the dresser. The hives *gurgled softly*. I giggled, deciding to go braless.

Exalted and terrified, I slipped on an emerald-green silk shirt. The smooth material cooled my shoulders, which had eased down to almost their normal size. During my fit, the ridges had extended a full four inches off my spine. Now, fully sated, the heads shrunk, little mouths puckered tightly together in sleep. I smiled at the mirror; fully clothed, my back looked perfectly normal. My skin glowed.

Thumping against my spine, my pinched heart fluttered in its cage all the way back to the Hotel Empress. It was nearly dusk.

Excitement whirred around my chest as I parked the car. The hives, responsive to every emotion, hummed vibrantly. I heard a soft hiss escape a blinking lip—"Sssh . . . aahhh."

Exhilarated and shaking, I wound my way through the crowded lobby to the elevator. As I pushed the button, a cool hand pressed gently but firmly on my left shoulder.

"Melanie darling, what a coincidence," said Todd, turning me around and inspecting me like one of his cherished bronze collectibles. His mouth twitched ever so slightly, as though he were annoyed but wanted to repress his feelings.

"You look truly marvelous." He studied my face. "Your skin . . . I believe the word is resplendent. How do you manage, with everything that's been going on?" He paused, eyeing me critically. "Are you trying a new therapy? You really have to be careful about some of the newer ones. They haven't been tested thoroughly."

"Yes," I answered, irritated, "very new. It's quite different. You ought to try it." His hand was uncomfortably warm on my shoulder. Could he feel the hives? They were aware of him but mercifully silent. The elevator reached the twenty-third floor and hovered there. I pressed the button again.

With feigned interest I asked, "How is the lecture? Who's speaking?" The elevator paused on floor nineteen, then resumed its descent. I tapped my foot.

"A novelist from London, Harris is his name. You're not here for the lecture?" He looked bewildered; then his eyes shone, ferret-like. He knew something was up. Sequestered behind his mask he said, "It's really rather boring, the lecture I mean. And I've been meaning to call you . . . I mean . . ."

I quelled an urge to spit on him, swallowing painfully. Where was the damn elevator?

His hand clenched tighter; Todd was being his most persuasive. Slowly, the hives began to extend their heads above the skin, the lips opening wider to suckle his hand pressed against my shirt. They hummed very softly, a lulling sound that Todd did not seem to notice. He stood very still, mouth twitching oddly, almost transfixed. I was aware the hives had changed: Hard little teeth pressed against the circular mouths. They rubbed against the lips, making a light smacking sound. My shoulders prickled and were getting itchy. I knew it wouldn't be long. Panic. I pressed the call button over and over and tried to pry his damn hand off my shoulder.

At last the elevator door opened and I leapt inside in one bound so strong and unexpected that Todd was thrown off balance. The hives really buzzed now and I flung him my best nuclear smile over my shoulder.

"I have to go; friends from Montreal are visiting. Maybe another time?" The doors shut on his astonished face.

My tremors were under control by the time I got to the seventh floor. The hives buzzed angrily for a while before slipping back into their envelopes of horny skin. A gentle rasping sound filled the air when the mouths pressed shut.

Carl's door was open and I went right in, anxious to avoid any more unexpected encounters. He reclined on the Elizabethan chaise longue next to the low-burning fire. A large black book lay face down on his lap, the cover splayed out from the spine like the wings of a dead crow. A decanter of brandy cast amber lights on the polished wood floor. I could smell some brandy warming inside a metal container which hung over the coals by means of small chains attached inside the chimney flue. Without a word he got up and poured a generous amount into a large, globe-shaped glass. His hands flickered slightly.

"You must be thirsty," he said simply, handing me the

drink, without smiling or giving any indication he intended a pun. He seemed preoccupied and distant. Self-absorbed. His distance angered me after the sobering incident with Todd in the lobby. What the hell was happening to me? Insensitive prick. He must know I'm in pain. I felt like hitting him, pounding him with my fists. But my voice was modulated when I spoke.

"I think it's time you tell me just what the fuck is going on, don't you agree?" I was shaking.

He smiled wryly, amused. He seemed to know how rarely I spoke that way. He lifted his head, piercing me with a cold, blue stare.

He spoke very clear and low, the sound of glass beads tinkling. "Are you finished 'teething' yet?"

I wanted to rake the high-bridged, elegant look off his arrogant face. I counted the stray hairs wandering between his smooth eyebrows. Then I spoke. "Is that supposed to be a metaphor for a symptom of this disease you gave me? Or perhaps you are suggesting I've contracted a rare case of dermatosis?" I paused, afraid I'd lose what thread of control I had left.

His eyes danced. "Disease? Disease is a condition of mind. All life is parasitic, don't you think?"

My hand jolted, ready to strike. "Cut the crap. Or I swear I'll remove your bowels with my nails." I couldn't believe I'd said that but I knew I meant it.

His hyena smile slowly transformed into a thoughtful, straight line. "You have grown," he demurred. I felt him repress a thrill.

He got up, poured himself another drink, and strode the room at a smoldering pace. I watched his magnificent shoulders with grim fascination, changing and shifting with each stride, the corded blades rippling like the haunches of a jaguar.

"This 'disease,' as you call it, has sprung from our

internal darkness; our soul . . . has spread its wings at last,"
he said, laughing, and then frowned, seeing the look on my
face. He continued. "The soul has always possessed the *capacity* to venture into physical form, from shadow into
hungry beast. Aeons of damnation pushed him into the deepest corners of the body where he has been left to rot. His
wailing pain now breaks through generations of denial. Modern
man has answered his call with insipid therapies, flushing him
from the nethermost regions of the human mind. Starvation
has driven him to the surface of the flesh where he can feed
freely at last, without hindrance. His physical appearance was
inevitable," he said, with great satisfaction. "Several of us
began to appear around the turn of the century. About the
same time AIDS began to mutate.

"Not to imply the two are actually *related*," he said, lips
flexing upward in a crooked smile, "except that both trans-
mute the essence of the blood."

"Primal red into blue . . . into? What was it?" I asked,
mouth tight, expressionless. "Oh yes. A banquet of desire."
I strove to remain calm.

He beamed. "Precisely. Haven't you noticed a change
in appetite?"

I checked my anger, feeling the hives stir. "And where
are these others? The ones who have this, this . . ."

He swigged his brandy like a musketeer, curvy lips almost
devouring the glass. He turned and grinned. The hives hissed
softly.

"I believe," he said, leveling his gaze so that his eyes
penetrated me with an amused look, "I am the only survivor."

I was shaken. He meant only one thing—he'd murdered
them all. The hives increased their incessant humming. "And
now I must suckle the beast's breast or die, is that it?" My
voice reminded me of darts hitting a corkboard, the sharp-
ness dulled by impact with a pliant surface. I felt dizzy.

"Melanie dear . . . it's not a fatal condition, at least as

far as *you* are concerned. On the contrary, your lifespan has increased by at least several hundred years—about as long as it takes existential pain to become meaningful.'' He laughed coldly. ''Humans,'' he said sneering, ''think they are so civilized. As if the soul's rage can be tamed and then placated with tepid 'therapies,' or subdued by scientific analysis—the fools. Soul is wanton, Melanie, it is desire, ever ascending and transmuting spirits' adventure. Without soul, spirit is a flaccid bag of decaying seed wasting on the vine of life. The symbiotic relationship between soul and spirit is the Divine Beast. His undying devotion to desire inflames the intelligence of the blood. Without the rapacious appetite of soul, Melanie, human spirit withers and dies. Don't you see?''

He slammed his fist against the stone mantel above the fireplace before continuing, voice rising in a menacing tone. Ancient. Wrathful.

''Spirit tried to abandon soul and imprison the dragon within. I have witnessed the revolution . . . and the *revelation* of the blood,'' he cried, exultantly, turning slightly. The heads of the hives were raising the shirt off his back. Mine responded with a hiss; I sat rooted. He faced me again. ''Devotion to desire, soul and spirit, together—is this not truly genius brooding itself into the future?''

He drained back the brandy in one fell swoop and suddenly whipped his glass into the fire grate. His brow glistened under a pool of shadow. He mouthed a silent curse, nose flaring, lips turning a voluptuous shade of blueberry mocha. I hated him and yet I wanted to seize him, pull him down and bite those lips. The hives were wriggling, rasping loudly, and my back and thighs were burning; I didn't dare move. He sighed, speaking softly.

''Rejoin the wisdom of the flesh, Melanie. Here,'' he said, pressing his hand to his chest, ''is where the primal substance of life is made whole, eternal. Here is pain and terror, rage

and lust. Waiting to transform from shadow into flesh. Metamorphosis need not be solitary."

He speared my heart with a look, eyes ringed in yellow.
A tiny gasp escaped my hives. They were salivating.

"You have great strength, Melanie. An indigo heart. I
would feed your heart if... would you drink?"

I was so amazed to see the glint of a tear on his eyelash
that I didn't notice the slender surgical knife arcing toward
his forearm until it was too late.

I didn't see the blood he offered; his arms folded over
me, reaching the small of my back. I heard fabric ripping.
My eyes rolled into my head.

The frenzy came from my deepest cave, a sunburst of
feathers crushed by human ribs, enveloping all but the race
of hunger up my spine. The strange taste—this time slipping
into many little mouths—descended farther than ever before
until it bottomed out and entered my throat from behind.
My dragon roared. Carl released an iron grip on my hair,
murmuring, turning me around. Our clothes fell away and
we stood in each other's eyes, irises wide open. When he
entered my twilight chamber, I took him fully, womb pulsing.
I screamed with joy. He bit my forearms till they bled and
I draped them over his back like a cloak. He rubbed, little
mouths suckling, nibbling, humming. The room vibrated with
our thrusting and sucking till the light of dawn forked the
ginger shadows sprawled on the floor by the fire where we
lay. We moved onto the bed and I remember dreamily showing Carl where the bite marks on my arms should have been:
The skin was shiny and smooth, like new milk. He smiled
and kissed me, then turned facing the wall. His ridges were
the size of baseballs, only supple, rippling and sighing as his
breathing slowed. "Sshh... ahhhmmmmm."

I dozed while Carl slept, my mind floating with strange
images. Diamond-shaped irises stared from within, lava red.

Tongues of fire rasped my genitals; I wanted, but I didn't know what. I sat up. My back throbbed and I heard the hives whispering. I ached to hear more.

The words came easily. I wrote them on a portion of the bedsheet, such was my heat to capture them before they could disappear like the bite marks on my arm. Curtains of taboo fell away, wrested from my intellect by thorny fingers dripping indigo blood. My ravenhearted feathers unfolded, and my musing desires grew sable wings, and I flew straight into the indigo heart. Inky tears blurred my vision, falling as lines of prose onto the red, red sheet. The last verse expelled from my womb in a shudder of finality, an afterbirth that left me exhausted. I dropped the pen and curled my arms around Carl's waist, falling asleep to the sound of the hives' low purr. A sound like bees gorged on honey.

"Melanie."

I woke. He sat with the knife, carving cheese. He had my poem scrunched up by his side, the last verse smoothed out over his stomach, easy to read.

"You must be hungry," he said, shaving a thick slice before setting the knife on the board on his lap. I shook my head, suddenly alert. The hives were awake and I sat up, watching his eyes on my poem.

I couldn't bring myself to ask him what he thought; I was still on the tightwire above the vision, feeling the power of it lifting me higher, higher. . . .

His smile was pointy-toothed.

My hives snapped; I sat very still, waiting.

"It is a good poem about teething," he said, laughing. "But this part here," he paused, with great enjoyment, tugging on the portion of poem-sheet on his belly, "is quite, well, it's actually *trifling*."

My hives began to drone. What were they saying? I thought I could almost make out words. Carl didn't seem to notice. He was laughing so hard.

"Surely you can do better than this . . . fussing bit of prose. It's rather like a handmaid's maudlin attempt to woo a king into bed. You've mistaken feminine emotionalism for primal desire—a tragic error which no doubt reflects your association with that paltry pseudo-poet's society. Never mind. In time you will learn. Poetry, my *dear* Melanie, is spartan. As any true survivalist packing for a long safari knows—you bring only what is necessary for your journey, what will serve your purposes along the way; bring only the things that will help you attain your goal. Poetry is like the safari—if you want to attain a good poem you must leave sentimentality behind, you must ruthlessly slash the superfluous—"

I severed his vocal chords in one clean stroke, the blade hitting vertebrae with a wet *thwack*. Blood spewed onto the pillowslip—a vivid splash of bluebell against the red sheet. His final words gushed out of his throat on a foaming bright wave which quickly faded, draining the blueberry from the irises of his eyes. I cut again. Then the hives jacked open their yaws and I lost complete control. But this time the vision became a quasar of irrevocable, blinding awareness.

The hives bubbled up, mouths gaping, chanting in tongues. My soul was babbling in rhymes, calling my name. I listened and listened, rapturous, laughing in pain. Answering.

I picked up the phone. Carl's bloodless body lay askew on the bed. The neck had made a feeble attempt to heal itself, the skin growing in prune-like patches toward the middle of the stump. I dialed for an outside line, pulled the ivory curtains away from the window. Autumn light streamed onto the stone mantel above the fireplace, illuminating the bone-white skin of Carl's head. Already the raw neck edges were black. A pang shot through me, deep within the hives. They murmured an incantation, flooding my internal darkness with evensong.

A voice came on the line. I spoke a few words.

"Melanie?" He sounded surprised.

"I think I'm ready for that drink now," I said. There was finally a reason to endure everything, even Todd.

I suddenly realized what Carl had meant.

Devotion to desire is *living poetry.* Only blood and desire could evoke the verses of the soul and slake the perpetual thirst of the dragon. Only blood and desire.

Given enough of both, I knew I would become a great poet yet.

Not Simply Blue
by
Gene Bostwick

ILLUSTRATED BY Allen Koszowski

About the Author

Like some other winners this year, Gene is a man who puts his concern for the environment to practical use— he owns a general contracting company where he specializes in designing and building solar-heated homes in and around Santa Fe, New Mexico.

Gene, who is in his late thirties, has been writing short stories consistently now for about four years. It normally takes writers several years to perfect their craft well enough to compete in the professional markets, and Gene has reached that point a bit ahead of schedule.

Gene's story, with its fast pace and enjoyable tone, was a strong contender for a prize in the third quarter. "Not Simply Blue" won a place in our hearts, as I am sure it will in yours.

• • •

Gene Bostwick's illustrator is Allen Koszowski.

When I looked up, she stood
in the doorway—she was beautiful, completely
naked, and she was blue. Not just pale blue
as if she were cold or anemic or something, but deep, ocean
blue. She flashed me a delicately blue smile as she stepped
into my office. My jaw hung open or I might have smiled
back.

"You are Tom?" she asked, her accent foreign, nothing
placeable.

Her hands glided slowly up her sides and around her
breasts. The coloring ran right out to the nipples, but that
didn't dampen my basic appreciation. The lady really was
beautiful.

I'm not your cynical type, but the only explanation I could
come up with was an office prank. What else would a siren
like her want with a dumpy little, half-bald guy like me? I
pictured the guys in Research laughing their heads off over
this little caper.

She stepped forward and offered a ladylike hand. "I Tom
Omara Omara are."

I stood before I realized how silly the scene looked and
reached over my desk to touch her hand. "Tom Bridges,
ma'am, Head of Procurement." Her palm felt surprisingly
warm. "Are you the replacement from General Services, Miss,
uh, Omara?"

I knew darn well she didn't work here at Diversified
Fields, but I really didn't know what else to say.

I plopped back into my seat as she glided forward. With

Illustrated by Allen Koszowski

a deliberate sway to her hips, she swung around my desk, grabbed the arm of my chair and spun me to face her. A weak chuckle dragged from my throat.

"I would you have me," she whispered as she pulled the knot from my tie, her voice smoother than her grammar.

"I bet somebody's being had here, lady." I choked back another nervous laugh and tried to brush aside her fingers. She had other ideas.

Blue hands fought open my shirt. Steely nails brushed across my chest. It was arousing, but not the way she intended. I grabbed her wrist and found her to be much stronger than she looked. Her arm twisted in my grip and iron fingers locked onto my forearm. She pressed my hand into the softest part of her rump.

Using my necktie as a choke collar, she yanked me forward and jammed my face into her chest. I tried to push away with my free hand, but she only tightened her grip. I couldn't shout, but my eyes rolled up to meet hers. They were half closed and drool welled at the corners of her mouth. Her voice sounded convincingly excited.

"Oh Tom, Oh Tom, Oh Tom, Oh Tom, Oh Tom, Oh Tom!"

She finished thirty seconds later. Her body quivered for a few moments before she relaxed her hold on my tie and my arm.

The air between her breasts might have been sweet, but it was limited in supply. I took the opportunity to push away. She let go suddenly, and my chair rolled back and banged the wall. I grabbed the edge of my desk and put a few feet between me and my blue Amazon.

"What the hell are you doing, lady? I could have suffocated!"

"Now we completed are Tom. You or I cannot refuse anything." Her words were all softness and indigo, and they scared the hell out of me.

I backed away another step, figuring I might have half a chance if she lunged.

"I love you too, sweetheart. But I think you'd better meet my folks first." I moved toward the door as she crawled up onto my desk. "So, now that we've uh . . . made acquaintance, you mind telling me a little about yourself, like who does your makeup, maybe, and planet of origin?"

"Oh Tom."

I didn't want to risk another mammary adventure. On all fours she could definitely be a theme for a photo session, but this Candid Camera shot was over. Office jokes be damned, I ran for help.

She left before I got back with Security. They thought I was nuts, even after I revised my story to include a gangster-style thug in a blue suit. Their questioning seemed to take forever. I doubt they heard a word I said after the first few repeats, but no prank would get the best of me.

I figured my next step was to uncover the inside story. I needed a person who knew the score, who wouldn't take sides, who wouldn't think I was crazy. I headed for Jim Brewster.

Jim's the granddad of Diversified's dozen research sections, a wispy old man without the patience for long words. Fifty years in the business has stooped his shoulders and whitened his hair, but he still brings a passion to his work. I sat in his office and stifled my impatience—after all, he might have been in the midst of another brilliant discovery—while I waited for him to disconnect from his monitor.

The winter sun dipped below the horizon, and automatic lumen sensors compensated the lights up a notch. That seemed to rouse him, and he glanced my way. "Still don't know how to knock, eh, Tom?"

"And you're still the grumpiest man in Solar Research," I said. "So, Jim, seen any blue ladies lately?"

"As a matter of fact, I have."

I grinned in triumph. "Then you know what happened in my office today?"

Jim frowned as if my question hid some deep meaning. "No. Should I?"

I felt my grasp of victory slip away.

"I've been scratching my head over a parhelion series recorded on the autocams," he continued. "The blue lady's got me baffled."

It was my turn to frown. I'd seen lots of parhelia, sun dogs we called them. On hazy days they are common enough, faint rings around the sun with two bright spots spaced to either side. Nothing to do with my troubles.

"Are we talking about the same thing, Jim?"

"You tell me."

He turned his monitor my way. The curve of a parhelion ring sliced through the picture from top to bottom. In the center, the sun dog traced a rough version of a female form.

"She's vivid blue in the original photo," he said.

"So you're telling me that you're into X-rated atmospheric phenomena. Does the Research Advisory Board know about it yet? They'll probably want to fund a major study. Maybe even look for a paranormal connection."

Jim shot me an evil glance. "I mean it, Tom. This parhelion series has a blue center. Not red or yellow like every other one ever recorded. Not just blue edges like some of the rarer ones. The damn thing's blue from the inside out. We didn't pick up the anomaly until after the sun dog had faded, so we're trying to recreate the conditions that made it blue. So far we have two main cases."

The way he said it, I half expected him to include alien spoon-bending on the list.

"The first theory holds that a change in atmospheric content occurred to alter its refractory properties over some undefined area."

"Correct me if I'm wrong, Jim, but are you telling me the air ain't air up there?"

He didn't laugh. "That's one way of putting it. The other hypothesis means a change in the solar side of the equation."

"So if the air's okay, the sun isn't?"

I meant to be silly. Honest. Jim just turned back to his monitor and studied it.

"No, it isn't that simple. Photons are photons, at least in this universe. But this blue lady almost looks like we're seeing a picture taken tomorrow."

I can't say Jim made a lot of sense, but his last comment rang an alarm in my head. "Just when did this sun dog occur?"

"In the middle of the afternoon. About three o'clock."

I swallowed very hard.

I headed back to my office without telling Jim any more. How could I? His theories were crazy enough without adding a naked blue lady to the scenario. I wished I still thought she was only a joke, but the coincidence of those sun dogs worried me.

I decided to dig into the company's data bank for a little research of my own. Diversified Fields occupies a rare position in the world of private enterprise. We are a bunch of dabblers with the uncommon ability to guess wrong and come out right more than half the time.

When the military needed a better way to damp the noise that limited their secret surveillance plane's listening range, we introduced a harmonic electron gun that fit the bill very nicely. Of course, we never told the generals that the guy who invented it was working on a zero-G can opener at the time. Likewise the kid's video maze game that just happened to solve the chaotic equations behind fluid turbulence. When you add it up, our computer has a gold mine of oddball info just waiting for the questions to fit its answers.

I ended up with a stack of reports that ranged from Fulani African tribesmen to aniline poisoning to body cosmetics. Somehow, it had gotten to be midnight, and my eyes blurred with fatigue. The proverbial office sofa was as far as I got from my problem for the rest of the night.

I woke to a gray dawn, my head still fixed on blue. The morning's first coffee cart run was two hours away, so I made do with a splash of water on my face. My back winced as I sat down to review my diggings.

The aniline poisoning and African tribesman articles took little more than a glance to dismiss. I flipped through a summary of medical conditions, but the woman I'd met yesterday seemed quite healthy. I turned to the article on cosmetics.

From fifty pages of data I learned two important things: Makeup definitely had its limits—inside the lips, around the eyes, under the nails and so on—and the blue lady was way beyond anything on record.

The day had barely brightened, and a few fellow employees stirred in the hall. Someone would come knocking soon, expecting another plain old business day, but I was in no mood for company. I grabbed my coat, headed downstairs to the front entrance and plowed into the solitude of the crowded sidewalks.

I'd refused to consider a lot of other possibilities about the blue lady up to now. Corporate espionage. Blackmail. Well, maybe bluemail.

The more thought I gave it, the more serious it looked.

I trudged along for several blocks before I noticed that someone was matching my steps. I stopped short. Before I could laugh at myself for being paranoid, a gloved hand grabbed my shoulder.

''What the . . .''

An arm slid around my waist. I tried in vain to push

away, but a trench-coated figure reeled me in until we stood face to blue face. Her hand shot up and covered my mouth before I could scream. "Please, we must go cover Tom under."

Maybe I should have tried harder to escape, but I felt dazed. She led me around the corner and through the door of a shabby diner. We slid into the first booth.

She wore the biggest sunglasses I'd ever seen, and pearly white lipstick. High boots, a turtleneck blouse and hood-like scarf edged the camouflage to near perfection. Nearly. What did show was still unmistakably indigo.

Enough of my senses returned for me to feel a wave of panic. I tried to scramble over her to the aisle. Her left hand clamped onto my leg like a vise. I sat.

Behind the counter, a pimply kid with a greasy apron pretended not to watch. The place was a typical dive. If you didn't go to him, you weren't looking for service.

The grip on my leg eased a little as the blue lady turned to me with a whisper. "You must care to take Tom. You have much to help me."

"Yeah, thanks for the help."

To distract myself from feeling trapped, I used an old trick of conference management and focused on the details of her face. The lipstick failed to mask the blue that ran inside her mouth all the way up the gums. I imagined her throat was little different. Azure on azure eyes showed no sign of contact coloring or dye and looked entirely human. Raven-blue hair pulled tightly back under the scarf. My growing curiosity surprised me.

"I have been English practicing, Tom. And I have learned much customizing in a day."

I didn't figure she meant body work. Her hand stayed firmly on my leg, more effective than any leash. I managed a feeble protest.

"Look, lady. I've got a list of questions. . . ."

"Time is very little, Tom. Wolf doors are at me."

She squeezed just hard enough to show concern without bruising. I appreciated her restraint.

"So skip the long explanations. Just tell me how you happen to be here in living color."

She flushed. The effect was unique.

"This blue color Tom is error. My genetic manipulation blueprint humans misunderstood. Printed blue in all coloring sequences."

Against all good sense, I believed her. I rubbed my forehead to push back the growing ache and wondered if I believed myself. Practical jokes, blackmail or espionage would have been so much easier to handle.

My distraction technique lost ground. I felt a little scared and a lot nervous, and looked around for help. Several robed, Arab tourists clustered at the cash register while they calculated their change. When they turned for the door I reached out.

Omara caught my hand in hers and turned my grasp for help into an embrace. She faced away from the group, and rubbed me nose to nose. Her lips locked over mine, and I tasted blue just before she inhaled.

The tourists looked away in embarrassment at the American display of lust. They were gone by the time I reared back, gasping and dizzy. Behind the checkout, the kid stared at us with open enthusiasm, more interested in our necking than Omara's colorful expression. That's city life.

"We are bonded, Tom," she said. "Humans are by manual forever full of faith once they have shared as we have. How can you not trust me?"

"What do you mean 'bonded,' Omara? Not yesterday's scene in my office?"

"And not why Tom? Did we completely not act in sex?"

"Not the way I remember it, lady. You were a solo performance."

Her lower lip settled into a pout. She reached into her pocket and pulled out a cellophane-thin book. Her fingers flicked through several pages and stopped. She read intently for a moment, and her face brightened. Apparently, her manual said she was right.

She was about to give me an *I told you so* when she realized that the instructions went on to the next page. As she read on, her cheeks darkened to navy, and the book disappeared back in her pocket. It seemed to be time for another subject.

"To please, Tom. There is but little time. Without a density meter I will never save before it grows late."

Her agitation was obvious, even if her meaning wasn't. "If you're trying to tell me you're not American-made, I'm convinced. If you're looking to keep the secret, don't worry. I'm not about to risk a straightjacket just yet."

"Please, Tom. A density meter I need."

I still didn't get it, but she misread my blank expression.

"I have technology not to offer you, Tom. But information would not trouble my returning. This is power?"

"Technology?"

"No Tom. Information. You would make this body, maybe?"

My back pressed into the wall as I pulled away. I thought for a moment that she was leading up to another episode of half sex, will travail. Then the lights went on. She meant *make this body* as in *assemble from parts,* presumably as she had done.

My heart raced. I also heard a warning voice in the back of my head. She was an alien, for crissakes, and I was considering doing business with her.

"You're talking human genome, a complete DNA map?"

"I am so pleased, Tom. I knew you are help."

"I are, lady, I are."

"We will at your office after sunset meeting then to give my needs to your parts."

She got up and left without another word. I thought about following her, thought about the police, the FBI and the CIA. Mostly I thought about the royalties.

When I came out of my daydream a while later, the kid behind the counter smirked.

"I owe you anything?" I asked.

"Naw, we get lots of deadbeats here. Most of 'em don't provide half the show that you and the lady with the paint job did."

I walked out with a smile. The kid hadn't seen anything yet.

The walk back to the office gave me time to think. My confidence softened. I no longer just wanted to talk to Jim, I needed to.

Unfortunately, he wasn't alone. A load of haphazardly arranged equipment and several technicians crammed the room. Jim looked up from a pile of readouts and managed a smile. "Great news, Tom. You're just in time to see another one-in-a-billion phenomenon. We're recording a blue sun dog."

I refused to be distracted. "We need to talk."

His expression said everything but go to hell. "This is big!" he said. "I've been on the phone with every climatologist, meteorologist and physicist from here to Moscow, and you want me to take a break and chat? We're talking two unprecedented atmospheric events in three days, and I *missed* the first one."

I thought fast. "I can see things are pretty intense here, but this is important—and related. We could step outside. You wouldn't want to miss a first-hand look, would you?"

Somehow my suggestion filtered through the analyzer

he called a brain and came out positive. Once he decided it was a good idea, he nearly dragged me out the door.

The sun dogs glowed like twin beacons. Jim stared, open-mouthed, as I guided him to a bench.

"So, Jim, let me tell you a little story."

He continued to peer upward, making occasional scratches in his notebook. I don't know how much of my introduction he caught, but when I told him my theory about aliens, he looked sharply at me. "Isn't this a matter for immigration?"

"I don't think they have quota regs for where she's from."

He kept glancing between me and the sky, but I had his attention.

"As much as I'd like to believe it's a joke," I said, "I can't. Omara's real, but I don't know what she's made of, any more than you know why your sun dogs are blue."

He shook his head and looked at the sky. His expression changed and I felt a little hope.

"These parhelia are just a theoretical problem at this point." He gestured upward. "I can't deny they exist. Somewhere way down on the probability curve there must be a point where they could happen."

"Where does your curve fit blue ladies in, Jim?"

He shook his head again. "I don't think it does. I'm not denying your story, but you've got to consider every possibility. If this isn't a practical joke by the boys around the office, that doesn't mean it isn't a set-up. As Head of Procurement, you could get your hands on some pretty sensitive stuff. There are people who would try to swindle it out of you."

Lots of people, sure. But what if the one I was dealing with wasn't quite human? I knew I had to find out that answer first. "I hope to hell it's that simple, but . . ."

"But you're not going to bring the authorities in on this, are you?"

"Not yet. I can't. Not until I'm sure."

"And you expect me to keep a lid on as well."

I managed a weak smile, and gave my friend a pat on the shoulder.

She stepped through my door within a minute after sunset. I recognized the trench coat and hat, boots and gloves, but her face was another story. She'd found makeup to hide most of the blue, done a fair job of it, really, except that she seemed to lack any more than a crude understanding of color. The skin tone was Crayola flesh, the lips cherry red. She hadn't even bothered to try and change her eyes. With sunglasses she could pass in a crowd.

"I hope I've come at a good time," she said.

My eyebrows furrowed. Something else had changed about her. She seemed to read my expression.

"I have adjusted my translator program. I think it teaches me correctly, now, but your dialect has so many inconsistencies that it took some time."

"English is like that." I motioned her to a chair and focused on acting businesslike. "We have a lot to discuss."

She sat. Her adaptation to other customs may have needed work, but she managed to cross her legs like a professional. Stockings hid her real color. Right up to the thigh, I observed.

"Indeed, Tom. And very little time left."

I knew the rules of the game, and I wasn't about to rush into things. It didn't matter if she was from Planet Zero. On Earth, business is business.

She got right to the point, a tactic usually reserved for the desperate or overly confident. She could have been both, and I held my cards close. Her agenda ran slightly over thirty items, ranging from a mass spectrometer core to three hundred feet of triple sheathed coaxial cable.

"That's the list, Tom. As my mate, I know you will do everything you can to help."

I finished my notes and returned her smile.

"About this mate stuff, Omara, I'd hate to think you're tied to some sort of commitment you can't keep. After all, we never really . . . uh, completed."

Her smile faded, and it occurred to me that I didn't really want to expose her unpleasant side.

"Not that I'm not grateful," I continued hastily. "But it might ease your conscience about leaving if we kept this as more of a business deal."

The light in her eyes changed and her posture adjusted subtly. Any sign of a flirt was gone.

So, the dealing began.

She laughed at my suggestions about Faster-Than-Light drives and time machines. But the human genome map was okay.

We never got very far on anything that involved real technology—artifacts seemed to be off limits. In the end, I got three things I knew the value of, including the gene map, plans for a cold-fusion generator and a diagram of a full-spectrum photoelectric converter. Omara added a treatise on complex numbers and a blueprint for silicon super-mono-filaments. She thought they'd be useful, considering the planet.

In the back of my head I'd been tallying her list of goods. It looked like a little over two hundred thousand would cover it, ten percent of Diversified's annual supply budget. Not bad for five potential theories of relativity!

I could tell the trading ended by a shift in her demeanor. Beautiful emerged again. Her body language control was impressive, but also unsettling. Did I have any real chance if she tried to pull a galactic con job on me?

I hesitated while I thought about it. She'd be the only loser if we cancelled the deal right now, but once I put the goods in her hands the exposure would reverse. My shopper's instinct decided the risk was worth it. But I also wanted a little insurance.

"I checked up on your calling card, Omara. The boys in Research say you've been messing with things in our upper atmosphere."

I swear she suddenly looked nervous—and vulnerable. My insurance.

"No, Tom. You aren't quite right."

"So, why am I wrong?"

"I had hoped not to alarm you. But I didn't cause the atmospheric anomalies your people are recording, not directly at least."

She was right about improving her program. It even provided for talking in circles.

"Alarm me, Omara. What are you doing up there?"

"Being watched."

My hackles raised involuntarily.

"I don't get the impression these are your friends."

"No. And they will have little qualms about burning the atmosphere right off this planet if they think it will flush me out."

It felt as if a hammer had hit me right between the eyes. I grabbed my head with both hands and just about tipped over backward. Omara hurried around the desk and steadied me. Her blue-on-blue eyes showed no sign she was kidding.

"I had hoped to spare you, Tom. It would have been much easier if you'd thought of me as just another alien looking for charity."

I stood outside an old barn and looked across a field of windblown snow. The moonlight, unchallenged here sixty miles north of the city, lit lonely countryside. A cold gust slid down my collar and urged me on.

The last few hours had been the most desperate in my life. I'd spent six days assembling her order, another fabricating a drop-shipment paper trail and diverting the goods to an unscheduled truck—one that had left our shipping dock five hours earlier. And that's when I guess I lost control.

Somehow, she had changed the drop by radio and conveniently forgotten to tell me. I'd spent two frantic hours locating the driver, who was half in the bag from celebrating a hundred-dollar tip. I managed to squeeze out the info I needed before he drank himself under the table. So, here I stood by the barn, trembling, not from the cold. It was time to consummate the deal.

Another puff of wind revealed the tiniest flicker of light from an opening on the second story. I forced down the lump in my throat and stepped inside.

Halfway up the straw-covered stairs, I spotted her—stripped bare, her blue-engineered body exposed to the cold. I gave her genome program credit. It hadn't messed up in the proportions department.

She'd worked fast. A mass of tubes and wires wound through an array of high-tech junk. At least it looked like junk, the way it lay tumbled about. I remembered a sci-fi phrase, "alien geometry," and suppressed a shudder.

It struck me why she chose me in the first place. Not many people could have provided her with the parts in so short a time. They weren't that technical, but definitely unusual. Take the spectrograph core and the ion pump, for examples, and the Linde liquefaction pumps, all six of them. Someday I'll have to sit down and find out what all these things do.

She fussed over a series of liquid-filled vats, adjusting interconnecting hoses and wires until the whole mess radiated a pinkish glow. Then she turned and smiled at me. Her innocent expression chased away my anxiety but lit a spark of anger.

"Tom! I was afraid you would not make it before I left."

"Scared to death, I'll bet."

She frowned with a genuine look of concern. "But you had my letter of instructions, no? I had it delivered to your office."

Damn, I wanted to call her a liar, but I hadn't looked at the mail all day.

"Even so, Omara, you wouldn't have left before making good on our arrangement, would you?"

Ignoring my sarcasm, she stepped toward me and extended her hands in a sort of Hawaiian island greeting. My reflexes imitated the motion uncertainly.

"Here they are, Tom. All the information I possess on the five subjects."

Around her wrists rested five black rings. In a smooth gesture, she spun them around her fingers and touched my hands. The rings danced over onto my wrists and settled like so many plastic bracelets, two on the left, three on the right.

"And now I must go. The skies will be clear tomorrow, and my enemies will be ready."

She leaned forward and gave me a gentle hug. Her lips brushed my cheek and our eyes locked for an instant. I let out a long sigh. Suddenly I felt ashamed of my distrust.

"Omara Omara, there's so much more to . . ."

"It's late, Tom. You must go. I must go."

I shook my head.

"All this equipment will self-destruct after I pass through. It isn't safe for you to stay here."

That was all she said. She turned back to her tangle of gear and made several more quick adjustments. A large screen lit up. Colors swam across it and then coalesced into an image of bright daylight, but the scene was skewed somehow, as if the tones weren't quite right and the angles were a little off.

The more I stared at it, the more I knew it was not a picture of Earth. And then Omara stepped into it—no, through it—like an open window.

She surveyed the place for a moment and then turned back to me one last time. Over her shoulder, a huge planet appeared through the clouds on the horizon. The scene began to break up, swirling and fading away. I couldn't hear anything, but Omara looked right at me and mouthed very clearly the word "Go."

My feet refused to move. I'd not only come to trust her, I liked her. There was more to her than skin-deep beauty— an intelligence, however alien, that I could understand and appreciate.

I raised my hand to wave, and three rings slid down my arm. As I realized what she'd done, a wave of outrage washed over me. I shouted at the screen.

"Hey! How am I supposed to use these things? Omara!"

A sudden overload sent sparks scattering around me. The screen blanked with a loud pop. I stood in the middle of the tinder-dry floor and stared at those plastic loops. They could have come from a toy store. They would cost me my career.

At least my feet had sense enough to carry me out of there. I nearly reached the car when the barn exploded into a ball of fire.

"You've been had, Tom." Jim Brewster laughed from across my dinette and poured me another beer. "Your eyeballs in the sky turned out to be nothing more than plain old sun dogs. Rare in color, but otherwise absolutely normal."

Omara's barn-burning finale was two days past, but its jinx on my life was far from over. My car had refused to run for me ever since, and Diversified's auditory axe would likely fall soon. About the only good thing—I think—was Jim's refusal to let me go out and lie down across the railroad tracks.

"But you told me that blue sun dogs were impossible," I said.

"Not impossible. Improbable. We had to dig pretty deep to understand them, but one of the boys came up with a polarizing wave integrator while we were at it. I think it might have some interesting applications as a replacement for microwave cooking or a localized anesthetic field. And we've got some new ideas in photonics, too—bizarre, but exciting."

"Like a woman with blue skin."

Jim smiled and raised his glass in mock toast.

"I've got to hand it to her on that one. If she was as well made up as you said, she must have been a sight."

"She was more than a sight. How do you explain her eyes and lips and under her nails?"

"I don't. But for the stuff she conned you out of, I'd say she could buy one sophisticated load of cosmetics." My stomach was sour enough. I would have been happy for Jim to stop. "And what about those bracelets she gave you? As far as we can tell, they're about as common as cheap jewelry. There's some residual radiation in the one we tested, but she probably got them from a contaminated dump."

"Common, huh?" I raised my arm to stare at them. "They cost me forty thousand apiece."

"Well, they're the least of your problems, Tom. I wouldn't give them another thought."

I wanted to cry, but, after all, Jim was trying to cheer me up.

Sometime in the middle of the night I woke up in my own bed with the worst hangover in history. I remembered leaning on Jim and stumbling down the hall. Old Brewster, grouch and good friend, had bruised my ego and prodded my subconscious into actually sorting things out. I knew what had really happened.

He'd been partly right. I'd been conned. The sun dogs were nothing alien or contrived. Omara must have known about them and used them to up the ante. And I faced major misappropriation charges over the lost equipment.

But Omara was no spy, corporate or otherwise. I figure she had found herself stuck on this planet with little or no resources. Maybe she'd come specifically to pull off a scam, the next stop on the low-life circuit of galactic backwaters.

And I can't really blame her just because she's alien.

It's not as if we don't have our own share of shysters. Whatever the case, I was her ticket to the next stop down the line. Only that's where she made her mistake.

She knew about humanity, about our technology, but she wasn't an expert. I gave Omara what she asked for. But I doubt if her specifications took into account a second-rate part here, a cut-rate, knock-off imitation there. She conned me, but I accidentally tripped up the con.

Sure, her contraption worked. She stepped into another world. But there was something else as well. It just took my brain a while to recognize it.

That blue body of hers confirms it. Except for the color, it would have passed perfectly among us. She's a smart one, Omara, and she prepared herself for each scam. If she expected to reuse that body, she expected another humanoid civilization. But that body won't do her much good in that world beyond the window.

Why? Because of that planet that rose in the sky behind her. At first I believed it was another aspect of strange in a strange place. I was right and wrong. It was strange, but it wasn't a planet. It was an eye.

I hope Omara can run.

So, Jim was wrong about one more thing. Omara played more than a cosmetic confidence game, and she really did leave me a note that day.

With five rings I can afford to experiment a little. For one thing, my mechanic says my car is just fine. It just won't start when I'm in it. So, I think I'll test a ring for magnetic field disturbance—something in the range of a fuel injector circuit. And I can check into that parts list for a window to the universe—I've got a friend out there I'd like to look up one day. Sounds crazy, I know, but that *is* the way we work at Diversified.

Write from the Heart

by
R. García y Robertson

About the Author

Rod Garcia, who writes under the name R. García y Robertson, first came to our pages with "Black Sun and Dark Companion," an immensely enjoyable science fiction/horror story which appeared in Volume IV. Since that time, Rod has gone on to a very promising career with over twenty short story publications in the past four years, including lead and cover stories for both Asimov's and Fantasy and Science Fiction.

His first novel, The Spiral Dance, has received wide acclaim. Kirkus Reviews called it, "surely the best debut of the year." His novel American Woman is forthcoming from William Morrow.

Rod lives in Washington State with his wife and children. Though he has a Ph.D. from UCLA in the history of science and technology, he is now a full-time writer, and we are all enriched by that.

The single best piece of advice I
can give to a new writer is this: Decide what
type of story *you* want to write, then *write from
the heart*.

There is a terrific temptation for new writers to say, "I
know what story I want to write—one that sells!" But writing does not work that way. Not for most of us. To find out
"what sells" all you need do is pick up a novel or magazine.
The real problem for a writer is not to psych out the markets,
but to cultivate your own creative spark. Whenever I
write a strong, heartfelt story—one that cries out, demanding to be written—it always does well. Whenever I write a
"good solid, commercial" story—it is often hard as hell to
sell. My reject files are full of them.

The story I wrote for the Contest, published in *L. Ron
Hubbard Presents Writers of The Future, Volume IV* is an
excellent example. I usually work from detailed historical
settings, or realistic SF futures—but "Black Sun and Dark
Companion" was a completely "cut-loose" story. I decided
to write only what I felt, not worrying about setting, or
markets. "Black Sun" was set on a burnt-over planet in a
far off universe (whatever that means) with only one completely human character. I thought the story was too bizarre
to really make it. Instead it won me a second place in
L. Ron Hubbard's Writers of The Future Contest, and
unlocked a whole new galaxy of writing for me. It was my
"third sale" that qualified me for full membership in SFFWA,

and my first non-magazine sale—a pivotal story as far as my career is concerned.

1) *So what type of story should I write?*

This is a very personal decision. One of the biggest benefits from Writers of The Future is going to the week-long workshop. We stayed in Malibu for a week (without ever opening a wallet), while we got in-depth tutoring from SF pros, including Algis Budrys, Orson Scott Card, and Kristine Rusch. This workshop helped me define the type of story I wanted to write. I realized I felt most comfortable with classic stories that have a strong, appealing central character— who overcomes grave crises through change, growth, and discovery. Algis Budrys laid out this basic story type in one of his lectures. I was not comfortable with straight horror— though many horrid things happen to my characters. Nor did I want to write broad comedy—though my stories always include humor. And I did not have the knack for romance— though love and sex are basic elements in my fiction. I just *liked* science fiction/fantasy adventure in the classic mold.

Other people will like other stories. You can make a lot of money writing horror, romance, or techno-thrillers—but I have had to leave those markets untapped. They are not what I want to write. So you need to find *your* own story and tell it. Don't be imitative. Trying to write the ultimate Heinlein or Tolkien clone is the kiss of death. But it is perfectly fair to say, "This is my twist on an old tale—take it or leave it."

2) *Writing from the heart.*

The advantage of writing what you want to write is that it unblocks the creative juices—allowing stories to burst out. When I got back from the Writers of The Future workshop, I looked over my files of story ideas, trying to see which plots or settings grabbed my fancy. In my files was a two-page account of a Catholic rebellion in 16th century England, called the Rising in the North. The incident that intrigued me was the story of how the leaders of the rising fled into Scotland, where Countess Anne of Northumberland lost her horse, her husband, her gowns and her jewels to Scots border bandits. She ended up spending Christmas in a bandit's hovel. Exile stories, *a la Casablanca*, etc., have always fascinated me. (Perhaps because I am named for the most famous Spanish exile—Rodrigo Diaz, El Cid.) This particular exile story had great comic-adventure possibilities, but it lacked two things to make it an adventure fantasy. (1) It had no fantasy elements—not so much as an elf. (2) And there was no character change, leading to any kind of upbeat resolution.

Very often the best way to fix a story idea is to "combine the weak points." I decided to introduce a fantasy element, and make Anne's acceptance of that fantasy element her salvation—she cannot save herself until she overcomes her Catholic bigotry, accepting the notion that people may worship the same thing in different ways. It gave the story growth, change, and a satisfactory ironic climax.

Once I had molded the original incident into *my type of story,* the tale began to write itself—characters, dialogue and dramatic scenes began to pop into my head as fast as I could get them onto paper. This is one key to creativity—make sure you are writing what you *want* to write, not what you *should* be writing. Since the basic story conflict was between Anne's blind Catholicism and older pagan elements, I titled the story "The Auld Religion." *Fantasy and Science Fiction* made it their lead story for the January 1990 issue.

Another good technique is to leave your stories somewhat open-ended. In real life, characters never resolve all their problems. This leaves open the possibility for sequels, novels, series, etc.—if you like your characters, and want to see more of them, maybe the reader will too. When I sat down to write a Countess Anne sequel, I stuck to the principle that "whatever is hinted at in the opening must be made manifest by the end." In other words, don't disappoint the reader. I had hinted at Anne's involvement in witchcraft and the dire threat of persecution. So in the sequel—"The Spiral Dance"—I had to deal directly with these themes. In "Spiral Dance" Anne is not just threatened, she is seized and accused of witchcraft. In a dungeon torture session she is forced to proclaim her belief in the Goddess Mary, even though it means burning at the stake. Only offering up her life and accepting her faith in Mary sets her free at the end of the story. Thus the original theme of "Auld Religion" is taken a step further, and played out against higher stakes.

"Spiral Dance" is true to its characters and setting. You cannot discuss the 16th century witch burnings without admitting the role of torture. (If you do not believe me, read the classic work in the field, *The European Witch Craze*, by H. R. Trevor-Roper.) For me, the only honest way to bring this home to the reader was to involve the main character— the person the reader had the most investment in. It was a difficult decision. The torture scene horrified me—and I thought it might be too upsetting for my readers. But I was not going to "prettify" the witch persecutions just to sell a story. Despite these misgivings, I sent "The Spiral Dance" off. *Fantasy and Science Fiction* picked it up for their May 1990 cover story. Chris Miller from Avon books called my agent and asked if I wanted to turn "Spiral Dance" into a novel. If you are true to your vision, good things can happen.

The general techniques of writing—pacing, setting, dialogue, etc.—are fundamental. But they can be studied and learned. All that takes is hard work and the willingness to learn. The stories themselves have to come from within you. So understand what type of story you want to write—then listen for that inner voice. Listen to that voice even if what it says does not sound safe, or marketable. If you stifle that voice, you stifle your writing.

Scary Monsters

by
Stephen Woodworth

ILLUSTRATED BY Yevgeny Rzhanov

About the Author

Steve tells us that he is a third-generation resident of Anaheim, California—home to that cultural mecca of the western world, Disneyland.

As a child, his interests included dinosaurs, Agatha Christie murder mysteries, U.S. presidents and magic—which led him to become a writer of the strange and fantastic. Since graduating from Pomona College as an English major, he has moved to Maine, where he now pursues his writing career.

Steve has held a number of odd jobs—working at an auditorium, at a movie theater and at a bookstore—trying to break into the entertainment industry via the distribution end. Like several others in this anthology, Steve has an interest in acting, and as I write this, he has the lead role at a community theater playing "Dracula," all of which might help you get in the mood for "Scary Monsters," which follows.

• • •

Stephen Woodworth's illustrator is Yevgeny Rzhanov.

"*G*et in, Holly," her mother said, pulling open the closet door. "Quickly."

"Can I take Misty with me?" Holly asked, cradling her doll in her arms.

"Yes, you can take Misty. Now please hurry, honey."

Holly obediently stepped inside. She was tall enough now so that she had to bend over to keep from brushing her head on the hanging coats and dresses inside. She knelt on the floor and looked back up at her mother wistfully. "Mommy?"

Hands trembling, her mother was placing the key in the keyhole on the inside of the closet door. "Yes, honey?"

"Won't you stay here this time?"

Her mother glanced down at her. Though her mother's face was hidden in shadow by the light from the hall behind, her whole silhouette seemed to quiver.

"There's lots of room," Holly insisted, settling herself into one corner and drawing her knees up to her chest to leave a clear space in the closet's center. "We could both play with Misty."

Her mother bent over, kissed Holly on the forehead, and hugged her tightly. "Oh, sweetie, I wish I could," she whispered. Then she gently pushed her daughter back and started to close the door. "Remember to turn the key, Holly. And don't come out till I tell you."

Holly nodded. "Mommy?"

Her mother stuck her head back through the narrow gap of light now entering the closet. "Yes, honey?"

"Is it the scary monster?"

Her mother remained silent for a moment then nodded. "Yes, honey." She glanced fearfully over her shoulder at the thump of heavy, irregular footsteps on the front steps, at the creak of the loose floorboard on the front porch. The line of a tear parted the purple patch on her cheek, and she hastily brushed it away. "Yes, it's the scary monster."

Then the light from the hall narrowed until the closet was sealed in darkness. Holly turned the key.

She sat behind the window like a wax gypsy in an old fortune-telling machine, waiting for me to put a quarter in her slot. Head bowed, pale face shadowed by a fall of curly brown hair, delicate china-white hands resting on an open paperback book. I rapped on the glass and she looked up, startled. The bluish light of the fluorescent lamp above made her face seem even paler, even more statuesque. But pretty. Very pretty.

"Sorry," she said, smiling nervously. "What can I do for you?" Her voice had a tinny quality due to the vent we spoke through.

"Ten on two," I answered, sliding a twenty through the steel trough below. I scanned the inside of the little hut, bounded on three sides by racks of cigarettes, chips, and road maps. "Looks cozy in there," I added as she gave me my change.

She smiled and shrugged. "It's a living."

"What happens if you have to go to the bathroom?" She giggled. "Don't ask."

I chuckled and turned to go back to my car. No one else seemed to be out that night—a little surprising for L.A., even at 2 A.M. I watched her in her little booth as I pumped my gas, and thought about my now-vacant love life. I decided I needed another pack of cigarettes, though I had a carton of Winstons at home. She looked relieved to see me come back.

I opened the box she handed me and shook out a cigarette.

"So, they let you out of there once in a while?" I asked casually, lighting up.

"Oh, once in a while. For good behavior."

Ah, I said to myself, a healthy sense of sarcasm. I like that in a woman. "I'm Doug, by the way. Deliver the *Times*," I announced, nodding towards the newspaper dispenser across the street.

She paused before answering. Uh-oh, I thought, giving me the once-over. Do I get the Good Housekeeping Seal?

"Holly," she answered finally. "Welcome to Insomniacs Anonymous."

I grinned. "Maybe we can share some coffee and No-Doz sometime."

She smirked back at me. "Maybe the Tooth Fairy will run for President."

"We should be so lucky," I said, and teased a laugh out of her. I decided not to rush things. This one might be a keeper. "But the *Times* they are a-callin'. See you 'round, Holly."

"I'll be here, Doug."

I smiled and waved as I left. At least she had the name. That was a foot in the door. And she seemed pretty cool.

Still, as I drove my route that night, I couldn't help wondering how someone could sit in a box for hours without going nuts.

The sudden darkness did not frighten Holly. The blackness was warm, close, comforting. Familiar smells embraced her: The sharp leather tang of her mother's high heels, the acrid miasma of mothballs in her grandmother's woolen coat, the stale aura of cigarettes and beer from her father's ragged military jacket. Just enough light leaked through the crack under the closet door to give soft gray outlines to the objects around her.

Holly hummed tunelessly as she and Misty explored the box of assorted knick-knacks in the corner, picking up items one at a time and feeling them, imagining what they might be. Sometimes Holly played Mommy, and shut Misty in the box, telling her not to come out until it was okay. Some kids at Holly's school said they were scared of closets, said there were monsters in them. But Holly knew they were just being silly. There was no monster in here.

It was outside.

She could hear its leaden, shambling footsteps treading back and forth through the house. "Holly! Holly!" it called, voice slurred, now growling, now pleading. "Come here, girl! Come here and give me a kiss!"

Holly fell silent and leaned against the sturdy wooden closet door, hugging Misty to her chest and listening.

It took two weeks of topping off my tank at 2 A.M. and several boxes of shared donuts before Holly said she'd go out with me. I got Rick to cover my route Saturday night and picked Holly up at her place. As she opened the door, I smiled and flashed the button I'd made at the mall that afternoon: "TOOTH FAIRY IN '92."

"Very funny," she said, nodding appreciatively as she leaned against the door frame. "You know, I could be watching *Tootsie* on cable right now. . . ."

"Yeah, but would you get a free meal out of it?"

"Well, since you put it that way . . ."

She locked up and followed me out to my Toyota. It was the first time I'd seen more than the top half of her. She wore a modest but elegant dress which highlighted her slight figure in black satin. Black nylons sheathed lean, smooth legs. And her face—a small red mouth, a straight aristocratic nose, perfectly arched eyebrows. Like a painted porcelain mask. Only the eyes seemed to peek from behind the mask. Brown eyes with large black pupils.

I spent the next couple of hours looking at that face as we ate dinner and danced. I twitched every time she nervously swept back her long, full hair to reveal the pale arc of her forehead. She danced better than any woman I'd ever known, floating in the midst of the cramped dance floor without so much as brushing someone else's shoulder. I put my arm around her waist, and I could feel the delicate impression of her spine through the fabric of her dress and the almost feverish warmth of her skin.

As the crowd began to thin in the club, Holly started to tense, glancing from side to side at the vacant places on the dance floor. "Maybe we should head out," she suggested, shouting in my ear to be heard over Billy Idol's "Rebel Yell."

I looked at my watch. Only midnight—early by my standards. But that was cool. It gave us more time for what I'd planned next. I nodded to her, and we made our way to the door.

She seemed to ease a bit when we got back in my car. "Thanks," she said, smiling adorably. "This was the most fun I've had in a long time."

"It's not over yet," I replied, starting the car.

Her smile wilted a bit. "Oh. Really."

I just grinned mischievously and drove. She began to fidget with her purse, snapping and unsnapping it as she peered at the road ahead. "Where are we going?" she asked as concrete and glass gave way to pine and brush.

"To the top of the world," I said, shifting down as the road began to climb. "Close your eyes."

"*What?*"

"You heard me. It's a surprise."

She looked dubious, but sighed and closed her eyes anyway. "It better be good," she said petulantly, crossing her arms.

"It is."

The car rounded another curve, and the floodlit dome of Griffith Observatory ascended into view. "Don't open 'em yet," I said as I parked the car.

I went around and opened her door. As she got out, I put a hand over her eyes.

"Hey!"

"Just don't want you peeking till it's time." I guided her toward the rail bordering the cliff. She chuckled nervously and put an arm around my waist for support. Below us, the vast, blinking grid of Los Angeles glowed magically beneath its permanent haze of smog. Above us were as many stars as you ever see in Southern California. It was the best view L.A. had to offer.

"Ta-da!" I trumpeted, lifting my hand from her eyes.

She blinked a moment, disoriented, then stared. Her eyes widened. She drew a sharp, deep breath, then another, then another. Then she started trembling and whimpering softly, her eyes roving over the panoramic landscape as if searching for an exit.

My smile died. "Holly, what's wrong?"

Biting the thumb of one hand, she felt for me with the other, unable to tear her eyes from the scene. She dug her fingers into my shoulder and staggered backward to lean against me. "Take me home," she croaked.

"What? Holly, what's the—"

"Take me *home! Take me home!*" she sobbed and beat her fist on my chest.

"*Okay. Okay.*" I glanced around the parking lot. Only a few people were left at that hour—mostly couples—and all of them were staring at us. I patted Holly's shoulder as I guided her back to my car, praying that no one would call the cops.

As I eased her into the passenger seat and turned to go around to the driver's side, I caught a brief peripheral glimpse of the view below. Suddenly, the brilliant patchwork of streets and freeways lining the L.A. basin appeared to stretch and warp upward, expanding, spreading across the horizon like some infinite web. I pictured myself falling . . . falling down between those endless threads of gold . . . into a square of bottomless black. . . .

Then I looked directly at the city, and the impression was gone. I shivered and got in the car. I think I was almost as glad as Holly to be back inside.

We said nothing to each other on the drive back to her apartment. I wanted to turn on the radio, but silence seemed more appropriate.

I pulled in front of her apartment and turned off the ignition. "I—I'm sorry."

"No, it's okay," she said in a distant voice. "Really. Good night." She got out and walked away without glancing back.

Well, so much for that, I thought as I drove home, and felt both frustrated and relieved. When I got back to my apartment, however, the phone was already ringing.

"Holly!" the monster yelled. "Holly! Come when I call, dammit!" It stomped upstairs toward her closet. Holly heard the light pad of her mother's footsteps follow it.

"I told you, Ray," her mother shouted. "She's not here. I left her with Mother—"

"Don't give me that crap, Marie! I'm not buying it this time!" the monster thundered. "Holly!" Its pounding came closer.

"Don't you touch her, Ray! Don't you dare—"

"Get off! I only want to give her a kiss. She's mine just as much as yours.   Holly!"

Holly reached up, grabbed the tail of her daddy's army jacket, and pressed it against her cheek like a security blanket. She wished Daddy were here now. All she really remembered about him was the feel of his strong shoulders as he carried her around and the gentle lull of his voice when he read her storybooks.

But surely he would know what to do about the monster.

• • •

Illustrated by Yevgeny Rzhanov

"Agoraphobia."

"Niagara-*what?*" Rick's brows knit over the rims of his ever-present dark glasses.

"Agoraphobia," I repeated, explaining it to him as Holly had to me that night two weeks before. "Fear of wide open spaces. She'd freak if she came in this warehouse."

"No shit?" He clucked his tongue and shook his head as he went back to stuffing the Sunday *Times*. "Doug, m'boy, sounds like you got another psycho-chick on your hands. Stoke-*moi* some more 'Calendars,' willya?"

I tossed him a bundle. "Yeah, well at least she's not a juicer," I countered, referring to Kris, my ex. I aborted that relationship shortly after Kris commented casually that, though the doctors had prescribed Valium to help her control her drinking, she'd taken thirty that day without any noticeable decrease in her desire for alcohol.

"No, she's a friggin' schizo-Niagara-phobic. She'll creep up on you in the middle of the night sometime and slice you up like Freddy Krueger." He waved his X-acto knife at me for emphasis, then used it to cut open the bundle. "Don't say I didn't warn you."

I tried to laugh, but it came out as a snort. "Shouldn't be that bad. Long as I keep her away from state parks, stadiums, large movie theaters, rooms bigger than a bread box. . . ."

"Whoops! Scratch that honeymoon at the Grand Canyon," Dave interjected.

"What's she look like, anyway?" Stan asked.

I dug out a photo Holly and I had taken in a machine at the mall a week earlier and passed it around. Most of the guys just nodded or shrugged. Rick sighed and shook his head again as he studied the picture. "Another flat one," he muttered as he handed the photo back. "I just hope she gives a good one, bro, know-what-I-mean?"

My jaw tightened, but I didn't let myself say what I had

in mind. I merely nodded and smirked, content in the knowledge that I had a B.A. in Communications from Berkeley and
they were mostly high school drop-outs, and that therefore
their opinions did not amount to a heap of ferret droppings.
Yet I had the same lousy job they did, so who was I to talk?

Still, I felt uneasy as I climbed the stairs to Holly's apartment the following afternoon. Agoraphobia. It seemed a harmless enough handicap—as if she had diabetes or something,
I told myself. I'd have to make certain adjustments, but I could
live with it . . . couldn't I? After all, Holly had.

I hesitated a moment outside her apartment door while
I tried to shake off the frown I felt creeping across my face.
Then I rang the bell.

I always had the sense that she was watching me through
the peephole even before I pushed the button. For a split
second, I seemed to see myself as she must have seen me—
my forced smile stretched wide and malefic by the fisheye
lens, nose growing hideously large as I leaned in and waved,
body small and squat below the harlequin face. I almost felt
her flinch back as I stuck my eye right up against the peephole and said, "Hey-ho! Anybody in there?"

An awkward pause followed, during which, I suspect,
she had second thoughts about letting me in. Soon, however,
she undid the Fort Knox assortment of chains and locks she
had on the door. The door opened just enough to reveal Holly's
pale, smiling face. "Peekaboo," she said, eyes gleaming.

"Do I pass security, or do you want to frisk me first?"
I asked suggestively as I squeezed through the opening
sideways.

"Hmmm. Sounds tempting," she replied, then rose on
tiptoes to give me a kiss. She broke it off prematurely, however,
in order to shut and lock the door behind me.

I blinked while my pupils swelled in the sudden darkness.
I don't think Holly had a light bulb bigger than 60 watts in
the whole place. To make matters worse, she had draped

paisley fabric over some of the lamp shades and most of the walls, dousing the apartment in a pinkish pall. The patches of wall that weren't covered with cloth had posters plastered over them, as if blank space were some kind of sin.

Holly scampered toward the kitchen, and I followed her, pulling a beer from the fridge as she stirred spaghetti sauce at the stove. I stepped up behind her and lightly kissed her ear. "So, what's cookin', Doc?"

She giggled. "Something edible, I hope—Wellington!"

The black-and-white demon she called a cat had jumped up on the counter and was stalking the strained spaghetti. She scooped him up in her arms and asked me to keep an eye on the sauce. "He just wants some food, don't you, tiger?" she cooed, nuzzling the beast in a nauseatingly coy manner that made me extremely jealous. Grumbling, I reluctantly set my beer on the counter and stirred the sauce.

As soon as the dear Duke had his feast of Friskies in front of him, Holly set the table for us lowly humans. I turned to grab my beer, and found a shiny, plastic coaster beneath the perspiring can. Coasters had a way of materializing like that around Holly's place. Like my mom, Holly was a neatness freak. I chuckled, and took both coaster and can to the table.

We sat down to our spaghetti, making small talk and exchanging coy glances while we ate. This was the "quality time" we spent together before we both had to go to work. We got on the subject of high school, and I was fondly reminiscing about the substitutes we used to torment.

". . . so he comes back in, slams his book on the counter, and almost *screams,* 'Where the *hell* is my *desk?*'" I quoted in my best Mr. Herman whine. But the expected laugh didn't follow.

In fact, Holly wasn't even looking at me. She was staring at the carpet, but her eyes seemed to focus beyond that, as if she were looking through the floor. She swept her hair back from one ear, a nervous habit she had when she wanted to hear something better, but she didn't notice that I had stopped talking.

"Something wrong?" I asked.

"Hmm? Oh, sorry. What did you say?" She leaned forward attentively.

"You okay?" I asked again, regarding her seriously.

"Yeah. Fine," she answered, prodding her spaghetti.

"You sure?"

"Sure," she said with a nervous chuckle and a shrug.

I halfheartedly finished my substitute story while she nodded and murmured "Uh-huh." I might as well have sung "The Twelve Days of Christmas," though, because her gaze continued to stray around the room anxiously, as if looking for a chink in her armor of paisley prints and posters. She shifted in her seat uncomfortably, and poked at her food.

Finally, I sighed and dropped my fork on my plate. "Holly, what *is* it?"

She cleared her throat and massaged her temples with her fingertips. "Nothing. Just a little headache, that's all." She drew a sharp breath. Her gaze went to the ceiling, to the floor, to the wall, to me. I knew that look—she was having one of her "attacks." "I'm sorry, Doug, I guess I'm just not feeling too good," she began. "Could you—?"

"Leave? Like last week?" I asked a bit more harshly than I intended. "Is this going to be a regular thing with us? 'Excuse me while I have a nervous—' Holly, what's wrong?"

Gasping, she pressed her hands to her ears. "Don't you hear it?" she breathed.

In the pause that followed, I held my breath and listened. For a moment, I didn't hear anything, and didn't expect to. Then I seemed to catch a muffled seashell roar coming from somewhere below us, so soft that it seemed more of an after-impression than a real sound, like the lingering whisper in your ears following a thunderclap. Holly, however, shrieked as if it deafened her. She jumped from her chair, whimpering "I'm sorry, I'm sorry," and ran from the room, hands clamped on her ears.

"Holly!" I called, and started after her. As I got to the door, though, something about the room behind made me do a double take. Possibly due to a change in air pressure, the paisley sheets adorning the walls seemed to have billowed outward, expanding and blurring the contours of the room. It became difficult to tell where one wall left off and the next began. I traced the chaotic pattern of the print and it seemed to go on and on and on. I felt myself sagging against the doorjamb, gripping it tightly, because I looked and looked and the pattern never ended.

A door slammed in the bedroom, and I snapped back to reality. I had to find Holly, I told myself as I ran toward the sound. And I had to get out of that living room, though I didn't admit that at the time.

I rushed to the bedroom, but Holly wasn't there. *Maybe she went to the bathroom instead,* I thought, but I didn't move to find out. The bedroom, like the living room, looked *wrong* somehow. As if everything in it had been subtly rearranged. The bed, the dresser and the chair seemed to lean away from each other, leaving a spreading vacuum of emptiness in the center of the floor. Darkening gaps had formed in the tightly packed assortment of books, stuffed animals and knick-knacks lining the shelves, as if the objects were repelling each other to the point of exploding.

"Holly!" I called, surprised at the quaver in my voice.

She didn't answer, but I heard that muffled roar from beneath the floor again. The sound defined itself into a shout, but muted, as if the person were stifling himself with a pillow. I was trying to make out the words when another sound caught my attention.

A tiny whimper from the bedroom closet.

"*Holly?*" I asked in disbelief, approaching the closet door.

The whimper stopped. Only a brittle silence answered, broken by the faint shouting below.

"Holly?" I tried the doorknob and found it locked. I rapped on the door. "Holly, it's me, Doug. Open up."

Nothing.

For a moment, I got the same impression that I had outside the front door: She was in there, watching me, sizing me up . . . deciding my fate. I suddenly became irritated. I bit my lip, and knocked harder. "C'mon, Holly! It's *me,* for Christ's sake!"

Pause. The bedroom dimmed, and I fought the urge to glance over my shoulder at the pulsing blank space on the floor. A key turned in the door's lock. The door opened a crack, and one misty, glistening eye peered out from knee-level. "Doug?" she whispered.

I saw that eye and felt my stomach constrict. Needles of fear, pity, sadness, and dread pricked my skin. I wondered if Anne Frank had looked like that when the Nazis finally found her. I cleared my throat and forced myself to smile. "Yeah, Doug. You were expecting, maybe, the Avon Lady?" I tried to chuckle, but only coughed.

Opening the door just wide enough for me to slip through, Holly started desperately tugging my arm, pulling me down into the closet. "Come *on,* Doug—it's *coming!*" she pleaded.

"What, in there? You've got to be—Holly!" I tried to yank her out into the room.

"No!" she shrieked, and let go. She was about to slam the door again, but I put my foot in the way.

"All right, all right," I said soothingly, and started to crawl inside. Before I could react, she yanked me off-balance and sent me stumbling among hanging skirts and blouses. The door slammed behind me, and the key turned in the lock.

I tried to sit up as best I could, scrunching myself in

a corner and carelessly shoving aside the flattened shoes I'd sat on. I had to tilt my head forward to keep from brushing against the hems of the blouses above me. I blinked and rubbed my eyes, but I might as well have been blind. From the opposite corner came the rabbit-quick panting of Holly's breath.

"Well," I said to the darkness in the other corner, "here we are."

She shifted position, but didn't answer.

I sighed. "You know, in most cases I would think this was kinda kinky, but—"

Nothing.

I dropped that thought, and decided on a different tack. "If you want to . . . you know, just talk or something . . . I'd like to . . . Ow!" Claws sank into my thigh, and I realized that Duke Wellington, the demon-cat, was in there as well. I swatted him aside and swore. "*Christ!*" Exasperated, I sat up and reached for where I thought the key should be.

"No!" she gasped. Her delicate hand locked around my wrist like a manacle.

I shook her off. "*What?* What *is* it, Holly?"

"Don't you *hear* it?" she asked.

I stopped short. I knew what she meant, and, yes, I could hear it. "Yeah. Someone downstairs is having a fight. So?"

"It never stops," she said wistfully. But I wasn't sure she was talking to me.

"Look, if *you* want to worry about other people's problems—fine! Let's do it outside." I grabbed the doorknob and shook it, vainly hoping I could jar the door open without unlocking it.

"Stop, please!" Holly screamed and pulled my hand from the knob. She kissed my hand then pressed it against her cheek as she began to cry, muttering "Please, please."

"*Okay, okay,*" I whispered. I put my arms around the blackness where I felt her to be. She sank against my shoulder and hugged me tightly. "It's okay," I murmured and rocked her gently back and forth. "It's okay."

But I don't think she really believed that. I know I didn't.

The monster roared. Glass shattered. Mommy screamed.

"It'll be over soon," Holly whispered in Misty's ear.

"Where is she, Marie?" the monster demanded. "Under here?" A wooden groan, then a crash rang in the air. "No? Over here?" A shrill creak and a thud followed.

"Stop, Ray! Just stop!" her mother shrieked.

"Getting warm, am I? What about here?" Another crash.

"That does it, Ray! I'm calling the cops!"

"You do that, Marie. You just go ahead and do that. Get off my back."

The monster's heavy footsteps grew louder. Two lines of darkness divided the narrow thread of light leaking under the closet door. The footsteps stopped.

Holly shrank farther into the corner.

The doorknob rattled violently, then fell silent.

"Holly?" the monster murmured, its voice unnaturally calm. "You in there? Open up, baby, it's me."

Holly sat perfectly still, but her heart raced. Something about that voice . . .

"Holly?" There was a tremor in the voice this time. "Come on, baby, it's Daddy. God, it's been so long. . . ."

Holly trembled. Daddy? Could it be? The voice . . . but Mommy had said—

The doorknob clattered again. "Please, Holly," the voice croaked.

What if it was Daddy? Holly thought hopefully. What if he'd come to fight the monster? Maybe he'd even brought some of his army men with him to help.

She hesitantly reached toward the key in the door.

"I said come out now, *dammit!" the monster howled, its*

fury returned, and the whole door shook. Holly jerked her arm back as if it had been shocked. "You hear me, you little bitch? Come—Out—Now!"

A shuddering blow struck the door, which buckled. Holly heard its good old wood crackle with the strain.

"Get away from there, Ray," her mother said gravely.

"Marie, didn't I tell you to—" The monster's shout dropped suddenly to a lethal whisper. "Where the hell did you get that?"

"Just get away from there," her mother repeated.

The monster laughed hollowly. "You wouldn't dare," it sneered.

A small click sounded. "Don't push me, Ray, I swear I'll—"

"Come on, then. Come on." Its footsteps thumped away from the door.

"Stay back, Ray! I'm warning you!" Her mother's voice was high and thin.

"You stupid— Give me that!"

There was scuffling down the hall, toward the stairwell. Holly's mother whimpered, then shrieked. A loud bang made Holly's ears ring. The monster let out a pained yowl. It grunted angrily, and her mother screamed. The scream ended with a dull thud.

Holly wanted to cry out to Mommy then, but pressed her hands over her mouth. It was still there.

"Oh, shit," it muttered. It made a soft, regular wheezing sound.

"Oh shit. Oh shit." *She heard it stagger and stumble, the stairs creaking as it went. "Marie? Marie?" It took a few steps, stopped. Took a few steps. Stopped.*

"Marie?" It coughed and spat. "Oh shit."

There was another small thud. Then everything became very, very quiet.

Holly remained perfectly still. She didn't cry out, though tears streamed down both cheeks. She just sat hugging herself, cradled in darkness.

She was still there when the policemen pried open the door.

"And they were both dead," Holly finished hollowly.

She sniffed and leaned her head against my shoulder. The Duke dozed contentedly across both our laps; I guess he'd probably heard the story many times before.

"And you didn't know he was your dad?" Our faces were so close now that I thought I could actually see the nervous twitch of her thin lips, the withdrawn stare of her glazed eyes in the darkness.

She sighed. "Nope. Mom never talked about him, and Grandma didn't tell me the truth until I was fourteen." She paused, and I felt a current of warm breath brush past my neck. "He left when I was two. Mom only said he had to go somewhere and might not be back for a long time. I waited and hoped. He never came." She let out a giggle that was almost a sob. "But the scary monster did," she said, and began to cry again.

"Jesus, Holly," I breathed, and hugged her. I wanted to say something wise, supportive, and compassionate, but everything I came up with sounded like the cheap sympathy of a Hallmark card. I figured it would be better just to hold her and keep my mouth shut.

We sat like that for several minutes, arms around one another, as her crying gradually exhausted itself. When it was over, she brushed my cheek with her hand and whispered, "Thank you for staying."

I touched her face and began to guide my mouth toward hers for a kiss when Wellington suddenly decided to sharpen his claws on my chest. Holly laughed, this time without tears. I grumbled, then started laughing, too. "Come on, let's get out of here," I said cheerily and leaned toward the doorknob.

Holly caught hold of my shoulder and held me back. *"Wait."*

I waited, and we listened. The people downstairs had apparently called a truce for the night, and peace reigned once more.

Holly's grip on my shoulder eased. "Okay," she murmured, and unlocked the door.

The sudden flood of light as the door swung open was almost painful, and a minute passed before I could even think of opening my eyes again. The bedroom looked its usual cozy self as I squinted at it now, and I tried to remember what had seemed so weird about it when I first came in. I moved to stand up, and the crick in my neck shot an instant headache to my brain. I had to brace myself against the door because my legs had turned to Jell-O. "God," I moaned, rubbing my face, "I feel like a sardine on parole."

"Yeah, it hurts sometimes," Holly said. She stood with Wellington in her arms, stroking his fur, and looked as fresh and relaxed as if she had just come back from a pleasant forest hike. "You get used to it, though," she added reflectively.

I nodded, and asked for some aspirin. *You get used to it, though.*

I kind of hoped I wouldn't.

On the way down from Holly's later that evening, I happened to pass the apartment directly below hers. The windows were dark, the curtains drawn. On impulse, I paused at the front door and was about to knock, but then chuckled and shook my head. No, I thought, better let them rest in peace. They'd had quite a bout that night. A little embarrassed by my own nosiness, I sighed and looked down at my feet as I turned to go.

And there, sitting beside the welcome mat, one leaning on top of the other, were two newspapers.

I stared at those two newspapers for half a minute or

more, and couldn't figure out what was so God-Almighty amazing about them. As if I hadn't seen newspapers almost every night for the past eight months!

But there were *two* of them. Today's and yesterday's. On the same doorstep. Which meant that—

—no one was home.

I turned and walked away quickly, without glancing back. I was late to work, after all.

Holly and I grew much closer after that. She relaxed and opened up more now that she didn't have to hide her big secret. I coped with her neurotic habit the same way I'd coped with Kris's drinking at first: I ignored it. When Holly went to the closet, I went to work. Out of sight, out of mind.

Except that I still got a queasy feeling in my gut every time I stepped out of my car into a wide, flat parking lot.

We might have gone on blissfully like that for months if I hadn't had the bright idea of talking Holly into coming over to my place for a change one Friday night. Getting Holly to go out *anywhere* was a job for Superman, and it took two weeks of hard-fought wheedling and cajoling to get her to come. Needless to say, I did not take the occasion lightly. I cleaned and dusted the place for the first time since the Reagan administration, and promised not to smoke for the full three hours. I even dug out Mom's old chicken cacciatore recipe, which I whipped up pretty competently once I deciphered her handwriting.

That much of the plan went swimmingly. By eight o'clock, we were cuddling on my Salvation Army sofa with Steely Dan on the stereo. I had my lips pressed to the warm, soft skin of her bare shoulder when I sensed that *it* was about to happen again. Maybe the faint quickening of the pulse in her veins tipped me off.

Or maybe *it* was happening to me too.

My kissing got a bit hotter, my petting a bit heavier, my

touching a bit rougher as I tried to bury the thought in what I was doing. But Holly pushed me away, maneuvering her face to avoid mine.

"No . . . *no,* I can't. . . . I've got to go," she whined.

"What?" I asked impatiently. But I knew what. I could hear them. Angry voices below us.

She looked away. "It's coming," she said softly.

"Oh, *Christ,* Holly!" I stood up. "You're twenty-three now, for God's sake. How long is this gonna go on?"

"I'm sorry, I just . . ." she mumbled as she tried to pass me.

I blocked her with my arm and pointed to the sofa. "No, we are going to talk about this right now."

"Couldn't we . . . later . . ."

"No. Look, Holly, your father is *dead.* . . ."

Her eyes narrowed. "You think I don't know that?"

"You act like you don't. Maybe you should see some-one—"

She let out a loud, humorless laugh. "I've 'seen' plenty of people. What about *you?*"

Before I knew I had done it, I slapped her across the face. Hard. I slapped her because she had agoraphobia, because my friends made fun of me for it, because she interrupted our lovemaking to go run in a closet. But mostly I slapped her because I remembered that this was *my* apartment, which was on the ground floor, because something was now pounding up stairs that didn't exist, because the dimensions and perspectives of the room around us had swelled with the queasy sensation in my stomach, and I just wanted it all to stop.

The look on Holly's face chilled me. Not one of shock. One of *recognition.*

"Oh, God, Holly, I'm sorry," I whispered.

She glared at me, then ran past.

"Holly!" I called.

Holly! another voice said, but distorted, as if on a record played at half-speed. It came from behind me, and I whipped around to face it. There was nothing there, but I had the impression that the roof had buckled outward as something tried to pry its way in.

A door slammed to my right. I thought it might be Holly, but when I turned I found myself facing a solid wall. I suddenly felt disoriented and helpless in my own living room.

I ran the direction Holly had gone. She must've discovered that my closet didn't have a lock, for she'd sealed herself in the bathroom instead. I rapped on the door. "Holly, please let me in."

No reply. *She hates me now,* I thought morosely.

Behind me, glass smashed and furniture toppled as the voice moved back and forth through the apartment, growling semi-intelligible words like a gorilla learning to speak.

I leaned against the bathroom door, gasping. "I believe you, Holly," I said. "I believe you."

The door eased open, and I took my cue to creep inside. I hugged Holly tightly and sighed. "I never wanted to hurt you. Can you forgive me?"

After a pause, she hugged me back. "Yes." Another, longer pause followed. "Can you forgive *me?*" she asked, as the voice outside swelled in our ears.

"Yes."

But I wasn't so sure when we finally came out of the bathroom. The scene in my apartment was far worse than I had imagined.

Nothing. Not a shard of shattered glass or splinter of broken furniture anywhere. The apartment was as clean as I'd made it that afternoon. Which meant only one thing.

I was going nuts.

I took several deep breaths and tried to hold back the tears of panic in my eyes. *You get used to it, though,* I thought.

"I'm sorry, Doug," Holly murmured.

• • •

"Looking a little pale, there, Doug, m'boy," Rick commented at work the following night. " 'Hot Holly' more than you bargained for, eh?" He laughed, and wiped off the top of his Pepsi can with the tail of his Metallica T-shirt.

I massaged my forehead. "You could say that," I answered in a strained voice. Rick adding his barbs to the other thoughts needling my brain was like giving acupuncture to a pincushion.

"How is it going, anyway?" Dave asked. "You haven't said two words about her in over a week."

That's 'cause it's none of your goddam business, I thought, then checked myself. Dave was an okay guy. But I still wanted to smack him and all the rest of them upside the head.

"Great," I answered curtly as I finished stuffing another bundle of the Sunday edition. "Three months and going strong."

Rick whistled sarcastically. "Three *months?* Call Guinness, guys. We got a record." Everybody laughed and clapped.

I forced my grimace into a smirk. "Yeah. And your last relationship was all of—twenty minutes, was it?"

Rick shrugged. "Guess I'm just a rolling stone. How's the Niagara-phobia, anyway?" he added without a beat.

I winced and ground my teeth. "Not bad. How's your coke habit?"

The snickering around us died out. Rick shot me an angry glance over the tops of his dark glasses. "Just watch your mouth there, bro."

"Practice what you preach, bro." I licked a drop of sweat from my upper lip and narrowed my eyes against the suddenly harsh light of the fluorescent bars above us.

"Hey, guys, lighten up," Stan cut in with a forced laugh. "Or we'll have to flog you with the Fashion section." The other guys gave an encouraging chuckle. Rick just stared at me. "Rick?" Stan prompted, nudging his shoulder.

Rick shrugged and pushed his glasses back up to the bridge of his nose. "Hey, man, it's not my problem. He's the one with the psycho girlfriend."

I stood up, letting a pile of newspapers slide off my lap. Rick got up, too, and suddenly it seemed as if we were all alone, two gunfighters standing off on a vast plain of concrete littered with newsprint. I realized I still had my X-acto knife in my hand. Distantly, I heard Stan say, "Easy, Doug, you know he didn't . . ." Then he was drowned out by a low growl that echoed off the warehouse walls, which were very far away.

I dropped the knife and ran to the small, scummy bathroom the *Times* had thoughtfully provided us. I rushed inside the first stall and slammed the door shut, sitting on the toilet without even wiping the seat. Breathing hard, I leaned on one side of the stall and pressed my hand to its close, comforting metal.

I heard the bathroom door open. "Doug? You okay?" Stan asked in a voice made hollow by the enclosed space.

I held my breath, and drew my legs up to my chest so my feet wouldn't show below the stall's door. I sat silently until the bathroom door squeaked shut. I didn't move again for several minutes.

I got Stan to take my route that night, telling him I felt as if I were about to puke. The drive home was like doing Disneyland on acid. Red stoplights dipped toward me out of nowhere. The road outside the circle of my headlights appeared to drop off into nothingness. Jagged silhouettes of buildings parted before me as if they were the teeth of a gigantic zipper. Glaring straight ahead through the windshield, I watched the dark world refract and flow around me, like a goldfish that swims around its bowl and always ends up at the same place.

When I finally made it back to my apartment, I went straight to bed, praying for a good night's unconsciousness.

Instead, I lay there rigid for an hour, staring at the ceiling which looked too far away.

I know what'll help you sleep, a mocking voice in my skull said. It sounded just like Rick. *That closet over there looks mighty comfy, doesn't it? I bet if you curled up in there, you'd be out like a light in no time. . . .*

I wrapped my pillow around my head and hummed Beatles songs to stifle the voice. After an hour or so, boredom finally worked its merciful magic and I dozed off. And dreamed.

Holly and I were running down a long corridor, bordered on both sides by rows of identical doors, its end a vanishingly small point in the distance. Behind us, I heard a distant growl, like the rumble of a subway train approaching its station. I didn't look back.

Holly kept stumbling and crying as I tried to drag her along faster and faster. The ceiling disappeared in shadow above us as we ran, and the sides of the corridor grew farther apart, leaving us in a spreading chasm of barren hallway. I expected a huge crack to break in the floor and swallow us whole.

In desperation, I yanked open the door nearest to us. It led to a closet. I pulled open another one. Coats swung on hangers inside. Holly pleaded for us to crawl inside and hide, but I held her back and dragged her across the widening hall to another door. I twisted the knob and pulled, and the rancid smell of mothballs poured out. The growl behind us swelled to a roar. More doors, more closets. Holly screamed and clawed at my face. The walls of the corridor looked as if they were about to fall off into space, letting in the surrounding void—and, with it, the thing that made the hall vibrate with its cry.

On the opposite wall, now almost a football-field away, I saw a door with a tiny spot of green light over it. Instinctively, I began a determined sprint to it, my fingers locked

around Holly's cold, frail wrist. The door receded even as
we raced toward it, but the green letters above it started to
come into focus: EXIT. I felt the floor quiver as another deaf-
ening wail engulfed us. I closed the gap to the door—which
opened *inward*—and pushed it open. Behind it was a
frightening vacuum of opaque blackness. But no coats. No
shoes. No walls.

"Holly—!" I breathed excitedly, and turned to face her.
I found myself looking at a creature of congealed darkness,
its burning white eyes staring at me, its bony claw still tightly
gripped in my hand. . . .

I woke, gasping, and the after-image of those white eyes
glared down at me from the ceiling. I lay panting on the
sweat-dampened sheets and thought, *This has to stop. I have
to stop it now.*

I considered not even calling her again. That had always
been the easiest way in the past—no arguments, no explanations, no apologies. A month of screening the calls on my
answering machine, and that would be it. Quick. Simple.
Painless. It even worked for the first four days I tried it.

Then I heard her voice on the tape.

"Uh, hi, Doug, it's me," she began after the beep. "Is
. . . everything okay? I just haven't seen you all week, is
all." A pause followed—her real message. "Well, anyway,
I just called to see what was up," she went on, a little too
brightly. "'Bye." She lingered on the line a moment more,
then hung up.

I almost called her right then. But I didn't. Instead, I
vegged around my apartment for the next three days, waiting
for her to call again and knowing she wouldn't. She was like
my mother, I thought bitterly, a master of the fine art of
guiltmongering. Oh, if I *really* didn't want to see her, she
wouldn't complain; she'd just quietly cry herself to sleep in
a corner someplace, don't mind her. I pictured Holly, cuddling that cursed cat, her hair hanging in front of her face

in frizzy strands, her eyes watery, her nose red and runny.

So, of course, I went to her apartment.

When she opened the door, she looked so much like my mental image of her that another jolt of guilt rippled through me. Then she brushed her hair back and beamed at me. "Hey!" she greeted, and moved forward as if to hug me, then shied back uncertainly. "Uh, sorry I'm such a mess," she said, glancing down at her baggy tie-dyed T-shirt and ripped jeans, "I didn't know . . ."

"Oh . . . don't sweat it," I said. "You look great." Seeing her then, I didn't know what I wanted to say. Certainly not goodbye.

The first part of the evening passed almost like normal, except that some emotional aura kept us apart. We ate dinner and made small talk, but we never kissed, never touched, hardly met each other's gaze—it felt more like a blind date than "quality time." Afterward Holly conned me into playing checkers, a game she nearly always won, and I was relieved to see her giggle and gloat with her usual sprightliness.

Then I heard the shouting.

I glanced up at Holly, and she quickly averted her gaze, fidgeting in her seat. The room wavered behind her. I shook a cigarette out of my pack, then remembered that Holly hated my smoking, so I sat tapping the thing on the table as I scanned my hopeless position in the game.

An overturned piece of furniture thudded heavily below us, and a woman screamed.

Holly drew a sharp breath and rubbed her temples. As our eyes met, she smiled weakly. But she didn't leave her chair.

Shadows deepened and grew longer as the walls gradually retreated. Irregular but purposeful footsteps pounded up unseen stairs.

I chose a checker at random and moved it, then pressed myself back into my chair, my hands gripping the armrests as if they were safety bars on a roller coaster. Holly mumbled something to herself that I didn't catch. "Your move," I told her.

A door slammed outside the apartment's curtained window, the sound pulsing in my ears with dream-like resonance. The paisley sheets shivered as darkness seeped over them. Holly stared at the table, eyes brimming with restrained tears, and whimpered softly, "Not tonight. Please . . . not tonight."

I wanted to cry, too. She was trying so hard. So was I.

"Holly . . ." I began.

Holly! an angry voice echoed.

That did it. She bolted for the bedroom. I jumped from my chair and managed to grab her around the waist. We pitched forward and landed on the floor in a wriggling embrace.

"*No!*" she shrieked. "*Let me go!*"

"Holly, wait—*listen* to me!" I tried to turn her to face me. "We can't *live* like this—"

She grabbed a fistful of my hair and yanked. I yelped in pain, and she squirmed free. She got to her feet and headed for the bedroom.

Part of me wanted to leave. But I think if I had, I would only have ended up in another closet.

I scrambled to my feet and sprinted after Holly. The bedroom seemed about to dissolve, its walls undulating like a desert mirage. Holly was half-inside the closet as I came and pushed her the rest of the way, shutting the door behind us.

We sat for a minute, panting and listening to the stomp of approaching footsteps, the smash of shattering glass. "Well," I said, my voice quavering as I tried to sound cheerful, "here we are again."

Holly gave an anxious giggle and sniffed. "Yep," she quipped, laughing through her tears. "We've got to stop meeting like this." Then her head drooped onto my shoulder, and she began to sob quietly. "I tried," she whispered.

"I know."

The doorknob rattled.

"Do you want to try again?" I asked gently. I felt her body go rigid in my arms.

Holly? a reptilian voice outside murmured. *You in there? Open up, baby, it's me.*

She whimpered and didn't move. But she didn't say no. "Holly . . ." I prompted.

Holly? the voice oozed. *Come on, baby, it's Daddy. God, it's been so long . . .*

Her fingers tightened on my shoulder. "You can go," she breathed. "It's okay."

"I won't go if you stay."

Please, Holly . . .

I leaned closer to her until my lips almost brushed her earlobe. "I'm scared, too," I whispered. And then I whispered something else.

I said come out now, *dammit! You hear me, you little* bitch! Come—Out—Now!

The door shook with the words, and we cringed. Slowly, I stretched my arm toward the doorknob. I could feel Holly's heartbeat speed up—or maybe it was mine. As I grabbed the knob, she caught hold of my hand in both of hers and pulled it away. Her skin was hot and damp. I sat back, resigned.

Then she drew a deep breath and turned the handle.

The door swung open. The bedroom was gone. We saw only a strip of wooden flooring and, beyond it, a wall of darkness.

And we looked up into the blazing eyes of the scary monster.

The creature towered over us, bloated and black, yet surrounded by an incandescent white aura, like an overexposed film negative. Cold white light shot from its blank eyes and from behind rows of needle-pointed teeth, light that signaled an emptiness that could never be filled. Its mouth opened in a grin. Rivulets of shining mercury drool dripped from its jaws.

It was the boogeyman Holly had made of her father.

Smiling, the thing stretched an arm toward us, claw open. Our backs pressed to the wall of the closet, Holly and I were too paralyzed even to shiver as it reached for us.

Get away from there, Ray, another voice said sternly.

The thing swiveled toward the woman who appeared next to it. She had a bruise on one cheek and a bleeding cut above her eye. She held a pistol straight out in front of her with both hands, barrel aimed at the monster's misshapen head.

"*Mommy,*" Holly whispered. She started forward, eyes glistening.

The creature advanced on the woman, jeering at her and snatching at the gun with its claws. She backed away and cocked the pistol. *Don't push me, Ray, I swear I'll—*

Holly crept forward onto the wooden flooring and stood up. I reluctantly followed her. The thing had cornered the woman against the banister of a stairwell which bordered a limitless cavern of empty space. They grappled. The gun went off like a cannon blast, the shot impacting the monster's chest. Roaring with rage, the thing seized the woman and lifted her, writhing, from the floor.

"*Mommy!*" Holly screamed, and darted toward the two figures.

"Holly, *no!*" I yelled, and tried to catch her. "You can't—" but she was already there.

The monster hurled the woman over the railing, where she vanished in darkness. Holly came up behind it, shrieking, "Stop it! Stop it!" And she laid her hands on its back.

The thing's black hide burned red, then orange, then blindingly white beneath her touch. It wailed in pain, as its massive head deflated and collapsed into its torso. Its legs and arms shriveled and shrunk like burning matchsticks, and it sank to its knees.

The white light dimmed and dissipated. Holly covered her mouth with her hands. Before her kneeled a gaunt, unshaven man with thinning brown hair who wore a pair of shabby fatigue pants and a tank-top with a growing spot of red on it. He gazed up into Holly's face with brown eyes that were infinitely tired.

I had seen eyes like them a hundred times before. The eyes of a Larry Talbot, a Henry Jekyll. They pleaded: *Let me die.*

The man mouthed some words, but only a wheeze came out. Then he fell back against the railing and lay still, eyes open. I can't read lips, but I like to think he tried to say "I'm sorry."

Quaking, Holly bent to touch him, but her hand passed right through his chest. Her fingers touched shag carpeting instead of wooden floorboards. She sat on the floor where he had been and began to cry.

I sat beside her, but I didn't put my arm around her; this was something she couldn't share with me, much as I wanted her to. I watched the familiar walls of Holly's bedroom shimmer back into view as if after a photographer's flash, and wondered if Holly even noticed. She cried longer and harder than I had ever seen her cry before. But this time she was sad, not afraid.

When she quieted to the hiccuping stage, I whispered in her ear. She looked at me, sniffed, and smiled. We got up and went to the apartment's front door. Hesitating only a moment, she opened the door and held it for me, bowing gallantly.

We laughed, then went out and stood under the big blue night sky. Even in L.A., it's something to see.

Pale Marionettes
by
Mark Budz

ILLUSTRATED BY Matthew Stork

About the Author

Mark Budz lives in Eugene, Oregon, where he is a
member of a highly successful writing group that has
included such past winners as Dean Wesley Smith, Nina Kiriki
Hoffman, Gary Shockley, and Lori Ann White.

Though Mark is new to publishing in some ways, he is
not in others. He works for Pulphouse Publishing as editor of
the Short Story Paperbacks, Axolotl Press and Author's Choice
lines of books. He is also managing editor of Pulphouse: A
Fiction Magazine. His first published story, "The War Inside,"
appeared in the premiere issue of Pulphouse: A Fiction Magazine and will be reprinted in Quick Chills II. He has since
sold stories to The Magazine of Fantasy and Science Fiction,
Amazing and Science Fiction Review.

As a fiction writer producing entertainment, you never know
who your audience will be. One reader may want to be immersed
in a strange world, while another admires the beauty of strong
prose, and a third is looking for an author with intelligence

and vision. As an editor, Mark understands this, so this very accomplished story combines all the elements—world creation, pacing, interesting and believable characters, voice, style, theme, and some fascinating ideas.

Mark is of a size that he could probably play professional football on the line if he wanted. Yet, with many other people in this anthology, he also shows that he is a big talent.

• • •

Mark Budz's illustrator is Matthew Stork.

I sat in the bar at the Posada del Mar, head throbbing to sheared-metal vocals, and waited for the Angel of Death to meet with me.

"You want a second beer?" Velasquez, the motel's owner, asked. It was hard to hear him over the high-voltage buzz of the band and the jumbled background noise of the tourists that had hovercrafted over from the north coast of Honduras to the Bay Island of Guanaja.

I looked at the half-empty bottle of Corona where I had been searching for the face of my lost sister Kaja, and shook my head. "Not yet," I said. "Maybe later."

"There's someone looking for you," he said, nodding to the door. "A French *multinacional*. If you want, I can tell him to go fuck himself."

"No," I said. "No obscenities. It might scare off your customers."

Velasquez squinted down at me, the skin around his eyes crinkling like a sun-dried mango rind. "I'm serious," he said. "I have a bad feeling about this job. Are you sure you know what you're getting into, Tomás?"

"I always know what I'm getting into," I said, hoping false bravado would cover the spring-loaded tension in my nerves. I fenced illegal nanoware to the molecular program black market. It gave me a lot more freedom than working for one of the companies that manufactured the stuff, and it paid a lot better because of the risks involved. There was big money to be made on both sides, but if I got caught, no one would bail me out.

"I'm not shitting," he went on. "A *bruja* is nothing to fuck with. They aren't human and they speak with the voices of the dead. If you're not careful, they'll steal away your soul, the way they stole your sister's."

I looked up at him through the thin haze of cigarette smoke and swallowed a sip of beer. "I'll be careful," I said. "Don't worry."

Velasquez looked at me hard, blinked, and finally walked off. We went back eight years. He thought of himself as my big brother because he'd taken Kaja and me in after our parents' helijet crashed on the way back from a Mosquito Coast desalination plant.

Back then, the Posada had been nothing more than a collection of tired bungalows, squatting on the white, palm-shaded sand at Robinson Crusoe Cay. My thoughts clicked on the long beach, the shallow water, and Kaja's face came to me, tossed in with all the other reef treasures I used to find— shells and tiny bits of coral broken off in a storm. I remembered looking into her quiet brown eyes the day she told me she'd decided to join the New Humanity, decided to reshape both her body and her mind in an image created by the society of artificial intelligences now living in orbiting colonies.

The *brujería*.

They had been created from nanotechnological templates of the human brain, templates manufactured by Couette. Kaja had wanted to join her consciousness with the *brujería*, wanted to leave the past behind and shed this life so she could be resurrected into another one, free of the nightmare memories and aborted dreams that had plagued her since the crash.

"Don't go," I had told her a year ago. I had held her arms and tried to make her stay. Once a year, the *brujas* shuttled down to baptize anyone who wanted to join. I could already feel the void that she would leave behind opening up inside me like a wound that would never close. I held her tight, thumbs and fingers pressing into bone beneath her satiny skin, bruising them both, love and selfish desire twisted into anger.

"Don't," she said. "You're hurting me."

"I'm sorry." I forced myself to let go, knowing that part of me wanted to hurt her, make her feel a little of the pain she would be leaving me when she left. Her fingers brushed my cheek, and then she turned and walked away. I knew I would never see her again.

Now, I stared at my hand holding the warm bottle in front of me, at the tattered label I'd been picking at. I could still feel the phantom touch of her fingers, like a dead person's, and taste in my beer the bitterness I felt for the *brujería*.

"Mind if I join you?" I heard a voice say close to me.

The Angel had dressed the enervated tourist part to the hilt. Loose cotton pants and polo shirt. He held a drink in one hand. His hair was rust-tinted and threaded with gray. He had a long smooth face as expressionless as bronze-glazed porcelain. His eyes were gilded hazel, as reengineered and artificial as his skin. I could read nothing in them as he smiled, pulled out the chair across from me and sat down.

I smiled back, lifted the bottle to my lips, and sipped the warm, flat-tasting Corona. The olfactory-pad behind my ear registered the pattern of designer pheromones the telecomm from my Couette contact had said the delivery boy would be wearing. He'd splashed it on like cologne so I'd know he was who he said he was and not some wetware regulatory agent out to bust my ass.

"You still interested?" he asked. He set his glass on the table and idly toyed with it.

"Yes. But to do the job I need to know a little more about what I'll be carrying."

"We can always get someone else." He scooted his chair back.

"You think so?" I waited for him to get up and leave, but he didn't. There were plenty of other fences willing to take the risk, but none that Couette wanted to take a chance on. Once the virus spread, every nanoware regulatory agency and watch group in the world would be trying to find out who had released an unauthorized program into the environment. Couette couldn't afford an information leak that would tie back to them, and I had a reputation for being as leak-proof as they came.

He finished off his drink and twirled the empty glass thoughtfully between his fingers. "The program is a meme-tic pathogen," he began. "A set of destructive ideas we want to implant into the collective consciousness of the *brujería*."

"Go on."

"They're trying to engineer a corporate takeover of Couette Micronics," the man said. "Establish an industrial foothold in the world economy."

I had a feeling there was more to it than that. In creating the *brujería,* Couette had manufactured something they couldn't control or understand and now they wanted to get rid of it out of fear, before things got out of hand.

"Programmable thought," I said. "I was under the impression that that was not possible."

"It's not as hard as you might think. AIs are even easier. Their thought processes are a lot more structured than our own."

"They must have a defense mechanism? An immune system of some kind."

"Yeah. Enzyme subprograms. We're not going to try and completely take over the *brujas'* thought processes, though, simply modify them."

I raised my beer bottle to my lips, felt it vibrating to the heavy undercurrent of the synthesized bass. "To do what?"

The delivery boy grinned, the tight-lipped smile of a snake about to strike its prey. "To kill each other," he said, watching me carefully. Ice rattled in his glass as he twirled it. "Is that a problem?"

I met his gaze, sipped. They weren't human. I'd told myself that a thousand times. They were pale marionettes of the mind they had been patterned after, nothing more than a linked network of computer code that had accidentally achieved a measure of independent awareness. Now, the AIs inhabited the nano-reengineered corpses they'd been installed in, like parasites in an unconscious host, feeding off the remains and searching for converts like Kaja to replenish them.

"No," I said, trying not to think of the alien presence behind my sister's vanished eyes. "What do I have to do?"

He seemed to relax then. "Deliver this." From beneath the edge of the table he produced a tiny loaf of *pan de los muertos*. Bread of the dead.

It was shaped like a human being with arms, legs and orange-bean eyes, and fit in the palm of his hand. The body was swollen and split down the middle. The loaf was supposed to represent a soul, and I imagined the skin of the dead person it symbolized spreading apart to release the spirit contained inside. A tiny blood-red bead sat in the center of the split, at about the point where the dead person's heart would be.

I stared at the bead. "What is it?"

"Thermal plastic around a wetware core. The virus is airborne. Above forty-one degrees centigrade the case will become porous, releasing the program through evaporation. There's a chemical strip inside the bread. All you have to do is twist the body and it'll heat up."

I thought of the sweat-box shanties of Guanaja, hot tin and tarpaper radiating heat into sauna-like rooms. "I don't see any problems," I said.

"You sure?"

Illustrated by Matthew Stork

"Yes. I will ask the *bruja* to save my soul, and in the process destroy hers."

"When?"

"Tonight, when she's taking the souls of converts."

"We haven't discussed payment," he said.

"My regular fee. Five-hundred-thousand International Dollars, credited directly to my Panamanian account."

"All right," the man said. He slid the loaf across the table. "Half now. The balance when we know the program has been delivered."

I picked up the hard bread. The loaf was lemon yellow against my palm. It was spiced with cinnamon, sesame seeds and anise. The heart stared out at me, and the throbbing of my own pulse made it seem alive against my skin.

"How long for it to take effect?" I asked, cradling the doll in my fingers.

The man pushed his chair back and stood. "A few days," he said. "Hours, maybe, depending on how fast they transfer the meme among their host bodies."

I nodded and then he was gone. Lost in the music as if he had never been there, like so many other people who came and went in a kind of phantom dance in which I was the only living participant.

I went back to my room, set the loaf on the night table next to my bed, and lay down. The window was open. Hot air whispered through the slats of the wooden shutter. Outside, I could hear the faraway shouts of children drifting across the blue stained-glass Caribbean, mingling with the smell of decaying palms and ocean garbage that lapped at the edges of Guanaja.

The town was a landfill of ramshackle tin and clapboard buildings that spilled out into the ocean, perched on wooden stilts against the rising waters of global warming. Some of the paint still remained, faded blue, red, green and yellow pastels that clung to the weather-beaten siding, but most of the vitality had rotted away with the wood. Now, the people who stayed there lived in little more than desiccated shells of the past.

I closed my eyes and thought of the *pan de los muertos* lying on the night table. Soon, though, my head filled with images of Kaja paging through the latest vidmag in her room, or picking flowers from the San Juan tree in the backyard of our company home. My chest swelled up tight. I imagined my skin splitting apart, and the memory of Kaja leaving me like some disembodied soul so that all that was left was a vacuum ache pulling at my ribs.

Sweet Kaja. Sucked into an orbiting dream built out of molecular assemblers, artificial intelligence and a promise of new life. At times I wished she had died with our parents, because it would have been easier for me to let her go—to bury her. I imagined the crash in my head. I pictured Kaja's face next to theirs, the helijet falling out of the sky, a bright flare arcing into some jungle hillside. I replayed it a thousand times, unable to stop the unfolding images, and hated the part of myself that wanted to see her dead—her face charred and gone in the Honduran night like a terrible dream I could forget in the morning.

I opened my eyes and sat up. I had dozed. It was four o'clock in the afternoon. Time to get ready. Time to find out exactly what I would be delivering.

I swung my legs over the side of the bed and went to the dresser. My portable disassembler lay in the bottom drawer, the one legacy of my father—and the multinational he had worked for—that I had decided to keep. I pulled the unit out, carried it to the bed and opened the graphite gray case.

The soul doll felt light in my hands, as weightless as a memory. I sat down on the crumpled sheets and stared at the orange beans, the banal heart. I could almost taste the cloying kiss of cinnamon, the sharp bite of anise as I pried the bead out, placed it on a slide and slotted the chip into the machine.

While the disassembler ran I went into the closet-sized bathroom, splashed warm water on my face and changed my clothes. I wanted to look the part of the disaffected North American searching for salvation—absolution. I put on loose cotton pants and a clean T-shirt, a short-sleeve shirt over it, unbuttoned and untucked.

When I stepped out, the analysis was finished. I paged through the readout on the screen, long strings of chemical code that looked like the equations for tailored electronic DNA—viral programming that would modify the AIs' neural net when inserted.

I saw one other thing. A micro-band transmitter tagged to each of the pathogen subprograms.

I smiled. With the tracers, Couette could track the spread of the virus through satellite boosters and relays. They would also be able to tell if the program had been transferred or not. It seemed that I wasn't as trusted as I'd thought.

I had the analyzer store the breakdown, and removed the slide. Then, with a micropore syringe, I pierced the heart and drew the wetware out, a single thick drop, seminal-white outside of its crimson skin. The needle barely stung when I slipped it into a vein on my wrist. From there, the virus would spread throughout my body, replicated by the internal programs I keep in my bloodstream to insulate me from, and make copies of, the nanoware I smuggle. In a half hour Couette's pathogen would permeate my skin like a normal virus, and evaporate when I sweated. Not the way Couette had planned it, but this way I had a copy I could modify and sell later on if I wanted to.

Outside, Guanaja Island began to stir beneath the blanket of simmering air that had suffocated it during the afternoon. The sinking sun reflected off the Caribbean in a sheet of molten silver that shimmered around the ring of long-abandoned oil platforms that circled the island.

I turned away from the window and went down to the main lobby, through the languid reggae rhythms undulating in the bar. Velasquez was nowhere in sight. A caged toucan shifted on its dowel perch to watch me leave.

When I stepped out of the air-conditioned foyer into the oppressive heat, I felt suddenly light-headed, as if I had walked out onto the dirt street of a different world.

Before offshore oil there had been no roads on Guanaja. The town had risen on toothpick legs out of the quiet water, floors hiked up above the waves. Most of the early town was gone now, submerged by the melting of polar ice caps. Over the years the buildings had crept inland to avoid the slowly rising Caribbean. Even so, more than half of the town was accessible only by boat, a kind of shantytown Venice.

It was a quarter of a kilometer walk down to the docks. The dirt roads were narrow, lined with mud-sealed wooden houses and *mercado* stalls that sold clay figurines, pottery and palm frond baskets. Squawking chickens kicked up dust that coated my teeth and the day-old vegetables. Overripe pineapples, grapefruit and bananas lay sickly sweet in their bins, and kids squabbled with each other for pieces of sugar cane, teeth rotten and gaping whenever they grinned at the tourists passing by.

For the foreigners, it was nothing more than a carnival sideshow. An isolated microcosm, like Disneyland, that held some nostalgic appeal they felt compelled to indulge every now and then. No arcologies here, or fusion reactors built out of diamond. Nothing here except the past. An island of memories.

The last light of the sun lay in an oily film across the palm-shadowed water at the edge of boat-town. Row after row of skeleton houses squatted above floating plastic bottles, discarded paper, mango rinds and coconut shells. A collection of battered dories thumped against the piers that staggered out across the water in crooked lines. Old rope creaked softly under the quiet lapping of waves, and a faint breeze mixed the offshore smell of frying fish and oil with creosote-preserved wood.

"You need a ride?" a taxi-kid asked. "I'll take you, no problem."

"How much?" I asked. He looked about twelve, and had straight black hair that hung down over dark brown eyes.

"First tell me where you want to go."

"The Temple of the *Brujería*."

"Five dollars," the boy said. "It's a long way around to there."

I shrugged and he led me to a flat-bottomed dinghy with a Plexiglas pane that looked down into the darkening water. I sat on a board and he pushed off from the pier and started the old gasoline-powered engine. It sputtered, then caught, kicking up debris as we sped out into the wraith-like sheds of boat-town.

"How long?" I asked.

"Twenty minutes, no problem. Too bad it's getting dark now." He grinned. "You can't see all the wonderful fish we have here. Strange and very exotic."

His teeth were bone white, but veined with streaks of lapis so that they looked like pieces of polished stone set in his mouth. His skin shone abnormally smooth in the dim light, like kiln-glazed clay. I imagined him being formed from one of the tiny figurines in the market, animated via the biological magic of the Christian healers who performed their curative rites without the alien consciousness of the *brujas*.

Artificial molecules were in almost everything now, tailored ribosomes and mRNA that had filtered into the eco-system when molecular engineering was in its infancy. The programs had become an integral part of the herbs and plants the healers rubbed into the skin of their patients to effect their physical and spiritual cures.

He grinned at me, not quite human. A chill breeze stirred between the sagging tin and tarpaper walls huddled around us, and I shivered.

Halogen lights began flicking on in the open windows of Guanaja's houses and buildings, painting the lagoon with acrylic streaks of red, green, and yellow. A ragged line of scrub brush and palms lay silhouetted against the periwinkle sky, hunched beneath the stars and the occasional flare of an orbiting colony snagged in sunlight.

"*Muy bonita, no?*" the boy said, his face ghostly behind the grin.

"Yes," I said. "Very beautiful."

"But not so beautiful to make you want to stay. Maybe someday I'll get tired and want to be reborn in heaven too."

Was that it? Had Kaja gotten tired? Bored with the world and its mundane beauties, so transitory in comparison to the timeless wonder of the stars floating in their frigid vacuum like some all-encompassing Grail.

I shook my head. Around the dark curve of the island I could see the dull lights of the Temple of the *Brujería*. It had been a large fish-packing shed and warehouse at one time. It leaned out over the water on thick pilings. The walls were corrugated metal, salt corroded and eaten through in places. A wide platform bordered it on three sides, littered with old oil drums and the remains of a small shipping crane that tottered to one side like the carcass of a mutated insect.

"Almost there," the boy said. I dug out what I owed and handed it to him.

There were a few other boats tied next to the dock and the short ladders that went up to it from water level. Not many, though. Most people who decided to convert were dropped off, with no plans of coming back. If they had decided on suicide instead, they would have been the people who used a gun instead of pills. No more cries for help from them.

The kid throttled back on the engine, drifting the boat

in. I grabbed a rung and stepped out of the dinghy, feeling
it slip away from under my feet.

"*Buena suerte*," the boy said. Good luck. "Maybe one
day I'll have the courage to give up being human." Then he
sped off into the night, the sound of the little outboard trailing behind him until it vanished into the soft creak of wood
and constant slap of waves.

Not courage, I thought. But disenchantment, and the alien
promise of new life that the *brujería* planted in the womb
of the imagination.

The dock area was quiet. An open tomb that smelled of
decayed wood and steel. I could taste the rotten air, damp
and acidic on my lips. A lone halogen burned over a single
office door, the sign above it unreadable, the letters faded
beyond recognition. Beyond life.

The door opened on rust-stiff hinges. Light filtered in
from a doorway behind a counter at the back of the room.
Through it, I could see the open area of the warehouse with
its array of conveyor belts, stacks of packing crates, and overhead network of transport cables with hooks dangling from
the support joists and I-beam girderwork that held up the roof.

An empty machine temple, I thought, carved out of post-
turn-of-the-century industrialism.

Inside the air was still hot, trapped by the corrugated
steel walls. The smell of burning copal hung in the greased
air, burned my eyes. My skin felt flushed and sticky with sweat.
Grit scraped underfoot as I went toward a flickering glow
at the far end of the building.

Candlelight, I realized. It came from behind a wall of
crates stacked to form a U-shaped enclosure around the
converts. They lay curled up on the bare floor, eyes closed,
a waxlike sheen on their fetal faces. Tiny soul dolls made
from strips of bark were attached to their necks. The dolls
looked like obscene flowers blossoming out of their skin. A

few of the bodies were faceless, as if they had begun to dissolve into some kind of shapeless goo inside a membrane of translucent skin.

My eyes stung and bile burned my throat. I wondered if Kaja had looked like that waiting for her metamorphosis, and knew she had. I felt suddenly queasy. My stomach knotted and I held my breath for a couple of seconds until the wave of nausea and a decayed image of Kaja passed.

The *bruja* sat near the back wall of the enclosure. She wore a cotton-print dress. Her gray hair was pulled back behind her ears. She looked like an ancient Mayan statue someone had put clothes on, only less human. Her eyes were polished obsidian and I shuddered at the alien intelligence lurking behind them, cold, distant and unfathomable.

A wooden table had been set up off to one side. It was covered with old soft-drink bottles that held flowers, paper soul dolls, woven-palm ornaments called "stars," and bunches of pepper tree branches, rue, and rosemary. Postcard-size holograms of the Virgin Mary and Jesus had been tacked up on the crates. Smoke from the clay incense brazier below them wreathed the cheap images.

"Welcome," the old woman said. "Come forward, please." Her voice was a soft sandpaper scratch in the air.

"You want to be reborn, yes? To leave this tired world behind and start your life over again."

"I want to forget the past," I said, the words sounding thick and hollow in the empty space. My palms were slick, my mouth dry.

"A new skin," she said. "New thoughts and desires. We understand how you feel."

I walked toward her. "I'm afraid," I said. "Afraid to die."

"That is normal," she said. "But there is nothing to fear. The program in the doll records the pattern of your mind and body so that it can be reborn later. What is your name?"

"Thomas." A trickle of sweat ran down the side of my

face. I wiped it off with the back of my hand and felt the perspiration splotching my shirt, smelled the metallic odor of Couette's virus evaporating into the air.

"A foreigner," she said. "An outcast, perhaps. Tell me. Is that why you want to be resurrected?"

"Yes."

Her artificial eyes held mine for a moment, cloudy and impenetrable as they probed me. "There is something else," she said.

"I had a sister . . ." My throat tightened. It didn't matter. She would misinterpret one outward show of loss for another. In the end it would work to my advantage. "We were very close. Last year she left to become part of your consciousness."

"And now you want to be with her."

"Yes."

"What is her name?"

I licked my parched lips. "Robertson," I rasped in a barely audible whisper. "Kaja Robertson."

She closed her eyes and pulled an inner veil over her, like an actress preparing to take on a different character. Her expression changed, and the way she sat. Her shoulders went back and her spine straightened. She appeared younger, and when she finally opened her eyes to look at me she tilted her head distractedly to one side the way Kaja always had whenever anyone intruded into her self-absorbed world of dreams.

I blinked. The crates closed in around me and wobbled. In the dancing candlelight, it might have been Kaja, brought back from the dead.

"I never thought I'd see you again, Tom. Not now. Not after what you said before I left."

I shook my head. Her face floated in front of me like an apparition, Kaja's voice and personality in an alien body.

"You're not here to join us," the puppet in front of me said. "I know that."

My chest tightened. My throat hurt and I forced myself to swallow. "Who are you?"

"You still don't believe," the woman said. It was the same thing Kaja had told me the day before she left, and now I could hear the same sense of sadness and disappointment I had then.

"A trick," I said. I wanted to stand, but my legs felt too wooden to move.

"No. I'm here, Tom, the same way you are."

My pulse hammered in my ears. "Not the same way."

"The part you remember," she said. "Isn't that enough?"

"That person died a year ago," I said. "When she came here."

"For you, maybe. But I'm still alive. Here and now in this body with twenty-seven other personalities who share my thoughts and dreams. If they agreed, in time I could become the person you remember, reshape this body so it matched the image you still carry around inside your head. Is that what you want?"

I stared at the wrinkled, sagging skin, the bird-thin wrists webbed with varicose veins and age spots, and then I closed my eyes. "Why did you leave?" I asked, remembering how she had turned away on the beach, hearing the sound of waves fill the void she left as she disappeared across the sand.

"I already told you once."

"Not everything."

Kaja paused. The eyes were brown now, softer. "To get away from you," she said at last. "To become my own person. To be free of the past you wanted to keep me locked up in."

The words struck me like a whip. "I needed you," I said to her. "When you left, it felt like the only part of me that was still alive died. I hated you for that. Hated and loved you at the same time. It would have been easier if you'd died the way our parents did."

"Is that why you're here now? To kill me, destroy what I've become?"

"I want to kill the program that poisoned your mind and took you away."

"It won't make any difference if you kill the body I'm wearing now. There are copies of me and the other personalities. I'll still be alive inside them, thinking, seeing through their eyes." She stood up and walked toward me, her dress rustling in the heavy air. When she was less than a meter away she stopped and stood quietly.

My spine prickled. I tried to tell myself it wasn't really her, that she had been absorbed into the New Humanity and twisted into something else, but I couldn't. Everything was the same, her memories, mannerisms and words—all that I remembered.

"What's it like?" I whispered. It wasn't something I'd intended to ask, and I wasn't sure I wanted to know, but the question slipped out before I could stop it.

"Different," she said. "The colonies are kind of like the hive arcologies back in the States, but not really. It's hard at first, sharing a body with different people and combining thoughts. There are a lot more memories and pain, but it doesn't hurt as much. It's a lot easier to deal with your own problems when you're able to experience all of the problems other people have. You don't think about yours so much."

She knelt in front of me, hair, skin and dress fragrant with incense and herbs.

"People hate us because they're afraid, Tom. Afraid not only of what we are and what we might become, but that they'll be left behind, unable to let go of the status quo they've spent their whole lives trying to be a part of."

"I'm not afraid," I said.

"But you're filled with hate the same as the people who hired you. A different kind of hate, maybe, with different roots, but hate still the same." She had a soul doll in one hand, strips of bark tied around a tiny vial equipped with a microinjector needle that pricked at the uneven candlelight.

"How much do you know?" I asked.

"Only that someone would come. We didn't know who, or how the attempt would be made."

Her hands took mine. They were cool and withered and I flinched at her touch. She bent closer and I remembered our final embrace, the light fleeting touch of her hands and arms.

"I can be more than a memory," she said, her gray lips centimeters from mine. "You can share my thoughts, and all that I am."

"No," I said, more to myself than her. I held her face in my palms. I knew by now that the virus had infected her. I knew that if I let her go I would end up killing the parts of her that were living elsewhere, and that I would never be able to forgive myself.

She reached out her empty hand, and bird-thin fingers stroked my face. I could smell the odd blend of herbs and symbiotic molecular assemblers that had shaped them.

"Join us," Kaja said. She raised her other hand. The soul doll glinted in her palm, waiting.

I shook my head slowly. "You were right to want to be free," I said. "To get away."

I looked into her quiet eyes. They reminded me of the toucan's. I thought of them staring at me from out of the past, caged by my memory. I had locked her up inside me, I realized, the same way the toucan had been locked up in the motel lobby, a bird imprisoned inside the empty cavity of my chest. My ribs felt like bars that had kept her from flying free, and her fingers on my cheek became a flutter of wings against my heart.

Her cheek felt frail between my hands, the skin dry and papery. "I love you," I said. I pulled her close to me. My fingers ran along the top of her hair. I cupped her face in my hands like a chalice and kissed her on the forehead.

"I never wanted to hurt you," I said. "I'm sorry."

And then I twisted her head sharply to one side. Tears stung my eyes as I listened to the loud crack of her neck, felt the weight of her head sag against my hands. I let her fall into my lap and hugged her tight as I watched the light fade from her eyes.

Something moved behind me in the mechanized carcass of the warehouse. One of the bodies twitching in its cocoon, I imagined. I turned and saw someone walking toward me out of the shadows. The taxi-boy.

"You killed her," he said. "You were supposed to let her go."

"Yes," I said. I pushed Kaja's body onto the floor and got up.

The boy paused a moment, and then hurried off into the greasy nest of conveyor belts. I had a little time, but not much. It wouldn't be long, I guessed, before Couette found out I had reneged on their contract. How else would the kid have known I wasn't supposed to kill her?

It didn't matter. I didn't care if they came after me. I felt freer than I had in a long time.

The *bruja's* eyes were still open. I closed them. Then I took the soul doll out of her hand and inserted the needle into her neck. I held her hand while I waited for the doll to copy the pattern of her synapses and the disassemblers to start breaking down the body. When I felt the bones in her fingers soften, I let them go and removed the doll. If what she said was true about there being multiple backups of her and the others, I wouldn't need it.

But I didn't want to take any chances. I wanted to be sure.

I let go of her.

And when I turned away the toucan was gone, a colorful flash of wings against some mental sky that left me feeling lighter, as if I, too, might one day be able to escape the past.

Running Rings Around the Moon

by
Kevin Kirk

ILLUSTRATED BY Omar Rayyan

About the Author

Kevin Kirk of Las Vegas, Nevada, was born in Vegas twenty-nine years ago to a great family which he describes as a cross between "the Addams Family and the Arthurian Mythos—close knit, quirky, and full of vision." He has a B.A. in psychology and recently landed a job with the Clark County Social Services where he helps the poor as kind of a legal Robin Hood, with paperwork.

Before this, he ran the gamut of jobs which seems almost a prerequisite for a writing career—library assistant, dishwasher, industrial laundry sorter, typesetter, front-desk hotel clerk on the Strip in Vegas, bus boy, security guard, doing grunt graphics work for print shops, and others.

Still, Kevin is a writer. He says he has been writing for as long as he can remember, and that writing is "basic to what

I am.'' This sort of an attitude is also a prerequisite to a writing career.

This is Kevin's first published story, but I suspect you will be seeing much more of him in the future. Kevin asked us to share one piece of advice for new writers, *"Please don't give up! It seems the trick is to keep submitting your work until you get noticed, that's all. Rejection is not a statement of not being good enough, it's a statement of limited access. Keep writing, keep sending it in.''*

You see, Kevin has also already developed a writer's thick skin.

• • •

Kevin Kirk's illustrator is Omar Rayyan.

Virginia was the one who actually **found the alien. The doctors were examining the alien ship while Virginia and I searched** the quarantine area to see if we could dig up anything.

It was a dangerous mission, searching in the arctic where snow can cover crevices that could drop you sixty feet or more, but we did it. We did whatever they asked for the duration of our hitch. We were young and on a mission, searching around an alien wreck in the frozen north. Paradise.

Virginia radioed on general band that she had found a body. I moved toward her location at close to a run. I got there just as the doctor's orders came through. It amounted to getting the corpse on a stretcher and bringing it back to the alien ship for study.

We didn't have a stretcher.

"What do you want to do?" I asked Virginia over our private field comm. Neither of us would expose our face to the freezing air if we didn't have to. I opened my mask only to spit, sometimes to wake up if I grew tired.

The alien lay half-exposed on the leeward side of a snow dune. Its manlike head had little spiked tufts. Ice and snow had robbed it of much of its original indigo. It looked like a person. At least I thought it could wear my gloves and boots. We dusted the snow off its lower torso, shoveling it by hand and by walking stick until we could free the body. I grabbed the legs, Virginia grabbed the arms, and we set off back toward the alien ship.

We talked on field comm as we walked, just the two of

us on line. No need to let the scientists in on things like "Let's rest a minute" or "Oh, he's slipping, hold on."

"Oh, god dammit!" Virginia swore, and I answered.

"What's wrong?"

"Well," she seemed hesitant. I waited. I knew she'd come around. "I stole a ring, Jack. The guy had a ring on."

"You *stole* an alien artifact?"

"Yeah." We marched on, not even slowing. "I thought it was made of crystal. I took my glove off, real quick to put the ring on, and now I discover it's only ice."

I laughed. "Natural formation, then?"

"Yeah, I guess so."

"No harm done, Virginia." I watched the back of her head, hooded and covered like the rest of her body, enough to appear sexless.

"Yeah. No harm. Except for a cold hand."

Virginia didn't say anything the rest of the way to the doctors and the wrecked ship, and it took a good hour and a half to get there. I thought maybe she felt a little ashamed for wanting to steal the ring, maybe going through a little personality crisis, so I let her weather it out.

We dropped the alien off at the ship, not a leviathan, almost a disappointingly small craft with octopus-like wings, but we loved it. The doctors became ecstatic and ordered us to return to our main base. We went outside and I started the snowmobile and with Virginia in back we headed to our temporary home.

She had a strange, faraway look in her eye when we took off our masks. I slung my arm around her still-bundled shoulder and started us off to the kitchen for our traditional hot chocolate, but she shrugged off my arm and glared.

"Don't touch me!"

I backed off, confused. She wouldn't let me touch her. If it were just sex, that wouldn't have been all that unusual, we were shaky as lovers at best. But she wouldn't even let me touch her after that, from avoiding a casual nudge to outright hostility if I tried to get too close.

Things were strange then, and during the final four days at base she stayed exactly the same.

Two years after the alien expedition, I had just finished my stint with NASA and I was on a two-month leave. I decided to visit Virginia. We had parted abruptly, she with something bordering neurosis, me with other things to do.

I tracked her via phone calls to a small town, and when I called she said she would be delighted to see me. I thought that meant she was back to her old self. It cheered me enough to give me the final impetus to map out the trip. Williamsport, Maine. I'd never heard of it, and it had no airport. Not even nearby.

I rigged my travel lines to include a rented car. It would take the better part of ten hours to get there, a small price to see the old Virginia again.

I was wrong about the trip. It took twelve hours.

At the tail end I stopped along the road at a general store to gas up and buy something quick to eat. They had all the usuals, so I grabbed a soda and a hot dog and went to the register.

The man behind it gave me a warm hello. "Not from around here?"

"No. San Diego, currently." He nodded and grinned, said it must be nice. I nodded inane agreement.

"What brings you to Williamsport?"

"Looking for an old friend."

He smiled wistfully at that. "You can find friends older than you imagine in Williamsport. Anyone specific?"

"Yeah, a Virginia Crane." I said quickly, to get the conversation over. "You know her?"

"Who doesn't?" He leaned forward conspiratorally. "Would you like to hear a story, young fella? About an evening on another world, about fishing in the air with nets made of glass thread? You made it sing, just right, with little vibrations to attract the fish, and they came to the center of the net if you did it right. Me and my friend, we were only eight years old that summer, but I wielded the net as well as an adult."

I shook my head, apologized to the gentle loony. "I really don't have time for this."

He gave me directions, wished me well. I started to leave. "You must have been on that expedition with Virginia."

I turned when I was halfway out the rickety, wooden door. "Yeah. We shared one or two."

"I don't think there's any left," he called over my shoulder. And then I was gone, to pump gas and down a hot dog.

Virginia seemed to be her old self, or something similar. She rushed out of a picturesque little house when she heard me drive up. I barely got out of the car before she grabbed me in a big hug. It was good to hold her again, good to feel her body under the stars. The last time I'd held her had been inside and under thermal blankets.

"Hi, Jack," she said shyly, her face buried in my shoulder.

"Well, hello," I said. "It's good to see you. It's good to feel welcome."

She sighed and held me, and it was pretty terrific. We just stood under the stars; I had forgotten how many you could see away from the city. The drive suddenly felt worth it.

"How was the trip?" she asked. "A little hard to find?"

I laughed, hugged her, and we walked arm in arm toward the house. "A bit. I just had the strangest conversation with the owner of the little market down the road.

"Pelano?" Virginia asked, "or Richard?"

Illustrated by Omar Rayyan

"Two owners?"

"No, just one," she said, and marched me into the house.

She fixed us a cup of tea and we sat in silence for a few minutes, looking at each other and looking around. It felt comfortable. I could tell she was doing better.

"It seems things are working for you," I said after the first cup of tea. She nodded. "I'm glad. Last time I saw you . . ."

"I know," she said. "But there was a reason for it. I couldn't touch you then, I didn't know if you wanted what that meant."

"Settling down?"

"No," she laughed. "An alien personality."

"Funny, Virginia." I poured myself some more tea. "I guess north was strange for all of us. Not your average trip, eh?"

She came to the couch, put her arm around me. "I meant what I said about the personalities. I have one, too. Back then I was a Distributor. If you touched me you would have received an extra persona."

"Right, Virginia."

"It was the ring. It melted into my skin. Remember the ring?" I grinned, a little weakly. I remembered all right. The guilt must have tripped her further than I thought. "It held thousands of souls, thousands of encoded personalities. I've distributed them all here in Williamsport. We live in relative peace, two lives at once."

I leaned back, tried to make light of it. "Just getting away from it all, Virginia?"

She smiled, with an amused expression. "There's kind of a city meeting tonight. We have little neighborhood get-togethers. Would you come with me?"

"Sounds . . ." I bit my tongue. "Okay, Virginia. Sounds fine."

• • •

The meeting was at someone's farm, where several fires had been lit for cooking, warmth, and seemingly for the kids to play with. I recognized the store owner, but stuck close to Virginia.

She introduced me to several people, always by their given name and then a second, odd-sounding alien name. The whole town believed it, and now I began to as well. If they thought they were the spirits of an alien race, who was I to say otherwise?

But when they spoke, circled around the fires in groups of twenty or so, I started to believe it.

Everything grew quiet, and even the kids stopped their shrieking play. A middle-aged woman stepped into our circle and just began talking, telling a tale. It was storytime, and it felt funny with a group of adults, but also kind of nice.

She had no particular charisma. Her voice was nothing special. She just spoke about what she knew.

She told about the boats of the plain. She told how she, a ranking daughter of her family, held command of one of her family's two boats. She described an outing one morning, a usual run to the city when a sudden storm developed. She and her little brother fought with the wind long after they should have anchored and turned off the grav device, but her pride would not let her surrender to the elements. The boat was tossed at high speed, dangerous speed should it have struck something solid, but she steered true and within an hour, by luck and by skill, the city gates came into view.

She said that at the time she had been proud of her abilities and regretted not having friends on board as witnesses, but that later in life she regretted only her self-absorption in the boat, and not letting her little brother steer in the quieter moments, even if it meant helping him grip the wheel, his hands beneath hers.

It was like anyone telling a story. It didn't seem a big

deal. People listened, then turned to gossip about the story or something else, then back to their own lives.

A boy skipped near to the fire. He sat down as close to it as he could, and started telling a tale about when he was a miner.

He said he had mined salt and that the days had been very long, and it held no reward. He said that this life on Earth was better, and that he was glad he chose to end his life and send forth his seed of memory.

Many present interrupted, calling him names and claiming that he was a pessimist, that life had never really been that bad. He frowned at the crowd in an expression far beyond his years, and told them that they had better remember the truth or not remember at all. This just sparked another round of catcalls. The boy stormed away, the circle parting to let him through into the night.

I was swiftly becoming amazed.

I noticed Virginia's eyes on me, a maddening I-told-you-so grin firmly in place. I frowned at her, hating the feeling of being wrong, hating the feeling of not belonging.

"And you, Virginia? Cleopatra in another life?"

She laughed, rose, and held out her hands to lift me to my feet. We began to wander away from the fires, back toward my car. "No. I am the Distributor. As for my persona, I was a weaver."

"Hardly glamorous," I noted.

Her arm slid about my back, her head rested on my shoulder. "It's something, though," she sighed. "Something wonderful."

"So you live your life out here? Reliving alien memories in town meetings?"

She held my hand, squeezed it tight. "Look at my finger."

For a moment, panic took hold. I imagined all sorts of alien tentacles from late night T.V., and I'm afraid I jerked away a bit. But only for a second. I held up her hand under the clouds and stars and distant firelight.

"My ring, Jack. Look at my ring."

I ignored the gold one, the silver one with the ruby. I looked at the ring of crystal, the ring of ice. "It didn't melt after all," I whispered.

"Oh, it melted all right," she said. "I'm growing another. To store people. Memories and lives. I am the Distributor, Jack." We kept walking.

"Whose memories? And who will you give them to?"

She turned to me under the big, starry sky and I felt as if I were in the third grade.

"To the people on the other planet, from the people of Earth."

"How do you get these memories stored? In the stories it sounded like you had to die to have it done. Virginia?" She hadn't heard me. She kept talking, kept explaining what had to be done.

"There is another ship, Jack. It has been revealed to me, from my other memory. It is time. I will go back, along with thousands of others held in my ring."

"Virginia!" I shook her, but I had nothing to say.

"I don't expect you to give up your life for this, Jack. There will be plenty of volunteers. There always are."

"Virginia." I held her to me, desperately tight, hoping that I could force some sense into her through sheer physical contact. "You can't go around killing people."

I could feel her shaking her head. It was as if I were a small child and she the adult, when once it had been the opposite. "Jack. They will want to go. They will live again in the bodies of others. The sharing is a wonderful thing, Jack. One feels very old, and very fulfilled."

I held onto her for a long time, and neither of us moved. And then she stroked my hair, and I cried into her shoulder.

She knew that I would leave, that I would go right away. That I would just drive off. She held me with tenderness and sympathy. And I cried, great racking sobs that tore the strength from me. For she, my friend Virginia, would go to the stars and tread on alien ground, and even touch an alien mind.

And I . . . with sudden, startling clarity I knew that I would remain here. My life—the adventures, the discoveries—all was a mockery. I did not have what it took to reach for the unfamiliar. I would never touch the stars.

Virginia watched me go. I could feel her looking at me with care and wisdom gained from more than one lifetime. As I drove away I realized that part of my fear and shame was anger, pure red rage that *we* hadn't done it. That our only way out was through an alien ring, from alien sympathizers on a student-exchange program.

I floored it, firing the car like a rocket down the dark highway. Maybe we had a chance. Maybe we could do it ourselves. We might store memories to reduce weight, maybe on computer chips. We could colonize with frozen sperm and egg. Or . . . *something!*

As I drove I hunted for the moon with my head half out the car window. But the moon was hiding in the clouds, and I couldn't see it. We hadn't been there in twenty years and might never make it there again, and I just couldn't see it.

The Augmented Man

by
Wendy Rathbone

ILLUSTRATED BY Thomas Whittaker

About the Author

While working for her degree in Literature/Writing from the University of California at San Diego, Wendy Rathbone's favorite class was a writing workshop taught by Kim Stanley Robinson, one of the finest science fiction authors today.

She has worked at various odd jobs, in a microbiology lab, at Sea World, in movie theaters, and she has published articles on media subjects, such as Star Trek. In addition to her nonfiction, Wendy has sold a large number of poems to magazines such as Asimov's, Aboriginal SF, Pandora and many others.

Wendy notes that her first success in writing came at age twelve when she won a savings bond for her poem "UNICEF." For her, as for many others here, publishing her fiction is the realization of a life-long ambition. This warm tale about love and commitment is her first professional short story sale.

About the Illustrator

Thomas Whittaker is twenty-three years old, and lives in Bricktown, New Jersey.

He began illustrating when he was young. In high school his murals garnered him several awards, and he won the state Teen Arts Festival.

Thomas says that he has no formal education in art, and is therefore always observing others and trying to learn something new, and he spends his free time at the drawing board, enhancing his skills. He has worked doing caricature portraits in a major theme park, and he now works as a custom framer and as a manager for an art supply store.

E**ver since she could remember, the little girl had been afraid of the *augie* guards who stood outside her door.**

Though her mother and father assured her that the guards were good people, very loyal, and hired for their protection, she still had nightmares about them. In one, the guards used their extra strong, flashing metallic arms to smash her father against a hallway wall. His bloodied body sank from view as they turned on her mother. One of the guards removed his human hand from the sleeve of silver that was his arm. The edges of his sleeve were sharp like a knife, and with one arcing swipe, he beheaded the little girl's mother. The dream always ended when the guards turned to face the little girl. She would try to run but her body was somehow paralyzed. Her own screaming would awaken her.

The little girl knew that her house and her family were somehow special, different from the rest of the people in The City, though she wasn't quite sure why. For that reason there were always *augie* guards outside and within the house.

The house itself was a mansion, according to her mother. She would say things like: "Our mansion has a plumbing problem." "Our mansion's windows need washing." "Isn't our mansion splendid?" The little girl didn't know what made the house a mansion, but she liked the word and was glad to live there, aside from the ever-vigilant presence of the guards.

In the mornings, a governess came in to take care of her.

The governess was a young woman with long, brown hair pinned back tightly from her lean face. She taught her games like counting and the alphabet. She encouraged her to draw and sing and showed her how to play short three-note songs on the piano. Sometimes, hidden in the governess' pockets, were special sweets which the little girl got to eat if she painted an especially pretty picture, or was very well behaved.

In the afternoons she would attend swimming or skating or dancing lessons. All were taught by her mother and father's personal fitness instructor, Mr. Mike. Though she loved her governess, the little girl liked afternoons with Mr. Mike the best. For her size and age—average build and five years—she was an excellent swimmer. The pool room was her favorite in the whole mansion. Its glass ceilings and walls revealed the blue sky and the sun. Sunlight made the water look like melting diamonds. When she tried to capture them in her hands, they eluded her. She would play at trying to catch them for hours, swimming and diving. Sometimes the very tall and athletic Mr. Mike would join her and challenge her to races, which he let her win.

One time Mr. Mike didn't let her win and when she got to the edge of the pool he caught her up and threw her toward the deep water in the center. She laughed loudly, enjoying the game and the feel of his hands when he wrestled with her in the water. His fingers, long and warm, touched her everywhere. Her suit came off during the rough play and he held her close as he helped put it back on.

She saw the *augie* guard then, standing by the shallow end, but Mr. Mike did not. Just as Mr. Mike was telling her to help him put his bathing trunks back on, which like her suit had accidentally fallen off during their game, the *augie* guard made a shallow dive into the water, came up beside her and picked her up with one arm around her waist.

The little girl screamed. She kicked. She pounded with her fists.

"Hey!" Mr. Mike said. But he didn't try to help her. Instead, he merely stood and watched as the guard, metal body streaked with water drops, carried her out of the pool.

She began to cry, terrified that the guard would hurt her. She called out for Mr. Mike but he didn't come.

Then her mother arrived and took her from the guard. "Midi," she said. She smelled of lavender and rum. "It's all right."

"Ma'am," said the guard, "I must have a word with you."

"Of course. What in the world happened?"

"Alone, please."

"Midi, everything's okay. You don't have to cry. Go off and change your clothes, okay?"

Even though her mother sounded confident and unalarmed in the *augie*'s presence, the little girl was still terrified, and felt betrayed because Mr. Mike had not come to help. She clung to her mother's leg, the stiff skirts scratching her cheek and chin.

"Go on," her mother said, firmer.

Still sniffling, she obeyed.

While Midi changed into her day clothes—a jumpsuit and gold belt—she heard voices, sharp and angered. One belonged to her mother. The other, to Mr. Mike. When she came out, dressed and dry, her mother waited for her by the entrance to the pool room. Mr. Mike was gone.

She ran to her mother. "Mommy, the augie tried to kill me!"

"No, dear. He saved you. Don't you remember all the times I told you they are here for our protection? Well, it's true."

"But he wasn't protecting me. The augie came after me!"

"Mr. Mike is not a good man. You won't be seeing him anymore."

"Why?" Tears stung her eyes again and rolled down her cheeks. "I like him. Where did he go?"

"He went away."

"Because of the augie?" The little girl pouted. "The augie made you send him away. It's going to kill me."

"No. That's not true. When you're older you'll understand. But believe me, Midi, no one, especially the guards, wants to kill you." As her mother spoke, the *augie* who had grabbed her came into view from behind some indoor bushes. In a low voice he said, "He is gone."

"Thank you."

And Midi began to cry again. Through her tears she saw him look at her and open his hands in a gesture of peace. "I'm sorry this happened," he said. She turned her face into her mother's skirts.

"She is afraid of me," she heard him say. She clutched at the lavender-scented cloth.

Midi, whose full name was Midori Melina Kosaki, had no swimming lessons the next day. Instead, she spent the whole morning and afternoon with her governess with the long brown hair, Ms. Dahl.

Midi was not a good girl. She received no special sweets that day and spent much of her time throwing paint, getting her numbers wrong, and decorating the table with various free-form sculptures which she'd made out of her lunch. She was sullen and argumentative. She spoke often of Mr. Mike and said she didn't want to be good unless he came back.

At dinner she openly defied her parents. When an *augie* came in and asked to speak privately with her father about a very urgent matter, she got up from the table, ran over to him, and kicked him in his metal leg. It hurt her toe.

"Midi!" her mother exclaimed.

The *augie* turned to look down at her. He was the same one who had grabbed her in the pool. His gold-brown eyes were soft and concerned. He had light hair, the color of the sunlight on the pool water, and skin several shades paler than

hers. His human head, attached to a metal body, was rather
handsome. But the way his neck fused into the silver torso
made her shiver. He was horrible to look at, and she could
tell by the way his human hands, which protruded from sharp
silver sleeves, clasped and unclasped that he wasn't to be
trusted. He looked like a murderer.

"Midi, stop kicking him at once!" her father yelled.

"It's all right, really," the *augie* said.

"No, it's not," her father said. Then he turned to her
mother. "What has this child's governess been teaching her?"

"You're not going to send her away, too," Midi cried.
"It's not fair!" And she collapsed in tears on the floor by
the *augie*'s feet. She pounded her little fists against his hard
boots. "I hate you," she sobbed. "I hate you!" She felt her
mother's arms go around her and lift her.

"I've tried to explain to her what happened, but she
doesn't understand," her mother said.

That night, she was put to bed early. The mansion felt
different. It was quieter, somehow, as if the air in the house
were being held in, tight, like a breath. When she finally
fell asleep she had the nightmare again, and woke gasping
in the dark, afraid to move.

For a long time she lay there, listening. Scurrying footsteps passed through the hall outside her door and scared her
more than the dream. She thought she heard voices, shrill
and rushed. Perhaps they were what had wakened her.

She imagined that her dream was coming true, that the
*augie*s had killed her parents and were now deciding whether
to kidnap or kill her.

Holding on tightly to her soft blankets, she lay shivering,
her throat raw, her sobs barely contained.

After a while, she dozed. Dark shades struck at her from
within her mind and she jerked awake several times.

Then, just as she felt herself melt into sleep again, the
door to her rooms burst open with a crack, letting in the eerie

ambered light from the hall. A large silhouette of a man
seemed to fly at her. She tried to scream but all that would
come out of her mouth was a squeak.

The man wore all black and grabbed her by the hair.
She closed her eyes and automatically put her hands up to
push him away. He didn't seem to notice as he gripped her
neck. Her lungs filled with the fear and the pain. Her eyes
rolled up into the back of her head. The grip suddenly
loosened, and she fell back to her mattress.

A strange breaking sound, followed by a wet plop, both
panicked and relieved her. She opened blurred eyes, scratching at her long black hair which had fallen in her face. The
light shone dim, but she could see enough. The form of the
black-clad man lay across her bed. But he had no head. Shiny,
dark liquid gushed, fountain-like, from where his head should
have been. At the sight, a strange sound escaped her throat.
She tried to scoot back on the bed but the pillows tripped
her. She jumped up, whimpering, just as someone grabbed
her from behind.

"No!" She kicked. From the feel of his body, he was
an *augie*. "No!"

"Hush, little one," said a soft voice, "or you'll get us
all killed."

Deep inside something told her that he spoke the truth
and she shut up. But that didn't stop her from continuing to
kick. Her movements didn't seem to bother him at all as he
carried her from her bedroom and out into the hall.

He walked quickly, through halls and down stairways.
She could see he was heading for the back of the mansion,
toward the pool and outside. Her kicking stopped and she
observed as though she were a separate entity outside her body,
watching.

There was no one about. The house, again, seemed
strangely quiet. In the dark it looked different, scary, big.
She wondered where her mother and father were and, at the

thought, felt another pang of fear. Her body jerked against his hard side. "I want my mommy," she said in a high, weak voice.

"Quiet!" the *augie* said.

For a moment she thought she heard footsteps behind them. The *augie* moved swiftly and silently into the kitchen, a place Midi had rarely been. Then, opening the door to what appeared to be a huge cupboard, he practically tossed her in. "Be quiet and wait for me," he ordered in a harsh whisper. He shut the door.

It was so black in the cupboard that Midi thought she might actually die there, paralyzed to death by her fear. She could see and hear nothing. She could only hug her thin nightgown against her chest and wait, crouched, like an animal caught in a cage. She was shaking so hard she felt sick. Tears welled in her eyes again, but she did as the *augie* had ordered and made no sound.

After what seemed like hours, the cupboard door opened. She blinked, holding her breath. A hand touched hers. "Come with me," a voice said.

The hand was human and she grasped it, her legs aching as they straightened. For a moment she couldn't move. Her legs just wouldn't obey.

"Are you okay?" the voice asked.

She looked up. It was the *augie* who had jumped in the pool and who had come in to speak to her father at dinner. His silver body looked dull now, tarnished and dirty, splashed with what looked like brown mud.

"Where's my mommy?" she asked. Her voice sounded timid but she didn't care. She was just a kid. She shouldn't have to be strong.

The *augie* did not answer her. Instead, he said, "You must come with me. I'll take you to where you'll be safe."

"Is my mommy there?" she asked.

He hesitated before answering. "Maybe."

"Take me to her." She unconsciously imitated the tone her father used when giving orders to his servants.

She'd never been out this late at night. The stars burned like jewels and she got dizzy looking at them. The sky was huge and the air cool and it seemed they had walked for a long time in places where there were no lights and where the ground was all loose gravel and dirt. She didn't see any houses, only low bushes like crouched beasts, and rocks as big as trees.

"Where are we?" she asked softly, not looking up.

"Are you tired?" the *augie* asked.

She shook her head though it was true. Her bare feet seemed unconnected to the rest of her, and her eyes felt dry and sore.

"How much further?" she asked.

"A bit," he replied.

She sighed heavily and he stopped walking. Though she refused to look at him, she could hear the rustle of him kneeling to her level. "Would you like to ride on my shoulders?" he asked.

She said nothing.

"It'll be quicker that way," he continued. "I won't let you fall."

She stared at the ground and tried not to blink. Her white nightgown, which came only to her knees, fluttered against her in a soft night breeze. A darkness against the volume of white averted her attention. She studied it. The stain was in the shape of a hand. She reached up to touch it and her fingertips came away sticky.

"Midi?"

"You got dirt on my gown," she said, eyes stinging. Finally, she looked up, voice quivering. "It's blood, isn't it?"

"I'm sorry," the *augie* man said.

Illustrated by Thomas Whittaker

"You killed my parents!" she yelled suddenly. She burst into tears and ran away, alone into the dark.

"I did not kill your parents," he called after her. "I tried to save them."

Starlight littered the path. There were rocks and potholes and weeds. She tripped and fell, her hands smacking the earth with a sharp sting. But she got up again and kept running.

The *augie* had no problem keeping up with her. Finally, ignoring her protests, he simply picked her up and set her on his broad, steel shoulder. At that point she was too tired to fight him, and she sat quietly, hanging onto the arm that braced her legs against his chest. After a while she felt comfortable enough to lean against the side of his head. While the rest of him was cold, he was warm there, and for some reason that made her less afraid. The muscles in her chest eased and for the first time that night she could breathe a little easier. Her head bowed and she dozed.

When she woke, the landscape looked no different. Large boulders loomed to the left. They were hip deep in scrub and the sky was still black as the cupboard where she'd waited for the *augie* to return. The stars blinked and guttered.

The *augie* kept such a smooth gait that she barely noticed any bumping or jerking as he carried her. Though she was sore from sitting, she felt much better now, more relaxed.

"Where are we going?" she said, forcing herself to sound matter-of-fact.

"Away from The City," came the immediate answer.

"Why?"

"It'll be safer."

"Why?"

"The people in The City are angry. It's not safe to be around them right now."

"But why are they angry?"

"For many reasons. You're a little young to understand

it all, but people fight. Sometimes because they're hungry or unhappy or angry. Sometimes for no reason at all.''

"Are my mommy and daddy fighting?" She pictured them hitting people with their fists and with sticks. It was a ludicrous image. Her parents had never hit anyone that she had seen.

"I don't know."

"Did they get away like me?"

"I don't know."

"Will you help me find them?"

"Yes."

"Okay." After a moment's silence, she said: "I have to go to the bathroom."

The *augie* stopped, lifted her off his shoulder and swung her gracefully to the ground. Her stomach flipped over in a pleasurable way and she almost laughed.

When she pulled up her gown to urinate on the ground, he politely turned away. When she finished, she stood at his massive side peering up at his pale head which, like his body, was riddled and sparking with starlight, seeming to flash in the darkness. He was so tall that she only came up to his thighs. At his knee, she could see the formation of a socket behind the shiny cap. Except for his head, which was real, and his hands which were bare and warm, he could have been a giant doll.

"Ready?" he asked.

She cocked her head and had to strain her neck to meet his gaze. "How do you go to the bathroom?" she asked, unabashed.

He seemed to bow toward her. Pointing to his lower right side, he said, "See this little door?"

It was hard to make out, but as she stared a slight indentation in the metal became clear.

"That," he explained, "is my waste compartment. Since

I do not need to eat as you eat, it only has to be taken care of about once a week.''

She frowned, nodded. The thought did not disturb her as it once might have. "What do you eat?" she asked.

"I can eat whatever you eat. But I do not need to. What I do need occasionally are special energy bars. They are like fuel. Without them my functions would weaken, just as you would weaken if you did not eat."

"Oh. Can you die?"

"Yes," he answered softly. "I can die."

The words, when spoken, were like a shroud over her mind and body. She quieted after that, and when he gave her the option of being carried, she chose to walk for a little while.

The air dampened as the night aged. Her skin chilled. She was a knot of ice, no more alive than one of the rocks on their path, or a saber-point of cold light that pricked from space.

The sleeves of her nightgown clung to her small arms. Her glossy hair lay in tangles along her shoulders and back. "I'm cold," she murmured, arms crossed tightly in front of her.

"Would you like me to carry you now?" the *augie* asked.

"You're even colder," she observed. "All that metal . . ."

He stopped in front of her and knelt. "Not always," he replied. He held out his arm. "Feel."

Shyly, she touched his smooth forearm. The metal was actually warm to the touch. The warmth made her body seem colder and she instinctively moved toward him. "I can control the energy flowing through my body," he explained. He held out his arms. "I can focus it into my arms. You can feel the warmth."

She contemplated him for a moment, one hand still resting on his forearm, then said, "Okay, I'm ready to be carried."

He held her cradled against his wide chest. Because of

his warmth, which remained constant, she did not mind the
unrelenting hardness of him. In the heat of his focused energy flow, she fell asleep.

A high, sharply pitched cry awakened her. She tensed,
dizzy and disoriented for a moment. A small moan escaped
her throat and she tried to turn over, thinking she was still
in her bed at the mansion.

"There's nothing to be afraid of," said a low voice.

Midi took a breath and opened her eyes. The night was
like a desperate mouth, the stars its teeth. And she remembered where she was. Shivering, she snuggled closer to the
augie's chest. "What was that?" She half-whispered.

"Coyotes. Listen."

She did. More cries, almost like screams, wavered through
the air. The lunatic chorus picked up power. The sound
traveled, like a spiked caress, straight to her spine. A few
moments later it stopped, just as suddenly as it started. Silence
wafted in, but it was still tainted with the memory of that
alien cacophony.

"What are they?" she asked, breathless.

"Like dogs," he said. "Wild dogs. They are scavengers
and survivors. They're everywhere. Like rats or roaches. An
admirable species, actually."

"Maybe they were crying like that because they're cold.
And hungry," Midi suggested.

"Maybe."

She dozed off again and when she woke she could feel
the wind pushing at her face and hair. Cool but not cold.
She watched the shadow shapes of brush and rock pass by
and realized they were moving quite fast. From her perch
in the arms of the *augie* she looked down. Ground disappeared
under his feet in a blur. His steps were long and quick, but
smooth, graceful. He was running, his gait even and untiring.
She wouldn't have noticed this if she hadn't looked. Where
his arms cushioned her, the movement was barely discernable.

"We're going fast," she commented.

"Yes," he said. "The night is fading and we're in the middle of a desert. We have to make it through as far as we can before the sun gets too hot."

"Oh." She thought about that for a moment, then frowned. "Where are we going?"

"To a place where you'll be safe."

"Oh. My mommy was right. I'm safe with you, aren't I?"

"Yes."

"I was afraid before."

"I know."

"I'm not now."

"Good." In his voice, she thought she could hear a smile.

She wasn't at all tired. The sky, a strange mixture of black and purple edged in gold low on the horizon made her think of the colors she liked to use when she painted. The dawn reminded her of an enormous flower. The next time she made a picture, she decided she would draw the sky at dawn as if it really were a blooming plant. Then she would draw people under it, herself and the *augie*.

She squirmed in his arms until she could rest her head on his shoulder. "Do you have a name?" she asked.

"Rinn."

"Rinn," she repeated. "Is that your last name, or your first name?"

"Both."

"How old are you?"

"That's hard to answer. Parts of me are older than other parts of me."

"That's funny." She laughed. "Which part of you is oldest?"

"My brain. It took five years to grow me, another two to augment and assimilate all the parts. That's why your people call us augies. Because we are augmented beings. After

I was completed, I went to work. I've been working for your parents since before you were born.''

"You mean you never had another life?"

"If you mean in the human way, like you, no."

"Why?"

"Because this is what I do. This is what I was made for.''

She scratched at her chin. ''But do you ever get to play?''

"I'm not like you," he answered.

"But you can't work all the time," she protested, tugging at a strand of her hair and curling it around her finger. The air seemed to be the color of violets. ''You have to have vacations.''

"I'm not like you," he said again.

"Rinn?"

"Yes."

"I have to go to the bathroom."

Standing on the ground she turned around and around. The sand squeezed up between her toes. "There's nothing out here. I can't see any houses or lights or anything."

"We're far away from The City," Rinn told her.

"But where will we eat breakfast? Where will we rest?"

"We can't stop until we get across this desert," he explained calmly. He knelt and touched the sand with his slender human hands. "You'll just have to try not to think about it until then, okay?" His brown eyes looked like deep velvet. He blinked languidly as he watched her on her level.

"But I'm thirsty."

"Try not to think about it, okay?"

She nodded, rubbing at her eyes which were gritty and dry. When he held out his arms to her she turned away, walking toward the sunrise.

Rinn followed. "We can go faster if I carry you," he said. So she let him.

• • •

The sun was just peeking over distant mountaintops when Rinn came to a halt.

"What . . . ?"

His "Shhh!" cut her off. He stared at the ground, his boots poking at an indentation in it.

Then, suddenly she was falling. She heard herself scream but behind that sound came another more guttural cry.

The sandy ground hit hard against her shoulder and back. For a moment, she was too stunned to breathe.

Resonant thuds of metal clanging against metal brought her fully alert and she sat up to see Rinn fighting with another *augie*. Their bodies clashed like great chrome sculptures caught off balance, crashing into each other. They fell heavily to the ground, heaps of squirming, dawn-lit steel. The fiery colors of the sky and land mixed upon their bodies. They seemed to sizzle.

The second *augie* was darker than Rinn, with black hair like Midi's, and sable brown skin on his hands and face. He was bigger, too, and had managed to straddle Rinn who lay on his back. The brown *augie*'s hands grasped Rinn's throat, and Rinn seemed to be choking.

Midi got up and ran at the other *augie*, pushing against his rock-hard shoulders. He backhanded her without even looking and she fell on her side again in the coarse sand. She stood up quickly, ignoring the sting on her face. Rinn struggled, pushing and kicking at the other *augie*.

"Rinn!" she screamed, the tears starting to come. The feeling of helplessness she'd had when waking from nightmares washed over her like a thick liquid. But a part of her fought the sensation with anger and outrage. She could be a baby and sit there and cry, or she could try to help Rinn. With an inner focus she'd never experienced before, she assessed the situation. It was as if time had slowed and she could see everything that had happened and was going to happen clearly for the first time. She understood that Mr.

Mike had been about to do something bad to her under the water and that was why Rinn had grabbed her from the pool. She understood that her parent's mansion had been attacked and that they might be dead, and that Rinn had risked his life to save hers. She understood that now another *augie*, not one who worked for her parents but one with another purpose, had come to kill Rinn and herself. In that instant, she was no longer a baby, but a human being who wanted to live. But in order to live, she needed Rinn.

Her hand closed over a rock bigger than her two fists put together. With a yell, she ran toward the other *augie* and slammed it into the back of his head. It stunned him enough for Rinn to flip him over and smash an elbow into his face. The *augie* went down but his body still moved.

Midi ran and picked up another large rock. When she came back she saw it wasn't needed. Rinn, covered in fresh red blood, had neatly severed the augmented man's head with a part of his sleeve.

"Oh," she said, and sat down hard, her body suddenly going numb all over. "Oh." The rock slid from her hands and into the dirt.

Rinn looked over at her. A large cut below his left eye seeped red blood. Blood bubbled from the neck of the dead *augie*. The pale sand was spattered with brick-dark clots. The sky reflected it, reddening as the sun slowly came up, spreading its light like the petals of a cinnamon rose.

Midi couldn't look away for a long time. Even when Rinn put his hand on her shoulder, she didn't move, didn't blink.

Finally, he just picked her up, his bloody hands leaving marks on her stained gown. She didn't protest and continued to stare at the carnage as they walked away. Only when they got far enough from it that all she could see was sand and rock and briary bushes did she finally close her eyes. But her body would not rest. Even as Rinn held her in metal arms, warm and safe, her muscles remained taut as cables.

• • •

It got hot fast. Rinn did not seem to notice. He continued
to run, Midi cradled in his shining arms.

She never once complained about hunger or thirst, though
both afflicted her. If Rinn felt the same, she didn't know. She
wasn't going to ask.

The land rushed by, craggy and desolate. The sun moved
higher and higher until the sky became almost white with
its light.

After what seemed like forever to Midi, the landscape
gradually changed. Thin twig-like bushes were replaced by
an occasional gnarled tree with leaves of dusty green and
branches thick as Rinn's arms. Instead of flat terrain, there
were little hills. Grass and weeds sprouted up by their path,
some of it several feet tall. Little yellow flowers dotted the
countryside.

"We're leaving the desert," Midi said, her voice cracking.

"Yes." Rinn sounded tired.

"That's good," she said, sighing.

"Yes, that's good."

They were silent for another long time, then Midi felt
like talking again. "Augies are a lot like people. Some are
good, some are bad, right?"

"I suppose so."

"Why did that one try to kill us?"

Rinn seemed to think for a long time before he answered.
"Just as your parents hire augies for your protection, other
people hire augies for protection. If two people who hire them
are at war, then the augies, too, are at war against each other
because they have the best interests of their employers at heart.
Some new people who have come to The City to change it
don't like certain things your parents stand for. The attack
on your house was expected, but not at this early date."

"But why do people want to kill each other?" she asked.

"Because they threaten each other's way of life, I would guess."

"Do you feel threatened?" She stared at his face even though his gaze was not on her but on some point far ahead.

"I am threatened when you are threatened."

"But when you're on your own, do you feel that way? Like when people hate you?" She took a deep breath. "When I hated you?"

"I don't think like you do, Midi."

She tilted her head back until her face was just under his ear. Wisps of blond hair curled against it. "Why? You have a real head and brain. Why wouldn't you think like me?"

"Because I am a created being. Like a tool."

"What does *created* mean?"

"Made."

She closed her eyes and thought about that. "My mommy and daddy made me. Am I a tool, too?"

"No. You're different." His running slowed.

She opened her eyes and saw there were more trees now, and meadows off to the right. "How?"

"I have one purpose only and no choices. You have choices. I am owned. You are not."

"But how can someone own a person?"

"I'm not a person."

She put her hands on his forearm and held tight. "I think you are."

They came upon a dirt road. It looked overgrown, unused, but they followed it anyway. The air smelled fresh, like grass and tilled earth. When they crested a tall hill, they finally saw it. A city. But not The City. This was another one. One where Rinn said they would be safe for a little while.

A party of uniformed *augies* met them before they got halfway down the hill.

"I'll take the child, now," one *augie* said. But Midi

held onto to Rinn's neck and would not allow herself to be removed.

They were escorted into town where humans and *augies* alike greeted them.

A voice called from the crowd. "Midi!"

Midi turned in Rinn's arms. "Mommy?" She looked at the many faces peering at her.

"Here." Her mother emerged to the front of the mob, smiling, her arms open, her face very wet.

"You're safe now," Rinn said softly, and put her down.

Once on the ground, Midi ran to her mother without looking back.

After being checked over by doctors, fed and bathed, Midi sat with her mother and father and told them everything that had happened.

"We looked for you everywhere," her mother said. "Your room was empty, and there were signs of a fight. We hoped you would be with Rinn. The underground speedway brought us here—we barely got out alive."

"Do you realize," her father said, "that Rinn brought you over a hundred miles on foot? And in less than a day."

But Midi barely heard. She was thinking of the man in her bedroom, and the dead *augie* in the desert. She was seeing the blood again, and thinking of being with Rinn who made sure she was safe.

Later, she entered a hazy sleep filled with dreams of dead bodies and Rinn. But in those new dreams the *augie* protected her, and the blood she saw was not her parents' or her own, but the blood of angry enemies.

She woke alone in a dark unfamiliar room and called out for Rinn. When he didn't come she left the warm cushions of her bed and ran to the door.

This new house, like the mansion, had high-beamed ceilings and long halls. An *augie* guard at the end of the hall turned as Midi stepped from her room. It was not Rinn. It had short brown hair and a wide face with high cheeks and full lips.

She hesitated, then felt a boldness enter her that had not been present two days before. With her hands at her sides, head high, she approached the unfamiliar *augie*.

"Where's Rinn?" she asked.

The *augie* looked at her with discerning blue eyes. "Maintenance overhaul, I believe." It spoke with a woman's voice, a woman's inflections. "I am Nisa. May I be of help?"

"I want to see Rinn."

"You shouldn't be walking about the house alone after dark. I'll accompany you." She went to a nearby intercom, spoke some unintelligible words, then turned back to Midi. "I'll take you to him."

Midi walked alongside her without comment.

They descended two flights of wide, marble stairways and passed through two sitting rooms and a kitchen. At the end of the kitchen, a door opened into a long, bare room filled with ugly machines and hard tables. Rinn lay on one of the tables. Wires from three different flashing apparatus plugged into his metal body.

Midi walked over to his side. He had a haphazard grey bandage over the cut on his face. "Rinn," she said softly, touching his shiny arm.

He turned his head toward her and opened his eyes. They widened, then relaxed when he saw Nisa. "Midi. You shouldn't be here. Is something wrong?"

"No. I wanted to see you."

"Are you all right?"

At the question, a part of her warmed. "Yes. Are you?"

"Yes."

She moved her palm down his arm and touched his hand. It felt warm and she squeezed it. "You should be in bed resting," she said.

"So should you." He looked away from her, then, and moved his hand out of her grasp. "This is where I rest."

"But it's so cold," she said, looking at the hard table, the bare walls and the humming instruments. "This is where you stay all the time you're not working?"

"Yes."

"Isn't it lonely?" Not giving him time to answer, she added, "Do you dream?"

A small smile curved his pale lips. He motioned toward Nisa and said, "I think it's time for Midi to leave." He looked at Midi and said, "I'm sorry. I'm very tired."

"Oh." She moved backwards toward the door which Nisa quietly opened. "Good night, Rinn."

"Good night." His voice was almost a human whisper.

More Than a Contest
by
Dave Wolverton

About the Author

Dave Wolverton won the L. Ron Hubbard Gold Award for his story "On My Way to Paradise," which was published in Volume III. After doing so, he immediately signed on with one of the best agents in the business and quickly signed a three-novel contract with Bantam books. His first novel, On My Way to Paradise, grew out of the story by the same name. It received wide praise from Orson Scott Card and other critics, and was first runner-up for the Philip K. Dick Award as one of the outstanding novels of 1989. His second novel, Serpent Catch, which is recently out, has received similar acclaim.

In 1990 Dave was invited to be the first "home-grown" judge for the Writers of The Future Contest, and in October of 1991 Algis Budrys chose Dave to assume duties as Coordinating Judge.

Very often in this book you have heard of L. Ron Hubbard's Writers and Illustrators of The Future *Contests*. As a writer, I've won a few contests, so I know whereof I speak when I say that this is more than a contest: It's an exciting program to inspire struggling new authors and illustrators, and then to honor, train, and promote them when they have proven ready to join the ranks of professionals.

For inspiration, the Contests are held quarterly, and we find that many aspiring authors and illustrators make it a goal to enter every quarter. To motivate them to this end, for the writers there are three prizes of $1,000, $750, and $500, with an additional $4,000 grand prize for one of the first-place authors at the end of the year. For the illustrators, there are three prizes of $500 each, plus the opportunity to win an additional $4,000 grand prize at the end of the year. (Trophies or handsome framed awards certificates also go to each winner.) Both Contests are judged by professionals, top names in the field, as you can see by the list on the back cover.

At the end of each Contest year, all winners who wish to participate are flown at Contest expense to the awards event, which is held at a different venue each year. The locations vary, but have included such places as the top of the World Trade Center, Hollywood and the United Nations. At the awards ceremony, the grand prize winners are announced, the winners get to mingle with judges, they are wined and dined.

At this time, the writers and illustrators get to participate in a workshop taught by the Coordinating Judges and other professionals in the field. Both workshops use training materials gleaned from articles written by L. Ron Hubbard, and the workshops are focused on helping new writers and illustrators make a career in their chosen profession. For example, writers learn ways to avoid burnout and generate story ideas, how to submit to major markets and treat editors in a professional manner.

Along with these, of course, comes publication. Bridge Publications has published all eight of the anthologies but is a separate organization from the Contests Administration. Bridge therefore pays separately for each story or illustration that goes into each anthology, and they pay very generously for sharply limited rights. When you combine the payment from Bridge with the Contest money, new authors will find that frankly this is one of the highest paying markets available, which is only one reason that the Contest continues to draw strong writers.

For most contests, once you have your check and trophy (if either are given), you are finished. But winners of Writers and Illustrators of The Future receive more. You also receive promotion. Bridge will send out news releases to your local papers, and, if you so desire, you can often participate in radio or television interviews. This helps promote the Contest, but it also helps promote you. Many illustrators find that they get phone calls from prospective clients. Personally speaking, in 1987 within one month after I won the L. Ron Hubbard Gold Award I received four separate full-time job offers over the phone from different companies. They all were looking for writers and saw my name in the paper. And you can keep receiving that promotional help as long as you want it.

As I say, this is more than a contest, it's a program designed to help new authors and illustrators, and it continues to fulfill the vision that inspired L. Ron Hubbard to organize these programs. L. Ron Hubbard, as a prominent author with over half a century of expertise in the field, founded the program with unequaled foresight and an abundance of goodwill.

We are very proud to present this year's winners and finalists and wish them the very best in their careers.

The Writers of The Future winners this year are:

First Quarter

> Michael Paul Meltzer
> Larry Ferrill
> C. Maria Plieger

Second Quarter

> Brian Burt
> Astrid Julian
> James S. Dorr

Third Quarter

> M. C. Sumner
> Mark Budz
> Sam Wilson

Fourth Quarter

> Stephen Woodworth
> Wendy Rathbone
> Mike Swope

Finalists included in this anthology:

Christine Beckert   Nicholas A. DiChario
Gene Bostwick   Bronwynn Elko
             Kevin Kirk

The Illustrators of The Future winners for this year are:

First Quarter

> John Caponigro
> Ira Crowe
> Bob Hobbs

Second Quarter

> Allen Koszowski
> Evan T. Thomas
> Jane Walker

Third Quarter

> Darren Albertson
> Matthew Stork
> Shaun Tan

Fourth Quarter

> Omar Rayyan
> Yevgeny Rzhanov
> Thomas Whittaker

A Note from
Frank Kelly-Freas

Co-ordinating Judge
L. Ron Hubbard's
Illustrators of The Future

About the Author

Frank Kelly-Freas is Coordinating Judge of the Illustrators of The Future Contest, and Illustration Director for this series of books. He began garnering awards in the 1950s, and has amassed ten Hugo Awards for Best Artist of the Year, and won the Lensman, the Inkpot, and the Frank R. Paul awards. Beyond that, his credentials are too long to list.

Despite his accomplishments, when he looks at the work of young artists, genuine respect and admiration show in his face, and new artists will often find that he freely gives both his praise and counsel. Distinctive, articulate, and intelligent, Frank Kelly-Freas always has a gleam in his eye that seems to be born of pure delight. Look closely at his characters next time you see his work, it's in their eyes too.

All of these qualities combined make him more than just a good Coordinating Judge, he is an excellent Coordinating Judge.

There are some advantages to taking a breather about once a year to consider just where you are/have been/are going to—and perhaps even *why*. For me, the publication of each succeeding volume of *L. Ron Hubbard Presents Writers of The Future* is all the above: It is the final distillation of a year of looking at, talking about, and selecting the very best storytellers from a veritable tidal wave of talent. "Conventional wisdom" tells us that the most beautiful women have never entered any beauty contests, the best novel is still looking for a publisher, the greatest picture has yet to be painted. That obviously implies the presence of a vast untapped reservoir of beauty and talent bubbling away Out There somewhere—and I'm beginning to believe it.

It isn't just the volume of entries we are getting from all over the world that is so mind-boggling, it is the implication of the existence of thousands of emerging illustrators, capable of putting a whole story into one potent visual expression—who haven't even given a thought to entering our Contest! And it's worth a thought. Several of them, in fact.

For instance, the top winner in the Contest is immediately nearly $5K richer. That's cash. Then there is the matter of what all the winners get in terms of exposure, promotion, career impetus, and just plain fun. (Oh, those Award parties!) They will also meet artists, writers, publishers and various sorts of art buyers that would take them months to see on their own. They will have the opportunity to display portfolios for sympathetic, critical and *informed* review by professional illustrators, potential clients, and especially by their true peers—the other winners in the Contest. Believe me, this is good company!

Our winners have proved their ability in competition with what must certainly be the most intelligent and talented generation of artists in history. There is no doubt in my mind that we will in the next two or three decades see that Renaissance in illustration of which L. Ron Hubbard dreamed; and which we at the Contest are doing our best to encourage.

One of the nicer things about illustration as a profession is that you can work from almost anywhere. One of this year's winners is from Australia. Another is from Russia. Who knows, any day we may get one from Poughkeepsie. Of course, it can be taken for granted that anyone who enters the Contest is a good artist: He can draw well; he has a good sense of values, contrasts, composition, and at least some awareness of methods of reproduction. But remember that what makes an illustrator is his THINKING: His ability to communicate the excitement of the story to a potential reader, to make the latter *want* to read the story, and to enhance the reader's enjoyment of the story.

Take a close look at the illustrations in this book. They reward study. Whatever their style or medium, these artists are ILLUSTRATORS: Storytellers using pens and brushes in place of typewriters—or campfires.

CONTEST RULES

1. No entry fee is required, and all rights in the story remain the property of the author. All types of science fiction and fantasy are welcome; every entry is judged on its own merits only.

2. All entries must be original works of science fiction or fantasy in English. Plagiarism will result in disqualification. Submitted works may not have been previously published in professional media.

3. Eligible entries must be works of prose, either short stories (under 10,000 words) or novelets (under 17,000 words) in length. We regret we cannot consider poetry, or works intended for children.

4. The Contest is open only to those who have not had professionally published a novel or short novel, or more than one novelet or more than three short stories.

5. Entries must be typewritten and double spaced with numbered pages (computer-printer output O.K.). Each entry must have a cover page with the title of the work, the author's name, address, and telephone number, and an approximate word-count. The manuscript itself should be titled and numbered on every page, but the author's name should be deleted to facilitate fair judging.

6. Manuscripts will be returned after judging. Entries must include a self-addressed return envelope. U.S. return envelopes must be stamped; others may enclose international postal reply coupons.

7. There shall be three cash prizes in each quarter: 1st Prize of $1,000, 2nd Prize of $750, and 3rd Prize of $500, in U.S. dollars or the recipient's locally equivalent amount. In addition, there shall be a further cash prize of $4,000 to the Grand Prize winner, who will be selected from among the 1st Prize winners for the period of October 1, 1991 through September 30, 1992. All winners will also receive trophies or certificates.

8. The Contest will continue through September 30, 1992, on the following quarterly basis:

    October 1 - December 31, 1991   January 1 - March 31, 1992
    April 1 - June 30, 1992   July 1 - September 30, 1992

The next Contest will continue through September 30, 1993, on the following quarterly basis:

    October 1 - December 31, 1992   January 1 - March 31, 1993
    April 1 - June 30, 1993   July 1 - September 30, 1993

Information regarding subsequent contests may be obtained by sending a self-addressed, stamped, business-size envelope to the above address.

To be eligible for the quarterly judging, an entry must be postmarked no later than Midnight on the last day of the Quarter.

9. Each entrant may submit only one manuscript per Quarter. Winners in a quarterly judging are ineligible to make further entries in this or any future Contests.

10. All entrants, including winners, retain all rights to their stories.

11. Entries will be judged by a panel of professional authors. Each quarterly judging and the Grand Prize judging may have a different panel. The decisions of the judges are entirely their own, and are final.

12. Entrants in each Quarter will be individually notified of the results by mail, together with the names of those sitting on the panel of judges.

This contest is void where prohibited by law.

1. The Contest is open to Entrants from all nations. (However, Entrants should provide themselves with some means for written communication in English.) All themes of science fiction and fantasy illustration are welcome: every entry is judged on its own merits only. No entry fee is required, and all rights in the entries remain the property of their artists.

2. By submitting work to the Contest, the Entrant agrees to abide by all Contest rules.

3. This Contest is open to those who have not previously published more than three black-and-white story illustrations, or more than one process-color painting, in media distributed nationally to the general public, such as magazines or books sold at newsstands, or books sold in stores merchandising to the general public. The submitted entry shall not have been previously published in professional media as exampled above.

If you are not sure of your eligibility, write to the Contest address with details, enclosing a business-size, self-addressed envelope with return postage. The Contest Administration will reply with a determination.

Winners in previous quarters are not eligible to make further entries.

4. Only one entry per quarter is permitted. The entry must be original to the Entrant. Plagiarism, infringement of the rights of others, or other violations of the Contest rules will result in disqualification.

5. An entry shall consist of three illustrations done by the Entrant in a black-and-white medium. Each must represent a theme different from the other two.

6. ENTRIES SHOULD NOT BE THE ORIGINAL DRAWINGS, but should be large black-and-white photocopies of a quality satisfactory to the Entrant. Entries must be submitted unfolded and flat, in an envelope no larger than 9 inches by 12 inches.

All entries must be accompanied by a self-addressed return envelope of the appropriate size, with correct U.S. postage affixed. (Non-U.S. Entrants should enclose International Postal Reply coupons.)

If the Entrant does not want the photocopies returned, the entry should be clearly marked DISPOSABLE COPIES: DO NOT RETURN. A business-size, self-addressed envelope with correct postage should be included so that judging results can be returned to the Entrant.

7. To facilitate anonymous judging, each of the three photocopies must be accompanied by a removable cover sheet bearing the artist's name, address, and telephone number, and an identifying title for that work. The photocopy of the work should carry the same identifying title, and the artist's signature should be deleted from the photocopy.

The Contest Administration will remove and file the cover sheets, and forward only the anonymous entry to the judges.

8. To be eligible for a quarterly judging, an entry must be postmarked no later than the last day of the quarter.

Late entries will be included in the following quarter, and the Contest Administration will so notify the Entrant.

9. There will be three co-winners in each quarter. Each winner will receive an outright cash grant of U.S. $500, and a certificate of merit. Such winners also receive eligibility to compete for the annual Grand Prize of an additional outright cash grant of $4,000 together with the annual Grand Prize trophy.

10. Competition for the Grand Prize is designed to acquaint the Entrant with customary practices in the field of professional illustrating. It will be conducted in the following manner:

Each winner in each quarter will be furnished a Specification Sheet giving details on the size and kind of black-and-white illustration work required by Grand Prize competition. Requirements will be of the sort customarily stated by professional publishing companies.

These specifications will be furnished to the Entrant by the Contest Administration, using Return Receipt Requested mail or its equivalent.

Also furnished will be a copy of a science fiction or fantasy story, to be illustrated by the Entrant. This story will have been selected for that purpose by the Co-ordinating Judge of the Contest. Thereafter, the Entrant will work toward completing the assigned illustration.

In order to retain eligibility for the Grand Prize, each Entrant shall, within thirty (30) days of receipt of the said story assignment, send to the Contest address the Entrant's black-and-white page illustration of the assigned story in accordance with the Specification Sheet.

The Entrant's finished illustration shall be in the form of camera-ready art prepared in accordance with the Specification Sheet and securely packed, shipped at the Entrant's own risk. The Contest will exercise due care in handling all submissions as received.

The said illustration will then be judged in competition for the Grand Prize on the following basis only:

Each Grand Prize judge's personal opinion on the extent to which it makes the judge want to read the story it illustrates.

The Entrant shall retain copyright in the said illustration.

11. The Contest year will continue through September 30, 1992, with the following quarterly periods (See Rule 8):

October 1 - December 31, 1991
January 1 - March 31, 1992
April 1 - June 30, 1992
July 1 - September 30, 1992

The next Contest will continue through September 30, 1993, on the following quarterly basis:

October 1 - December 31, 1992
January 1 - March 31, 1993
April 1 - June 30, 1993
July 1 - September 30, 1993

Entrants in each quarter will be individually notified of the quarter's judging results by mail. Winning entrants' participation in the Contest shall continue until the results of the Grand Prize judging have been announced.

Information regarding subsequent contests may be obtained by sending a self-addressed business-size envelope, with postage, to the Contest address.

12. The October 1, 1991 - September 30, 1992 Grand Prize winner will be announced at the L. Ron Hubbard Awards event to be held in the calendar year 1993.

13. Entries will be judged by professional artists only. Each quarterly judging and the Grand Prize judging may have a different panel of judges. The decisions of the judges are entirely their own, and are final.

14. This contest is void where prohibited by law.